The Bluffs of Devil's Swamp
Mack Cameron

Mack Cameron
517 Keyword Circle, Suite 1-C
Jackson, MS 39232

Visit our Web site at http://www.msbluffs.com

First Edition: March 2008

Library of Congress Control Number: 2008902183

Cameron, Mack.
        The Bluffs of Devil's Swamp / Mack Cameron. – 1st ed.
                p.cm.

        ISBN-13: 978-0-9801434-1-6
        ISBN-10: 0-9801434-1-1

Dedicated to all of my friends and family,
without whose support I could have not completed this novel.

Chapter One

It was the last week of February 1927 when Nick Gable, at age 30, made his first trip from New Orleans to Bay St. Louis, Mississippi. The weather was as warm as a July day in Detroit, where he had lived for the past few years.

The three-hour drive to Bay St. Louis proved more arduous than Nick had thought it would be. He found that though the narrow roads leading out of New Orleans were paved with oyster shells, they did not invite speed. The ferry crossing of the Pearl River at the Louisiana-Mississippi state line took longer than he had expected. During the crossing, he got out of his car and took a brief walk around the deck of the small ferry for fresh air and the view. Once in Mississippi, he noticed the heavy concentrations of pine trees mixed in with large areas of low-lying swamp land. He eventually began to see small houses along the roadway which indicated to him that the little town of Bay St. Louis was probably not too far away.

The road Nick had taken came to an end at Front Street in Bay St. Louis. He found himself looking out over a body of water known as the Bay of St. Louis, from which the town derived its name. A portion of the water reflected sunlight off of its surface so that it appeared as if there were thousands of mirrors showing themselves. From the waterfront road, he looked at the numerous large, expensive looking houses that were sitting on the high ground overlooking the Bay. Not wanting to linger, Nick turned his car away from the water and drove toward buildings that looked like a small business district. He noticed a large granite building with a sign in front of it which read "Hancock County Courthouse." It was almost eleven o'clock in the morning when he pulled into a parking spot in front of the courthouse.

Not much went unnoticed in the town of Bay St. Louis. Everybody and everything were observed and commented on by almost everyone. There were only around nine hundred people living there this early in the year. In the summer months it was a different story as many residents of New Orleans escaped the insects and oppressive heat of that city by coming to beach front homes they either owned or rented in Bay St. Louis and near-by areas. So when a stranger drove into town in a black Lincoln during this time of the year, members of the local citizenry took notice.

Nick stepped out of his car and gave his six-foot, slender frame a full and long stretch. Although physically fit, the stretch felt good; the drive over had stiffened his muscles. He looked out over the courthouse square and liked what he saw. It was so different from Detroit which, when Nick had left a few days earlier, had not had any sunshine, but instead, had near-freezing temperatures. Nick noticed a sign for the law office of Dudley Marquette hanging on the front of a small building across the street from the courthouse. He walked around to the trunk of the car, pulled out a large suitcase, and walked across the street.

Nick was greeted by a slender woman behind a desk when he entered Marquette's law office. He noticed that, dressed as she was, she could have gone straight to church from the office. The high-necked collar and length of her dress told Nick that this woman probably spent a lot of time in church. Either that or she was covering up another lifestyle, and doing it rather well.

"Good morning," Nick said. "I'm Nick Gable. Mr. Marquette is expecting me."

"Yes, I'll tell him you're here."

Nick looked around the front office after the secretary had walked down a narrow hallway toward the back of the building. Files were everywhere, on chairs, tables, and on top of file cabinets. How anyone could find anything in the stacks and stacks of files was beyond Nick.

"Mr. Marquette will see you now," the secretary said walking back into the front office. "Just down the hallway. His office is the last door on the right."

"Thank you," Nick said as he began to make his way down the dim hallway, carrying his suitcase in front of him to avoid bumping the walls. He noticed the rooms off the hallway had not escaped the disorder of the front office. Every room was the same. Files were stacked everywhere. Reaching the end of the hall, Nick tapped lightly on the office door before pushing it open.

"Hello, hello," said a whiskey-and-cigar voice. Marquette, with cigar in hand, was already up from behind his desk and walking toward Nick in a cloud of cigar smoke.

Marquette did not look the way Nick thought he would. He was shorter than Nick, probably five foot six or so, and his belly showed the results of someone who sat behind a desk all day. Marquette had an informal air about him in person that contradicted his formality over the telephone. Nick guessed Marquette was in his early forties.

"I'm Nick Gable, Mr. Marquette," Nick said as they shook hands.

"Yes, yes. Welcome to Bay St. Louis, Mr. Gable," Marquette said and motioned to a chair. "Please have a seat. It's a pleasure to meet you in person. I trust you had a safe trip over and had no trouble finding my office."

"None at all, thank you. I have to admit I'm very impressed with the natural beauty of the area. This is quite a pleasant-looking little town you have here."

"Well, good! I am glad to hear that and hope you have a very profitable business here."

"Thank you," Nick answered as he settled into his chair. "Let's get straight down to business. Have you been able to handle my request? Was the money I wired sufficient?" he asked.

"Things have gone as you requested," Marquette replied. "An option to buy the nine thousand acres of land that you wanted has been placed in your name. To do that, I used some of the funds you wired to me which will be applied to the purchase price should you decide to close on the property. Since the property is mostly in a swamp, the land was cheap, about six dollars an acre, and the option went through without any problems."

Nick thought for a moment and then said, "I have made the decision to go ahead and close on that property sight unseen, Mr. Marquette, so please do what is necessary to take care of that. Would it be possible to buy additional acreage in that same area?"

"Mr. Gable, you could buy most of the county if the price was right, and it really wouldn't be that expensive," Marquette said with a laugh.

"Okay, then. Double the size of the purchase; buy eighteen thousand acres," Nick said.

"Why, that's a lot of acreage. That will take more money, not to mention more of my time and effort," Marquette responded, looking straight at Nick.

"I am sure that a man of your many talents can take care of that in a way that will be beneficial to both of us, now can't you Mr. Marquette? Our mutual friend in New Orleans told me I could depend on you for anything I needed."

Through the haze of cigar smoke, Marquette continued to look at Nick and came to a conclusion. Yes, sir, this Nick, although younger than he, was not a person that Marquette wanted to cross. He had tried enough cases and judged the character of enough people to know that this was a man he wanted on his side. Besides, Marquette stood to make a lot of money and Dudley Marquette loved making money.

"I will need to have the funds readily available to buy the additional acreage you want," Marquette said. "These people, once you get in touch with them about buying their land, well, it's always easier to just pay them the money on the spot so they don't have a chance to talk with their neighbors, cousins and all to compare prices. No, sir, if you want to buy that land, I need to be able to pay them right then and there, when I ask them to sell. Money talks and a lot of the people need it."

"Okay, that can be arranged. Now, how did you do locating a building for my office?" Nick asked.

"I found you a nice one, a brick building on Second Avenue, a few blocks from here off of the square. It's in the downtown area just like you wanted," Marquette said. "It used to be a grocery store, but it was too small and the store lost money. The owners have moved to Georgia and are eager to sell."

With that, Marquette wrote the building's address on a piece of paper and gave it to Nick along with a key. Nick looked at Marquette's almost unreadable scribbling.

"Go ahead and check it out for yourself," Marquette said. Noticing Nick's difficulty reading the address, he said, "As you go out the front door of my office, take a right. Go to the corner and turn right. Go four blocks and it will be on your right."

"I'll do that," Nick said taking the key and sheet of paper. Nick stood up and then put the large suitcase on Marquette's desk. Nick opened it and, making sure Marquette was looking, removed the pistol from the suitcase and secured the weapon in an ankle holster. He then turned the suitcase around so that Marquette, whose mouth was already half open after seeing the gun, could see its contents.

Nick said, "There is enough money here to take care of the rest of the payment on the land under option, and to purchase the additional acreage we just discussed. Get a good deal on the additional land purchases and you will receive a substantial bonus."

Looking at Marquette, whose mouth was now fully open, Nick continued, "My only requirement is that the various land sales be signed and a deed to each piece of property be in your possession before any money changes hands. I would not want to come back here looking for you, Mr. Marquette, if the money is gone and there are no deeds. Understood?"

Staring at the money in the suitcase, Marquette barely heard a word Nick said. There was easily $50,000 in that suitcase, he thought. Together with the $75,000 Nick had wired earlier, there was more than enough money to buy the swamp land acreage Nick wanted. Even if it had been selling for more than just $6.00 an acre, no one wanted to buy it.

"Ah, yes, understood," Marquette replied. "I can get it done."

Marquette reached for a wooden box on his credenza and, opening it with his hand shaking a bit, said, "Would you like a cigar?"

"No, thanks. But do go ahead."

As Nick settled back into his chair, Marquette removed a cigar and brought it up to his nose to smell the aroma. It was a ritual Marquette had gone through many times. Smoking a cigar had always made him feel special. It had also settled him down on occasion and he needed that now. He reached into his pocket, pulled out a small knife and clipped off the end of the cigar. He then struck a match to light it.

After the cigar was lit, Marquette blew out the match and looked at Nick. What Marquette really wanted to do now was ask Nick how a young man such as he had the money to buy all this land.

Nick, sensing a question he may not want to answer, brought Marquette's attention back to the property.

"Now, when can I visit the property?" Nick inquired.

"Arrangements have been made for you to go out there tomorrow."

"Ah, good!"

Marquette added, "I also took the liberty of reserving a room for you tonight at the Bayside Hotel just a few blocks away down on Front Street. It's our nicest hotel with good views of the water."

"Thank you, Mr. Marquette. That was thoughtful of you."

"Please, please call me Dudley. I hope we have a long and profitable relationship."

Nick stood up to leave. "I do too, Dudley, and by all means, call me Nick. I suppose I will see you tomorrow then. You are going to the property with me, aren't you?"

"Yes, yes, of course. Meet me down at the city docks, just below the hotel, in the morning at seven o'clock. I have hired a guide to take us up Bayou Le Croix to the property. A person can easily get lost going up there. You'll see what I'm talking about tomorrow."

"Then seven o'clock sharp at the city docks it shall be." Nick shook hands with Marquette and turned to leave.

"Take care of that money, Dudley," he said looking back over his shoulder.

"I will, I will," Marquette said nodding his head.

"Nice to have met you," Nick said to the secretary as he passed by.

"It was a pleasure to meet you, Mr. Gable," the secretary said as Nick opened the door to fresh air and sunshine.

As Nick crossed the street to his car, Helen Patterson, the wife of Sheriff "Wild Bill" Patterson, was bringing her husband lunch, which she did every Tuesday and Thursday. Helen was a graceful woman who always dressed carefully before leaving home. She was unusually pretty. Many people often commented on her classic features. On this day, as she carried a picnic basket to her husband's office, she saw the most handsome man she had ever seen getting into a car on the opposite side of the street.

"Someone has a new car," she thought to herself, among other things.

Nick could not help but notice the beautiful blonde as he drove past her, following Marquette's directions to the address on the piece of paper. He almost hit a parked car while attempting to look at her as he drove and tried to read the directions, all at the same time. He made a mental note to find out who she was. Surely there weren't that many women who were that attractive in this small town.

He quickly located the two-story brick building. Parking in front of it, he unlocked the front door and went in. The building appeared to be well-built and in fairly good shape, Nick thought. It was three times as long as it was wide. Turning to go upstairs, he noticed a side entrance to the building that he had not seen when he had driven up. He guessed it had served as some sort of service entrance. It was hidden from the street by thick shrubbery. Nick found the second floor in good shape. The first floor would be his office and the second floor, he thought, could easily be converted into an apartment. He would check with Marquette tomorrow about workmen.

Satisfied with the building, Nick locked up and spent the rest of the afternoon touring Bay St. Louis, taking in its small-town charm, its innocence. The massive courthouse with its huge columns was offset by the open area of a nearby park that was almost a complete city block in size. Grand live oak trees were everywhere, along almost all of the streets leading from the park, but especially around the park's edges. The tall trees provided ample shade and were not affected by the gentle breeze coming off of the nearby salt water. The bright sunlight accented the smaller commercial buildings surrounding the square with the shade from those buildings providing a sharp contrast. Well-kept houses could be seen down the street for several blocks.

It was so different from Detroit. For one thing, the weather was much warmer. In late February of any year, Nick thought living in Detroit was depressing. It was cold to be sure, but it also was definitely depressing. Here though, the azalea bushes, which seemed to be everywhere, were already blooming and spring was in the air. The nice, constant breeze off of the water was something to enjoy. Yes, by sunset, Nick was convinced the right place had been selected.

Chapter Two

Nick spent an uneventful evening at the hotel. The next morning after breakfast he walked down to the dock, arriving promptly at seven o'clock. Marquette was there waiting for him along with a man whom he introduced only as Sam. Sam was the boat owner and would serve as their guide on the trip to view the property under option. Sam worked, as did a lot of the people in Bay St. Louis, as a fisherman, and he looked it. His face showed years of exposure to the sun and the wind.

After finding out that Sam was an oyster fisherman, Nick pointed to the six large wooden buildings that were located along the beach front road running south out of Bay St. Louis and asked, "What are those large buildings there along the road?"

"Seafood processing plants, Mista Nick," Sam answered. "They do a really good business. They each almost have more than they can handle. Waters 'round here are just full of every kind of fish folks love to eat. All the oysters anybody ever wants and people wants lots of 'um. Shrimp by the boatload. So many shrimp dey take'um there at all of those plants and take dat shell off of'um, fix'um up so a person can eat 'um and dey so good. People do love dem shrimp. Ship 'um all over the place by boat and by train."

"I heard loud whistles from those plants at about six this morning," Nick said.

"Those be to let the people who want to work know that that plant be hiring for today," Sam answered. Nick thought about Sam's answer and remembered seeing groups of men making their way down the street as he had been walking to the boat dock.

Soon the three men were headed up Bayou Le Croix into the middle of a vast swampy area. Nick had never seen anything like this swamp. The marsh grass grew so tall that it was almost impossible to see beyond the area immediately surrounding the boat. There were constant turns, first one way and then another. This went on for about forty-five minutes, long enough for Nick to know that it would take a person very familiar with the area to ever find his way in the swamp.

They finally rounded a bend in the bayou and were able to see, because the bayou opened up somewhat, three bluffs not too far in the distance. The middle bluff was the largest and highest of the three, being about twenty feet in height and at least over eighty yards in width. Several large oak trees were scattered around the high ground. Since the first of the three bluffs would be the easiest to climb because of its lower height of only about ten feet, the guide put their boat into the bank as close to that bluff as he could get.

Nick stepped out of the boat and looked around. It was another absolutely beautiful day. The blue sky complemented the golden hue of the marsh grass. Those colors blended in nicely with the various light and dark greens of the trees and shrubs. The water of the bayou was generally murky, but in some places it was almost completely clear.

Nick and Marquette walked around the base of the first bluff. Nick saw why he had not been able to see the bluffs until they were almost on top of them. It was because of the high marsh grass which, even in the little area of open water around the bluffs, limited what could be seen from down at the level of the water.

As they climbed higher on the first bluff, they were able to see much farther over the swamp. Nick walked over to the highest of the three bluffs, the middle one, slowly moving to the edge of the bluff to overlook the open water. Finally, standing still at what he felt was its highest point, he could see an even further distance over the vast bayou. Nick knew this was the place that he wanted.

"I like this high ground here," Nick said to Marquette as he looked over the bayou.

"I thought you might like it," Marquette said.

Turning away from the bayou and gazing over the high ground, Nick noticed the trees that were scattered around the area. Most of them had trunks that were large, in some instances probably taking up twice the area of ground that the three men would have occupied if they had stood closely together. The crowns of the trees were massive. Nick thought some of the trees might be as tall as a hundred feet.

"What kind of trees are those really big ones?" Nick asked as he became awed by their sheer size.

"Most of them are water oaks, a few live oaks," Marquette said, enjoying the opportunity to show off his knowledge.

"What is that stuff hanging from their limbs?" Nick asked as he looked at the numerous tufts of grayish green filaments hanging from the branches of the trees and swaying in the gentle breeze.

"That's Spanish moss. It's found all over the place down here. You boys probably don't have anything like that up where you're from," Marquette said with the hint of a smile on his face.

After a few more moments of observation, Nick turned to Marquette and said, "This is a good location. When can you complete the purchase?"

"Oh, in a week or so," Marquette answered.

"What's the name of this swamp? Does it even have a name," Nick asked.

"It's called Devil's Swamp," Sam answered.

Nick turned and looked at him. "Devil's Swamp? How did it get that name?"

"Cause sum says dat tha ole devil hisself lives out har," Sam answered.

Turning his head to look at Sam, Nick stared at him for a moment and then asked, "Why do people say that?"

Sam paused for a second and then said, "Thar's strange thangs that happ'n out har."

"What do you mean strange things?" Nick asked, keeping his eyes focused on the guide.

"Strange thangs," Sam said again, now looking around nervously.

"Strange things like what," Nick asked, making sure with his tone of voice that Sam understood that Nick wanted more information in the answer.

Sam looked down at the ground, pausing again, and when he looked back up, said, "People sometimes disappear out har, jus don't cum back. Ner seen agin."

Nick continued to study the guide's face, noticing the furrows in his brow. He realized that Sam was serious, very serious.

"Well, now, there has been no proof of any of that," Marquette said. "There has not been anybody that has just disappeared out here, now has there? Tell Mr. Gable the truth now," Marquette said, his voice rising so that Sam would understand that he really needed to clear this up as quickly as possible and then keep his mouth shut.

The guide gave Marquette a quizzical look but said nothing.

After a few moments, Nick insisted, "What other types of strange things are you talking about, Sam?"

Sam looked at Marquette and back at Nick. Sam decided that if Nick wanted to hear more, regardless of Marquette, Sam was going to tell him more. That way if anything ever happened, at least the guide could sleep at night knowing he had made Nick aware of what he was talking about.

"Sometimes out har, thar's parts of livin thangs hang'n from trees and thangs," Sam continued in a very low and shaky voice. Marquette shook his head from side to side. He knew now, just knew, that the sale was gone.

"Sometimes thar be thangs hang'n from poles and sticks in tha wat'r. Jus hang'n thar, twist'n in tha wind," Sam said.

Sam glanced at Marquette and looked back at Nick and said, in a whisper after looking from side to side, "Thars lots of voodoo symbols and thangs all ovar tha swamp." With that, he turned and faced away from the swamp, as if the devil, or someone or something, was going to come and get him for talking about it all.

If the guide was telling him that to scare him, Nick thought, it wasn't going to work. Nick Gable didn't scare easily, and he certainly wasn't going to be scared by a story told by this old man. Besides, those kinds of stories would fit his plans. They could keep curious people from nosing around his property. Nick chuckled to himself. He might even start a few more rumors himself just to make sure the curious stayed away.

Nick walked to the edge of the center bluff to take a last look. He caught a faint glimpse of movement down in the swamp. Shielding his eyes to cut the glare coming off of the water, Nick was certain he had seen a person out there. Ah! He had seen somebody. A person seemed to be standing in the swamp! What was a person doing standing in this swamp in the middle of nowhere?

The other two men joined him. "What are you looking at down there?" Marquette asked. Nick now thought he could see that the person was standing in what seemed to be a very small boat.

"It's a man in what looks like some sort of boat. What kind of a boat is that?" Nick asked.

Marquette answered, "It's called a pirogue. It's a little flat-bottomed boat that's used by the fisherman out here because they can go almost anywhere in the swamp in those things. See how it sits so low in the water?"

Nick, squinting in the sunlight, said, "Who is the person in the boat?"

"Probably one of the swamp people," said Marquette as he cast a glance at Sam. Sam quickly looked away, a move which caught Nick's attention.

"Swamp people? Okay, now who are the swamp people?" Nick asked as he continued to shade his eyes from the glare.

Marquette answered, "They are the descendants of the Acadian French people that left Canada in the 1700s after England took over up there." Knowing he was probably going to get asked more questions about that, Marquette decided to just continue, explaining, "Most of the French up there didn't want to live under the rule of the King of England so they came down the Mississippi River and eventually settled in a large area called Baratarria that ran all along the coastline of Louisiana and parts of the coasts of Mississippi and Texas. For a long time their leader was a guy named Jean Lafitte, a pirate who helped General Andrew Jackson win the battle of New Orleans for the United States at the end of the War of 1812. Some of their descendants have lived in this area ever since then. They are rarely seen since they usually stay to themselves. The ones around here mostly live in this swamp. They have a language all their own, part French and part English and a whole lot of their own made up words."

"Interesting," Nick said as he began to make his way down to their boat. Marquette and Sam followed.

After Nick and Marquette had gotten back into the boat and Sam had shoved off from the bank, Nick said, "Take us over to the man in the pirogue."

Sam immediately protested, saying "Now Mista Nick, you really don't want to do dat."

Marquette quickly pitched in, "I agree. We really need to get back so I can start closing on those options."

Nick replied, in a low and determined voice, looking directly at Marquette, "Look, if I am going to buy this property, I definitely think it would be a good idea to talk with someone from this area. Don't you agree, Mr. Marquette?"

Marquette knew he could not win this one.

"Whatever you say, Nick."

The man, with long, wavy hair and wearing an unbuttoned shirt, saw them coming but knew he could not get out of where he was in the inlet in time to avoid them. He waited warily as they approached.

As they neared, Nick saw what looked like a large creature in the water behind the pirogue. Nick reached under his pants leg and pulled his pistol from his ankle holster. The man in the pirogue saw Nick pointing a pistol in his direction and shouted, "*Non, non!*" Nick fired four shots in rapid succession. The terrified boatman turned at the sound of a creature thrashing about in the water. It was a huge alligator!

Looking at the gator and then back at Nick in disbelief, Sam was the first, in almost a whisper, to say anything.

"He shot a gator." Looking back at the now thrashing gator and then again at Nick, Sam said, "He shot dat gator and didn't miss 'em. Not one shot missed 'em."

Marquette was just as stunned. Marquette slowly took his eyes off the alligator and looked at Nick. Nick had already put his gun back in his ankle holster. It was as if it had never existed.

"Pull over there to him," Nick said motioning in the man's direction.

As they pulled up alongside, the thin, wiry man in the pirogue, now standing up, looked first at the final slow twistings of the alligator and then at Nick.

"*Merci, merci beaucoup,*" the man said and extended his hand. "I was in trouble and *je ne le connais pas.* I did not know eet. Thank you, *monsieur.*"

Nick smiled and reached over to shake the man's hand. "You would have done the same thing for me. You don't have to thank me."

"*Mais oui, mais oui,* I do," the man answered, now with a big smile on his face. "Oh! *C'est possible que j'etais mort.* I could be dead. *Merci, monsieur, merci beaucoup.* Thank you!"

Nick answered, "He probably would not have done anything but he was so close to you and I didn't think you knew he was there. *Il n'y a pas de quois.* It was nothing."

The man's face lit up. *"Vous comprenez francais!* You understand French."

"Un peu. Un peu, just a little," Nick responded. "I have visited France a few times and learned a little of the language."

"Je m'appelle Claude." Then realizing he had spoken in French again, the man apologized saying in broken English, "I am so sorry. My name ees Claude."

"Hi Claude. *Je m'appelle* Nick." Pointing to the two men with him, Nick said, "These are my friends, Mr. Marquette and Sam. I have just bought a large piece of land out here and we came to take a look at some of it. I hope we can be friends since it looks like we are going to be neighbors." Claude nodded.

Nick then asked Claude, "Where do you live?"

Claude looked at him, smiled and just waved his hand toward the swamp, "Out there." With that he pushed away and said, "Again *monsieur, merci beaucoup.* I owe you."

Within a matter of seconds, Claude disappeared into the swamp.

Chapter Three

By the end of the second week in March, Nick's office building in Bay St. Louis began to come together. With Marquette's help, local workers had been obtained to clean the place up and do improvements to the building. The downstairs wooden floors were refinished and that helped brighten up the entire room. Portions of the brick walls now had varnished wood on them. Small paintings were hung that Nick had managed to obtain at one of the local art stores, the Bird's Nest, endearing himself to the shop's husband and wife owners.

As the workers finished cleaning off the remaining portions of the brick walls and began working upstairs on his living quarters, Nick knew that it wouldn't be too long before he would be able to move into his new office. He was looking forward to that day since he had been staying at the Bayside Hotel for the two weeks after his trip out to his land in the swamp. He was looking forward to having his own place to call home, at least until he could get something more substantial built on the property he had bought. Nick also visited New Orleans looking for architects and contractors to work on the buildings he had in mind for the Bluffs.

During the third week in March, Nick's living quarters at his office building were finished and the limited amount of furniture he had bought, also locally, was assigned to its proper location. He moved in as the workers were finishing their efforts. Nick Gable now had one of the local offices in town.

Knowing how important the Catholic Church had been to him and his family, Nick thought it would be a good idea for him to start attending the St. Richard's Catholic Church in Bay St. Louis. It would be a good way to meet people and get acquainted with some of those who provided leadership in the small community. When Nick was being raised as a young child in Sicily, his father and mother, Giavonni and Gabriella Gabolini, would take him every Sunday to the big Catholic Church in the town nearby to their land. His parents had been given eleven acres of relatively poor farmland just outside of town by his father's parents after his father and mother had married. Giavonni raised sheep and a few goats on their farm and with the help of his wife, who worked part-time in the town at a clothes cleaner, they were able to barely make ends meet. They were helped from time to time by relatives who owned land nearby. At age five, Nick began attending a small school run by their church which was located on the edge of Messina. Nick had met many of his childhood friends through church activities.

Nick attended his first Sunday service at St. Richard's the weekend after moving into his office. While leaving the service, he was encouraged by one of its members to come to a picnic the church was sponsoring the next Saturday at the downtown park not too far from his office. At first he just passed it off as an act by someone associated with the church to get him to attend something where they might be able to try to find out how to get some of his money. The more he thought about it, he realized it may be a good opportunity to meet more of the residents of his new town. Thinking it might also be a chance to evaluate people and listen to what they had to say, he decided to attend.

When the next Saturday arrived, a little after ten o'clock in the morning, Nick drove up in his sleek, well-discussed Lincoln to the city park area across from the Hancock County Courthouse. He found a place to park, pulling up under one of the magnificent live oak trees that he had noticed his first day in Bay St. Louis.

Surveying the open area not too far from where he had parked, he saw children of all ages in casual outfits playing various games. He had been told that this was the church's first fundraising picnic of the year and that it was being held now since warm weather had arrived. Nick quickly realized that, while he might keep his hat on to shade his eyes, he needed to take off the coat he had worn because it was hot and because none of the other men were wearing jackets. As he was taking off his coat, he continued to look around the picnic area to decide where he should go to try and mix with those in attendance.

As soon as he began walking around the area, people started speaking to him, saying "hi" even though he had no idea who most of them were. What he didn't know was that they had all come to know of him simply by word of mouth. He was quickly becoming the supposed close friend of everybody who was anybody in the small town. These good ol' boys did not necessarily want to be associated with anyone from north of the old Mason-Dixon Line, but each one of them wanted to be the friend of the man who was spending all of that money. While no one could understand why anyone would buy such a large amount of swamp land infested with alligators, mosquitoes, snakes and the always-strange descendants of Jean Lafitte's band, everyone wanted to know how they might get Nick to spend some of what seemed like an endless amount of money on something that they could sell him. It had been repeated many times that if Nick wanted more of that worthless type of property, there were plenty of people who would be glad to sell him some. Nick knew that type of attitude was present, but he also knew that there were not that many people who actually owned property in the swamp other than a few large landowners, and Nick had already dealt with most of them through Marquette.

While slowly walking around, Nick felt someone approach him from his right side. When turned to see who it was, all he saw at first was a hand stuck out almost in his face. Reacting by pulling back a bit, his eyes focused on the man holding the hand out. The man was in a white suit and had a small moustache and slicked back dark hair that had too much hair oil on it.

"Brantley Foucher's my name. I'm the mayor of this little town. Don't believe I've had the honor of meeting you."

"I'm Nick Gable," Nick answered as he shook the mayor's hand.

"Yes, I have heard of you. Yes, indeed I have. You are the man that spent all that money buying land out in the swamp."

"Well, I have bought some property recently. I had the good fortune of doing well in the stock market the past couple of years and have been able to spend some of the money I made around here. Not all of it has been on land in the swamp."

"Yes, yes. That would be true, I've heard. Well, may I officially welcome you to our little community. I hope you are enjoying yourself here. We are always happy to have someone move to the area who spends money," the mayor said with a forced laugh at the end of his last sentence.

Nick joined in with an equally forced laugh and said, "Why thank you, Mr. Mayor. I have enjoyed my stay here so far."

With a broad smile on his face, Foucher said, "I am glad to hear that and hope that you continue to enjoy our friendly people and our wonderful weather."

"Thank you, sir. I appreciate that and look forward to meeting more of the citizens here."

The mayor then said, "I am so sorry, but I must go now. I understand I am supposed to judge a pie-making contest about now so if you will, please excuse me."

"Most certainly. It was a pleasure meeting you, Mr. Mayor."

"And you too, sir. Hope to see you again soon." With that, the mayor turned and began walking over to a row of tables set up in the shade under several of the huge oak trees on the far edge of the park.

As Nick continued to wander around the picnic area, he saw Helen Patterson. He remembered that he had seen her on the sidewalk in Bay St. Louis the first day he had arrived in town. He recognized her immediately since she was easily the best-looking woman he had seen in the area. Since then he had seen her several times downtown near the courthouse and had discreetly asked about her. He had found out that she was the wife of Sheriff Wild Bill Patterson. Her first husband had died in a lumber yard accident, leaving her a widow at the age of twenty-three. The sheriff had been like a rock for her in the painful months that had followed. She was childless and, because she was so attractive, she had soon gotten the attention of every bachelor in the county who had even a modest amount of money and several that didn't even have that. The sheriff had protected her and given her comfort. She had felt safe with him. When, a year later, he had asked her to marry him, she had said yes. Nick was told that Helen and Bill Patterson had recently celebrated their third anniversary.

Nick was also told that a stranger looking at Helen and the sheriff would never think of them as husband and wife. For one thing, Sheriff Patterson was eighteen years older than Helen. Another thing was that Helen was a well-mannered, proper, southern lady. The sheriff, however, was a brawny man with a brusque manner. Yet, the people of Hancock County had repeatedly elected him as their sheriff. Though not a vain man by any means, he did, when out of the office, wear his Stetson hat to cover his receding hairline. Nick now wanted to meet his wife.

When he saw Helen talking with two other women under one of the large oak trees, he meandered around the picnic area making sure that he happened to go near to where she was engaged in her conversation. After standing by himself nearby for a few moments, he decided he would just walk over and introduce himself.

"Hello, ladies," Nick said, removing his hat. "I'm Nick Gable. I am new to town and when I saw you lovely ladies I thought it might elevate everyone's opinion of me if they saw me talking with you."

Laughing, the beautiful woman said, "Hi, Mr. Gable, I am Helen Patterson, and this is Julie Covington and Anna Brown." Helen continued, "We heard you had moved to town. Not much goes on here that everyone doesn't know about. Where are you from?"

"I'm from Detroit," Nick answered, his hat slowly being turned in his hand. Julie said in her strong southern accent, "Why, I do believe you are a Yankee, sir." This little southern belle had immediately put him on the spot and he knew that she was well aware of exactly what she had just done.

"Yes ma'am, I am, but I am one Yankee who appreciates the southern beauty that he is presently surrounded by." With that, Nick had taken the potentially rough edge that Julie had put in the conversation and turned it into a cream puff.

Anna did not appreciate Julie putting their new visitor on the spot. She also recognized that this handsome gentleman seemed to be just that, a gentleman, even if he was a Yankee. Anna immediately took over the conversation from her friends, as if to say to Julie, "Just stay quiet now while I show you how to be polite to a northern stranger."

"How does the gentleman from up nawth like it down here in the Deep South?" Anna asked.

Nick responded like a true southern gentleman might have.

"I cannot believe how wonderful this weather is. This beautiful day is just not something that we see this time of the year in my part of the country. Where I am from, up in Michigan, there is snow on the ground and it is awfully cold right now."

Noticing that a brief smile crossed Helen's face, he turned his attention to his ally in this encounter. Nick asked, looking at Anna, "Are all of you ladies from Bay St. Louis?" This brought smiles from each of the women.

"Yes, we all grew up and went to school together," Helen answered, briefly looking at Julie as if to also let her know that her type of comments were not to be made anymore. Nick noticed the look on Helen's face. He would have liked to find out more about Helen but, because of the situation, that would have to wait. He also didn't want to find out what other little statements Julie might make that may put him on the spot or tempt him say something he might regret.

"Well, I don't want to get all of the other men here mad at me for taking up your time so I will bid you beautiful ladies a good-day." With that he put his hat back on his head and, after tipping it to the women, quickly moved away from them. They immediately huddled, all three talking at once about the charming, rich man from up north that they had just talked with. Yes, it was the same one that they had heard spent lots and lots of money buying things all over the place and drove that Lincoln.

Nick walked around under the huge live oak trees. As he surveyed the area, he noticed a man with the distinctive priest's collar. He watched the priest for a little bit, walking generally in his direction. The priest finished his conversation with a small group with smiles and handshakes and, noticing Nick, walked towards him.

Taking his hat off and sticking out his hand, Nick said, "Good morning, Father. I'm Nick Gable."

"Good morning, Nick. I'm Father Patrick Ryan. It is a pleasure to finally meet the man I have heard so much about," the Father said, smiling and looking Nick right in the eye.

"Well, I don't know what you have heard about me. You have me at a disadvantage there, but it is a pleasure to meet you, sir" Nick answered. Yes, this Father Ryan was a man who should definitely be a minister. Nick could sense his goodness and kindness. He had first noticed it during the service he had attended.

"I think I saw you at our church last Sunday," the minister said, continuing to smile.

"Yes, I was there and really enjoyed the service," Nick responded. "And this is certainly a nice event here today," Nick said.

"I am glad you enjoyed your visit to our church and I am glad you are here with us today. We need to enjoy days like these by being outside in this wonderful weather," the Father said as he looked around the area.

"Yes, I couldn't agree more." Recognizing the opportunity to talk further with the priest with no one around, Nick continued, "Father, as you probably know, I am new to the area. One day, at your convenience, I would like to come by and meet with you. I would hope that in some way I may be of assistance to the church," Nick said while closely watching the Father for his reaction.

Father Ryan looked at him and responded, "Any help you can provide would be greatly appreciated. We have so many things that we need help with. It is very nice of you to offer. Just check with my office to make sure I am going to be there, and I will be happy to meet with you."

"I will do that, Father. I am still trying to get a few things put together from my move here, but once things get a bit more settled, I will certainly do that."

The Father, continuing to look at him with a pleasant, peaceful look on his face that made Nick feel comfortable being in his presence, answered, "Good. I will look forward to hearing from you."

Before Nick could further discuss getting together with the Father, he noticed the same group of women he had just talked with, which included the sheriff's wife, now walking toward him and the Father.

"Just let me know," Father Ryan said. Hearing their approaching chatter, he turned to greet the three women.

"Hello, ladies. Have you met Nick Gable?" the Father asked turning toward Nick.

"Yes, we met him just a few minutes ago," Anna answered for the group. She then took Father Ryan by his arm and said, "Father Ryan, you just have to come with me to see my daughter Sally. She has grown up so much during the past winter. You know she thinks so much of you."

With that, she put her arm in Father Ryan's and began walking him away. As he walked away, Father Ryan looked over his shoulder at Nick and said, "Nice to have met you, Nick. I'll look forward to hearing from you."

Julie quickly determined she was not going to stand there and talk with Nick without Anna there so she followed Father Ryan and Anna. She looked back as she walked away as if to motion to Helen to come with them, but Helen was not looking at her, and she was not walking away. With the two of them leaving, Nick was now standing by himself with the beautiful Helen Patterson.

"Do you think you should go with them? They may need you to keep them out of trouble, you being the sheriff's wife and all," Nick said smiling.

She looked at Nick and, with a big smile, said, "No, they'll be alright. Now how did you know I'm married to the sheriff?"

"I guess I will have to confess and tell you that I do know a little bit about you," he said looking intently at her. "I saw you in town one day. Being a single man, I made it a point to find out who you were and all I could about you. You are hard to find out something about, even though you are the sheriff's wife."

"I am?" Helen said, while trying to shield her eyes with her hand from the bright sun.

"Yes, you are," Nick said in a mock determined voice. "Part of it might be because you are the sheriff's wife and nobody wants to say anything about the sheriff's wife, especially anything bad. With you though, it is also that people seem to like you and usually when people like a person, they don't say anything about them in great detail, except that they like them. They will say a lot about somebody if they don't like them."

"Oh, really? You asked about me, did you? Well, you should have just asked me. There is not really much to tell," she said.

"Well, we had not officially met. Now that we have, can I find out everything I want to know about you by just asking you?" Nick continued.

"You can ask me anything you want, but I may not answer you," she said coyly.

"Oh, okay. Well, let's start out with your telling me why the sheriff is missing this wonderful event today," Nick said.

"I thought you wanted to ask questions about me," she teased and then continued. "Bill was here for a while but had to leave. One of his deputies came and got him to go check on something. You just missed him," she said.

"Oh, that's too bad."

"What else would you like to know?" she asked, still holding her hand up shielding her eyes.

"Well, let's see. Earlier you mentioned that you grew up and went to school with the two ladies you were chatting with. I bet you had all sorts of boyfriends in high school. Now tell me the truth. You did, didn't you?" Nick's teasing brought an immediate reaction.

"I did not! As a matter of fact, I dated only one boy all through high school and we ended up getting married. He died in an accident where he was working a little over four years ago."

"I am so sorry," Nick quickly said, now noticing a sad look on Helen's face.

Wanting to get past that information, Nick moved on with the conversation. "So now, you are married to the sheriff. He is a very lucky man."

Tilting her head to the side, Helen said, "Thank you. I am lucky also." Then looking directly at him, she asked, "Are you married, Mr. Gable?"

"No, I am not," he answered.

A brief smile crossed her face. With the sun on her face while she smiled, she looked gorgeous, Nick thought. She was still relatively young, he guessed. He remembered the first time he had seen her when she was walking on the sidewalk as he was pulling away from Marquette's office and he had almost hit a parked car. She had stood out that much. Oh, maybe she was not, and that was only a maybe, as beautiful as one or two of the women he had seen in Detroit. She had her own way about her though, the way she had walked when he had first seen her, the way she had talked when he had first met her a few minutes ago, and the way she was looking at him. With her hair up and standing straight with her hand now on her hip, she was simply elegant. She was the very definition of a classy woman.

"There is one thing I would like to ask you though, something that I cannot get an answer to and that nobody seems to be able to figure out," Nick said looking intently into her eyes.

"What might that be?" Helen said with a quizzical look on her face.

"How in the world the sheriff got to be so lucky as to have you for his wife?" Nick said with a smile on his face.

"Of all the things you could have asked me, that is what you want to know? Why do you ask me that?"

"Because it is important to me how you answer. Since I first saw you and started asking about you and about the sheriff, almost nobody I talked with could tell me about when you and the sheriff started seeing each other. Also, nobody has been able to tell me that they even knew the two of you were seriously dating. Don't get me wrong. Most people like the sheriff, but nobody says they thought the two of you were seeing each other, much less getting married," Nick answered. He said it all with sincerity because that is exactly what had happened.

After a moment's pause, Helen said, "We tried to keep it quiet, as quiet as anything can be kept in a small town like Bay St. Louis. I was still in mourning but he was good to me, and I was terribly lonely. Do you know what it is like to be lonely, Mr. Gable?"

"Yes, I know what it's like, and please call me Nick."

"Okay, Nick," she said with a smile and then continued. "After my husband died, I needed someone. I needed someone really badly. I did not know what to do with myself. I could not stand the loneliness. Bill was nice to me. He spent time with me. He was there when I needed someone. He is well-respected here, and he's a good man," she said looking around again.

"But you didn't say you love him. You do you love him, don't you?" Nick asked.

"Yes, I do. Like I said, he is a good man and good men are hard to find," she said with the flicker of another smile at the end of the sentence.

"From everything I hear, he is a good man. And like I said, he is very lucky to have you for his wife."

Looking her in her eyes, Nick then said, "You are a most interesting woman, and I would certainly like to get to know you better. I hope we can be friends. I bought the building over there on the corner of Lemuse and Second Avenue. The old, I think they call it, Bynum Building. Come over sometime and let me show it to you. It has a front entrance, which I never use, and a side entrance. I would love to know what you think about what all has been done with the building."

"Thanks. I appreciate your offer." She stuck her hand out and Nick took it, shaking it formally. To Nick, everyone at the picnic seemed to be watching him as he stood with the most beautiful woman there. He had to make himself not watch her as she turned and left, walking over to a group of nearby women and children. He would have to be very careful around her. Very careful. After all, she was the sheriff's wife.

Marquette walked up.

"I see you have met one of our county's sweetest and most beautiful residents," Marquette said as he held a white, wide-brimmed hat in his hands.

"Who would that be?" Nick asked as he turned his attention to Marquette.

"Mrs. Helen Patterson, the wife of our esteemed Sheriff Wild Bill Patterson," Marquette said as they both now watched her as she made her way to the refreshment table.

"Don't know why she married the sheriff. Nobody does. They got married about three years ago now. He's forty-five. She's about seventeen or eighteen years younger than him. Just doesn't make sense, but it surely did happen." Nick was almost wishing Helen was standing there listening to Marquette say what he had just said. If for no other reason, maybe she would understand better why Nick had asked the question that nobody seemed to know the answer to.

"How did he get the nickname Wild Bill?" Nick asked.

Marquette shook his head from side to side. "Now that's a story." Looking back at Nick, Marquette said, "Bill has been sheriff here now for over fourteen years. You haven't met him yet, right?"

"No, not yet," Nick answered.

"Well, he's a big fella, about six foot three. He was a Bay St. Louis city policeman for a little while. Then when he first got to be sheriff, he started wearing boots and a cowboy hat; the boots because sometimes he had to walk in places where it's just best to have boots on because of animals like snakes and such trying to bite him all the time when he was out in the county. He started wearing that cowboy hat of his because he was going bald and was out in the sun a lot. He wears those boots and that hat everywhere he goes. Oh, he'll take his hat off when he meets a lady or when he goes to church. But usually, when you see him around, he will always be wearing that hat. The other thing you will always see him wearing is a Colt .45 pistol, in a holster just like ol' 'Wild Bill' Hickok did. You know, that really tough U. S. Marshal that was out west somewhere. I think it was Dodge City."

Nick was listening closely to what Marquette was saying about this interesting person whose wife he had just met. He wanted to know all about the county's chief lawman.

"The story goes that not too long after he was elected the first time, he was wearing a hat, boots, and that pistol, and while patrolling out in the northern part of the county, he went into one of those honky-tonks up there, one called the Screaming Rabbit.

"The Screaming Rabbit," Nick said laughing. "Come on, Dudley, you can't be serious about that name."

Marquette gave one of his boisterous laughs and said, "Serious as I can be. It's called the Screaming Rabbit. We have five or six of those ol' tonks up there. The Screaming Rabbit, the Red Maple, the Cracked Nut, and a few others. That Screaming Rabbit, why it's one of the roughest places in the whole county."

"How in the world did that place get such a name?" Nick asked. He had to hear about that.

"Oh the man that owns it, ol' Sonny Burdette, just swears that while he was building it, late one afternoon after almost working himself to death, he was sittin' there on the ground at the site and he looked over and saw this rabbit, a rabbit of all things, just sittin' there lookin' at him. Sonny swears that all of a sudden, that rabbit started screaming at him. Can you imagine that?" Dudley said, letting out one of his big belly laughs again.

"He told the whole county that story. Some of my friends think he got to drinking some of that hooch stuff, that white lightening that he was probably making out there, and he got drunk. He got so drunk that while he was sitting there on the ground, he was looking at a rabbit alright. The rabbit was so scared it wasn't moving, probably thinking if it moved it would let the human know where it was. Well, as ol' Sonny sat there looking at that rabbit, he heard something screaming at him. Only thing was that he was so drunk he thought it was that rabbit!" Marquette let out another booming laugh at that one.

He continued, "Turned out it was his wife who was yelling at him. She was standing right behind him while he was sittin' there on the ground! She was mad at him for being so drunk!" Nick had to laugh at that one himself, which he did, along with Marquette.

"Now back to that Wild Bill thing. Finish telling me about that," Nick said. After that news about the Screaming Rabbit, he had to hear the rest of the Wild Bill story.

Marquette began, saying, "Well, ol' Bill goes out there to the Screaming

Rabbit, being a brand new sheriff and all, and not five minutes after he gets there one Saturday night, there was one of those genuine bar room brawls that got started. Now, I don't know about you northerners, but every now and then down here these good ol' southern boys just like to get together and fight. I mean, some people go huntin' or fishin', some people go dancin', some people go to church. But some of these good ol' boys down here, especially up in that part of the county, they just like to go somewhere and get drunk and fight. Doesn't really matter what the reason is. So on this particular night, Bill walked into the Screaming Rabbit, checking to make sure everything was alright. I mean, he was sort of new at his job so he wanted to do the right thing and all. Back then, whiskey was legal, before that 1919 prohibition amendment to the constitution that made sellin' booze and makin' booze illegal like it is now."

Taking a big breath, Marquette continued. "Well, like I said, Bill hadn't been in that bar five minutes and, about that time, one of those ol' boys walked over and asked Tommy Bob Pruitt if the reason he had two first names like he does was because his momma didn't know exactly who the daddy was and just gave the boy both names of the men she had been with. Well, the fight was on!" Marquette chuckled.

"Tommy Bob and his brother, ol' 'Snuff' Pruitt, well, they worked in one of the lumber yards up there and they just started doing what they love to do best on the weekends and that's drinkin whiskey and fightin'. There they were, fightin' with that ol' boy that said what he did and one of his buddies that had been listening to it all. So Bill just stood there at the corner of the bar and when ol' Tommy Bob got over there close to where Bill was standing, and while ol' Tommy Bob was fightin' with the boy that had said what he said, why Bill just pulled out his pistol and hit ol' Tommy Bob on the back of his head, really hard, with the butt of that there gun he was carryin', just like ol' Wild Bill Hickok used to do with that Buntline Special pistol of his that he used to always carry with him out west. Well, Tommy Bob went out like turning off one of those new fangled light switches," Marquette said, shaking his head at this point. Looking around quickly and seeing no one nearby, he continued.

"Then, if that wasn't enough, a few seconds later ol' 'Snuff', who was still fightin' the other boy, got close enough to Bill and Bill clobbered him on the head too, just like he had done ol' Tommy Bob. The other two boys they was fightin' with, well they was already beat up pretty bad anyway. That bar fight was over. Ol' Bill has been called Wild Bill ever since then."

Nick was amazed. This was certainly different from Detroit, or any other place he had been, that was for sure. But as he looked at the various groups of people at the picnic, he determined that he wanted to know one more thing, the one piece of information Marquette had left out so he decided to ask.

"Dudley, I have just got to ask you."

"What's that?"

"You wouldn't happen to know how 'Snuff', as you call him, got that name, now would you?"

Marquette immediately let out another one of his big laughs.

"Sure do. I was in school with him at the time. It was in the sixth grade. His real name's Ronnie. Ronnie decided he was gonna be a big shot, show his brother, ol' Tommy Bob, how grown up he was so he got himself some snuff and one day during recess, of all things, he tried to sniff it but couldn't do it. Then he tried to chew it and ended up swallowing some of it. Got dog-eared sick, you hear me. I mean bad sick!"

Marquette again let out a big laugh.

"Had to be sent home. Whole school found out about it. He never got past it. That ol' boy's been called 'Snuff' ever since then."

Nick stood there, continuing to be amazed at what he had just heard. He began to wonder about what type of place he had moved to.

Turning back to face Nick, Marquette quickly changed subjects.

"Are you going to do any building out at that Bluffs property out there?"

Coming back to the present, Nick said, "Yes, I think so. Think I am going to do something special out there. Hope to get started on it in the next couple of weeks, after I get all of the construction under contract and all." Nick was almost glad that Marquette had changed the subject. He didn't know how much more of things like he had just been told that he could believe, especially if he heard any more today.

"I think I am going to have a nice party out there once everything is finished. What do you think, Dudley? Maybe ask a lot of these people and some of my friends from New Orleans," Nick said, watching for any reaction at all from Marquette to the New Orleans "friends" part of his statement.

"That would be a nice thing to do," Marquette answered, with no noticeable recognition of the New Orleans reference. Nick had found out that most of the people in the area usually had some sort of connection with New Orleans, whether it was relatives or friends who lived there or shopping or just going there for good food and fun.

"A party would also be a very smart thing to do, you being from up north and all. Would let all of the unrepentant rebels down here know that, even though you're from up north, you're not such a bad person after all," Marquette said, giving another of his trademark, boisterous laughs.

A nicely dressed woman walked up to the men and greeted Marquette as an old friend.

"Hello, Dudley."

"Hi there, Jenny! It is so nice to see you," Marquette greeted her and began to look all around him.

"Where is Jimmy?" Marquette asked. Then a young boy about twelve years old appeared, smiling.

"There he is. Hi, Jimmy," Marquette warmly said.

"Hi, Mr. Marquette," the young boy quickly answered. With all of the enthusiasm of a twelve year old, Jimmy continued, "You told me before that when there was another hanging in the swamp that you would take me out there to see it, but you didn't let me know about this last one. Promise you will take me out there to see it when there is another one. Promise?" Jimmy pleaded.

"Now, Jimmy, you stop that," interrupted his mother. "You are going to give this gentleman here the wrong impression of us."

"A hanging? Why Mr. Marquette, you have never mentioned such a thing to me," Nick said, looking at Marquette for an answer.

"I am Nick Gable," he said turning towards Jenny. "I don't believe I have had the pleasure of meeting you."

"I am Jenny Green, Mr. Gable, and this is my son, Jimmy. Nice to meet you." The boy politely said, "Nice to meet you, sir."

Marquette jumped into the conversation, "Jenny and I have known each other most of our lives, haven't we, Jenny? We were in school together. Her young boy is the best fisherman anywhere around these parts, aren't you Jimmy?"

"I bet that is true, and I bet there is a real fisherman's story about that knife there," Nick said, noticing a folded knife hanging from a metal ring on the side of the belt on Jimmy's torn jeans.

"Not really sir," Jimmy said. "I just like to have it with me all the time."

"He likes having a little bit of his dad with him," Jenny said as she brushed his hair.

"His dad gave him that knife on his tenth birthday and he has kept it with him ever since. His dad passed away not too long after that," Jenny said.

"I am so sorry," Nick said. "And I understand why you keep it with you, Jimmy. I know it helps to have it with you."

Jimmy just nodded his head and looked off into the distance.

"Well, we just wanted to say 'hello' to Dudley. Hope you gentlemen have a blessed day," Jenny said, as she held Jimmy's hand and led him away from the men.

"Nice to have met you, Mrs. Green. Someday you will have to tell me what ol' Dudley was like back in school," Nick said.

"I will, Mr. Gable. I will," she said back over her shoulder as she laughed.

Jimmy yelled back as he and his mother walked away, "Promise you won't forget next time, Mr. Marquette. Okay?"

"I promise," Marquette quickly answered.

Nick turned to Marquette as the two disappeared into a group of people and said, "You didn't say anything about any hangings of people when I was talking to you about buying that property, Dudley. The only thing I have heard is what Sam said out there that day about there had been parts of living things hanging from trees and poles out there in the swamp."

"No, no, t'weren't anything to mention beyond what Sam said that day," Marquette said. Nick remembered that Sam had also mentioned something about "strange things" happening in Devil's Swamp.

"What hanging was Jimmy Green talking about? Why don't you try telling me what else there is I should know that you didn't bother telling me about while we were out there, Dudley. Or at any other time when we were talking about my making that purchase!" Nick said sharply.

"Okay! Okay! It probably isn't anything that will concern you. It's just that sometimes, not often, but sometimes, there's a body that will be found hanging in the swamp, just hanging there. The last time it happened was about five months ago," Marquette said.

"Don't you think that is something that is significant enough to at least mention to me?" Nick said with more fire in his eyes than Marquette had seen before.

"I know, I know. You might feel that I should have told you about it, but if I had of mentioned it, you would probably have just left, on the spot. And besides, the bodies, and it has only happened a couple of times in the past few years, have all been of people who nobody knows."

"People who nobody knows?" Nick said, now not paying any attention to the church picnic attendees who were not that far away. "Dudley, how in a small town like Bay St. Louis can somebody be hung, even in the swamp, and nobody knows who it is? How is that? Doesn't it matter that somebody was hanged, whether that person was known or not?"

"Most people seem to think that the dead folks are some of those swamp people, like the one you saw out there that day. Nobody knows them at all. They don't come to town. They don't talk to you the few times you ever see them. They run away when you come up on them, just like that man wanted to do that day we ran up on him out there in the swamp. Nobody knows them, so we think it must be some sort of ritual or justice system just amongst them."

Marquette looked at Nick and decided that, since he had helped Nick buy all that land out there, he needed to go ahead and tell Nick the rest of it.

"That's not all. I guess I should tell you the rest of it," Marquette said as he looked at the ground.

"What do you mean, the rest of it?" Nick demanded.

Taking a big breath, and looking around to make sure no one was close by, Marquette said, "Each one of the bodies is usually really messed up."

Nick looked at Marquette, now with a quizzical look on his face. "Messed up?" Nick asked. "Messed up how, Dudley?"

Marquette took a deep breath and said very quietly, "The last two bodies were mutilated and had all sorts of things written on what was left. Nobody could figure out what the writings said. They were in some sort of language that the swamp people use. From what was left of each body, it also looked like some sort of blood, maybe their own, had been smeared over what was left of them."

Nick continued to look at Marquette, waiting for him to continue.

"The best anybody could figure out was, like I said, that it was either some kind of sacrifice or some kind of a justice thing the swamp people were involved in.   Nobody ever figured out what really happened. The sheriff looked into it, but I think he just finally decided to drop it, mainly because nobody out there would ever talk about it. I told Jimmy about it to keep him out of the swamp. I mean, like I said, his mom and I grew up together. The one that was found about two years ago was right after his dad had died. I just didn't want him going out there by himself. I am afraid that he would do that. If anything happened to that boy, his mom could just not handle it."

Nick kept his gaze on Marquette. He was impressed. He could see Marquette was telling what he thought was the truth and that he was sincere in his desire to protect Jimmy. Nick would have to keep an eye out now that he knew this. He suspected Marquette was probably right, that it was just something between individuals in the "swamp people," but he began to wonder about the writings that had been seen on what was left of the bodies. He wondered if they were variations of the swamp people's language, or if they had been voodoo symbols that Sam, the guide, had talked about. Genuine voodoo symbols. All of a sudden he had lost interest in the church picnic.

Chapter Four

While work on his Bay St. Louis office was being completed, Nick began meeting in New Orleans with an architect he had decided to work with whose offices were downtown on Canal Street. The design Nick selected for a big house at the Bluffs was based on plans for a huge, extravagant home that the architect had drawn up for a location on St. Charles Avenue, the area where most of the upper-class houses in New Orleans were located. Nick made changes to the plans, keeping the same basic design appearance, but making his house smaller which meant that it would be possible to build the main house at the Bluffs in much less time. It also meant Nick would soon have a fabulous house that everyone would talk about. Nick reached an agreement with a New Orleans construction company to come out to the Bluffs, as he now called his house site in the swamp, and begin to immediately make his plans a reality.

Having access to seemingly unlimited amounts of money, Nick was able to commandeer the services of many more workers than were normally used on construction sites in the area. Five weeks after Nick's first visit to the Bluffs, construction started on two large cement boat docks and a 20-foot-high cement wall covering the edge of the bluff next to the docks. In addition, a loading site about twelve miles further up Bayou Le Croix, which was given the name Cypress Landing, was cleared so that the main road coming into the area from New Orleans could be more easily accessed. Once docks had been completed at the Bluffs and at Cypress Landing, construction materials could be brought in and unloaded more easily.

Construction also began on two bunk houses and two barns that were located on the back of the highest of the three bluffs. The bunkhouses were to be used as living quarters for some of the construction workers, making it unnecessary for them to stay in Bay St. Louis hotels which caused them to waste time each day being transported to and from the construction site.

As the two bunk houses and two barns, which took only a little over a week to build, were being finished, construction began on a small guest house. The guest house was built on the edge of the flat area overlooking the bayou at the top of the highest bluff. A swimming pool was built not too far from the guest house. There were no shallow areas in the pool. This pool was built for grownups, not kids, and had a depth of ten feet over the entire pool. It was twenty feet wide and fifty feet long with a cement walkway around the entire pool and stair steps leading down into the pool from one end. A diving board was located at the end of the pool opposite the steps. Standing on the diving board, a person could look out over the bayou and the swamp. Separate male and female bathhouses were built on opposite sides of the pool. Both bathhouses were almost the full length of the pool with six doors leading to the six dressing cubicles in each building.

Nick was on a tight time schedule. He wanted to finish everything being built at the Bluffs as soon as possible. With oversized work crews, he was told that it would be possible to finish construction on everything, including the antebellum mansion, by the beginning of July. The two story mansion would be located next to a large cluster of live oak trees in the center area of the middle and highest of the three Bluffs.

Nick had been staying in the upstairs portion of his office while the first buildings at the Bluffs were finished. He traveled out to the construction site by boat almost every day with some of the construction workers who were staying at the Bayside Hotel. The oversized construction crews quickly finished the small guest cottage near the pool and Nick began to spend an occasional night out on the property. While out at the site, he closely monitored all of the building activities. Seeing space available, Nick directed that a race track also be constructed.

Some days he stayed in Bay St. Louis to keep up with local gossip by going to Marquette's office or by spending time with one of the local politicians, who were all too happy to have him in their company for everyone to see at lunches and on the streets. Around noon most days he was in town, Nick would walk over to the Bay Café on Front Street overlooking the Bay of St. Louis. The Bay Café was small with a beautiful view of the water from its back deck. It was only six blocks from his office and two blocks from the courthouse. He was usually able to have Mayor Foucher or other politicians at his table, often along with a judge or two. He also made sure he got to know the city policemen and any deputies who might wander in for lunch. Nick anticipated that it wouldn't be long before he would be doing favors for some of his new political friends, such as making contributions to their campaigns or giving them a little cash for spending money from time to time.

About two weeks after work on his downtown office had been completed, Nick was sitting at his desk in the downstairs portion of his office building reviewing paperwork dealing with all of the construction at the Bluffs. He was there by himself since he had not had the time to hire someone to work in his office nor had he run into just the right person for that job. From time to time, people who were his new friends would drop by to say "hi," but Nick knew they were just there hoping to find out more about the latest rumor concerning him or what sort of business he was going to be involved with. Nick always answered by saying that he was checking out numerous options and would not make a hasty decision since he was new to the area. Because he usually did not know who it might be, Nick often kept the front door locked even when he was there. A person never knew when he might need a few extra seconds to grab something to defend himself with, like the pistol that Nick had pulled from his ankle holster in the swamp the day he met Claude.

The knock on the side door to his office was totally unexpected. That door was well-concealed and not generally used, though a few people had been granted access through that entrance for cleaning purposes. Nick got up and walked over to find out who was there. He opened the door and to his surprise a female figure quickly walked through the open door and past him.

"Hello, Mr. Nick Gable," the sheriff's wife said. Nick, thoroughly surprised by Helen's visit and quick entry through the door, looked around from the doorway to see if anyone was with her or had seen her come in. He did not need to have the sheriff as an enemy. With anyone having the nickname Wild Bill, Nick knew he had better be careful. After a quick glance told him no one was watching and, even if they were, could not have seen her unless they had been there looking at just that door, Nick closed and locked the door.

"Well, I have to admit I had about given up hope that you would actually come visit," Nick said.

"Since it finally looked like you finished working on this old building, I thought I would drop by. It seems that you have managed to make it livable again. I wasn't so sure that could be done with it," she said, now slowly walking around the office. Nick watched her admiringly as she looked about.

"I'm glad you like it. It took quite an effort, I have to admit, but it all seemed to come together nicely," Nick said.

She turned and began walking over to the stairs in the middle of the room. Looking back over her shoulder as she started to climb the stairs, she said "What do you have up here, Mr. Nick Gable?"

Nick thought to himself that the sheriff's wife knew exactly what she was doing and had known that well before she had come to Nick's building. He followed her upstairs. Reaching the top of the stairs, which came up to the second floor over next to the wall, Nick said, "This is my living room." Pointing to his left, Nick said, "That couch over there and the sitting chair are where I do most of my reading." Now pointing towards the far back side of the room, he continued, "Over there is my little kitchen." Walking over to a small table next to his sitting chair, Nick said, "If you promise not to tell the sheriff, I will show you a secret."

"Why, Mr. Gable! You have a secret up here?" Helen asked with feigned surprise. Nick pulled a drawer open and pulled out a bottle of whiskey.

"Mr. Gable!" she exclaimed in mock indignation. "You just got to town and already are in possession of illegal beverages. Shame, shame, shame! But I know the sheriff's wife so maybe I could put in a word for you," she said with a wide smile.

Holding the bottle up, Nick said, "I have three other types in here if you want something different. Would you like a drink?" he asked as he turned to face her.

"No, I don't drink, but thanks for the offer," she replied with no rebuke in the tone of her voice.

"Then let me show you my kitchen," he said as he put the bottle back in its place. She made no comment as he guided her to his kitchen which was just behind where the stairs came up to the second floor.

"This is it and I try to avoid using it at all costs," he said, laughing while waving his hand in the direction of the small area as she faintly smiled.

He continued, saying, "If I have to rely on my cooking up here, then I am in serious danger of starvation." She broadened her smile as he said that to a lovely, full smile. He then walked to the doorway at the back of the upstairs level. He stood there at the door and said, "And this is my bedroom."

As he said that, she walked over to where he was now standing in the doorway and stopped to face him, inches from his face.

"I am a lonely, married woman, but then you knew that, didn't you?"

She stayed in Nick's bedroom for more than two hours, spending a large part of that time viewing the ceiling of his bedroom and giving him the best sex he had ever had. He was totally surprised by that, but not as surprised by what happened next. Easing herself on her side and propping her head on her hand, she said, "Okay, Nick, is that what they call you? Nick or Nickey? See how much I don't know about you? What do your close friends call you, or do you even have close friends?"

Nick had wondered when this was coming, all of the questioning that most of the women he had ever been with felt like they just had to put him through. At least Helen had waited a little bit and not started the verbal exercise until the physical exercise had finished.

"For you, Nick will do nicely," Nick said turning to face her and showing a smile. "And I do not have any close friends here, just yet, except maybe now you."

Helen looked into his deep blue eyes. There was a lot more to this man with the dark black, brushed back hair than probably anyone realized, she thought. She could sense by how he guarded his answer to her first question that this effort of hers, to gather information about this man she had just been intimate with, was not going to result in her obtaining a lot of that information easily. That was going to take time, which was a thought she was now beginning to think might be very attractive.

"I bet as a young boy you gave all the girls fits," she said as she playfully stuck her finger in his ribs.

Flinching at her poke in his ribs, he answered, "No. Not me. I was too busy working. Also, I had all of my relatives always keeping me in line." He thought about his answer as he finished it. He did not necessarily want this beautiful being to know about his family's poor life raising sheep and goats on their eleven acres of farm land in Sicily. There were other things he did not want her to know about his family also. After making the comment about his relatives, he briefly thought about his aunts and uncles on both his father's side and his mother's side that had all lived within three miles of their small farm. His answer seemed to inspire her as she propped her head even higher on her hand and, interrupting his thoughts, continued with her effort.

"Where up north were you raised?" she asked.

He knew he had to make a decision about what to tell her. It was a decision that he had made many times before in other situations. There was so much that went into making the decision about what to say, but the result was always the same. He was not going to get into things about his family, even though this woman appeared to be harmless and was only asking the questions because she seemed to be genuinely interested in finding out about him. Still, his background was just not something he was going to talk about, at least not now and not with her.

"Well, let's just say I spent a lot of my recent years in Detroit and now here I am." Nick knew he was going to have to guide this conversation, whatever limited amount of it he was going to have to be involved with, in another direction.

"My life is not nearly as interesting as yours probably was. Being the prettiest girl in the whole area was probably very hard on you, having to fend off all of those boys who I know, even though you won't admit it, were after you all the time!" With that, he playfully poked her in her ribs and she jerked back using both hands to defend herself from such an attack.

"There you go changing the subject and talking about me. We were talking about you," she said, now sitting up on his bed, but with a radiant smile on her face.

"No, you were asking questions about me. We had not gotten to the point of my talking about me."

Seeing her face sadden a bit with that comment, he said, "Okay, I will let you have three questions and that is all. That is more than enough for you to find out all you need to know about me. And remember how you said at the picnic that day we met that you might not answer my questions? Well, I am not saying I will answer yours now. At least not until I know what they are." His smile at the end of his last sentence eased the effect of what he had just said.

"That is not fair, Nick Gable. Three questions? That's all? And you may not even answer those?" She looked at him with a somewhat quizzical look on her face.

He smiled at her and said, "That's it. Go ahead. That's more than I was going to let you ask at first, but go ahead."

She moved so that she was now sitting up on the bed with her legs crossed and said, "Okay. Let's see. You told me at the picnic that you are not married. Have you ever been married, separated or divorced?"

Nick laughed, "Are you going to use all three of your questions up at once?"

"No! That is one question!" she said laughing.

"Didn't sound like it to me. Sounded like three questions to me," Nick said, looking at her wonderful smile.

"No! That is one single question," she answered, still trying.

She was still waiting for an answer, and he wanted to get this over with so he said, "I have never been any of those. Next question."

She thought for a moment and said, "Do you have any brothers or sisters?"

Nick looked at her and thought about his response. His quick response to this question would have him almost through with what he had let himself be taken into by granting her the questions in the first place.

"I have one sister, Madeline, who is three years younger than me and lives in Detroit. Now see, I even told you more than you asked. Look how cooperative I am? Now for your third and final question, Madame Interrogator."

Helen smiled, and then prepared in her own mind how she was going to ask her last question. She knew what it was going to be, but she had to make sure it was phrased correctly to get the most, she hoped, in return. While looking at him, her smile left her face as she then glanced down at the bed before she looked up at Nick. Then she asked it.

"Nick, what is a man like you doing in a place like Bay St. Louis?"

Nick had to control himself. This was a very good question! While the question might seem to be something a person like Helen might want to know just for information purposes, it had the potential to lead to other areas that Nick in no way wanted to get into. Nick wondered how many men this Helen had led to believe that she was just another pretty blonde. Pretty blondes didn't ask questions like this woman had just asked. This wife of the sheriff was ahead of the crowd. He would definitely have to remember that. That question didn't just come out of nowhere. She had thought about getting the answer to that question, probably before she ever made the decision to come see him. That may even be the reason why she was there.

As quickly as he thought about that though, he felt that she was just interested in finding out the answer to the question, being the intelligent person that she was. He had to admit, it didn't make much sense. He had thought about what his answer would be for that very reason; it just didn't make any sense, especially to someone who had any sense at all.

He looked at her and could tell she was going to listen very intently to what he had to say. Just as carefully as she had phrased her question, he would have to carefully phrase his answer. He remembered what he had told Marquette when asked a similar question in Marquette's office that day. He didn't know if Helen would talk to any of her friends about him or not. She probably would not, but then a person never knew. There was no question in his mind, though, that if she did talk to someone, to anyone, at some point whatever he said next would probably be mentioned.

"I came down here to the south because I was tired of the weather. I know that sounds simple but I was born and raised in Sicily, and it was warm in Sicily. I had the chance to come to the United States because some of my relatives had come over here and I took that opportunity to come where there is so much more of a chance for a better life than I ever could have had in Sicily. I went to Detroit because that was where my relatives and many people from Sicily went to." He continually looked at her while he talked and could see she was listening. He decided he would take the same tact with her as he had taken with Marquette.

"Have you ever been to Detroit, Helen?" he asked.

She shook her head and said, "No, I have never been much outside the coast."

Nick nodded and said, "Well, Helen, today in Detroit it is probably

25 degrees with about a foot and a half of snow on the ground. Having snow on the ground may sound like fun but, believe me, after about the first two days of it, you would hate it. At least I did. Here today, in the nice little town of Bay St. Louis, it is probably what, seventy-five degrees, without a cloud in the sky. Remember when I met you, I told you and your friends how beautiful it was that day here."

He looked at her as she took in what he had been saying. She was not going to say anything else. She had listened, but now she really had to go before too much time went by. She would have to wait until another time to ask more questions. She had to worry about other things now, like getting out of this man's bedroom and back into her so-called "normal" life.

She soon left by the same concealed side door through which she had entered. Nick was glad he usually kept the front door locked. She would become a frequent, but always discreet, visitor.

A few days later, while out at the Bluffs, Nick saw Claude in his pirogue on the bayou and waved and yelled at him to come over to the dock at the Bluffs. Claude guided his pirogue over to where Nick was standing on the dock. After Claude had gotten out of his small boat, Nick said, "Claude, I need your help."

"*Monsieur* Neek, if I can help you in any way, the pleasure ees mine, afta what you deed for me," Claude answered in a deeply sincere tone of voice.

Nick asked, "Do you know of anyone that could help do things around here to keep people living in the Bay St. Louis area from coming to the Bluffs uninvited? You know how hard we are working out here to build this place. I just do not want anybody who does not live out here in the bayou to be near what I am putting up on my property."

"Ah, my woman, Carlotta, might be able to help you with taking care of dat problem. She ees a voodoo queen, a priestess. I weel talk wid her and let you know. Me and my people do not want anyone out here either."

"Okay, just let me know. While you are here, there is one other thing I would like to ask you," Nick said. Having Claude's attention, Nick said, "What can you tell me about the bodies that have been found hanging in the swamp?"

After briefly looking at Nick as if to determine exactly how he was going to answer that question, Claude responded, "Theengs like dat have happened in the past, but they are not theengs dat you need to worry about. After all, I owe you and I will keep an eye on theengs for you as long as none of my people are bothered by you or your friends at the Bluffs." With that statement, Claude climbed into his pirogue, and said "I weel talk to you agin soon." He then disappeared into the swamp.

Chapter Five

A large party was held the night of the second Saturday in April 1927 at the Pine Hills Hotel, a very elegant, first class hotel that had just been built by one of the railroad barons who was building rail lines to service the area. The hotel, which had been built at the head of and overlooking the Bay of St. Louis, was certainly one of the finest hotels in the mid-south region. The railroad baron, Harold Trafalgar, had spent an enormous amount of money on railroad construction along the coast and wanted to have a place that could be enjoyed by visitors from all over, but especially by the people of New Orleans and the Gulf Coast. The tellers and officers at the New Orleans bank where Trafalgar conducted his business were always amazed at the large sums of money that were deposited into his accounts from Chicago from time to time.

People who were attending the party from New Orleans had taken the train over and were let off at a station just a short walk from the lobby of the hotel. The train running on the route from New Orleans to Mobile had been stopping there for the past several months since the hotel had opened. The parties at the hotel were becoming famous in New Orleans and gave those needing a reason the opportunity to get out of that city during the already hot spring days.

Nick had decided a few weeks earlier to ask Jenny Green to go to the party with him. He couldn't take Helen, of course, which he would rather have done, but she was going to be there anyway with her husband, Sheriff Patterson. He had seen Jenny numerous times on the streets of Bay St. Louis, and they always enjoyed a brief conversation. Jenny was delighted that such a nice-looking and apparently wealthy man such as Nick had asked her out. She was very seldom asked out, mainly because there were not too many men in the Bay St. Louis area that would behave themselves on a date. Jenny was not interested in having to fight off some man all evening, especially when the men were not the type of person Jenny wanted to be seen with anyway. She attended church regularly and spent a lot of her time taking care of her well-mannered son.

Jenny had been surprised when Nick had come by her nice little home on Sixth Avenue in Bay St. Louis and knocked on her front door. She quickly accepted his invitation to attend the party, even though she knew there would probably be some drinking and carrying on there, which she did not approve of. Being with Nick, though, would make her the envy of almost every girl in Bay St. Louis. After all, everyone knew that this new man in town was spending so much money building on his property out on the bayou. She couldn't pass up the opportunity to be seen with him. Besides, the party just might be fun.

Nick went to Jenny's house to pick her up for the party in his beautiful new car, a Stutz Bearcat, which had just been brought down to him from Detroit. When they drove up at the Pine Hills Hotel in this stylish, top of the line, exquisite convertible, it created quite a stir. No one had seen a car of its type in the area and all of those arriving for the party could not help but notice the cream colored, sleek racing car that was so different from all of the other cars there. The Stutz Bearcat had been the winner of over twenty-five racing titles in recent years and was well-known for its capability of reaching high speeds. It was also known for its high price. Most people in Hancock County had heard about the Stutz Bearcat, but few had ever actually seen one.

A young attendant opened the driver's door and said, "Welcome to the Pine Hills Hotel, Mr. Gable." Jenny was impressed that the attendant knew Nick's name.

"Thank you. Make sure you take good care of my car," Nick said with a smile, giving the youngster a twenty dollar tip and knowing that, because of the size of that tip, the kid would spend a whole day just polishing the Bearcat if he were allowed. After taking the metal parking tab for his car, Nick stood there for a second letting his white cape, an item that only the most upper of upper class men seemed to be wearing, swirl around him while he pulled his white gloves tight, adjusted his white top hat and made sure his white tuxedo and vest were all in place. Jenny soon joined him after having her car door opened by another attendant. She was appropriately attired in an attractive, but not flashy, white dress that was just right for her, not too low cut and with a length of just above her knees. The jealousy in the looks from several female observers toward Jenny for her being with Nick was noticed and appreciated by him, and her, as the couple moved toward the hotel doors.

Nick greeted several people who recognized him and called out to him by name, even though he had no idea who they were. He tipped his hat to all of the ladies with the greeters and kept moving toward the door leading to the lobby of the hotel. Jenny stayed dutifully by his side with a constant smile on her face.

"Good evening, Mr. Gable. Will the two of you be staying with us tonight?" the bellman asked as he held the door leading into the lobby of the hotel open for Nick and Jenny.

"No, not tonight. We are just here to enjoy the party," he said as they prepared to enter the lobby. Looking over to his left, the presence of the train tracks and the train platform not too far from the lobby of the hotel were impressive, though he had seen it many times in Europe when he had been a child. He looked around the grand lobby entrance area as they walked toward the ballroom. Jenny had been to social events at the hotel before and was familiar with it and its lobby area.

The couple made their way to the ballroom entrance where Nick checked his hat and cape at a counter, along with Jenny's purse. As both of them left the check counter, another uniformed hotel worker opened the door for them to enter the grand ballroom. They walked onto an elevated balcony from which grand stairways led down on both sides to the dance floor. Large floor to ceiling windows ran all the way down the left side of the ballroom, giving the attendees an unobstructed view of the beautiful moonlit waters of the Bay of St. Louis. The wall on the opposite side of the ballroom was completely mirrored. Three large chandeliers hung from the center of the ceiling of the room.

As they stood on the balcony taking in the view of the dance floor, the loud sound of fast music led by the band's signature instrument, the clarinet, engulfed them. The dance floor was almost completely covered with dancers. All of them were dressed in formal wear, and all of them tried, the best each one was able, to keep time with the fast pace of the exciting music.

Nick and Jenny made their way down the stairway to their right and then began to work their way around the edge of the dance floor. They were greeted by several party goers, some of whom had already had too much to drink. One particularly attractive young lady dragged her inebriated and disheveled date over and, ignoring Jenny, loudly said, "Nick! Promise me that you will dance with me before the night is over! Promise me!"

Nick remembered the girl as being the daughter of the state senator from Bay St. Louis and who, if his memory served him correctly, was much too young to be at a party like this.

"I have a date with Miss Jenny here and will be spending my time with her. Besides, you seem to have your dance card filled for the evening," Nick answered, nodding toward her very drunk date.

"Oh, he will be passed out soon. I will come find you," she said, smiling and waving to Nick as she was pulled off into the dancing crowd by her staggering date.

Nick and Jenny continued to walk around the edge of the dance floor, looking at the dancers and continually returning greetings and waving to those too far away to speak to.

Leaning near Jenny's right ear, Nick said over the loud noise of the music, "I need to be excused for a few minutes. Do you see someone you could talk with while I am gone so you won't be standing alone?"

Looking around the crowd, she said, "Yes. I can go talk with that group gathered over by that table." She nodded in the general direction of a small gathering of women standing nearby who seemed deep in conversation.

"Good. I won't be gone long," Nick said. Jenny smiled and left Nick to walk over to the group.

After she had left, Nick began to work his way further along the side of the room with all of the mirrors. As he waited at one point for people to move so he could walk further, he felt a presence to his left and turned to see who it was.

"Hello, Mr. Nick Gable," said the presence. It was Helen Patterson, looking absolutely stunning in her low-cut dress, heels, long earrings, and with her hair up.

"Well hello, Mrs. Patterson," Nick answered with a big smile on his face. "Where is the sheriff?"

"He is over there plotting his next campaign," she said with a gesture towards a group of men across the room seemingly involved in a serious conversation. Nick noticed the sheriff had removed his hat for this occasion.

"I see you brought a mouse," she said, now looking straight ahead.

"What?" Nick answered, not quite sure what he had heard and leaning toward Helen so as to hear better what she had to say.

"You brought a mouse," she said again, with a glimmer of a grin on her face as she nodded her head towards Jenny. Realizing now what the reference was she was making, Nick chuckled.

"Oh, you mean my date. She is a very nice person," Nick said smiling as he looked in Jenny's direction.

"Yes, she is. She is a very nice mouse," Helen said again, now with a full grin on her face.

"Mmmm, do I detect a little, uh, jealousy maybe?" Nick said, now looking at Helen.

"Me? Jealous? Mr. Gable! Not me! Your girlfriend might be, but not me. You do have a girlfriend, Mr. Gable, don't you?"

"Well, I would not tell many people this, but I will tell you, confidentially, of course. I do have a girlfriend, a very beautiful woman that I have just started seeing and care a lot about, but she could not be here with me tonight."

A look of surprise came over Helen's face and she quickly said, "Oh, really?"

Nick leaned over closer and said in a lowered voice, "Yes. You see, she's married," Nick whispered. "Don't tell anyone."

"Oh, Mr. Gable! I will certainly not say anything! Does the mouse know?" Helen asked, her beautiful smile back on her face.

"No! Nobody knows."

Looking back at Nick, Helen said, "Well, be careful taking the mouse home tonight. We wouldn't want anything to happen to that sweet, furry, little thing while it was on its way home."

Nick let out a full laugh. As he did, Helen edged away and disappeared into the large crowd.

Once Helen was out of sight and after checking to see that Jenny was still comfortably associated with her small group of ladies, Nick began edging his way further along the mirrored wall of the dance floor. Doors were located about every seventy-five feet or so along the wall, but they could only be identified by the presence of their gold plated door knobs because the doors were covered with mirrors also. He gradually moved to an area next to one of the doors and paused there, observing all of the fun and frivolity.

After watching the dancers and the crowd for a few moments and seeing that Jenny was now fully involved talking with her friends, Nick discreetly reached down and found the door knob he was looking for. Twisting the knob he quickly opened the door and slipped behind it, closing it just as quickly as he had opened it. He started walking down a dimly-lit hallway to an intersection with another hallway. Turning left at the intersection, he walked down that hallway to its end, pulling his gloves off as he walked.

At the end of that hallway, he turned to the right and walked until he reached the second door on the right. Stopping in front of the door, he looked briefly both to his right and his left before knocking on the door. Softly, his knuckles struck the door: knock-knock, knock, knock-knock. After a few tense seconds, the door opened and Nick walked in, looking around the room as the door was quickly shut behind him. Seeing the man whom he had come to see, Nick walked over to him, smiling, with his hand out to greet him.

"Welcome to the Mississippi Gulf Coast, Mr. Capone."

Chapter Six

Nick was always skeptical about talking with Al Capone in front of other people, even those people he knew Capone felt comfortable being around. Capone was involved in illegal businesses, mostly the shipment of liquor, but also drugs, prostitution and other things. He was the very definition of the term "gangster." The one piece of information that people talked about the most, besides the long scar on the left side of his face that had led to the nickname he hated of "Scarface," was that Capone was rumored to have murdered so many people himself. What most people didn't know was that Capone had been so successful that, if all of his operations had been considered legitimate businesses, those businesses would have been listed among the largest and most financially successful businesses in the country.

Because of everything they had been through together, Nick always felt that he and Capone had a special relationship. The big bear hug Capone now gave him after shaking his hand added to that feeling. Capone just didn't give out hugs like that. He didn't trust many people; and, because of that, he didn't like letting people, especially men, get that close to him physically. However, Nick had done things for Capone that nobody knew about. Those things could cause both him and Capone a lot of problems if they ever became known. Oh, he had seen the two men in the room now with Capone quite a few times. Still, he was just a little bit uneasy. But they were Capone's men and if Capone felt he wanted to talk in front of them, then Nick had to go along with it. Still, Nick liked doing things nobody knew about. Nobody, that is, except Capone. Now he knew Capone wanted to find out how much progress Nick had made down here in Mississippi. After all, he had given Nick a lot of money to set things up down here.

"Good to see you, Nicky," Capone said with his distinctive accent as he motioned Nick to a chair next to where he was now sitting. Cigar smoke filled the air, but it was not as heavy as Nick had seen it on many other occasions. That was a sure sign that Capone had only been there for a little while. As Nick settled into his chair, Capone said, "How are things going out at the Bluffs?"

"Everything is coming along fine. Not much construction work is left to be done. The shipping docks are finished as are the two large storage barns where we can keep the liquor until we get ready to send it out. The guest house is finished also. The big house will take a while longer but, with the extra crews, it should be finished by late June or early July. It has all gone very well so far."

"Good! Good. I knew you would handle things. You always do. So you are ready to store everything that is shipped to you until it is ready to be sent out, right?" Capone asked while taking another puff from his cigar.

"Yes, sir. By the time it all starts getting here, we will be ready at the Bluffs," Nick answered, glancing at each of the two men leaning on the dresser drawers which were up against the wall on the side of the room. "We might want to wait until the construction crews are finished with the big house and gone so we don't have any of those guys asking questions about what's in the barrels being shipped in there."

"Yes. I agree. I want you to be all set up before we move to the next stage of this operation down here. Now that you are getting closer to being ready, it's time for you to go visit each of the local lumber yards. Just like we talked about at our last meeting in Chicago. They ship a lot of lumber out of this area. Go get their cooperation, Nicky. Do what you have to do, but get it. They may be happy to get some additional money. Try the easy way first, but if that doesn't work, do what you have to do. You make sure that those large boats that they use to ship lumber out of here to Cuba come back carrying what all we have waiting for us down there. Buy the yards if you have to, Nicky, I'll make sure you have the money you need for that, but just make sure you get it done. You did a good job for me in Detroit, and you have done a good job here so far. I know you will take care of it."

"Yes sir, Mr. Capone. I will."

Capone leaned forward toward Nick and in a low voice said, "Nicky, on Saturday three weeks from today, go to New Orleans and at eleven o'clock be at the Canal Street docks. Find a boat there named the *Sea Witch*. It will take you to Cuba so you can meet your contact there in Havana, a man named Fernando Gonzales. Fernando is already receiving the shipments of liquor that are coming to Cuba by boat from Canada and the Caribbean islands. He'll see to it that the lumber boats will be coming back to you loaded with our shipments. We need to start moving the stuff in here as soon as we can. We are working with a guy named Kennedy up in the northeast and Canada, but I don't really trust him yet. Just make sure everything is all set to go in Cuba and match it up with your end here. Get everything coordinated between down there and up here, Nicky."

"Yes sir, Mr. Capone. I will."

Capone stood up as Nick was answering and walked over to the closet in the far corner of the room. Taking something out of the closet, he then came back to where Nick was sitting. He had a light blue handkerchief in his hand. Giving it to Nick, Capone said, "Carry this in your left hand when you get off the boat at the Havana docks. Fernando will be carrying in his left hand a handkerchief the same color as this one. You can trust him, Nicky. Listen to what he says while you're there."

"What if he doesn't show up at the docks?"

Capone answered, "Oh, he'll be there, but if for some reason he is not there, go on to the Cabana Hotel just off of the docks, check in and wait. If somebody tries to meet you and doesn't have this same colored handkerchief in his left hand, don't deal with him. If Fernando does not show up in twenty-four hours, take the same boat and return to New Orleans and call me immediately. I'll be in Chicago. He will be there unless something goes wrong."

Capone then said, "Now it's time for you to go, Nicky. People at the party will start to miss you."

Nick stood up and began walking with Capone toward the door to the room.

"Just so you know, Mr. Capone. The county sheriff, Sheriff Bill Patterson, is in the hotel ballroom at the party. I just wanted to make sure you knew that."

Capone stopped and, looking at Nick, said, "You mean Sheriff Wild Bill Patterson. Is that who you mean?"

"Why, yes," Nick answered, a bit surprised to say the least.

"Do you know him?" Nick was very interested in how this question was going to be answered.

"Let's just say I know who he is," Capone said. Nick immediately thought, why should he be surprised that Capone would know something about Sheriff Patterson? One of Capone's biggest assets was that he always tried to know as much as he could about any situation he was going to get involved with. This would be no exception. If Capone was going to set up a major operation shipping illegal booze into the southern United States through Hancock County, Mississippi, it stood to reason that he would at least find out something about its sheriff.

"You'll have to decide how to deal with him, Nicky. That will be one of the most important things that you will do here, how you deal with him. I have been told that his word is his bond. I am going to leave how he is dealt with up to you, for the time being. If dealing with him is mishandled, things will be much more difficult here. So don't mess it up. A man standing by his word is a lot different from what we had to deal with in Detroit, right Nicky?" Capone said.

Nick understood completely what Capone meant and said, "Yes, sir. That is for sure."

Capone now put his hand on Nick's shoulder.

"Nicky, you did a good job for me with that terrible situation up there. That is why I put you in charge down here. I appreciate what all you went through, but I also greatly appreciate the fact that you took care of things there."

Then Capone turned more toward Nick and said, "That brings us to one more thing, Nicky. Your sister, Madeline, is going to be coming to stay with you at the Bluffs. She wants to get out of Detroit because she keeps thinking about her husband dying up there and all. I will let you know when she is going to come down here. With her down here, you can sort of keep an eye on her. It's alright if you go ahead and include her in some of the things that will be going on down here, if you can. That's up to you. Including her in some way may help her get her mind away from everything that happened up there. Maybe she can help you with furnishing the big house or help you with some of your political connections down here. She would probably be good at both of those things. She knows generally about why you are down here; but, Nicky, she does not know all of the details about what happened in Detroit."

Nick was startled, but tried not to show it. He was surprised, to say the least, to hear that his younger sister, Madeline Benedetti, was coming to the Mississippi Gulf Coast, but he understood what Capone was saying. Several thoughts quickly crossed his mind, but there was one thing he was absolutely sure of. Things would definitely be different here for Nick with her around. He didn't necessarily like it, but knew there was nothing he could do about it. She would be a distraction though.

Nodding at one of the men now standing just a few feet away, Capone said, "Carmine here will be coming down from time to time to check on things. When he is here he will be speaking for me, so if he says something that's the way it will be. Understand?"

"Yes, sir, I understand." Nick decided to go ahead and bring up one more rather important subject.

"Mr. Capone, I need to mention one other thing to you. I think it would be helpful to have some muscle down here now instead of waiting until later. I could use five or six of the boys from Chicago or Detroit, boys that I know I could count on, if you can spare them, especially while we are getting all of this started."

Capone looked at Nick as they began to slowly walk towards the door and said, "Okay. Sure, I'll send a few of them down here to help you out. I agree that it would probably be better to have them come on down now rather than later. We have to make sure they would be what you need here. What about 'Tiny'? I think he might be a good fit for this area."

Nick remembered Tiny. How could anyone forget him! Tiny was probably the biggest man he had ever seen, a 6 foot 7 inch black man that weighed over 250 pounds, but Nick remembered him as being fit and very agile for his size.

As they neared the door to the room, Capone continued. "And 'Rocko'. What about Rocko? He would probably be good down here, too. You remember him, don't you? He might be good here taking care of some of your more difficult problems."

Nick thought about Rocko and how utterly cruel he could be. Rocko was certainly the right person to get a point across to anyone anywhere, much less people in this area. Rocko in the small, quiet southern town of Bay St. Louis would be like the proverbial bull in a china shop. Nick would have to try to restrict him to the Bluffs as much as possible.

Turning to face Capone, Nick said, "Yes, they both would be good here."

"Okay. I'll have them down here along with a few others within the next couple of weeks or so. They will all report to you while they are down here."

"Thanks, Mr. Capone. Good to see you again. Have a safe trip back."

Capone grabbed the door knob and, holding it, said, "Thanks, Nicky. I will. You have a safe trip to Cuba. Be careful down there, and here. Don't take any chances here while we are getting all of this started up. It's been good to see you, Nicky. Like I said, you've done a good job here so far. I know you will keep it up. Let me know if you need anything else. "

"Thanks, Mr. Capone. I will."

Capone opened the door and Nick, with a nod of his head to the other two men in the room, stepped through the doorway, hearing the door shut behind him.

As he walked down the hallway back to the ballroom, Nick thought about what they had just discussed. He also thought about how successful the man he just met with had been in Detroit. Capone had seen the wisdom of reaching an agreement with the Purple Gang, the group they had literally been at war with in Detroit. The Jewish guys running that gang were tough, very tough, but they were also good businessmen, just like Capone. It had been beneficial to each side to stop doing things like shooting each others' men and breaking up each others' shipments and just co-operate with one another. After they had reached an agreement to help each other instead of fighting each other, they both ended up profiting so much that it took large suitcases to deliver the money to where it was supposed to go.

Yes, it had turned out fine for Capone in Detroit and, despite his relatively young age, Nick had been in the middle of it and had helped actually bring it all about there. He also quickly remembered some of the bad things he had done for Capone there, especially that last thing Capone had made Nick do just before sending him down here. But Capone had given him the time and the money to set up the operation down here the right way. Now they were ready to move forward and go the next step.

Having reached the door to the ballroom, Nick opened it and stepped into the packed room, slipping back into it and the unsuspecting world of the Mississippi Gulf Coast.

Chapter Seven

Three days after his meeting with Capone at Pine Hills, Nick received word that Madeline would be arriving on Thursday morning at ten-twenty at Union Station in New Orleans on the daily train from Chicago, the *Panama Limited*. The train was scheduled to leave Chicago at six-fifteen the evening before and Nick was to meet her upon her arrival. Having gone over the operation in his mind, Nick thought that Madeline would be helpful in picking out furnishings for the main house being built at the Bluffs and in overseeing the household staff that would be working out at the Bluffs. He also thought that Madeline might actually be helpful with some of their efforts on the Gulf Coast, such as participating in the cultivation of political contacts in the area, and also with attempts to find out information about those who might try to stop or interfere with their operations.

As Nick sat in the New Orleans station waiting for the train to arrive, he thought back over his and Madeline's early days together in Sicily. She had been born three years after him. When she was five, she had gone to the same church school Nick had attended when he was that age. She had been an ugly duckling then. However, as she grew older she had developed into a beautiful young woman. Not only did she have a lovely face, but her figure eventually developed to the point where she was constantly noticed by almost every man, regardless of age. Whenever she had been around any male, she was the subject of numerous gazes, looks and comments, and the topic of a lot of conversation, much to the despair of her family. Nick's father constantly had to keep boys away from her. Her mother had little to do with her because of the long hours her mother spent working in town at a cleaners to bring in extra money for the family.

Nick remembered when he began to have to go have "talks" with Madeline's young suitors. In two instances, he actually had to punch the young men out in order to make the point that they should not come around any more without the permission of their father. This only made Madeline mad since she loved the attention and would get bored because no one was usually around. Nick remembered that, when Madeline was only fifteen, she used to try to meet with boys two years or more older than her. One of them, Nick remembered, was Johnny Bertucci, who Madeline thought was exciting and worldly. Nick found out though that Johnny was telling everybody that he had met Madeline several times after school on a bluff overlooking the ocean for her first experiences with the opposite sex. Their father had told Nick to go convince Johnny that he should keep his mouth shut and also should not even think about seeing Madeline anymore, which Nick had reluctantly done.

Not too long thereafter though, Madeline had her eyes on another boy just a year older than her, Anthony Scabelli, and Johnny was just a memory. With her sights now on him, it had not been long before Anthony had begun to show this younger girl with such a great figure some flirtatious attention. Not too long after, Anthony was the boy Nick had to worry about Madeline meeting at her favorite spot overlooking the ocean. Those meetings ended though, not because of what Nick tried to do to stop them, but because Madeline began to work at the same place her mother worked. Nick remembered that Madeline was always trying to meet Anthony because they seemed to like the same things, but most of all because, Nick sincerely thought, they began to truly care for each other.

Nick sat on his bench thinking about so many other things that had happened with Madeline in Italy. He kept coming back, though, to

Madeline and Anthony. Anthony was a good person; and, in Nick's opinion, did the right things for the right reasons. When Nick had gone to talk with Anthony, just as he had done before with Madeline's other suitors, Anthony had just been a nice guy. He finally convinced Nick that he really, truly loved Madeline and would do anything to protect her.

Anthony was not the typical male from that area at that time. He was not involved in all of the gang related activities going on, but instead had his mind set on being good so that one day he might join the army. His dad was an officer in the Italian army and Anthony, who looked up to him, wanted to be an officer also. While the dad would never be rich, the family led a comfortable life. The dad was able to support his family and adequately provide for them. When Anthony turned seventeen he joined the army, with the help of some of his dad's friends who pretended to not know he was a year younger than the age for military service.

Nick remembered how tearful Madeline had been when Anthony had left to go to training camp. She constantly asked Nick why Anthony had left her if he loved her. She loved him and he said he loved her. Nick had no answer for her. He did remember though that it wasn't long after Anthony had left that Madeline began seeing other men. Nick tried to talk to her about it, but she was bitter over Anthony voluntarily leaving her when she loved him. Nick remembered how Madeline loved attention and had toyed with the new men she was seeing. None of the men, in Nick's opinion, were anything like Anthony.

Nick had not liked the men Madeline had started seeing. It all seemed to be a game to her. One of the men was the son of wealthy parents that owned a shipping company in town. Nick noticed how the man would always pretend to not know Madeline when he saw her in public, as if she wasn't good enough for him, but that same man was always after her to spend time with him when few people were around. Nick could not stand the man; fortunately, after almost a year, Anthony came back from training camp for a visit. While back in the area he asked Madeline to marry him. A date was set for six months later when Anthony could return on another leave from the army.

Madeline and Anthony's wedding had been a big family affair. The day had been one of those without a cloud in the sky. The ceremony had been held in the church in which Madeline and Nick had been raised.

Nick was Anthony's best man and was proud of his sister that day. Madeline had looked beautiful in her wedding dress and her smile had been radiant. It was probably one of the happiest days in her life that Nick had ever witnessed. She had been so happy and so had Anthony.

Everybody had liked Anthony. He was such a fine person. His dad had been there dressed in his finest military uniform. He and Anthony's mother had been so proud of their son. Nick's parents were happy because they both liked Anthony and his parents also.

There had been a big party with lots to eat and drink. It had lasted well into the night though Madeline and Anthony had left early in the evening. They had enjoyed a brief honeymoon and Anthony had gone back to the army. Not too long after that was the worst day of Madeline's life. World War I had started and Italy became involved. Within four months of Italy entering the conflict, Anthony had been killed fighting for his country.

"The *Panama Limited* will be arriving on track four in ten minutes," a porter announced as he came walking by, interrupting Nick's recollections.

As the porter disappeared into the crowded station, Nick began thinking about Madeline and Detroit. Not such pleasant memories. After Nick had arrived safely in the United States, his mom and dad kept trying to get Nick to find some way for Madeline to join him in the land of opportunity. Europe was so dangerous with what they were now calling a "World War" going on. There was never going to be any type of future for a young woman who was widowed, even though her being a widow had been caused by the war. Nick felt that he had looked out for Madeline enough. It was time for her to make her own way in life. Nick's parents had gotten him out of the country just before he was to be drafted into the army for the war. The boat trip over to the United States had been horrible. For one thing, the boat itself was crowded with too many people. Nick had also stayed seasick almost the entire trip. It had gotten to the point during the trip that there was not much he could eat and what little he could eat was not enough.

After he had finally arrived in New York City, it had been additionally difficult for him, being a young Italian immigrant in such a vast country as the United States, to find a job. That was the main reason why he changed his last name from Gabolini to Gable and why he eventually ended up in Chicago. That was also why he had ended up working for

Capone. There were simply no jobs for Italian boys, and it had gotten to where Nick had to do something to survive. That something ended up being introduced to the leader himself through one of Capone's men, who also had been a refugee from Sicily. After doing a few minor jobs for him, Capone had been impressed with Nick and began to give him more and more things to do.

Nick had finally been able to get Madeline to Chicago. There she met her second husband, Carlo Benedetti, a dashing Italian playboy who, Nick thought, had no backbone at all. Madeline enjoyed the good times that Carlo showed her, and at Carlo's insistence, constantly began asking Nick to get Carlo involved in Capone's operations. Since Capone was trying to move into Detroit and needed additional members for his gang, Madeline repeatedly asked Nick to help Carlo become part of Capone's activities in that new market. Nick had been sent over to Detroit when Capone first began to move into that area. Capone almost immediately began to assign Nick more and more responsibility there. Finally, with Nick's help, Carlo became a member of Capone's gang in Detroit. It hadn't been too long afterward that the gang war there with the Purple Gang had broken out.

Not too long after Carlo had been made a member of Capone's gang, under Nick's sponsorship, he was assigned tasks that, for whatever the reason, never seemed to get performed. There seemed to always be a reason that he did not make a pickup at the scheduled time of some of the bundles of cash generated by Capone's operations. Other times he would fail to be on time for meetings or just not show up at all. Capone had told Nick how displeased he was with Carlo, but let Nick handle the situation with Carlo because they needed the manpower. The war with the Purple Gang had been taking its toll and then the federal government, through its lead agency in the prohibition fight, the Internal Revenue Service or IRS, began trying to bring a halt to the illegal manufacture and shipment of liquor in the Detroit area.

It was during those difficult days that Nick became aware of Carlo's attention to various barmaids who had become impressed with the money Carlo was spending or the big diamond pin he wore in his lapel. Madeline loved the playboy, though, mainly because Carlo spent a lot of money on her. He always put on a big show about how much he loved her and cared for her. Then Nick thought about how, in Detroit over the short period of three weeks, the Purple Gang and Capone had reached a truce and decided to work together. As a result of that agreement, information had changed hands that had dramatic results. Now Carlo was dead and Madeline had not been able to take being alone in Detroit anymore.

"The *Panama Limited* is now arriving on track four," the porter announced as he again made his rounds.

This announcement brought Nick back to the present. In just a few moments he was going to see Madeline. He didn't think she knew much about the details of the more immediate past. Capone had told him she would never know everything.

When she got off of the train, Nick was again struck by her beauty, even though she was his kid sister. She was a gorgeous brunette Italian woman, now twenty-seven years old. She was still well-proportioned at five feet six inches with black hair, which this day was up in a bun. Her big hips and the size of her abundant bust let everyone know that this was one person who was all female. She was impeccably dressed with appropriate and expensive jewelry to match her outfit of a long skirt with matching jacket and blouse that she might wear on Sundays to church. Nick hoped that she had recovered from the death of her husband whom she had loved so much. It had been almost a year since he had been killed in Detroit.

"Hello, big brother," she said with a smile.

"Hello, little sister," Nick answered back with a smile of his own and a big hug. He was glad to see her. After all, he had spent a lot of time in his life trying to protect her. Nick did not note any sadness though he knew that she had been devastated by the death of Carlo. She had lost Anthony in Italy just a few years earlier and then had lost Carlo in the United States. Now, she was in New Orleans and seemed genuinely happy to be there.

Finally getting all of her bags unloaded and put onto the train for Bay St. Louis, Nick was able to settle himself into the seat next to her.

"Now I can give you the official welcome. Welcome to the sunny South," Nick said with enthusiasm.

Madeline replied, "Why thank you, brother. I appreciate your letting me come down here. I really do. Carlo's death has just been too much for me."

Nick tried to soothe her. "I know it has been tough for you. You will like it down here. It's a new start for you. At least it's warmer here."

"I was just so lonely there, Nick, with Carlo gone. It just seemed to always be so cold, so dreary. Not at all like Sicily. It was hard to do anything for fun anymore, with Carlo not there."

"I can imagine," Nick said. He realized this was his chance to ask a question that he really needed to know the answer to. She had known that Nick and her husband Carlo had worked for Capone, first in their war with the Purple Gang in Detroit, and then in their joint efforts to ship illegal liquor into that city. He needed to know something else so he went ahead and asked it.

"Madeline, I know Mr. Capone has financially helped each widow of the members of our outfit killed by the Purple Gang during our war with them. Has he helped you financially since Carlo was killed?"

Madeline turned to look at her brother for a moment, and then said, "He has helped me like he has the others, but I don't have money like I did when Carlo was alive. I have had to worry about having enough to live on ever since then and I used to never have to worry about that. It really bothers me, having to worry about money, and also just being so lonely, so bored. We had a fun life together. Now, I spend almost day after day crying. I just couldn't take it anymore. So here I am. Thanks for letting me come."

"You are most welcome, little sister. You knew I would help you if I could."

She turned her head facing the front of the railcar and, after briefly looking out of the window of the train, she continued.

"Mr. Capone didn't give me an answer when I first asked him about coming down here. He just said he would think about it and talk to you. Finally, he had one of his men call me and tell me it was alright. I knew you were trying to set up something down here for him, but that didn't matter to me as long as it didn't matter to Mr. Capone. I was just so glad it was alright. I had to get away from up there because of those bad memories."

Nick watched his sister as she talked. He had to agree with the conclusion of everybody that laid eyes on her. It was unanimous. She was still absolutely beautiful. Age, which usually had been hard on their female relatives by their mid-twenties, had not hurt her at all so far. If anything, it had made her even more attractive. It was hard to believe that the little girl who had really been so plain as a young child had turned into such a striking woman.

Madeline looked out the window of the train viewing the scenery for most of the remaining portion of the trip over to the town of Bay St. Louis. They both knew it was best to not talk too much while there were other people close by. When they arrived at the train station at Bay St. Louis, a driver with Nick's Lincoln was there waiting for them, which impressed Madeline. After a short ride around the quaint downtown area, they were on their way to Cypress Landing to meet one of the transport boats there.

Madeline was amazed in a contradictory sort of way as they traveled. She could not believe how nice the town of Bay St. Louis was but when they got to Cypress Landing, which was several miles away from town, she could not believe how far out in the swamp Nick's property was. As they got on the barge and began their trip on the bayou, Madeline was almost speechless, a fact not lost on Nick. He had known his sister all her life and, though she had never been a woman who just talked all the time, he took notice that she was observing everything, but not saying much at all as she experienced her first boat trip in the swamp going to the Bluffs.

Coming around the last bend of the bayou, Madeline saw the construction on the massive structure that was going to be the mansion on the center of the three bluffs fronting the bayou. After the boat docked, Nick led her up the stairs to the top of the center bluff. On the way up the stairs he told her, "Wait until you see this, little sister." At the top of the stairs, they stopped and she looked at the view in front of her and around her. She started looking from the very beginning at the open area in front of where the big house was being built. She then looked first one way, at the bathhouses and race track and then the other way, to more bathhouses and the small guest house. She then looked in the distance at the bunkhouses and the barns. But then she focused her gaze back on the foundation and brick piers holding the frame that was already in place for the big house. She couldn't wait to walk closer to the site.

As they walked up to the location, Nick said, "Just so you know, all of the modern comforts will be in the house. It will have indoor plumbing so that you won't have to go to an outhouse."

Nick saying that utterly pleased her. Though many houses in Detroit, and Chicago for that matter, had indoor plumbing, finding out that it would also be out here in the middle of a swamp at this house under construction was something that impressed her.

"You will be the mistress of the house, Madeline. I have already employed a small staff of two cooks, a maid who will also be a laundress, and a butler. They are all Negroes and live in the small bunk houses that have been built on the back side of the Bluffs."

As they stood there looking at the site for the big house, Nick said, "Anything that you want will be provided for you here, within reason of course." Madeline smiled and thought that was wonderful, especially with her having had only limited funds in Detroit.

Madeline settled into one of the two bedrooms in the guest house and began to oversee the activities of the household staff. Nick spent the first few nights Madeline was there in the other bedroom of the guest house. He then began to sometimes spend the night in town so he could stay in better touch with what the latest local information was.

Five horses had been brought out to the Bluffs by Nick. Madeline began riding the horses almost every day and soon was riding well. She would don her riding clothes, walk down to the stables, where word had usually been sent as to the exact time that she would be there and which of the five horses she wanted to ride. She quickly became an excellent rider and seemed to be able to sense which horse would be the best one for her to ride that day.

A little over a week after her arrival, Madeline even went fishing with Nick on the bayou one afternoon. It was then that she saw voodoo symbols for the first time. Nick decided that while they waited for the fish to start biting, he would give her a brief history lesson on the area and its people.

"There are people who live out in this swamp, Madeline, that you might see from time to time but they stay away from everybody, especially people they don't know. If you try to get up close to them in a boat or on land they usually go the opposite way and disappear. Most of these are what we call swamp people. A large portion of the swamp people are creoles. They have their own language, a mixture, as my lawyer friend Dudley Marquette says, of French, English, and their own made up words," Nick said with a chuckle.

Continuing he said, "They are descendants of the French-speaking Acadians that left Canada over a century ago when the British took over that area. They didn't want to live under British rule so they got into boats and came down the Mississippi River to the area mainly around

New Orleans, which was under French control for part of that time back then."

Seeing that Madeline was listening intently to what he had been saying, he took a breath and continued.

"Creoles usually have darker color skin because when the Acadians got down here many of them lived with and had children by the black slaves, freed blacks or Indians. Some of their ancestors were associated in the early 1800s with the pirate Jean Lafitte, who was in this area. Lafitte and his friends helped General Andrew Jackson win the Battle of New Orleans in 1814 against the British."

Thinking for a moment, Madeline said, "Why do they run away from you? I would think they would want to get to know you so that you could help each other out here in the swamp if someone needed it."

Nick had always appreciated that his sister, in addition to being beautiful, had a lot of common sense, so it was not surprising to him that she would ask that question.

"You would think so, but for whatever the reason, they stay to themselves. I have gotten to know one of them a little bit, a man named Claude. I don't know where he lives out here, but I do see him from time to time. His girlfriend is a woman named Carlotta. He has told me she is some type of voodoo queen or priestess. When I heard that, I thought it might be good to have this area marked off with voodoo symbols. Anybody who may be out here checking things out or possibly have gotten lost might get scared enough to go somewhere else if they were to run across voodoo symbols. I am going to talk to them about that in the next couple of weeks or so. We are in pretty good shape here because nobody has ever found our dock unless we sent a guide to bring them. It is really easy to get lost out here, which helps us."

Thinking for a moment, Madeline said, "I have heard about voodoo, but really don't know much about it. What is it?" she asked, intently looking at her brother.

"I've asked around, and I guess one way it could be described is that, like Christians worship Jesus and sometimes use the symbol of the cross in church, voodoo is the worship of the devil and his symbol which, I am told by people I have asked in New Orleans, is the upside down cross, like a cross driven into the ground."

"Oh, that is horrible!" Madeline exclaimed.

"I know. I felt the same way when I was told about it. I guess that is because of our upbringing in the Catholic Church, but that is not the worst of it. Supposedly, they do some really strange things, like drinking the blood of animals such as pigs, goats and chickens, and sometimes dancing with snakes," Nick said.

"Oh, no! I like this place less now that I know about that," Madeline said, clearly a little uneasy by what she had just been told. All of a sudden, the place didn't seem quite so beautiful anymore. After all she had been through the last few years though, she quickly made the decision that she wasn't going to let it affect her if some of these mixed breeds out in the swamp somewhere might be really weird with their religion, if a person could call it a religion. After all, Nick had said that they didn't want to be around people like her anyway. That was fine with her. They could stay strange, as long as they stayed away from her and also out of her way.

Nick continued to talk, trying to make Madeline feel a little less uneasy about her new home.

"I have been working real hard to set up Mr. Capone's plan for a shipping operation down here. We are going to have the booze brought by boat to Cuba from Canada by that Kennedy fellow and from all over the Caribbean by other people. We are going to try to use the boats of lumber companies down here that take lumber to Cuba to bring back barrels of rum, whiskey and a few other things into here. From here, it will all be shipped to various places all over the south, from Texas to Tennessee to Alabama and Florida. So far, we have been able to do everything we needed to do and not attract a lot of attention. We need to keep it that way in order to continue being successful. We have gone out of our way to not draw any attention to ourselves. All I have mentioned to people here is that over the past two years I made some good investments in the stock market and that I came down here to get away from the cold weather."

Taking a moment, Nick then continued, "Oh, we are going to have a party out here when the big house is finished, but that will be just so everybody can come and see for themselves that this is a first-class place, even though it is in the middle of a huge swamp. After the word gets around from those who attend the party about how nice it is out here, that should satisfy most people's interests so that they can begin to talk about other things. That is exactly what we want them to do, talk about other things. Meanwhile, we will continue on with our special business."

Madeline looked at her brother while he talked. He had done well for Mr. Capone and it all was beginning to come together. She had to ask, though, what was on her mind.

"Nick, what part can I play in all of this, besides managing the help at the house? Is there anything I can do to help you and Mr. Capone with everything that will be going on?"

"There may be. You could really be helpful by keeping your eyes and ears open for us. See if you can find out anything that might help us avoid a really bad situation like we found ourselves in with that Detroit war we were in with the Purple Gang. We really don't need something like that happening down here. Right now, it seems that things here are wide open for us to get established. In time, after you get sort of acclimated to the area and familiarize yourself with what all we are going to be doing down here, I think you could be a big help to us. After all, you are beautiful," Nick said with a smile. She returned Nick's smile with a faint smile of her own and Nick continued.

"You do have to be careful down here though. People here are very leery of outsiders, especially people from up *nawth*, as they call it," he said with a grin at the expression of the word using an exaggerated southern accent.

"You will have to be introduced gradually. Also, I guess I should tell you, most southern women are very reserved compared with northern women. They are more likely to talk about a person behind their back than be confrontational like a lot of northern women we know," Nick said with a wide grin, the reference to Madeline's normal way of doing things being readily apparent.

"I will do my best to be uncontroversial, big brother, but I have to tell you that I really don't care what they think or say about me. I am way past worrying myself about something like that," she said with firmness in her voice.

Nick continued, "It would help a lot if you would take on the responsibility of furnishing the mansion. Just treat it as if it were your own. We will have more than enough money to make it extremely nice. I talked with Mr. Capone before I came down here and he said he understood that if I was going to be out in this swamp and doing everything I had to in order to discreetly run this operation that I had to be able to build something nice out here to make it livable."

Looking at Madeline so as to make his point, Nick said, "So, Madeline, that means that you can go to Rome, pick out things there, and have them sent here for this house, if you want."

A big smile appeared on Madeline's face. "Really? Oh, Nick! Shopping in Rome!" she exclaimed. "Does that also mean while I am there that I can go see our relatives and friends in Sicily?"

"If you would like to do that, that is exactly what it means, Madeline," Nick answered with a big smile.

"That is so wonderful! Thank you, brother. Thank you, thank you, thank you!" she all but yelled.

Nick smiled. It was so good to see her happy again, genuinely happy. Nick knew Capone would not have a problem with her making that trip or for the purposes that she was going. After all, it was Capone that had said she might be helpful in picking out furnishings for the house. Since Capone would probably be spending nights at the Bluffs from time to time, of all people, he would appreciate the mansion being furnished in a first-class manner. If there was one thing Nick's sister could do, it was act in a first class manner. She would see to it that what was put in that house out in the swamp would be second to none.

At that point, the tip of Madeline's fishing pole bent as she felt the telltale pull on the line indicating she had just caught a fish. While again squealing with delight, Madeline realized that this was the first time, in her whole life, that she had caught a fish using a fishing pole. She fully anticipated that there might just be other firsts down here for her as well.

Chapter Eight

As Madeline spent time recovering from her train trip from Chicago and learning more about riding horses, she also became familiar with the floor plans of the mansion to the extent that she now felt she was ready to travel to Italy on her shopping trip. Nick found out that there were numerous ships making the various legs of the trip Madeline needed to make. There was a demand for goods from the old world, as well as a demand for various raw materials from the new world. Therefore, it had not been as difficult a trip to plan as he had first thought it might be. He was able to make arrangements for her to leave in the next week by boat from New Orleans to Havana, Cuba and from there to Rome.

Madeline was fortunate in that two prominent couples from New Orleans were making the same trip to Rome at the same time also for shopping reasons, plus taking short vacations. State Court Judge Marvin Tullos and his wife, Delores, and Federal District Court Judge Jonathan Parker and his wife, Betsy, found time from their busy court and social schedules to finally make the trip that they had all often talked about in the past. Nick's concern for Madeline's safety on the trip over was now alleviated. Soon Madeline and the two couples departed from New Orleans. Madeline's expected travel time was approximately ten weeks.

His sister's departure allowed Nick to focus on his responsibilities. He had no trouble identifying the owners of the three largest lumber yards in the area. He already had heard a little bit about each one of them. After asking a few questions of his new-found friends in the days following his meeting with Capone at the Pines Hill Hotel, he felt he was ready to go see the owners of two of the largest lumber yards in Hancock County. He had to work quickly because of his own upcoming trip to Havana. He had hoped to have everything in place for making his shipments before he made his trip to the Caribbean, so he could identify the boats that he would be using for the shipments.

The day after Madeline left on her trip, Nick was contacted by Claude. Claude told Nick that he and his girlfriend would meet with Nick to discuss what they could do to keep people away from the Bluffs. It was agreed that they would meet at the Bluff's dock at noon the next day.

When Claude arrived in his pirogue, with him was a thin, nice-looking, olive-skinned woman. She had very long black hair, brown piercing eyes, small hips and small breasts. Her slender figure seemed to almost flow with the light breeze that day. As their boat came close to the dock, Nick helped secure the bow rope. He then offered his hand to the woman now standing in the pirogue. She had obviously stood in a pirogue many times since she had no problem with balance, a common problem when standing in such a narrow boat.

"*Monsieur* Neek, thees ees Carlotta," Claude said as he also helped the woman as she stepped onto the dock.

"Nice to meet you. Thanks for taking the time to meet with me," Nick said, quickly trying to make the woman feel comfortable when, in fact, he was the one feeling a little uneasy. After all, this was the first time he had stood next to a voodoo priestess, something he found hard to believe as he glanced at the woman now standing beside him. She smiled a guarded smile and nodded her head. Nick wondered if she understood what he had just said. Claude got out of the boat and Nick greeted him with a handshake and a light pat on his shoulder.

"Carlotta ees a special person in my life, Neek. She ess my woman."

Nick caught exactly what Claude was saying. Claude wanted Nick to know that this creature was off limits, not just to Nick, but to everyone, and Nick could not blame him. Looking at her, Nick still could not believe this was, indeed, a person who was involved in the dark practices of voodoo. He had been told by various people in town that voodoo believers were definitely different people. Yet, this woman did not appear right now to be different from any other woman.

Nick was brought back to the moment as Claude continued talking, saying, "Carlotta ees a voodoo priestess. She can do theengs dat weel help you keep peeple away from your place out here."

Looking at Carlotta, Nick decided he might as well get one thing clear up front. "Carlotta, can you understand me when I talk?"

Nick knew that several townspeople had difficulty understanding his northern accent. He thought, especially since she had not said a word so far, that she might have an even harder time understanding him.

Looking directly at him, she said, "I can understand you perfectly."

Nick was surprised. She spoke better English than most of the people in Bay St. Louis, even though it was with what he thought was a French accent. So much for communication being any sort of a problem at all. He immediately wondered, though, why was it she spoke such good English when she lived out in the swamp with other people who did not speak well at all. That did not add up, but he also knew that was something that he would not ask about right now. Right now, he needed her help.

"Carlotta, I have spent a lot of money out here building things and fixing things up. Because I am not from here and for other reasons, I think that some people might try to come out here sometimes to see what all has been built and to see what is going on. If possible, I don't want that to happen. That would lead to just too many problems. Is there something you can do to maybe make this area off-limits, a place where people, who may just come out here, once they see strange things, might decide that maybe they should not go any further or that maybe they should go back where they came from?"

After looking at him for a moment, she said, "You don't want anyone to be out here seeing what you have here or what you might be doing."

Nick almost laughed out loud. He did laugh to himself. Although he had tried to phrase it in a particular way so as to not cause any suspicion, she had gotten right to the point of the whole discussion.

Looking back into her big brown eyes, Nick said, "That's right, Carlotta. I came down here to get away from people, especially certain types of people. I don't want anyone coming out here and maybe getting into places they should not be." She understood, very clearly, what he was saying.

Using her brown eyes to make sure Nick now understood what she was saying, she answered, "Mister Nick, we have noticed the boats coming to your dock and have seen what is going on here. We don't care what you are doing as long as your people are not a problem for us. As for everyone else, we don't want anyone else out here any more than you do."

Nick understood exactly what she meant. As long as Nick's people left them alone, they were fine. As far as anyone else, then they were both after the same thing. She continued, "Yes. We can do certain things out here. We already have some things out in the swamp to discourage people from getting close to areas where we are. We can add some things, especially at certain locations, so that your place is taken care of."

Nick said, "Good. Can you get started with putting those things in place soon?"

Claude intervened at that point and said, "Anytheeng dat she wants put in place weel be done by me and a few of our friends. Yes, we can get started in the next week or so. Some theengs will have to be prepared first. Then, after beeng prepared, they can be put in place."

Nick heard the word "prepared" and wondered what that meant, but at this point he didn't really know if he wanted to find out exactly what that meant. That was another thing he decided to not pursue at the moment. He would let them do what they had to do. If it got to be a problem, whatever the preparation was, he would deal with it then.

"Thanks. Your efforts will be most helpful, I am sure."

Then Claude made a statement Nick would later find himself thinking about on several occasions.

"*Monsieur* Neek, just be sure and tell your men, your workers, to not touch what we put out in swamp. At all!" Claude looked straight at Nick when he said that.

Nick noticed Carlotta looking at him also. Nick thought about what had been said for a brief moment and then answered, "I will tell them, in no uncertain terms, that they are not to so much as touch anything that you place out in the swamp."

Claude answered, "Okay. We will get started soon."

With that, he turned and guided Carlotta back into the pirogue.

Then he carefully seated himself behind her in the small boat. As they began to pull away, Nick said, "How will I know for sure what you have placed in the swamp?"

Claude answered, a big grin now on his face, "*Monsieur* Neek, believe me. You will know."

As Nick stood watching from the dock, Claude and Carlotta pulled off into the bayou.

A few days later Carlotta and some of the swamp people, all men when Nick saw them, began to be seen from time to time placing voodoo symbols all around the Bluffs so that anyone who came into the area would see them long before they arrived at the Bluffs. The symbols were such as to almost defy description. There were all sorts of markings on posts and on boards hooked to posts. Some of the boards and posts had what seemed to be parts of dead animals, usually chickens, but sometimes pigs and goats, hanging from them along with the markings, which appeared to be dried blood. Nick had told his workers, after his meeting with Claude and Carlotta, that they should make sure to not touch the symbols. With the passage of time, he found that he would not have to worry about them wanting to touch the symbols. In fact, when the men first saw the symbols, the last thing any of them wanted to do was touch them.

Nick also brought peacocks out to the Bluffs. He had been told that peacocks were very inquisitive and would not let any intrusion take place without loud exclamations which would quickly serve notice that an intruder was nearby. Nick thought that peacocks would be much better suited for the Bluffs than any type of guard dogs. They were given free rein to go anywhere around the Bluffs they wanted to go. It wasn't like they were going to run away. After all, there was nothing but miles of swamp all around them, and numerous alligators.

Two of the lumber company owners received Nick well and they easily reached agreements. These owners were more than happy to receive payments for the use of their ships on their return trips. They even agreed that Nick could supply the individuals to serve as captains of the ships for the round trips. Normally, the return trips from Cuba had not made any profit to speak of for them, and they did not really want to know why they were being paid twelve hundred dollars a piece each month for the use of their ships for only one leg of their trips. When Nick also gave each one an up-front cash payment of ten thousand dollars for them letting him use their ships on the return trips, they did not care who the captains of the ships were as long as their lumber was successfully delivered to Cuba. The ships were two masted schooners that were about sixty-five feet long and fifteen feet wide. Each vessel was sleek-looking and certainly did not have the appearance of being capable of hauling the heavy cargo that they actually carried.

Under Nick's plan, lumber would be shipped out to Cuba on two lumber boats, the schooners *Dark Shadows* and the *Molly Bee*. Those same ships would bring back the booze that had been shipped to Cuba from Canada and the Caribbean. Nick also had found out that without their heavy loads of lumber, the two ships were extremely fast and would still be fast even when loaded with the barrels and cases of rum and scotch instead of their heavier lumber cargo.

Everything had worked out fine until Nick went to visit the third and largest lumber company, the Western Lumber Company, a little over two weeks after he had met with Capone. Nick drove out to the company offices in northern Hancock County in his Lincoln. He knew better than to even think about driving the Stutz Bearcat out there. Taking the Lincoln was almost certain to cause enough conversation itself.

As Nick pulled up and parked his car near the front of the old wooden office building, several of the workers stopped to look at him, but mostly to look at his fine automobile. It was an extremely hot day and Nick's white three piece suit looked terribly out of place. As the men admired his automobile, Nick made his way up the stairs of the office building where he was met on the small porch near the front door by a large, bald, muscled white man.

Nick said, "Hi, I am Nick Gable. I'm looking for Mr. Billy Johnson."

"Wat chu want wid him, Mista," the man asked as he wiped his hands with a dirty rag. Seeing the man wiping his hands, Nick made no effort to try to shake hands, figuring out that based on this man's answer he was not the owner. Billy Johnson, the owner of the Western Lumber Company, was supposedly an arrogant man from the backwoods of Hancock County who, Nick had been told, had worked very hard and put together a local lumber empire under sometimes harsh circumstances. Nick had also been told that Johnson was very proud of what he had accomplished and was not shy about letting anyone know about it.

Nick had heard that Johnson had hired a bald, muscular white man

78

named Bubba Earl as an enforcer to intimidate his workers. Nick assumed that was who was now standing in front of him. Nick had also been told that Bubba Earl liked to show how tough he was and was constantly getting into fights that he knew he could easily win, hurting whomever he fought with so badly that a trip to the only doctor in Bay St. Louis was the usual result. Yes, this was not going to be easy.

"I have come to see Mr. Johnson," Nick said, trying to make the point nicely that he had come to see Johnson, not his enforcer. "Where might I find him?" Nick asked, keeping his gaze now on Bubba Earl.

Bubba Earl looked him over, noticed the fine white straw hat Nick was wearing, and said, "Ya stay heah and I'll see ifen he wants ta see ya."

Stepping into the building, Bubba Earl carefully knocked on the door to Johnson's office in the back of the building. Only after hearing Johnson grunt his usual response to such knocking did Bubba Earl know it was all right to open the door. He then opened the door, walked in and waited for Johnson to look up. Only when Johnson looked up did Bubba Earl start talking.

"Thar's a man out front dressed in a white Sunday school suit. Drove up in a real fancy car. Seys he wants ta talk wid ya."

Johnson cut him off at the end of his sentence saying, "Well, who is he?"

Bubba Earl shook his head saying, "Don't know. Nev'r seen him before, but he looks like dat feller dat everybody been talkin' bout dat come into town with all dat money."

The mention of money got Johnson's attention and he said, "Well, let's see if it's him and if it is, let's find out what he's doing out here. Bubba Earl, you should have found out what he wants. Have I got to tell you everything to do? I've heard he's been talking with the other lumber companies, but nobody has said anything about what he wanted. Show him in and let's see if I can find out what is going on since you didn't."

Johnson was looking at Bubba Earl with a scowl of disappointment on his face after he finished his last words. Bubba Earl walked back to Nick, who was now standing at the front doorway.

"Com'on back, Mista. Mr. Johnson will see ya now," he said pointing generally in the direction of the door to Johnson's office at the back of the room.

Nick walked back toward the office doorway. There were two women clerks in the room watching him as he walked by.

As he entered Johnson's office, Nick shook hands with him and said, "Mr. Johnson, I am Nick Gable. It is a pleasure to meet you."

Nick could see Johnson eyeing him up and down before Johnson said anything. Nick had heard that this man was successful because he was a cunning businessman. He sensed that Johnson would not be as easy to deal with as the other two had been.

"What brings you out here?" asked Johnson, getting to the point immediately as they both sat down. Nick noticed that Bubba Earl had come into the office behind him, closed the door and was standing there next to the door with his arms crossed.

Nick said, "Well, I was hoping to have a conversation just between the two of us."

Johnson quickly answered, "Bubba Earl here has been with me for twenty-seven years and I hope he will be with me for twenty-seven more. Now, Mr. Gable, you can say just anything you want in front of him as far as I am concerned, and you had best get about doing it right now!"

Nick was taken aback. This man had no tact to him at all. He probably owed his success to being tough and persevering, not because he was someone anybody wanted to work with or for. He would have to be careful how he approached his need for Johnson's cooperation.

"Okay, that's fine. I am here to offer you a business deal. You ship your lumber to Cuba on three ships, and I understand that they come back from Cuba usually empty. I would like to use those ships for the shipment of goods from Cuba on their return trips."

Johnson immediately answered, looking straight at Nick, "I don't want anything put on those ships when they are coming back from Cuba. I don't care what type of goods, as you call them, you are shipping. So Mister, take your offer and get out of my office."

"I wish you would hear me out," Nick began but was interrupted by Johnson, whose voice was now louder and firmer.

"Look Mister! I just told you, didn't I just tell him, Bubba Earl? I don't want you using my boats at all! Don't you understand me? With that accent of yours, you sound like a Yankee. Don't you Yankees understand anything? I just told you, I don't want you using my boats and I meant it. Now get out of here! Bubba Earl, show this Yankee fella out of my office!"

Johnson was now standing up, pointing toward the door. Before Nick could say anything else, Bubba Earl had grabbed the back of Nick's coat near his neck and pulled him up out of the chair.

"If you would just give me a minute, we could talk about maybe my buying your company. It would be for a good price," Nick said, remembering Capone's directions about offering to buy if that were necessary to complete the shipping deal. He hoped that the mention of money would get Johnson's attention.

"I don't care about any of your Yankee money! Bubba Earl, get this damn Yankee out of my eyesight! Now! Do you understand me, Bubba Earl," Johnson asked, almost yelling. Bubba Earl still had a strong grip on the back of the collar of Nick's coat and Nick had no choice but to go in the direction Bubba Earl was taking him, which was out of Johnson's office and toward the front door.

Near the exit Nick looked at Bubba Earl and said firmly, "Let go of me." Bubba Earl continued to drag Nick toward the front door.

"I said let go of me, Bubba Earl," Nick said a little louder.

"Don't you listen to him, Bubba Earl! You get him and his Yankee ass out of my eyesight now, Bubba Earl," Johnson yelled in a loud voice from the doorway of his office as Bubba Earl continued to literally drag Nick through the front doorway as the two women in the front office watched with their mouths open.

When they got to the edge of the front porch of the building, Bubba Earl pushed Nick one last time after letting go of him, causing Nick to stumble down the steps of the building and fall to the ground. His straw hat, which had been in his left hand while he was in Johnson's office and while he was being dragged out of that office, fell onto the porch floor when Nick had been pushed. Bubba Earl picked it up and threw it down on the ground next to Nick. While lying in the dirt at the foot of the stairs, Nick looked up and saw that the workers, who had watched him peacefully drive up just a few minutes earlier, were now standing there just looking at him, none of them saying a word.

Nick slowly got up off of the ground and brushed himself off. Looking at the front door he noticed Johnson standing just inside the doorway looking at him. Nick bent over and picked up his crumpled hat. He then slowly walked toward his car. Reaching his car, he opened the door while looking back at the top of the stairs. Bubba Earl was still standing there, now with his arms folded across his body, watching to make sure Nick was doing what his boss wanted, which was to leave the property.

Nick looked around at all of the people who were watching him. He looked back at Bubba Earl and said in a cold, even voice, "Bubba Earl, you shouldn't have done that."

He then got into his car, started it up, and with the engine roaring, spun his tires on the dirt road spraying dirt and dust as he left.

Chapter Nine

Nick had to go to Cuba and establish contact there like Capone had told him, regardless of the fact that he had not reached a shipping agreement with Johnson. He had a feeling that while he was in Cuba, Johnson might have a change of heart. He hoped so. Capone had made it real clear that he did not want any loose ends. Nick did not like loose ends either.

Nick dreaded the trip to Cuba. He thought about when, just before his eighteenth birthday, he had taken a job on the mainland of Italy at the Gabelli Winery even though he was living near Messina on the coast of the nearby island of Sicily. Since the job was going to pay well and Nick's family could use the income, Nick had begun making the daily three mile boat trip from Sicily across the Straits of Messina to the small town of Vila San Giovanni, which was not too far from the larger town of Reggie di Calabria where the winery was located.

There had hardly ever been a day that the sea in the straits was not rough. The small boat Nick traveled in would, daily it seemed, be on the verge of floundering and only through the excellent seamanship of the small boat's captain were they able to make it safely to the other side of the straits. Late in the afternoon, when the straits were almost always much rougher, he would travel in the same small boat back over to Messina. The money had been good though, and it helped his family through many hard economic times, but the family had still remained in dire financial straits. Eventually, Nick had gotten to the point that he hated the daily boat trips, getting seasick several times when the seas were really rough. Capone had told him to go to Cuba however, and so he had to try to put those memories behind him and do the best he could making the trip.

On the Saturday Capone had designated during their meeting at the Pine Hills Hotel, Nick took the early seven-thirty train from Bay St. Louis and traveled to New Orleans. When he got there, he made his way down to the docks and found the *Sea Witch*. She was a beautiful ship with a sleek look. Her black hull was an unusual color for a ship in that area because of how hot it got along the coast and in the Gulf of Mexico. Also, her triple masts were a bit unusual for the Gulf Coast since most ships he had seen only had one or two masts and shallow draft hulls. Nick discovered that this ship also had one of those new engines on board, as well as a propeller, generally called a screw propeller, which only the top of the line boats had and which allowed it to obtain high speeds on the water.

Thinking about it, he realized that this vessel was probably not from this area, but was here for some reason, one of which was now to take Nick to Cuba. Nick hoped this would be a pleasant trip, one he could enjoy, instead of the almost daily fear he had experienced in his travels across the straits of Messina. He had been able to enjoy some of his trip across the Atlantic Ocean when he had first come to the United States, although he had gotten sick even on that trip. Of course, that trip had been on an ocean-going liner, a much larger vessel than this one.

Nick found out the *Sea Witch* was carrying various items produced in Louisiana, such as sugar and cotton. There were also six other passengers on board, all men, in addition to Nick. He did not know any of them and made it a point not to get to know any of them too well, offering only a cordial "hello" when he encountered one of them on the deck. The trip was relatively short, lasting a little more than three days. Leaving a little after eleven, they pulled into the harbor of Havana at around two in the afternoon on Tuesday. Fortunately, Nick did not have any occurences of seasickness during the trip. Most of that may have been because of how placid the Gulf of Mexico had been all during the trip, at least when compared with the rough waters Nick had previously experienced.

Nick did as he had been instructed by Capone and wrapped the blue handkerchief Capone had given him around his left hand. With his light colored pants and his white shirt, the blue handkerchief made a perfect match. Whoever Fernando was, he should have no problem finding him, providing of course that Fernando was not having problems of his own and was able to get to the docks.

As Nick watched the workers unload the *Sea Witch*, he looked around but did not see anyone who had a blue handkerchief in his hand. Nick continued to watch the travelers' luggage being unloaded, which did not take long, and then watched the unloading of the large bags of sugar and bales of cotton from the ship.

After about an hour, just as the unloading was about to finish, Nick felt a tug on his sleeve. Looking around, he saw a smaller, thin man with dark hair and piercing brown eyes. In his left hand held down by his side was the blue handkerchief.

"You are Mr. Nick?"

"Yes, I am and you must be Fernando," Nick answered.

"Yes. Please follow me to the Cabildo Bar. These docks are closely watched," Fernando said as he put his blue handkerchief in his pants pocket and started to walk down the dock toward the city.

Nick followed closely behind, putting his own blue handkerchief in his pants pocket and watching Fernando discreetly survey the crowd around them as they walked.

They turned onto a side street near the docks, and Fernando soon ducked into a doorway under a sign for the Cabildo Bar with Nick right behind him. Fernando took a seat at a table near a window. Nick was motioned to sit in a particular chair, one that also gave him a good view of the streets outside.

A woman immediately appeared and came over to them. Fernando spoke to her in Spanish and she quickly disappeared.

"So, welcome to Cuba," Fernando said with a flicker of a smile. "How are things in the States?" he asked, giving Nick the impression that the answer did not matter as much as it mattered that they appeared to be talking.

"Things are going well. I take it you are familiar with what I am involved with," Nick said looking at Fernando as Fernando nodded his head. Nick continued, "We had one little setback, but that will be worked out soon. I think we should be ready to start shipments by the first week of July. The facility will be completely finished by then. The operation is in position for the most part. Are things ready here?"

"Yes," Fernando answered. "We are ready when you are. The sooner the better. I have a warehouse here that is half full. We need to start as soon as you can handle the shipments. We will, of course, use only the two boats to start with, the *Dark Shadows* and the *Molly Bee*. They are big boats that bring lumber down here, but they will both be fast carrying just our barrels. We have taken them out and tried them and they can fly, even when fully loaded. They will do just fine. The main problem will be making sure the captains do what we tell them, just do their jobs and don't ask a lot of questions or drink all the time, but I will take care of as much of that as I can from here. At least, I will try. You did a good thing getting those two ships for us. This is a different business we are in. You know what I mean."

Nick agreed, as both men casually looked around them. The woman Fernando had spoken to appeared with two drinking mugs, placing one in front of each man and quickly turning and leaving. Nick figured she somehow knew to not hang around the table. After she left, Nick continued the conversation in a low voice.

"I hope to have access to three more soon. If we get them, once things are finalized we will let you know what their names are and when we can start using them. The owners of the boats we will be using have agreed that we will be supplying the captains for the trips down here and back. I will try to have that same agreement on the other three boats."

Nick occasionally moved his eyes over the crowd as he spoke. Fernando continued to casually observe the crowd, but said nothing, just nodding his head in understanding and agreement.

"Is there anything else here I need to know about?" Nick asked.

"No, *señor*. We have covered the most important things. Our Canadian problems have been taken care of. We now have, let's say, understandings with those we will be working with up there. Shipments have already been made from there and from Haiti and Jamaica. More shipments are set to come in from those places. Everything is alright here. Now, it is up to you to get the product into your part of the country and get it circulating so that it is available for those who want it."

The two both took a drink from their mugs as they sat there watching the people in the streets. Nick immediately recognized the rum taste of the contents of his mug. After a few moments of silence, Nick decided that all was well and it was time to move on.

"Well, is there a hotel here that you might recommend to me? I guess I will go get a room and try to get some rest," Nick said thinking about how nice it would be to just relax for a little while. He was even looking forward to maybe enjoying a night out in the bustling city of Havana.

"There will be no need for a hotel room, my new friend," Fernando quickly responded. "You will be leaving on your return trip on the *Sea Witch* in about 2 hours."

"Two hours?"

"Yes, we need to get her, and you, out of here. There are too many crooked local policemen and officials here. Too many people who want to put their hands out so they can be convinced to look the other way. We have things all set up here, but the shorter time your ship is here, the less attention she will attract. Besides, you need to return so that you can make sure things fall into place as soon as you think. We have so much already waiting to be shipped to you, Mr. Nick," Fernando said now smiling.

Nick smiled and also thought of something else he needed to mention.

"One more thing," Nick said as he watched Fernando continue to move his eyes over the nearby crowd in the street. "Make sure the captains and your people know that they will need to wait at the farthest southeastern inlet of Cat Island. Tell them to not leave there without our guides meeting up with them. It is really easy to get lost on the bayous going to the docks at the Bluffs. Our guides are excellent. They really know the area, and they can be counted on by your people, but your people have to wait for them."

"Okay, I will make that clear to everybody," Fernando answered, feeling better about doing business with this Nick from the States. As for Nick, this thin man was all business and Nick liked that.

"Just to make sure you and I understand what the plan is, you will be sending your shipments to us when notified from Chicago. Chicago will let us know of the date and time of the arrival of your shipments at the Cat Island meeting point. All of the payments for what is being shipped will be taken care of through Chicago, Canada, and here," Nick said.

"Yes. That is what I was told also. Okay. We both understand how it will work. I must tell you also, Mr. Nick, that sometimes there will be other, shall we say, 'cargo' that will be shipped on these same boats with the barrels. You will find out more about that soon when you return to your ship. So now enjoy some of this Caribbean rum, and your trip back to the States will go much faster," Fernando said, now raising his cup for a toast.

"It was a pleasure meeting with you. May we have a long and prosperous business arrangement," Nick said as he raised his cup.

With that, the two men put their cups together and drank a toast.

After their toast, Fernando said, "I must be going. You do not need to be seen with me, and I don't need to be seen with you. I have taken care of our drinks here. Have a safe journey, Mr. Nick, and be careful. *Hasta luego!*"

Fernando quickly stood up and disappeared through a side door and out into the street traffic. Nick wondered about what Fernando meant about other "cargo," but with Fernando's abrupt departure, he would just have to wait and see for himself.

Nick stood up, moved slowly over to the bar and, now leaning on the bar, took his new friend's advice and continued to drink from his mug. After consuming the remainder of the mug's contents, Nick made his way back to the *Sea Witch*.

Once he got on board, he heard some voices coming from inside the front storage compartment of the ship. He walked over and looked into that area and was completely stunned by what he saw. There were people, who looked to be Chinese, both men and women, tightly packed in the hold, almost shoulder to shoulder. The thing that caught his attention though, as he looked closer, was that each one was attached to a long chain by locks that connected with metal collars that were around their necks. There was another chain that ran around each person's waist that was also locked to the person next to them.

As Nick stood there with all sorts of questions going through his mind, the captain of the ship walked over to him. He was the same man who had guided the ship on its trip from New Orleans. Nick found him to be a genial man and had carried on a few discussions, brief though they had been, with him on the trip down. Nothing had been mentioned about the people now on board.

"Are those people Chinese?" Nick asked gesturing toward the crowded compartment holding what, Nick guessed, were about forty-five people.

"Yep, they sure are," the captain replied, now standing next to Nick and also looking into the hold.

"What are they doing on here?" Nick asked, not yet completely understanding what he was seeing, but remembering the statement made by Fernando about other "cargo."

"Our growing country needs manpower. Our government seems to have a really hard time letting enough people in to satisfy that need. We are just trying to help out the best we can," the captain said with somewhat of a sneer.

"Isn't that illegal?" Nick asked still looking at the group of people.

"Yes it is, but so are a lot of the other things that are being shipped, or going to be shipped, in these waters."

With that comment, Nick shifted his eyes from the hold to the captain, who now had something of a smile on his face. Nick couldn't help but smile also.

"What happens if we get chased by a government boat when we go back north?" Nick asked.

"The most important thing is to save the ship. So the first thing we would do is lighten the load so the ship can go faster." Nick nodded his head, understanding to some extent what the captain was saying.

"So you would start throwing overboard any barrels you might be carrying as fast as you could?" Nick stated almost as a question.

"Oh no!" the captain said laughing. "Not the barrels first." Then looking at Nick he said, "The Chinese would go over first, one at a time, with some of those chains wrapped around them so they would go straight to the bottom when they hit the water." With that statement, the captain walked away.

Nick stood there quietly, with all sorts of emotions flowing through him. He had also come over to the United States by boat, but, obviously, not under the same conditions as these people. He realized that his being seasick for most of his trip in no way compared with the dangers these people faced, and they probably didn't even know it. All of a sudden he began to feel sick to his stomach.

It was two-thirty when the boat left for the United States, not too long after Nick had gotten back onboard. Nick stayed sick for most of the return trip. The one thing he could look forward to was that with this quick return trip, he would have to spend some time in New Orleans when he got back. He didn't want to get back to the Bluffs too soon. Besides, he had told everyone that he would be out of town for a while. He would have to find something to do for a few days in New Orleans. That shouldn't be too hard to do.

The Chinese were kept in the hold during the entire trip. The smell was horrendous since sanitary conditions were almost nonexistent. When the boat docked back in New Orleans long after the sun had set, Nick watched as the Chinese were quickly taken off of the ship and put into several waiting trucks, still in chains. The hold they had been kept in was immediately washed out by the deck hands. Nick had no idea what fate awaited the Chinese. That was not something that he had to worry about, at least not yet. He had his own concerns to deal with.

Chapter Ten

During Nick's trip to Cuba, fires took place late in the evening on different nights at four of Western Lumber Company's seven lumber yards. The first time Johnson was told about a fire, he did not think too much about it. Sometimes around lumber yards fires took place, but they were usually small fires and they did not happen too often. Then, another fire occurred two days later which caused more damage. Johnson began to wonder, but was more alarmed when the very next night additional fires took place at two other lumber yards.

The day after the latest two fires took place, Johnson was told about them and immediately began thinking that this was too many fires to just be a coincidence. Somebody was setting them. He immediately started screaming at Bubba Earl as soon as he saw him.

"What do you know about these fires, Bubba Earl?"

"I don't know nuthin bout 'm, Mr. Johnson."

"What do I pay you for, boy? Am I wasting my money paying you to protect me from this type of crap? Somebody is setting fires to my business and you haven't stopped it? You had better get to work, boy, or I am going to get me somebody who can find out who is doing this!

Do you understand me?"

Bubba Earl was scared. He had to have this job. He had been with Mr. Johnson for years. He was Johnson's man. He didn't take any offense when Johnson called him "boy." Johnson had always called him that, along with a lot of other things, but Bubba Earl knew, by the tone of Mr. Johnson's voice, that he had to find out what was happening and soon.

"I'll find out, Mr. Johnson. I promise I will. Just give me a little bit of time, and I'll find out what's going on. I promise I will, Mr. Johnson. I won't let you down," Bubba Earl said while looking for a sign of encouragement from Johnson.

Johnson looked at him and remembered when, about three years earlier, Bubba Earl had gotten those two teenage boys that had been going out to the lumber yards and turning the machinery on while so drunk they couldn't even walk. Yes, ol' Bubba Earl had stopped that by beating the two boys almost senseless. The only problem had been that Bubba Earl had enjoyed doing it almost too much. Johnson would have to watch Bubba Earl this time and make sure he didn't hurt, too badly, whomever it was that was setting the fires.

Johnson had been the target of a lot of criticism when those boys had been beaten so badly. Sheriff Patterson had even come by and had a little talk with Johnson about Bubba Earl. The sheriff had mentioned that the boys should have been turned over to him and he would have taken care of the situation. Johnson didn't know exactly what that meant, but he sure knew that the two boys, in fact the whole community, had gotten the message after Bubba Earl had worked on them for a while. There had been no more trouble out at Johnson's lumber yards, at least not until now. Only someone who was new to the area, and not around when all of that had happened, would not know about how it had been handled.

Bubba Earl got eight of Johnson's employees to use as night watchmen. They all were sent out to stand guard at each of the lumber yards, even the ones that had already suffered fires. One of the eight was sent to stand guard at Western's main office. Two of the fires had been pretty bad, but the others had not burned too much. Some of the machinery, including the cutting saws, had been damaged in the two worst fires. At the other locations, the fires would have been worse except that they had burned themselves out before getting too widespread.

Each of the night watchmen sent out to the various yards was given a shotgun and told to use it if anything strange happened. Bubba Earl assigned himself the task of checking on all of the men. He would continuously go from yard to yard checking on things all during the night. After four fruitless nights, Johnson was even more upset.

"Bubba Earl, you are so worthless! Here it is days after all of those fires and you have not found me anybody, not one person, who was responsible! You are not doing your job!"

Bubba Earl felt bad. Johnson had assigned him this big responsibility. Worse than that, everybody knew Johnson was expecting Bubba Earl to find out who it was that had been setting the fires, if somebody, indeed, was setting them which appeared to be the case. Bubba Earl had talked with some of their clients, but none of them had any ideas about who might be setting the fires. He talked with a few of his friends in Bay St. Louis to see if they might have heard anything, but none of them had. He also went by and saw Sheriff Patterson and told him about what had taken place. Sheriff Patterson told Bubba Earl to have Johnson keep his guards out on his mill sites, if at all possible, and to wait and see what happened next. Other than those contacts, there was nothing else Bubba Earl could think of to do. The lumber yards had hundreds of thousands of dollars of equipment and product at their locations and Mr. Johnson, because of his profits at the yards, was one of the most financially successful people in the whole county. Yet nobody had any idea about what was going on, and Bubba Earl certainly had no idea.

Making his rounds at the mills late the next night, Bubba Earl drove out to the Possum Creek Lumber Yard near the community known as "the Kiln." It was pitch black with clouds hiding the quarter moon. It was so dark Bubba Earl could hardly see his own hand in front of his face when he held it up.

An employee, Reggie Thompson, or "Coonass" as he was called by almost everyone, had been assigned by Bubba Earl to the Possum Creek Lumber Yard, but ol' Coonass was nowhere to be found. Bubba Earl had made his appearance at two of the other yards and the guards assigned to those yards had been there, but when he got to the Possum Creek yard, Coonass was missing. This was unusual. Reggie was a good, dependable worker and it was not right for him to not be there and not have somebody let Bubba Earl know about it.

Bubba Earl drove into the lumber yard and got out of the truck. Looking around he yelled out, "Coonass!" He expected to hear an immediate answer, but heard nothing. Waiting a moment, Bubba Earl again yelled out, "Coonass! Where are ya?"

He stood there looking into the darkness, waiting for a response. After watching and listening for a few moments, Bubba Earl reached into the truck and grabbed his shotgun. Better to be safe than sorry. He began to wonder if something was wrong and felt a whole lot better with that shotgun in his hand. If there was a trespasser out there, they were not going to scare him. He was Bubba Earl, and everybody knew better than to mess with him. Whoever it was, if they had any sense, had better stay away from him.

"Coonass! Where are ya?"

The silence was deafening. All of a sudden Bubba Earl heard a noise down to his left toward a large pile of posts about fifty yards from his truck. He stood still and listened. He heard what sounded as if a small piece of wood had hit the ground. They cut literally hundreds of fence posts at that yard almost every day. It sounded like one of those fence posts had fallen off of a stack, but there had been no answer to his calls. Why would it have fallen off unless somebody was there?

Bubba Earl started walking toward the noise. He knew about where the sound had come from. He hunted all the time and knew his way around the outdoors. Besides, he had his shotgun and if somebody was there, he was going to find them and do something to them almost as bad as he had done to those two drunken kids. But where was Coonass?

"Coonass! Where are ya?" he yelled as he walked toward the pile of wood. He just knew he would probably find Coonass lying face down on the other side of the woodpile drunk as he could be.

Just as Bubba Earl walked around the edge of the woodpile, he felt a sudden explosive pain in the back of his head. In the few short moments before he passed out, he knew what it was. Someone had hit him on the back of his head with one of those fence posts.

When Bubba Earl woke up, his head was really hurting. "What happened?" he tried to say as he groaned. He could barely open his eyes. He tried to put his hand on the back of his head to feel where the pain was coming from, but he couldn't move. Had he been hurt that badly? He blinked his eyes, again and again, trying to see through the pain and the darkness. He gradually began to remember that he was at Possum Creek and had been walking around the edge of a stack of lumber when his skull felt like it had been cracked open.

He heard voices. He tried to yell out for Coonass but he couldn't. Why was that?

At the sound of his mumbling, he heard a voice say, "I think he's waking up." Then Bubba Earl saw the form of a man leaning over him. He felt a light slap on his face, once, then again.

"Bubba Earl, wake up," the voice said. He didn't recognize the voice, or did he? He tried to sit up for a closer look, but still couldn't move. He was under a pile of logs! Under a pile of logs? How had that happened? Then he realized each of his hands was pulled out away from his body and tied to the log he was laying against with wire! And what was that in his mouth? It was something round and long and looked like a stick of dynamite. It was a stick of dynamite, and it was tied with wire into his mouth! A man leaned over to make sure Bubba Earl was conscious.

"Tiny, he's awake now," the man yelled over his shoulder.

Leaning back towards Bubba Earl the man said, "Now stay awake, Bubba Earl. You gotta be awake for what's gonna happen next."

Another man, a huge black man, came over and struck a match and held it down so Bubba Earl's eyes were not far from its glowing end. The giant black man said, "Bubba Earl, remember dat man you threw outta yor boss's office? You never shudda did dat."

With that, the man named Tiny lit the fuse to the dynamite, turned and disappeared. Bubba Earl frantically tried to dislodge the dynamite out of his mouth or at least pull the fuse out, but he couldn't get his head close to either hand. He tried to shake his head from side to side, even though it hurt to do that, but it was too securely tied in his mouth. Then it happened.

WHAMMMMMMMMM!

The sound of the explosion was heard by people living nearby. The dynamite had accomplished its mission. Other fires were set following the explosion and became more widespread until they consumed almost half of the lumber yard.

Chapter Eleven

The next morning Bubba Earl did not show up for work at five-thirty a.m. like he normally did. Johnson began getting concerned about an hour later. He asked other employees about Bubba Earl but no one had seen him or knew anything concerning his whereabouts. Then Bob Satcher, the man who worked for Johnson as the foreman at the Possum Creek Lumber Yard, came driving up very fast to Johnson's office and stopped as a cloud of dust swirled around his truck.

Johnson heard Satcher drive up and was standing in the doorway when Satcher threw his door open and jumped out yelling, "Mr. Johnson! Mr. Johnson! Bubba Earl's dead!"

Johnson was shocked by the news. "Bubba Earl's dead? What happened?"

"Come go with me, Mr. Johnson. You're not going to believe it. You've got to come see it for yourself," Satcher said in a tone of voice that Johnson had never heard come from Satcher before.

The two men got into the truck and sped over to the Possum Creek Lumber Yard. Along the way Satcher had a hard time talking about what he had seen when asked by Mr. Johnson.

"It's horrible, Mr. Johnson. I mean, there's just pieces of Bubba Earl all over the place. It's bad, really bad. I mean, I really didn't have that much to do with Bubba Earl other than working with him here, but what happened to him...." Satcher's voice trailed off, followed by silence.

"What did happen to him?"

"Mr. Johnson, some of the workers that live there near the mill said they heard this large explosion really late last night. They said after that explosion there were fires. A few of them even went over to the yard last night, but there was not much they could do. The fires were mostly out of control and parts of what was left of Bubba Earl's body were everywhere."

Taking a deep breath, he continued, "When I got there this morning it was still dark. It was horrible! I can't tell you how bad it was, trying to walk around and not step on parts of the body. I didn't even realize it was Bubba Earl until first sunlight this morning. That was when I found a part of Bubba Earl's left hand with his ring on it, which was the only thing I could recognize him by, and that was only because I knew he was so proud of that ring."

It was then that he looked over at Johnson and said, "There's something else I have to tell you, Mr. Johnson."

Johnson looked at his driver and could see that this was going to be something serious. He shifted himself so that he was a little closer to Satcher and could hear him better above the noise of the truck motor.

"The part of Bubba Earl's hand with his ring on his finger? It was tied to one of those logs with wire!"

Satcher watched Johnson's reaction to what he had just been told. The bottom part of his mouth fell open as he stared at Satcher, taking in the information.

"Mr. Johnson, not too much else was left of Bubba Earl and what was left of him was all over the place and in pieces."

Giving Johnson time to understand what he had just been told, Satcher continued.

"The man Bubba Earl had put at that yard for last night, a man called Coonass, he hasn't been seen yet today. At least he hadn't when I left there to come over and tell ya. His body was not found in the mess made by the explosion and fires."

Johnson continued to just stare at Satcher as the truck bounced along.

Only after several moments was Johnson able to turn his head and look down the dirt road in front of him.

When they arrived at the Possum Creek Lumber Yard, Sheriff Wild Bill Patterson, wearing his customary hat, boots and gun, was already there, having heard about the explosion earlier. Now the sheriff was also finding out about what was left of Bubba Earl.

"What do you know about all of this?" Patterson asked Johnson after they had acknowledged one another and began following Satcher across the lumber yard towards what Satcher wanted to show them. Johnson just shook his head back and forth but could not say much, just mumbling under his breath about what a good ol' boy Bubba Earl had been.

The sheriff then surmised, "It seems to me that either Bubba Earl had some enemies or was at the wrong place at the wrong time."

Johnson briefly thought, as they continued to follow Satcher, about what the sheriff had just said and replied, "I can't hardly think of anybody that you could say would want to do something like this to anybody, much less to Bubba Earl."

The three men approached a burned log. Johnson looked down and saw what was left of a burned hand and part of a forearm, tied with a piece of wire to the log. Then he saw the ring on the hand. Johnson knew that hand was Bubba Earl's. He turned his head quickly. He couldn't bear being near this fragment of a human being, especially a person who spent as much time around him as Bubba Earl had. Johnson didn't want to see any more.

The sheriff stayed and gave the scene a closer look, even squatting down near the hand and looking at the way it had been tied to the log. Yes sir, whoever tied that hand to that log definitely knew what they were doing. Even with all the burned flesh, the sheriff could tell Bubba Earl had really struggled to get that hand free. He looked up to see Johnson and Satcher slowly walking back up towards the vehicles.

Johnson's mind was racing. Who had dared do this to one of his employees? His first thought was that it must have been someone seeking revenge on Bubba Earl, maybe one of Johnson's former employees. The more he thought about it, the more he felt that it was not one of his former employees. Who else would have wanted to harm Bubba Earl?

What about that Yankee, the one he had Bubba Earl throw out of his office? There had been something about the look on that man's face while Bubba Earl was dragging him out of Johnson's office. It had not been a look of fear. It had been a look of extreme anger. Even after being dragged out of the office building in front of so many people, Johnson remembered that the Yankee had said something to Bubba Earl just before he had left in his car.

Then again, this seemed like a local thing maybe, something someone might do if they had a grudge against Bubba Earl. The sheriff would find out. In the meantime, Johnson would have to be extra careful, just in case.

As Johnson reached the foreman's truck, the sheriff called to him, "I've got a couple of my boys coming out to look around and see what they can find."

"They can check with Satcher if they need anything, sheriff," Johnson said.

Just as Johnson was getting behind the wheel of the truck, two deputies drove up.

"Bob, stay here and help Sheriff Patterson and his deputies as much as you can. Sheriff, he can catch a ride back to my office with your deputies if that's all right," Johnson said.

"Sure," Patterson said. With that, Johnson pulled away in the truck.

The sheriff stayed only a short time, taking one more look around. There was nothing more he could do at the lumber yard. His deputies would check everything out. This was the first outright murder in his county since the last time a body had been found hanging from a tree in Devil's Swamp about five months ago. The sheriff considered killings in the swamp to be a different matter from anything else that happened in the county. He felt those killings, for whatever the reason, concerned only the swamp people because of where those bodies had been left and how they had been displayed. He had never figured out what had happened when the last body had been found in the swamp. Normally, it was pretty easy to figure out who did what to whom in Hancock County and, usually, just as easy to figure out why, but not with this. This was different.

The sheriff left after instructing his two deputies to gather whatever evidence they could find, and be sure to let him know if they found anything that really caught their attention. He told them that he wanted a preliminary report from them by the next morning. In his mind, he was beginning to piece together what might be going on, and, if he was right, he needed to be really careful with this investigation. Just in the past week while he had been in New Orleans, he had heard a rumor that illegal liquor might be shipped through Mississippi. He hadn't thought much about it since then, but this just didn't make sense, unless something like that was somehow involved.

Johnson thought about what he had just seen all the way back to his office and went over and over in his mind about who might have done it. During the past two weeks, there had been all of those fires at his lumber yards and, now, an explosion had killed Bubba Earl. There was only one person who really stood out that he had had a face-to-face run-in within the past four or five years and that had been Nick Gable. Somehow, there had to be a connection. Normally, nobody interfered with Johnson. Nobody. But now, Bubba Earl had been killed. Not only killed, he had been blown apart!

Chapter Twelve

A few days after Bubba Earl's death, Johnson was in downtown Bay St. Louis at the food market. A man who Johnson had never seen before, and he knew everybody in Bay St. Louis, came up to stand by Johnson. The stranger said, "These sure are nice tomatoes for this time of year, aren't they?"

Johnson glanced at the man, noticing an accent while wondering who would just walk up to him and start a conversation. Didn't this man know who he was? Johnson turned to leave when the man said, "Sure was bad about ol' Bubba Earl. It would really be too bad if an accident happened to your wife and her head ended up like this tomato." As soon as the last word was out of his mouth, the stranger squeezed the tomato in his hand until it was completely squashed, and tomato juice squirted all over Johnson's shirt. Johnson yelped.

The store clerk ran over to him. "What's the matter?" she said. After wiping juice off of his shirt, Johnson turned to point out the idiot that had squashed the tomato on his shirt and looked around, but the man was nowhere to be seen. The stranger had disappeared, vanished into thin air.

The next morning at six, when Johnson left his house to go to work, he saw something sticking up in his front yard. He walked over to see what it was. What he saw shocked him. It really shocked him. Hanging from the stick in his front yard was what was left of a chicken with blood spread all over the stick! Horrified, Johnson grabbed the stick and pulled it out of the ground. Hoping no one had seen such a vile thing in his front yard, Johnson put it in the back of his truck and drove out to his nearest lumber yard, the Dalton Lumber Yard, to dispose of it. Not many things scared Johnson, but anything having to do with voodoo was certainly one of them. He broke out in a cold sweat thinking about what was in the back of his truck as he drove out to the yard. At least when he got there, he could get rid of the awful display without any of his neighbors knowing about it, whatever it meant.

When he pulled up to the headquarters building at the lumber yard, Johnson noticed a small group of men gathered in what seemed to be a circle. Johnson got out of his truck and walked over to the group to see what they were doing. There, in the middle of them, was another one of those sticks with part of a dead chicken hanging from it and blood everywhere.

Seeing the object, Johnson was stunned. After a few moments spent gathering his wits about him, he looked at the few men standing around and stuttered, "Does anybody, anybody know anything, anything at all about this?"

After a moment, one of the men spoke up, "Dat's a voodoo symbol, just as sure as I'm standin' here. We all need to really be careful. People get sick from things like that being put at places like where they live and all."

"Well, I've got another one just like that in the back of my truck that I pulled out of my front yard this morning," Johnson said.

"Mista Johnson, you better get rid of dat thang, right now. Some of the boys have already left, saying they not gonna be workin' at no place that has a voodoo hex or curse or something on it. You ain't gonna have no workers want to work here with all dis going on," one man said as a few of the men started easing away from the already small group.

During the day, voodoo symbols were found at three more of Johnson's lumber yards. Almost a third of his work force left the yards after seeing the displays.

That night Johnson sat on his front porch, looking to see if anyone might be coming by to put something else in his yard. His wife was scared since some of the neighbors had seen the symbol and word had spread like wildfire around the neighborhood and the town. The entire time he sat there, he thought that maybe he needed to go see Mr. Nick Gable as soon as he could. Johnson was no fool. If he could, maybe he would sell his lumber yards to Gable while he and his wife and family were still alive and while he still had something to sell. Gable wanted his yards, let him have them. Now, Johnson just wanted to get away from them. There weren't too many things that scared Johnson, but the more he thought about the voodoo symbols he had seen the more scared he became.

Thinking about selling everything was painful. He had started his business in 1915, had worked hard in hot, rainy weather and with mosquitoes and snakes. With the money he had made from his hard work at his first mill, he bought another mill not too far away. He gradually built his business up to where, now with seven mills, his was one of the most successful lumber companies around. Because of his successes, he was also one of the most respected men in the county, even though that respect was based mostly on his success and not on any genuine affection for Johnson. He knew that most people thought that he had taken advantage of other people's hard luck, and that he had done so time after time with no remorse. Johnson had always tried to present himself as just being a hard-nosed businessman.

Then all of these strange things began happening. First, the confrontation with Gable at Johnson's office, the numerous fires at his lumber yards, and Bubba Earl being literally blown up. Then there had been the stranger with the tomato at the food market threatening his wife. Now, to top it all off, voodoo symbols were found at four of his lumber yards and at his house. All of that had happened since Nick Gable showed up at his office. Johnson then remembered that he had heard that Gable lived in Devil's Swamp. Johnson had also heard that more and more voodoo symbols were appearing in the swamp. Johnson already knew about the legend that said the Devil, himself, lived in Devil's Swamp, and this man, Nick Gable, had moved out there!

Yes, he hated to do it, but he needed to go talk with Gable. Maybe such a visit would give Johnson some idea if he could still get a good offer from Nick to purchase his properties, before the others reached the same conclusion to sell that he had now reached.

Johnson needed to go talk to Nick immediately, before the others did, and see if he could somehow get a sale done. He was not stupid. After everything that had happened, there was no way to tell what might happen next. He considered himself a brave man, but he was no fool. Johnson would go to Nick's office in the morning and let Nick know that he would consider selling his lumber yards to him.

The next day Johnson parked his truck on the courthouse square and walked over to Nick's office. He didn't think anything bad would happen at Nick's office that close to the courthouse in mid-morning, but he made sure to wave to several people as he walked down the street. A few of them had strange looks on their faces because they had never seen Johnson wave at anybody first, and wondered if he was feeling alright. That was definitely out of character for Johnson.

Johnson knocked on the front door to Nick's office. He did not have an appointment and, as far as he knew, Nick might not even be there. He cautiously tried to open the door, but it was locked. Suddenly, it swung open and there stood Nick Gable.

"Well, this surely is a surprise," Nick said as he opened the door wider for Johnson to walk in. "Come on in."

The room Johnson walked into looked strange. It almost had a sort of light, red haze to it even though the day outside was sunny and beautiful. Johnson thought that it possessed an eeriness almost like what a place in hell might look like. Feeling that it was cold in the room, he felt himself shiver as he took his next few steps. Johnson's eyes attempted to adjust to the odd hue of the dimly lit room. He saw Nick walk over behind a huge desk and sit down. He then noticed two men in vested suits sitting in high-backed chairs in front of Nick's desk.

"If you are busy, I can come back another time," Johnson said, looking first at Nick and then at the two men.

"No, no. I have just gotten back from spending a few days in New Orleans, but I am never too busy for a man who had me thrown out of his office," Nick said very slowly. "However, I will treat you better than you treated me."

Motioning to the two seated men, he said, "One of these gentlemen will gladly let you have his seat." Whereupon, both men immediately stood up, each motioning for Johnson to have a seat in their respective chairs as they moved aside.

After Johnson gave each of the men a quick look of evaluation, he slowly walked over to the closest chair, having to almost edge himself by one of the two men. The closest man gradually moved back just far enough so Johnson could walk by him. Johnson stepped toward the chair to Nick's right and, after another quick glance as if to make sure the two men were still there, he sat down. As Johnson did so, the man who had been sitting in that chair stood just behind him. Johnson glanced back behind him and saw the large, well-dressed man, just standing there with his arms folded. The other man, to Johnson's right, was standing behind the chair he had previously been seated in with both of his hands now placed on the back of that chair.

Johnson began, saying, "I would like to talk to you about some business, privately if that is alright." Nick looked at Johnson and after a few moments, replied in low, firm voice, "Anything you have to say to me, you can say in front of these two gentlemen. They are business associates of mine. Just like that man you had in your office that day I visited you."

Johnson cast a quick glance at the man standing with his hands on the back of the chair next to his, then looked out of the side of his eyes at the man standing behind the chair where he was seated. Feeling he had no choice but to continue if he was going to get down to business, Johnson took a few moments to gather himself. Finally, he was able to get the words out of his mouth, words he really did not want to say, but knew he must.

"You had mentioned before that you might want to buy my lumber yards. I may be interested now in selling them."

Nick, not saying a word, took a cigar out of a humidor, lit it, and sat back in his chair.

"Go on," Nick said, now directing all of his attention towards Johnson.

"Well, I thought that if you were still interested in buying my yards that we might talk about a price," Johnson continued.

Nick didn't say anything as he began puffing from his cigar while staring at Johnson. After what seemed like forever to Johnson, Nick said, "I've heard that there have been several bad fires at your lumber yards. I've also heard that you have had some sort of voodoo symbols at some of your yards, and at your house. Your yards are not worth much any more. You've lost a lot of your workers who will probably never go back to work at the yards. I'm not interested."

Johnson had not expected that answer. Maybe he had been wrong to come here, but, with everything that had happened, he still had to try.

"But you were interested in buying them, remember? Just a few weeks ago," Johnson said, now in an almost pleading tone of voice. Nick stared at Johnson as he sat in his chair, smoking his cigar.

"I have everything now that I have to have. I don't need your lumber yards any more. Besides the voodoo symbols showing up, didn't somebody die recently at one of your yards? I don't want lumber yards that have a bad reputation, you know, some kind of taint to them," Nick said firmly as he peered through the cigar smoke at Johnson. Over time, he had perfected a firm stare similar to one that he had seen his mentor, Al Capone, use many times, always with great effect.

Johnson still couldn't believe it. He quickly looked at both of the other men standing near him and then said, while looking directly at Nick, "You told me that you were interested in buying them. Are you sure you aren't still interested?"

"You don't really want to sell, Mr. Johnson. You're a tough guy. You were such a tough guy that day I came to see you, the same day I offered to buy your lumber yards. You didn't want to sell, remember? You had your muscle man, what was his name? Bubba something? Wasn't that it? Was that his name? You had him throw me out. Remember? Throw me out! Do you remember that? Now you are asking me to buy your business? Do you think I am stupid? I got your message. It was very clear to me. You don't want to sell. A tough guy like you is not going to be bothered by something like voodoo symbols."

Still glaring at Johnson while taking puffs from his cigar, Nick continued, "You convinced me that you were a person I certainly did not want to tangle with. You also convinced me that a guy like me, a Yankee of all people, should not even think about buying your business. You made that very clear to me. Now, you want me to buy you out? What happened to you, Mr. Tough Guy? Where is your muscle guy that you had throw me out? Where is what's his name? It was Bubba something. Bubba Earl? Is that his name? The guy you had grab the back of my coat and throw me out of your office that day? Where is he? Does he know you want to sell to me? He might not be happy if he knew his boss was trying to sell to me. He might lose his job if you did that."

After pausing for a moment to think about whether he should say anything about what had happened to Bubba Earl, Johnson decided to mention it.

In such a low voice it was almost a whisper, Johnson said, "Bubba Earl's dead."

"I didn't hear what you said," Nick said, as he slowly turned his head to one side as if to hear better.

"What did you just say about Bubba Earl?"

"I said that Bubba Earl is dead. He's the guy who died at one of my lumber yards," Johnson said, not much louder than he had spoken before.

"He's dead? Now just how did he die, Mr. Johnson? What happened to him?" Nick asked as the other two men in the room suddenly moved closer to Johnson as if to make sure they heard every word he said.

"He died in an explosion," Johnson said softly.

"In an explosion? At a lumber yard? You must not be taking very good care of your yards, Mr. Johnson. You have somebody dying at your lumber yards, fires at your lumber yards, voodoo symbols showing up at your yards and your house, and now you want me to buy your yards?" Nick said looking intently at Johnson. Johnson glanced at Nick and then fixed his gaze on the floor in front of him, not saying anything in response to Nick's last statement.

Nick didn't say anything for what seemed to Johnson like an eternity as he continued to stare at Johnson. Johnson also felt the glare of the other two men standing near him. At one point, Johnson wondered if he would ever be able to just walk out of that room or would he be thrown out like he had Nick thrown out of his office. He continued to look at the floor, occasionally glancing from side to side to see if the men were moving closer to him to grab him. How he wished he had been nicer to Nick that day Nick had come out to his office. He also wished he had not come alone today to Nick's office, but he had not wanted anyone to know about his visit, and he certainly would not have wanted anyone to see him like this.

Finally, Nick broke the silence.

"Okay, I will make you an offer, but it will only be for what I think your business is worth now. It will be for a lesser price than I would have originally offered because of the damage from the fires," Nick said as he pulled a large checkbook out of the desk drawer. He opened it and slowly wrote out a check. There was total silence in the room. He tore the check out of the checkbook and handed it to Johnson.

Johnson looked at the check and saw an amount of $325,000. He looked up immediately and said, "This is for a lot less than my yards are worth! They are worth much more than this and you know that. There are seven of them, you know."

Nick cut him off, saying, "Look, I told you. Your yards have had all of those fires, somebody died at one of them, and now you've had voodoo symbols showing up all over the place. That's a lot of problems, Mr. Tough Guy. They are just not worth as much to me as they were before. You should have talked with me when I came to see you that day. I am not paying you any more than that."

Shoving a blank sheet of paper across his desk, Nick said, "Write 'bill of sale' across the top and then write that you are selling me, Nick Gable, all seven of the lumber yards and property holdings owned by you and the Western Lumber Company for the amount of that check, then sign your name and date it."

Johnson hesitated, thinking about it all, looking at Nick and then at the man to his right leaning on the back of the other chair and finally looking over his shoulder at the man standing behind him. Johnson then adjusted the sheet of paper in front of him on the desk, leaned forward and slowly began to write what Nick had told him to write. Then, he signed and dated it. After taking a deep breath, Johnson took the check Nick offered him, folded it up and put it in his pocket. He slowly stood up, defeat showing by the look on his face and by his slumping shoulders. Continuing to hold his hat in his hands, he began to turn to take a step to leave.

"Oh, one other thing. Where do you plan to live?" Nick asked, still seated and looking at Johnson.

Johnson turned and answered, "Where I live now. I have lived there for over 35 years."

Nick studied Johnson for a second and said, "No, I don't think so. See, I don't want you around here, you arrogant jackass. If you cash that check, you need to sell your house and move away. You need to take that money and your attitude and go somewhere else to live. That's plenty of money for you. Anyone with the bad judgment you have needs to live somewhere else. So where are you moving to?"

Johnson could not believe what he was hearing.

"Do you mean I am supposed to move away from here? I have lived here all my life! I have a lot of relatives here. You can't just tell me to move."

Nick leaned forward across his desk and looked directly at Johnson and said, "I just did! Listen to me, Mr. Tough Guy. If you take my Yankee money, I don't want your rebel ass anywhere around here anymore. I don't even want you in the state of Mississippi."

Johnson constantly moved his hat in his two hands as he looked at the floor and tried to understand the magnitude of what he had just heard. Looking at the other two men in the room, who were now standing uncomfortably close on both sides of Johnson, Johnson decided that he had better do and say whatever it took to get him safely out of that room. After several moments of heavy silence, Johnson said, "Well, I do have some kinfolk in Texas. I could move there, I guess," he said, meekly looking up at Nick.

Nick looked at his two associates. Then, looking directly back at Johnson he said, "No, I don't think so. That's still too close. I still might smell you if you were that close. Besides, you might have some type of voodoo hex thing on you now and the farther away you get, the better it might be for you. I think you need to move to California. Yes, California would be good for you. It has all of that fresh air. You need fresh air, lots of fresh air, so you and your arrogant attitude and your wife can stay alive and maybe be lucky enough to see your kids and grandkids from time to time when they go out there to visit you. Yes, you need to go to California, don't you, Mr. Tough Guy?"

Johnson backed away only to bump into one of the two men now standing right next to him on either side. Looking first at one and then the other, he said, "Well, I guess I do need to move out there. I guess I really do."

Nick slowly stood up, and, staring intently at Johnson, said, "You do that. You do that, and do it within the next two weeks. We wouldn't want anything like what happened to Bubba Earl to happen to you or, possibly, your wife, would we? Now, get out of my sight and don't ever let me see your face again."

Nick and Johnson stared at one another. After a few seconds, Johnson broke off the eye contact and, slowly and carefully, eased his way between the two men standing next to him and walked to the door leading out of the office. After opening the door, he glanced over his shoulder into the room one last time as he prepared to walk through the doorway. He saw Nick standing there, still looking at him as were the two other men. The light red haze he had noticed when he had first walked into the room had turned into an almost dark red. Also, there seemed to be a strange, low-pitched humming sound coming from the room.

After walking through the doorway and closing the door, Johnson was glad to be outside on Second Avenue. He had always thought of himself as a guy who could handle most anything, but this Nick Gable was like nobody he had ever met before. He almost didn't seem human. The colors had been so strange in that room and it had been so cold. There was also a strange odor, and the room had some sort of vibration in it. Thinking about what he had just seen, heard, and smelled as he left the room, there was only one word to describe what he had witnessed, and that word was "evil."

Johnson was glad to feel the fresh breeze of the air coming off the Mississippi Sound. Very glad. Even though he had just sold everything he had worked to accumulate for all those years for two-thirds of their value, he was glad to be out of that room. More importantly, he was glad to be alive. Now, he had to go tell his wife they were moving to California in two weeks. Thinking about what all had happened recently, she might even be grateful for that.

Nick felt good after the meeting. He had accomplished what he needed to accomplish, and that was getting the arrogant Mr. Johnson out of the way. Capone had always operated on the premise that nobody crossed him. In order to get that point across in the past, Capone and Capone's men, anytime it was necessary, had been absolutely ruthless. Nick knew that Capone wanted and expected him to make sure that anyone causing any problem was harshly dealt with, cruelly, if necessary. Nick felt confident that Johnson was taken care of. Word about what had happened with Johnson would make its way around Bay St. Louis, Hancock County, and even over to New Orleans. That should make it easier to get other things done.

The next day, Helen made one of her visits to see Nick. On her way over to see him, she thought about her relationship with Nick. She had thought about their relationship a lot during the past few weeks. She was beginning to fall in love with this handsome man from up north. She didn't want to hurt her husband in any way because he had stood by her when times were hard for her and was good to her, in his own way. He just wasn't a very warm person and certainly not as interesting as this northerner. The sheriff's dull personality was something she had not been prepared for when she married him. He had provided her with safety and standing in the community, that was definitely true, but on a day-to-day basis he might be more interested in going fishing than being with her. Yet, she was still relatively young and full of life and wanted to live her life. She felt bad when she spent any time thinking about what she was doing with Nick. It was not something she was proud of, and the more she thought about it, the worse she felt.

The thing that really got to her about Nick was how much he really seemed to like having her with him and being with her, which was so unlike her husband who very seldom showed any emotion at all. Today, she noticed that Nick seemed even happier than usual. He was smiling and much more at ease. Something good must have happened for him. She wanted to ask, but thinking more about it, she just decided to enjoy the moment. Seeing her, his excitement manifested itself by the amount of time it took him to get her into his bed, which was every bit of forty-five seconds. She quickly remembered that there was that one thing that kept getting in the way of her thoughts about him. The sex was fabulous!

Chapter Thirteen

Construction on the mansion was well on its way to its scheduled completion date of early July. The massive building was beginning to take shape at its location about fifty yards behind the swimming pool. Nick decided to plant an apple orchard on the grounds, mainly for the benefit of his horses. The apple trees, which were planted near the barns, were for the Yates apple, a late-ripening apple that could survive in the Deep South.

Because there were no roads to the site, all of the building materials were either being made at the site from the trees that were there and in the immediate area, or being brought in by boat from the Cypress Landing dock farther up the bayou. Cypress Landing was not too far from where the nearest back road ended in the swamp. Different types of trees from various areas of Nick's land in the bayou were used in the construction, such as short leafed pine, swamp pine, loblolly pine, sweet gum, black gum, water oak, live oak, maple, hickory, and myrtle. Most of the workers were brought in from New Orleans with a few having been brought in from up north. Nick wanted to make sure that he got the quality of work he wanted done at the site, but he also wanted to make it so that the details of what was being built at the Bluffs were not readily available for just anyone locally to know about.

Two large transport boats were brought in to carry materials and workers to the Bluffs' work site from the Cypress Landing dock. Both boats were fifty-five feet long and twenty feet wide and had flat bottoms, which were necessary in order to navigate the sometimes shallow bayou waters.

With the magnitude of such construction work being done out in the bayou, it was inevitable that word began to get around Bay St. Louis, Waveland and the county about what all was being built out at the Bluffs. Details began to be discussed such as how much money was actually being spent at the site, how expensive the buildings were that were being built, and how many additional workers were being used on the various projects. Rumors also began to circulate about how furniture and drapes for the main house were going to be obtained from Italy.

Madeline and the two couples from New Orleans made it to Rome without too much trouble. Their connection in Havana departed three days after their arrival there, giving them a couple of days and nights to tour that city. The two couples asked Madeline to go along with them as they explored the large city, to which she agreed so she would not spend her time alone. Once they arrived in Rome, the couples invited Madeline to accompany them as they traveled around that city. They were glad to have Madeline with them because she spoke the language so fluently and they enjoyed her company. She was of immense assistance to everyone as they made their way around the city on their trips shopping and visiting historical sites.

During the shopping excursions and the occasional lunches and dinners with the two couples, Judge Tullos and his wife both mentioned that they were avid golfers and wondered if Madeline ever played golf. Having played that game on occasion in Detroit, Madeline had numerous animated and humorous conversations with them about their respective golf games. She also had several discussions with Judge Parker about his friendship with the President which had resulted in his appointment as a federal judge. He told her about some of his successes as a trial attorney before being appointed to the federal bench for the southern district of Louisiana. Madeline also listened as the judge's wife, Betsy, discussed her work as an employee with the federal government's Treasury Department in New Orleans and her involvement in numerous charitable organizations and events in that area. Because she had no children, she was able to devote her time to as many of those types of activities as she could fit in.

Nick had made arrangements with a bank in Rome to have funds available for Madeline as she shopped. She enjoyed not having to worry about money, a fact duly noted by the two judges and their wives. They looked on as Madeline indulged herself with purchases of items clearly demonstrating quality workmanship. Embroidered curtains, exquisite chandeliers and hand-carved fireplace mantels were among the many items that she purchased. Italian marble, the kind found in the most expensive houses, not only in New Orleans, but around the world, was selected, cut, and made ready for shipment. The cutting of marble for the mantels of the fireplaces was so specialized that both right-handed and left-handed marble cutters were used in order to ensure the quality of the sculpturing. When combined with inlaid tables, chairs of various types and original paintings, Madeline was sure her purchases would make Nick's home the envy of everyone along the Mississippi Gulf Coast as well as many of the upper class in New Orleans.

After completing her shopping in Rome, Madeline bid a "good-bye" to her four new friends so that she could travel to Sicily to see her mother. Madeline and Nick's father had passed away while they had been in Detroit, but it meant a lot to Madeline to be able to see their mother. She had not had a close relationship with her mother because they both seemed to always be working so that the family could make ends meet. Unfortunately, the visit ended up being a rather unpleasant experience in that her mother took no time off from her work to be with Madeline. Even when Madeline offered to pay for any time she might miss, her mother insisted that she still needed to go to work.

Madeline began to realize that her interests had changed since she left Sicily. She was reminded time and time again how poor her family had been. That realization, along with being frustrated and convinced that her mother had no appreciation of Madeline's effort to see her, convinced Madeline to cut her visit to Sicily short and to return to Rome for her trip back to New Orleans. She was now more interested in being back at the mansion site when everything she had ordered began arriving.

There was one thing she had to do before she left, and it was one of the most difficult things she had ever had to do. Just before her departure, she set aside time for a visit to the grave site of her first husband, Anthony Scabelli. Feeling better about life since her move to the south, and especially after her shopping trip to Rome, she was reluctant to go to the cemetery. However, she knew that she might not ever come back again and while she was there, that was something she had to do for her beloved first husband.

As she walked up to the little knoll where the cemetery was located, she remembered how she had felt the day of his funeral. She had been mad at the world, especially at the politicians for sending him off to get killed instead of them going and getting killed themselves. She was furious with the generals for putting him in the situation where he had been killed. It had happened during a battle to take a small hill that Italian forces, once the hill had been taken, retreated from due to conflicting orders from their commanders. She remembered being mad at Anthony for getting killed, although she quickly pushed that thought out of her mind. He didn't want to die. He had loved her, and she had loved him. He had wanted to make his parents proud of him and joined the military just like his father. However, the difference was he was killed, but his father lived to be fifty-seven and died from natural causes.

Why did men want to go off to fight wars when they had loved ones, like Madeline, wanting them to stay? Oh, she had tried to talk Anthony into leaving for America, but he wouldn't even discuss the matter. He would do his duty, her hard-headed husband had told her, and he was killed doing that duty. If his death had accomplished something, then maybe she would feel better. If he had died so that others in his country might live, then that would have been a noble, maybe acceptable, cause. But nothing, nothing at all, had been accomplished by Anthony's death.

As she placed a bouquet of flowers at his tombstone, she cried. She had lost her young love, through nothing she had done, and it had greatly and adversely affected her life. Over and over, she kept thinking how nothing at all was better because of Anthony dying. A wonderful human being had died and she was still waiting for someone, anyone, to tell her that his death had not been in vain. What a wonderful life they would have had together.

As she stood up and looked over the cemetery, she thought about what other women in her situation might have done. She had been fortunate enough to go to America, to find another man she had also loved and enjoyed life with. That in itself was rare. She knew of so many women who never found another man to take the place of a loved one who, for whatever the reason, had died at an early age. She had been lucky. Her second husband had spent money on her and showered her with attention and affection. He had not been the same sweet type of person that Anthony had been, but he had been attentive and had done whatever he could to make her happy.

So there she was, standing at a cemetery, next to the grave of her first real love, knowing that her first husband had essentially died for nothing, and her second husband had been taken from her under circumstances she still did not fully understand. The death of her first husband had traumatized her; the death of her second husband had devastated her because, once again, she was a single woman who did not know what the future held. How could this have happened to her twice and she was just twenty-seven years old? The insecurity brought on by her thoughts caused her to stop crying and to leave the cemetery. Whatever it took, she had to find some way to survive and to once again find the security that had been taken from her. Most importantly, she had to try to find happiness again.

* * *

Joey Demarco was one of the construction workers who had been brought in from New Orleans. He was five feet ten inches tall with long, wavy blond hair to go along with his blue eyes and overall good looks. He had a solid build and did not have an ounce of fat on him. He had been born in Houma, Louisiana, but his parents had divorced when he was fifteen. Soon after their split, he found it easier on his mother if he was not around. His presence seemed to constantly remind her of how much she despised Joey's dad, who had disappeared for parts unknown. After his mother jumped on him one too many times in one of her drunken rages, Joey dropped out of the twelfth grade in high school and also disappeared. He had never been much of a student anyway. Enjoying his new independence, he ended up in New Orleans.

Being a physically strong boy for his size, Joey began working for a construction company that was very busy at just the time he needed a job. He was a quick learner and worked hard to make sure he kept his only means of support, his job. He stayed in a flop house near the Mississippi River where other construction workers often stayed. It was a rough place, but it was cheap and available. It had now been a little over three years since he had dropped out of school.

One day his boss called the workers together and told them that the company would soon be working on a major building project over on the Mississippi Gulf Coast. One of the problems with the job was that it would be done in the middle of one of the largest swamps on the gulf coast, Devil's Swamp. The boss was looking for volunteers to go work on the project, and asked the assembled workers if any of them would like to sign up. He told them that those who volunteered would be paid bonus wages because working conditions in the swamp would not be pleasant.

After seeing several of the more experienced workers raise their hands to volunteer, Joey decided that he would too. He wanted to make as much money as he possibly could. First of all he needed it, and second of all, if he had a lot of money he thought he could impress more women. That was important to Joey because, since he had been out on his own, he had become quite the ladies' man. His impressive good looks, along with a talent for talking his way into almost every woman's heart he had met or been interested in since he had left home, had given him a feeling of invincibility. After he had dropped out of school and was on his own, he had enjoyed almost constant successes with women. Simply put, he had proven time and time again that no woman could resist him. Yes, he was a ladies' man, and with every conquest he gained more and more self-confidence. Having more money, he felt, would make those conquests much easier.

Joey reasoned that the biggest disadvantage of working in the swamp was that he would be away from all of his women. The way he looked at it, his absence would be depriving so many of them of his presence. Yes, Joey had gotten cocky, and arrogant, very arrogant. Yet, he knew how to turn on the charm.

He thought it might be a good thing for him to take a break and get away from New Orleans and go experience other things. He was also interested in getting a rest from the continuous efforts by several of the women he was seeing to get him to marry them. The thought of being married scared Joey. He had seen how some of the men he worked with had wives they could not make happy regardless of what they did or how hard they worked. He had also seen how wives tended to have babies one after the other in an effort to keep their husbands around, but the additional mouths to feed only seemed to make their situations more hopeless. Yes, maybe it was time for him to go where there were fewer women, which certainly would be the case in a swamp in Mississippi.

When he first arrived at Cypress Landing, Joey began to have doubts. He had already heard about Mississippi swamps, but he had not been worried. Being raised in Houma, he had been in a few swamps before. At least, he thought he had. This Mississippi swamp was unlike any he had ever seen. Devil's Swamp, as they called it, was huge. Mile after mile of nothing but swamp. Snakes, alligators and millions of mosquitoes that seemed determined to feast off of some portion of his body.

Until the bunk houses were completed at the Bluffs, the workers stayed during the week at various hotels in Bay St. Louis and Waveland. Each day, they were picked up at the Bay St. Louis city docks by the construction transport barges that took them into the swamp to the Bluffs. In the first few weeks, Joey could never figure out how to get to the Bluffs from the city docks. He wondered how the guides found their way, but they always did. He quickly stopped worrying about that and began to sleep on the barge until it arrived at the Bluffs.

The workers were usually picked up at the city docks as the sun began to show itself on the eastern horizon. By the time they arrived at the Bluffs, there was enough sunlight to begin work, although it was still early in the morning. During the week it was usually quite boring. However, on Friday afternoon, they boarded a train and were taken to New Orleans where they spent Friday and Saturday nights before being returned to their hotels in Mississippi late Sunday afternoons.

Once the bunk houses were completed, the workers were moved out of the Bay St. Louis hotels and into those buildings. Now, on Friday afternoons, they were taken by the barges to Cypress Landing to meet trucks that took them into New Orleans for the weekends. The workers were expected back at Cypress Landing Sunday afternoons so they could be taken back out to their bunk houses at the Bluffs. It did not take Joey long to settle into the routine. He was now helping finish work on the mansion.

Chapter Fourteen

By early July, Nick had control of everything needed to begin the shipping operation. His contractor stated that the interior of the mansion would be finished in the next seven days, at the most, and then the remaining construction workers would be gone. Most of the workers had completed their responsibilities and already left.

Helen was the one that tipped Nick off that phone conversations were being listened in on by those whom she called "busy bodies." Helen had found out about such activity almost by accident. She had been interviewed by the church board two months earlier about playing the organ and piano for church functions. She had been taking lessons on both the organ and the piano for six years and had become proficient in both. Needing the extra money and also beginning to genuinely enjoy her playing efforts, she discovered the church needed to fill the position of organist since the former organist had recently moved to Texas with her husband.

When she mentioned her interview with the church board on the phone to one of her best friends, Carol Landry, she was confronted on the street not too long thereafter by Bessie Mae Childry who accused her of trying to steal the job Bessie Mae claimed she had been promised by the former organist if she ever left town. Helen knew her conversation had been listened in on when Bessie Mae told her that it didn't matter if Helen had taken lessons on the organ for the previous six years. Helen was sure that the only person she had ever told she took lessons for six years was her good friend Carol while on the phone. She hadn't even mentioned it to the board members because she was worried that someone might have had lessons or experience for more than six years. Bessie Mae told Helen that she had been promised that job and that Helen just needed to withdraw her name as a candidate.

To Helen's delight she was selected for the position. When Nick was told by Helen what had happened, he knew that future conversations by telephone from Bay St. Louis to Chicago would need to be very brief and in some sort of code. It would be better if the calls were made from New Orleans, especially those concerning shipping details at the start of operations. By doing that, he thought that there was far less likelihood of having the call listened to since there were so many more people in that city.

With this information in hand, Nick made a trip to New Orleans so that he could call Capone and notify him that everything was on the verge of being ready. He made the call from his room at the Monteleon Hotel in the French Quarter in New Orleans. Nick reached Capone at his hang-out in Chicago.

"Hello." Nick immediately recognized Capone's voice. It was so distinctive he could recognize it almost anywhere, he thought, even on one of these new fangled telephones.

"Hello, Boss. It's me." Nick knew better than to identify himself on the phone, especially with the message he was getting ready to deliver.

"Good to hear from you. I hope you have some good news for me." Capone had spent a lot of money and allowed a long period of time for this southern operation to be set up. Nick could understand if Capone was a little anxious for things to get started.

"As a matter of fact I do. Everything is basically ready. Finishing up will only take about one more week," Nick said proudly.

"Good! Good! That's good news!"

"I had hoped you would be happy to hear that."

"I am. I knew you would get it done. I really did. That is good news. I will pass that along and things can get started. It will be set up so that the first one should be met at the southeastern cove we talked about exactly two weeks from today. Unless you hear from me, have your guide there at five p.m. At exactly that time. Is that understood?"

"Yes, sir, boss. Five p.m. two weeks from today."

"Right. Good. That will be fine. Good job. We will make a trial run with a small load to see how it works out. Let me know if there are any problems. I want to know after the first trip how things work out on your end so let me hear from you a day or so after that arrival. You got that?"

"Yes, sir. I understand. I'll be back in touch after completion of the first effort." Nick said.

"Good! Good. I knew I picked the right guy to handle this operation when I picked you."

"Thanks, Boss. I've done my best. You know that."

"I know you have. Keep up the good work. Let me hear how it goes. Bye for now."

"Yes, sir. I will. Good-bye."

The well-financed, extensive operation was now set up and almost ready to begin. The potential return was enormous.

The first trip bringing barrels of liquor from Cuba was made by the *Molly Bee*. As Capone directed, the ship was met at the southeastern inlet of Cat Island by Nick's waiting guide. The guide took the boat through the Mississippi Sound and into the Bay of St. Louis, past the town of Bay St. Louis, and then up Bayou Le Croix. Once in the waters of the bayou, the guide's expertise was invaluable since the bayou's many twists and turns, along with parallel and dead-end channels, had often confused many an experienced seaman as well as supposed knowledgeable locals.

Work on the mansion had been completed just a few days before the ship's arrival. Once again, Nick did not need any of the citizens of Bay St. Louis passing on information about his shipments to law enforcement officials. As before, Nick called Capone from a room at the Monteleon Hotel to let him know that the first shipment had come in and that everything had gone well. Nick was able to speak in a way that let Capone know that Nick, if given permission, would notify Fernando Gonzalez in Cuba that boats would be coming to pick up the cargo stored at their warehouses on a regular, established schedule.

Capone gave his permission to start the shipments, and he also told Nick that the lucrative lumber shipments to Cuba should continue since there was money to also be made from that legitimate business. The demand for the lumber from the Mississippi yards in just the Caribbean islands more than took care of what was being shipped down to Cuba. The *Dark Shadows* and the *Molly Bee* had already made several trips just to haul lumber from the first two yards Nick had reached agreements with. Indeed, Nick soon realized that he could immediately use at least two more boats for the lumber shipment business alone. Of course, that meant that more of the other types of "contraband" could be shipped north on the return trips.

Subsequent trips delivering the barrels of liquor took place without any problems. The early shipments were mostly made up of rum and whisky. The cove on the southeastern side of Cat Island was designated as the rendezvous point for all of the boats to meet their guides for the trip into the Bay of St. Louis and up Bayou Le Croix to the Bluffs. The operation was soon being conducted on a regular basis with almost a military-type precision. Not too long after shipments began, the two barns at the Bluffs were packed with barrels of an assorted variety of booze.

Shipment plans were consistently increased to satisfy the demands for the illegal contraband. Once full operation was achieved, shipments were being brought in on the five different, extremely fast sixty-five foot long, two-masted lumber schooners. The liquor was stored at the Bluffs before eventually being taken upstream to Cypress Landing on the former construction barges. Another dock was eventually set up on the eastern shore, or opposite side, of the Bay of St. Louis a mile or so up a stream known as Rotten Bayou.

Once the illegal liquor made it to the docks, cars and trucks were waiting to be loaded for their delivery trips throughout the southern region. All of it was coming through the Bluffs of Devil's Swamp. Transportation capability became so needed that, among other things, Nick even struck an agreement with the two drivers of the ambulance of the local Bay St. Louis hospital. The ambulance was equipped with a special tank underneath the portion of the vehicle that the patients were in while they were being transported. The tank was routinely filled with booze which was then taken to various places around Hancock County without arousing any suspicion. Nick also incorporated black people into his shipping operation. As one black man told him, "Mista Nick, black folks drink just like white folks do."

Chapter Fifteen

Madeline returned to the Bluffs and, almost immediately, things she had ordered or bought in Italy started to arrive in New Orleans. Arrangements were made to transport, either by rail or truck, everything from New Orleans to Bay St. Louis and then to have it shipped out to the Bluffs. Since most items had been paid for in cash, there had been no delays in shipping. The builders were finished with the construction of the main house, which was a good time to start hanging curtains, moving in furniture, putting the marble mantels on the fireplaces, hanging wall paper, putting the chandeliers in their proper places, and doing all of the other things necessary to complete the magnificent mansion. Madeline was glad to be back.

As construction at the Bluffs moved toward completion, Nick realized that he was going to need some of the workers to stay around permanently to keep the place up and perform any maintenance jobs that may become necessary. All of the workers had been watched very closely by Nick, and he alone had made the decisions as to who would be asked to continue to work there, if they wanted to. The pay that was offered was much higher than in New Orleans, and that was what had encouraged Joey to stay. The two small bunk houses that had been built by the construction workers when work at the Bluffs had first started were much nicer places to live in than the flop houses that Joey had inhabited since his departure from Houma. For the employees, there was always a boat leaving for Cypress Landing on Friday afternoons and returning on Sunday afternoons, as it had while construction had been under way.

Each worker who was asked to remain had a meeting with Nick. All of the meetings were held on the front porch of one of the bunk houses. When it was Joey's time to meet with Nick, he stepped up on the small porch of the bunk house and found himself standing in front of Nick, who was sitting on a crude work bench behind a small table. Joey had not spent that much time around Nick and had been concerned that he might not be asked to stay because of that very reason. Joey had actually been a little surprised when he was told by one of his co-workers to be available to meet with "Mr. Nick" that afternoon.

"You're Joey, aren't you?"

"Yea. Joey Demarco."

"Well Joey, I have kept an eye on you while you have been working here and I have decided that you are one of the boys I want to keep around here now that construction is finished. You will be working here with our horses and doing maintenance work around the Bluffs. Now, if you stay, I want it understood that you won't talk about what goes on out here with anyone else." After a short pause, Nick then pointedly asked Joey, "What I want to know is, can you keep your mouth shut about things around here when you leave here on the weekends because, if you can't, you need to go on and leave right now."

Joey was surprised at what Nick had said to him and it took a second for it all to register.

"What things are you talking about?" Joey asked.

"You'll find out in due time, but that really means everything," Nick answered.

Joey said, "I don't want you to think by me asking that question that I don't want to stay here because I do. I need the job and I kinda like it out here. Yea, Mr. Nick. I can keep my mouth shut."

Nick slightly nodded his head and after a brief moment said, "Well, you have worked hard out here. So you can stay, but be sure and keep yourself in line. I'll be bringing in somebody to manage things, and you will report to him. I'll let you know who that will be when it is all set up. That's all for now."

As he left the meeting, Joey was almost excited about the unknown. Now he knew for a fact that there would be things happening out at the Bluffs that he was not supposed to talk about under any circumstances. While that might be hard to do, it didn't bother Joey. He would be staying at the Bluffs during the week and everybody there would know about what all was going on. However, during the weekends he would just have to mind his own business, and be careful to not say anything to anybody about what might be going on, whatever it might be. For all of that, he was going to continue to get paid far more than he could make in New Orleans or anywhere else in the surrounding area.

Also, there was no telling what exciting and interesting things he might be able to get into out there. If there was going to be anything illegal happening, and he was beginning to think that was definitely going to be the case, then all the more opportunity for him to make more money and maybe move up to a more responsible job. It might just end up being really exciting. Thinking that way, he had no problem at all telling Nick that he would not say anything to anybody outside of the Bluffs. Ever. He said that as easily as he had promised things to many of the women he had been with. Only with this, he knew he really did need to keep his mouth shut. He had also seen that beautiful woman with the fabulous body out at the Bluffs. He had seen her several weeks ago and now she was back again. He hoped she didn't leave any time soon because he never got tired of looking at a woman like her, especially out in the middle of nowhere.

* * *

It was now the third week of July and construction was finally completed. Nick decided it was now time to throw a big afternoon cocktail party at the Bluffs. He set the party for the first Saturday of August and invited all of his new political acquaintances and local officials, along with their wives, or dates, to come see the results of all of the hard work that the attendees had heard so many rumors about.

Madeline asked Nick to invite her New Orleans friends that she had met on her trip, Judge Marvin Tullos and his wife, Delores, and Judge Jonathan Parker and his wife, Betsy. Nick saw to it that the two couples were invited. He thought that it might be good for him to have such respected citizens of New Orleans talking about him and what a wonderful place he had built on the water over in Hancock County.

On the day of the scheduled event, the attendees for the party were picked up at the Bay St. Louis city docks and transported out to the Bluffs on the construction barges, which had been converted into ferries for the party by adding padded benches and pillows for the comfort of the ladies. Everyone wanted to see what had been built out in the middle of what was now over nineteen thousand acres that Nick had bought in Devil's Swamp.

The lawn party started at around eleven o'clock that morning. What the guests saw when they arrived was a massive, elegant plantation home located on the central bluff overlooking the bayou. The party was held around the swimming pool which was located in front of the house. Madeline greeted visitors by the pool near the top of the stairs leading up from the docks. Dressed in a white linen, skin-tight, spaghetti-strapped cocktail dress, she became almost as much of a topic of conversation as the facilities.

The two-story brick mansion had six large columns along its front, three on each side of the stairway leading up to the front porch on the first floor. The huge building was built up on brick footings which allowed for the circulation of air and water, if there ever was any flooding, below the first floor. Large chimneys rose from both sides of the house and towered high above the pitched roof. Two white, solid wooden doors were at the center of both the first and second stories of the house. An arched glass skylight, trimmed in wood, was over the doorway on each floor. Two windows were on each side of the front door on the bottom floor and also on each side of the center doorway on the second story. Dark green wooden shutters were on the sides of each window on both floors, as well as on each side of the downstairs and upstairs doorways. White lattice work was located on each side of the house to soften the point where both the downstairs porch and the upstairs balcony completed their wrap around the front of the house and halfway down each side.

In the center of each floor behind the doors was a wide hallway that went all the way from the front of the building to doors at the back of the building. The locals called that open area a "dog-trot" because, in the houses of the poorest citizens, dogs were allowed to trot down the center portion between the two sides of the house. Many houses were built that way, especially in the country, in the hopes that if a fire started on the side of the house that had the dining room and kitchen, which is what usually happened, then maybe the fire could be put out before it got to the bedrooms and living room on the other side of the house. Also, when it really got hot, the front and back doors could be opened to allow any breeze to circulate through that area of the house, thereby easing the burden of the high temperatures.

On the bottom floor, the first room off to the right was a dining room with twelve foot high ceilings, which height was uniform throughout the house. By having high ceilings in every room, the lower areas of the rooms would stay cooler since hot air rises and would thus be in the upper reaches of the ceiling. The floor of the dining room, as with every floor in the house, was made of wood that was cut from the massive oak trees that had been located at the site. The furniture in the dining room area had been imported, and its quality was something that had only been seen in a few of the high society houses in New Orleans and on the Mississippi Gulf Coast.

The chandelier in the center of the dining room was of such elegance that it could have been found in the White House in Washington. How such a magnificent fixture could be located out in the swamp was a source of continual conversation. The walls of the room were covered with a burgundy colored wall cloth trimmed with gold. The wall cloth had been purchased by Madeline at a shop in Rome. The shop had imported the cloth from France. Silk drapes were hanging on both sides of each of the big windows and were hung, as they were in every room of the house, from the top of the windows so that the bottom portion was lying spread out on the floor. Such was the display of similar drapes in the most elegant and expensive houses in New Orleans. A fireplace was located near the center of the far right, outside wall of the room.

The dining room was connected to the kitchen by a doorway in the wall common to both rooms. A sliding wooden door that retracted effortlessly into the wall could be pulled to separate the dining room from the kitchen to allow more privacy. A large dining room table occupied the center of the room. It was complete with ten matching chairs with four on each side and one at each end. Two large candelabras were placed on the table.

The adjacent kitchen was really a serving room which was centered around a carving table, with a pantry and numerous cabinets placed around the walls. Since Nick was fearful of a fire breaking out in the kitchen of this massive structure in the middle of nowhere, most of the cooking was usually done in a small, separate building behind the house.

Behind the serving area was a door which opened onto the hallway. It led to an indoor toilet room with a free-standing bath tub. This caused as much conversation by party-goers as anything in the house since indoor plumbing was a relatively new creation. Even the famous palace of Versailles in France did not have indoor plumbing like this house did. This new amenity was only available to the uppermost of the upper class. It was made possible by the large copper vats located toward the back of the house on top of the roof where they collected rainwater. When days without rain led to there being no water in the vats, an extensive pulley and bucket system allowed the vats to be refilled so that they could continue to serve their functions. Wire screens were placed over the vats to keep birds and other animals out. Hot water was provided upon request by being heated on an oven.

On the opposite side of the center hallway, the first room was a living room. The floor was covered with a large, thick rug that had been imported from England. As with the dining room, a large chandelier hung from the center of the ceiling of this room. Two ornate couches faced each other, separated by a small table with fold-up end pieces. Two large, high-backed chairs were located at each end of the small table, making the seating in the room ideal for small conversational gatherings following dinner. Two large paintings of the Italian countryside near Messina that had been specially ordered by Madeline during her trip were hung on opposite walls in the room.

The second room on the left side of the center hallway was a smaller room that served as a library. A small, elegant chandelier hung from the center of the ceiling of this room. Row upon row of full bookcases were located along each wall, except for the wall where the fireplace was located. A desk was in place facing the entrance to the room with a big window behind it. On the other side of the fireplace was the second large window of the room. Two high-backed chairs were placed facing the desk with a small round table between them. This room was connected to the living room by a doorway with a retractable door.

The third room on the left was the downstairs bedroom. A large, four-poster bed with a canopy was the centerpiece of that room. The head of the bed was against the wall to the right as one entered the room. Mosquito nets were rolled up on each side of the bed along with one for the foot of the bed. The tall and wide wooden headboard made a net for the head of the bed unnecessary. A large, heavy looking chest of drawers was located at the foot of the bed against the wall common with the adjacent library room. A high-back leather chair was angled facing the bed with a window behind it. A closet was located behind a door in the wall at the head of the bed, as well as another toilet and wash area with access through a door that could be closed.

Visitors found the second story of the house to be almost as interesting as the first story. The stairway going upstairs was located in the middle of the house and gradually curved from the right side of the central hallway until it reached the top floor more to the center of the upstairs hallway. The banisters provided something to hold onto as one worked their way to the top of the stairs. Once upstairs, a central hallway was the focus of the floor. There were two bedrooms on the right side with the front bedroom being larger than the rear one. On the left side of the hallway in the front area was the master bedroom with a smaller bedroom located behind it.

All bedrooms were well furnished with beds, dressers, chairs, closets and wash basins. Also provided in each bedroom was a small ladder, called a bed step, which consisted of three steps that made it easier for the person sleeping in the bed to climb up into it since the top of the mattress for each bed was at least three and a half feet from the floor. The windows on the second story were actually doors made with glass panes. The doors could be opened to allow any breeze the opportunity to circulate through the upstairs rooms and also allow any rising hot air an avenue for release to the outside area. On both sides at the end of the upstairs hallway, behind doors that opened onto the hallway, were the combination toilet-wash closets that were the same as those in place downstairs.

The view from the front upstairs balcony was something to behold. Most visitors had heard about the elegance and height of the house and wanted to experience the view from the second story balcony during their visit. Such elevation was not common in the swamp, and the view from so high was not something that most visitors had ever witnessed in that area. From the balcony, one could see quite a distance into the nearby bayous. The colors of the trees, the water and the sky all seemed to change almost by the minute as one enjoyed the scenery from that location.

Almost without exception, those attending Nick's party were impressed, if not stunned, by what all they saw. If the bathhouses, guesthouse, stables, or the racetrack Nick had built over near the two barns did not impress them, they were impressed by how utterly first-class the main house was and by the quality of the construction of such a place out in the middle of the swamp, as well as the furniture and accessories for the entire house. Although most of the furniture had been purchased in New Orleans, Madeline had excelled by purchasing only the very best of chandeliers, wall cloths and drapes during her trip to Italy.

Upon the arrival of her New Orleans friends, Madeline gave each one a big smile and a hug.

"It's so nice to see each of you! Thanks so much for coming. I hope it wasn't too much trouble for you to get here," Madeline said, genuinely happy at seeing her friends.

"Madeline, you did not tell us how beautiful this place is!" Delores exclaimed, unable to restrain her enthusiasm over what she was seeing.

"Well, I didn't know myself until I got back. Nick, my brother, is responsible for most of it. He has really worked hard on everything and I really didn't know it was going to be this wonderful until I got back from the trip."

"The only thing that seems to be missing is a golf course, Madeline," Judge Tullos quipped as he gazed around as if looking for the first tee. Everyone laughed and Madeline answered, "Give us time, Judge. I'll let Nick know you would like for us to put in one of those out here."

Everyone politely laughed and Betsy Parker said, "Well, it certainly looks wonderful from here."

"It looks like you have your duties for the moment welcoming your many guests," Judge Parker noted.

"Yes, I do," Madeline responded. "Please feel free to take a look around. Go up to the main house and be sure you look at the water from the second story. The view is so beautiful. We have bathing suits in the changing rooms if you would like to take a swim. Just look around and find a suit that you like and enjoy the pool. Later, I think Nick has some horse racing lined up so, hopefully, you might enjoy that also."

"We might pass on the swimming, but I think Judge Parker and I would be most interested in the horse racing, strictly as observers of course," said Judge Tullos, everyone chuckling at his comment.

Madeline answered saying, "Thanks, all of you, so much for coming. It is wonderful to see you again. Nick is at the main house so please introduce yourselves to him. Hopefully, I will get to see you all later."

Excusing themselves, the two couples began moving toward the mansion as Madeline greeted another group of attendees to the party. After walking along a short pathway to the front of the mansion, the group climbed the stairs and was greeted by Nick.

"Hello. Welcome. I am Nick Gable," he said as he shook Judge Tullos' hand.

"Hello, Nick. I am Judge Marvin Tullos and this is my wife, Delores. While traveling on our trip to Italy with Judge Jonathan Parker, here, and his wife, Betsy, we met your sister, Madeline."

"Yes. Yes, of course," Nick said, now shaking Judge Parker's hand and nodding his head to both of their wives. "It is so nice to meet you. Madeline had such wonderful things to say about each of you. Please accept my sincere appreciation for letting her tag along with you and for including her in so many of your activities. That was so kind."

"Well, it was our pleasure," Judge Parker said, with Judge Tullos adding, "It was nice having her along with us."

Delores said, "Having her with us during our shopping trips was like having our own interpreter," to which Betsy added, "She was always so helpful and so considerate."

"I am glad she was able to be of assistance to you, and, again, please accept my sincere appreciation for including her in so many of your activities there. She told me how much it meant to her, since she was traveling by herself, to have people that she was comfortable being with for so much of the trip."

"We are all looking forward to seeing more of this house. It is so beautiful," Delores said as everyone concurred with her statement.

"By all means, please do. Enjoy yourselves. If you need anything, just let any of the serving staff know. I have been told that, in a little while, some of the horses have a little competition planned between themselves so I hope you will stay around to see that," Nick said while taking a step to the side so the group could walk through the front door.

After laughter all around, Judge Tullos said, while glancing at Judge Parker, "I think we would all like to hang around for that. You never know what those sneaky horses might cook up. It could be fun to see. It was nice meeting you, Nick."

Judge Parker added, "Yes, Nick. Thanks for the invitation."

The two ladies showed their enthusiasm for their upcoming tour of the home by already moving toward the doorway, both saying almost in unison, "Nice to have met you." The group had nothing but positive comments to say about Nick after they left his presence.

Nick had brought in several workers from the New Orleans area to serve as waiters for the party. Tables had been placed around the pool and were covered with white table cloths. Food was plentiful at several locations. Chairs were in their appropriate locations at each table and were also covered with white cloths.

As two o'clock neared, the party attendees, now numbering over a hundred, heard an announcement by a waiter who circulated saying in a loud, booming voice, "The horse races will begin at the track behind the bunk houses in fifteen minutes." Jockeys had been brought in from New Orleans to ride Nick's horses, as well as several other horses that had been brought out to the Bluffs for the event. The races began promptly fifteen minutes later.

Madeline made her way over to the large tent that had been set up next to the finish line and joined her friends from New Orleans. They laughed as Madeline managed to pick more winners just by going with her favorite numbers on the horses than both of the Judges and their wives, who had all participated on many previous occasions in the sport of speculative betting on horse races.

After the races, Madeline enjoyed the company of the two wives as they sat overlooking the bend in the bayou in chairs adjacent to the pool while their husbands, who had changed their minds about taking a swim, enjoyed the coolness of the pool's water along with a few other men.

"This place is so wonderful," Delores said as she enjoyed a sip of her cool drink.

"It really is," seconded Betsy. "It is so peaceful out here, and so beautiful."

"It is. But it is also very dull out here," Madeline said.

"How can you say that when there is so much to see out here?" said Delores. "I bet you could just sit here and the wildlife would put on a show for you."

Madeline looked at Delores and almost laughed. She then realized that these two women had not lived like she had the past few years in Detroit with her life-of-the-party husband. She chose not to make a comment as she began watching the two judges swim an impromptu race from one end of the pool and back with the federal judge winning the race by a very small margin.

After briefly listening to the banter between the two judges about their race, Madeline continued the ladies' conversation by saying, "I would rather be somewhere that has great music, dancing and a lot of people."

Betsy said, "That's because you have not been at a place like this with the right person. If you had, the music, dancing and everything else would not matter. You would just be happy being with that person."

Madeline looked at Betsy and thought about what she had just said. Maybe she was right. If her first husband were still alive and with her at the Bluffs, Betsy would probably be right. But he wasn't, and her fun-loving second husband wasn't either. As Madeline watched the two judges get out of the pool, she realized she was very lonely.

Joey had been assigned duties as a stable hand and, along with some of the other construction workers who had been hired, had worked hard putting saddles and bridles on the horses during the races. They had been responsible for making sure the horses were exercised before their races and then cooled down after racing so hard in the hot weather. Joey had gotten a glimpse of the woman he now knew was Nick's sister, Madeline, in her tight, white dress, something he and many others who attended the party would clearly remember. She remained on his mind.

As dusk began to approach, and before mosquitoes began to come out, the guests made their way back to one of the transport ferries at the Bluffs' docks so that they could be returned to Bay St. Louis. Both Nick and Madeline saw their guests off, with promises when the New Orleans couples were leaving that, hopefully, they would stay in touch with one another.

The numerous kerosene lamps and lanterns provided more than an adequate light both inside the houses, along the walkways and on the grounds. Reflections of light off of the pendent Spanish moss in the nearby trees also provided an eerie glow to the area as darkness settled in. The Bluffs were going to be the topic of conversation for quite a while, not only on the Mississippi Gulf Coast, but also in New Orleans.

Chapter Sixteen

The week following the party at the Bluffs, Nick began making inquiries about joining a Mardi Gras krewe in New Orleans. The approaching end of the year 1924 meant that, early in the New Year, it would soon be Mardi Gras season in New Orleans and along the Mississippi Coast. Krewes were groups that were formed, many of them by members of the upper-class of society in New Orleans, so that they could have parties and socialize with one another. During the Mardi Gras parades each year, the members of the krewes would ride high floats and wear masks so that their identities would remain anonymous. Nick was told that it was hard to join one unless a person was from an old New Orleans' family, or had a lot of money, or both.

With the help of Bay St. Louis Mayor Foucher and the recommendations of some acquaintances in New Orleans, Nick made application to join the Krewe of Nobles, one of the oldest and most respected krewes. By attending the organizational meetings and parties held by the krewe at the New Orleans Country Club, he was able to get to know several officials from the New Orleans area, including the New Orleans mayor, the city's police chief, the district attorney, several state and federal judges and their wives and families. People had heard about Nick and his wealth and how much he had been spending in the Bay St. Louis area. Many of the members of upper New Orleans society had recently built "beach cottages," as they called them, in Bay St. Louis or Pass Christian, a small town located on the opposite shore of the Bay of St. Louis in Mississippi. The "beach cottages" were almost as big as some of the houses lived in by those same families in New Orleans. Nick's attendance at the meetings and parties gave the membership the opportunity to meet him and evaluate him to see if he was worthy of membership in the prestigious organization.

Nick had been going to church regularly and decided it was time to go talk more with Father Ryan about making a contribution to the church. He wanted to continue to leave a good impression in the local community, and it would be advantageous if he and the priest could agree on a project that Nick could support. Nick learned that Father Ryan usually met with parishioners who wanted to talk with him on Tuesday mornings of each week. He drove to the church on the bright Tuesday morning of the second week in August and walked around to where Father Ryan's office was located. Finally, seeing Father Ryan's secretary, he introduced himself and asked if the Father was available.

"I am sure that he would be most happy to see you, Mr. Gable," said Father Ryan's secretary. Nick could see by her name plate on her desk that she had been with the church long enough to have the pull necessary to get her own name plate, or else she knew somebody special. Loraine Mueller got up from her desk and walked the few steps it took to get to Father Ryan's office. Gently knocking on the door, she announced, "Mr. Nick Gable is here and would like to know if he could see you, Father Ryan."

"Surely. Have him come on in," said a voice from through the doorway.

Nick walked into Father Ryan's office as Father Ryan stood up and, with a smile on his face, extended his hand in greeting.

"It's a pleasure to see you, Nick," the priest said as he motioned Nick to a chair.

"It's a pleasure to see you also, Father," Nick replied as he sat down.

"How are things going with you?" the Father inquired.

"Everything is fine, Father. If you remember, I mentioned to you at the fundraiser picnic a few months ago that I wanted to do something for the church after construction was completed at the Bluffs. Well, we are now finished, for the most part, so this might be a good time to start thinking about what project I can contribute to."

"Yes, I remember our conversation. We have such great needs here. I was very glad to hear of your interest. Since our discussion, have you thought about anything in particular?" the priest asked, settling back in his chair.

"I did not have anything in mind when we talked then. Now, having thought about it and seeing what the church is doing for its members and in the community, I thought it might be nice to help some kids who are not able to afford tuition to the elementary school you have here. I have heard many good things about it," Nick said.

"That would simply be wonderful. You are so correct. Every year we have a number of local kids who are from families that cannot afford our tuition, but really need to attend our school. As you may have heard, our school starts the second week of next month. Any contribution you make we could designate for scholarships for this year. Is something like that what you might have had in mind?" the priest asked.

"Yes, that is something that might be just the right thing for me to do. If you would, Father, give me some idea about how much it might take to help the number of kids you have had approach you, say over the past six months, about going to your elementary school, but who couldn't afford tuition," Nick said. He was thinking that this may be a perfect fit for the type of assistance program he wanted to support.

"I would be happy to, Nick. That would be wonderful if you could somehow help us with that," Father Ryan said, now with a big smile on his face.

Nick knew that his original evaluation of the priest had been correct. Father Ryan was a good man, and the community was so fortunate to have him there.

"If you will, give me a few days, say about a week or so, and get back in touch with me. I will have that figure for you then," Father Ryan said.

Nick left Father Ryan's office that day with a positive feeling. He was going to do something good. He went back to see Father Ryan a little over a week after his initial visit. Father Ryan was not in, but his efficient secretary had the figure ready for him. She told him they had determined that it would take $16,500 for them to be able to admit every potential student that had applied in the past six months for the coming year that they knew probably would not have the money. She also told Nick that there were possibly two or three more who may make a late application.

Two days later, Nick delivered a sealed envelope to Father Ryan's secretary. After he had left, she opened the envelope and pulled out a bank check made out to the church for twenty thousand dollars.

Chapter Seventeen

Madeline settled into the upstairs bedroom on the front left side of the mansion. She made occasional trips to New Orleans to meet the remaining shipments of items she had ordered in Italy that had not already been delivered. Under her guidance, the mansion continued to have things added to it, the last being hurricane doors that could be placed over all of the windows. Even the workers who had been kept were impressed with the quality of this building out in the middle of the swamp. Both Nick and Madeline were anxious for improvements to continually be made on both the mansion and the other buildings and the grounds.

After a few weeks back at the Bluffs, Madeline determined that about the only thing she could really do for pleasure out there was ride horses. There was nothing exciting at all there for her to do. While she did have a lot of responsibility for making sure the shipments of items for the mansion were properly taken care of and assigned to their appropriate locations, she began to get bored now that the mansion was basically finished. Her life was so different from when she often went out in Detroit with her flamboyant husband whom everyone seemed to know and who always seemed to be the life of every party.

Joey had seen Madeline the first day she returned from Italy and at the party. He now began to see her on the days that she came out to ride. He would see her walking towards the stables in her tight black riding pants with her white long-sleeved blouse, black riding boots, black gloves and black hat with her hair pulled up. He was usually getting hay for the horses when she walked up, and she was on her horse and out before he had the chance to meet her. He knew he would have to change that, whatever it took. He was convinced that she was absolutely the most beautiful woman he had ever laid his eyes on.

During the next week, Joey hung out near the stables as much as he could so that he could find out when the stable hands were expecting Madeline. He then began making sure he was at the stables when she came. At first Madeline didn't even notice him. She didn't seem to recognize that this gift to all women was even there. As soon as she got to the stables, Madeline would put on her black riding hat, mount her horse of the day and ride off by herself.

There were usually at least three men, Tiny, along with two stable workers, Jason and Jeff, standing there to make sure everything was in order for her both when she left and when she returned, which was usually an hour or so later. Nick had told Tiny to make sure Madeline enjoyed her riding because Nick knew she needed something to hold her interest and make her happy in her new environment. Nick realized that, as far as Madeline was concerned, there was a major difference between the big city where Madeline had lived and now living out in the middle of a swamp.

Riding became boring during her third week back at the Bluffs. Because there was nothing else to do with her time, she decided she needed to start going out. She had done all she could do getting the staff organized and efficient, in addition to getting items that had been ordered for the house put in their proper places. It was time for some fun. She knew she had to tell Nick she was going to go out, just in case there were things she needed to know, such as where she should go and exactly what all she could tell someone about the Bluffs.

Walking into Nick's office at the mansion one morning, Madeline said, "Nick, I have got to go out and have some fun. I am going crazy here. I really am. Being out in this swamp with absolutely nothing fun to do. I can't stand it any more. I want to be happy. I need to do something exciting. Where in Bay St. Louis can I go? What about somewhere in New Orleans? There is nothing to do here."

Nick looked up and could see his sister was on edge. She was probably going crazy, with no men to tell her how beautiful she was and no place to go dressed in very expensive clothes, which was the only way she would allow herself to be seen in public. He had to hand it to her. She always dressed very classy and usually stopped conversation when she walked into almost any room. Most of the men and some women, usually the jealous ones, would just stare at her and follow her every move.

"There are not many places to go around here. Really, Madeline, until we get things running more smoothly here and until you are more familiar with the area, I would prefer you not go into Bay St. Louis or New Orleans. You will be asked too many questions and draw too much attention. If you just have to go out, then you should probably go up in the northern part of the county, to a place like the Red Maple."

"The Red Maple? That definitely sounds like some joint in the country. Look, I promise I will not draw attention to myself if I go into Bay St. Louis or New Orleans. I have to go somewhere at least a little more civilized than a place called the Red Maple."

"Maybe in a few weeks, Madeline, but not now. Not while we are still getting this operation underway. Wherever you go, you know you are going to attract attention. If you go out to a bar in Bay St. Louis, that news will be all over town tomorrow. I would much rather that you get attention at the Red Maple than in Bay St. Louis or New Orleans. It's the safest place up there to go to."

Madeline knew her brother was probably right. After Carlo died, she had a hard time in Detroit from guys she had never even seen who would not leave her alone. She knew that with there being less people here and fewer nice-looking women, she would have even more men chase after her. The more she thought about that, the more she began to love the idea. For the time being, she had to agree with her big brother and try to not attract too much attention, at least for now.

Nick offered to send someone along with her as her driver to be there if she needed them, but Madeline decided to go by herself. She found out that the Red Maple was a true honky-tonk that was definitely out in the country in the middle of nowhere on a dirt path off of a shell road. After literally stopping conversation when she first walked in, approaches were made by almost every man in the place. She eventually decided to focus her attention on a short, paunchy traveling salesman. After dancing with him a few times and deciding he was no threat in any way, she pulled him by his tie out of the bar and led him to the back seat of her car. He could not believe that he had ended up with what was the best-looking woman to ever be seen in the Red Maple. The more he thought about it, he felt it was because he was much more distinguished than all of the other men in there. The real reason she had picked him was because, although she did think he was kind of cute, she also thought he was dumb enough to not ask too many questions or be a threat to her. A brief one night stand was all she needed at the moment and he was the man who got lucky. He did wonder why, after a short time with her in her back seat, she had almost thrown him out of her car and left so quickly.

While Madeline was dealing with her situation in the back seat of a car in south Mississippi, in Chicago, Al Capone was evaluating his illegal liquor business in that area of the country that was being run by one Nick Gable. It was a very profitable business, more so than Capone had ever hoped for. The black market was so lucrative that couriers soon began taking suitcases of cash on the "City of New Orleans" train from New Orleans to Chicago twice a week. An average week was now resulting in over $300,000 in cash being deposited with Capone's operation in Chicago.

Chapter Eighteen

The "revenuers," federal government liquor agents working for the Internal Revenue Service of the Treasury Department, which had been charged with enforcing the prohibition amendment, began trying every way possible to figure out where all of the illegal liquor was coming from. They rode the highways of south Mississippi, Alabama, and Louisiana. They put two small boats on patrol out in the Gulf of Mexico. Neither the highway nor the water patrols could ever catch the shipments. Agents sometimes saw boats they thought might be carrying liquor, but the boats were so fast that they seemed like ghost ships gliding over the water.

One night the head man of the local revenuers, Charles Lovelady, was out on patrol by himself. He decided to wait on the side of a road in rural Hancock County that he had been told was being used by trucks taking booze to New Orleans. He had just recently been assigned to the area and wanted to make his name known as soon as possible, not only to any locals who might be involved in the booze trade, but also to his superiors. If he could make a seizure by himself, he reasoned, he would be on his way to quicker promotions.

As a truck was getting close to where he was waiting, Lovelady jumped out in front of it and yelled at its driver to stop, but instead Lovelady was hit by the truck, which really had no chance of stopping before hitting him because of how late Lovelady had waited to jump. The driver of the truck and his friend riding with him got out and saw that Lovelady was in pain with what was possibly a broken leg. Feeling sorry for him, they offered to take Lovelady to the hospital in Gulfport, which was several miles away. Instead, Lovelady persuaded them to take him to his house in Bay St. Louis.

When they arrived at his house, there were several cars parked out front. The two men helped Lovelady get out of the truck and up to the house, almost carrying him for most of the way. After knocking on the front door, a burly man in a suit opened the door and, upon seeing Lovelady, exclaimed, "Chief, what happened?"

Several men who were inside, also dressed in suits, came up to Lovelady and his helpers to assist them in getting Lovelady into the living room. While Lovelady told the men what had happened as he was being carried to a back bedroom, two of the men in suits eased outside. The two suits began a quick, but thorough, search of the truck in which the three had arrived.

After the two men had found the booze that was being transported in it, they came back to the house and notified their friends. Soon the driver of the truck and his rider found themselves being handcuffed as the men identified themselves as federal revenue agents. The two handcuffed men were then taken down into the basement of Lovelady's house where they were questioned. The two men said they only knew who their contact was for the shipment of the booze and nothing else. They were not going to say who that contact was. For several hours, both of the men were beaten in the basement of the house by agents who took turns putting gloves on their fists when it was their turn. After being made to watch each other go through that, one of the men could no longer take the beatings and told the revenuers that their contact was a man named Simon Montgomery. At last, the revenuers had their first solid lead.

* * *

Nick was now meeting regularly with the sheriff's wife in the apartment above his office. She told him about everything happening in town, and any other gossip she knew. She had overheard her husband talking about shipments of liquor being made all over the county, and that he had stopped a few on rural highways going north into Pearl River County. She also told him about the revenuers and what all her husband had said law enforcement officers were trying to do to catch the booze runners. She did not seem to have any idea that the person responsible for those illegal shipments was in bed with her.

Nick enjoyed his time with Helen and was not seeing anyone else. He had stopped taking Jenny out because he did not want her thinking he was leading her on, but also because he was so happy spending whatever time he could with Helen. He decided that there was really no reason to tell Madeline about Helen and did not mention Helen to her.

While Helen enjoyed being with Nick, she had been playing the organ and piano for church events now for several months. She thoroughly enjoyed her music, and constantly received compliments on how beautifully she played. However, she was beginning to have mixed emotions about the circumstances under which she was meeting Nick. After all, she was a married woman and her husband just happened to be the top law enforcement official in the county for the State of Mississippi. She was beginning to feel uncomfortable about her trysts with Nick.

* * *

After getting the information from the drivers who had been beaten in the basement of Lovelady's house, Lovelady decided that his operation needed more men and an office. He found vacant space in Bay St. Louis not too far from Nick's office building and leased it as the official headquarters for his group, although they continued to use Lovelady's basement for special occasions. They also increased the number of agents at their new office from six to nine. There was simply so much booze being made available from New Orleans to Pensacola and in the rest of Louisiana, Mississippi and Alabama that they just had to try harder to find the source of all of those shipments.

The revenue agents continued to be regularly frustrated by their lack of success at stopping the shipments. It seemed that whoever was making the liquor available knew their every move. Lovelady was recovering from his hurt leg, which had not been broken, and was adamant that his men find out more about what was going on, and especially where this man was named Simon Montgomery. The few bits of information Lovelady had been able to get, which had mostly come from the IRS office in New Orleans, indicated that some place on the Mississippi Gulf Coast was the center for shipments being made over most of the southeastern United States. Lovelady and his men were asking a lot of questions as they looked hard for one Mr. Simon Montgomery. They also began to take a closer look at everything around them. They had even heard that black people may be involved in the shipment of booze.

One afternoon as Lovelady and three of his men were leaving their office to go on patrol, they drove by the local black funeral home on their way out of town. As they approached the funeral home, they saw a brand new hearse pull into the garage area of the establishment.

"Pull over there to that Negro funeral home," Lovelady said to his driver as he pointed toward it.

"How do they make enough money to get a brand new, expensive hearse unless they are somehow involved in making some of these shipments?" he asked out loud as they parked in front of the funeral home. The agents nodded in agreement. They never questioned anything Lovelady said, at least if any of them wanted to get promoted.

Lovelady and his agents got out of the car and walked to the front door. Lovelady opened the door, somewhat cautiously, but still forceful enough so that whoever was inside would know that the law enforcement arm of their national government was making an entrance. Adjusting his eyes to the darkness of the room, Lovelady saw two black men sitting in chairs against the wall to the right. The room had very little furniture in it, although a few chairs were lined up against the walls.

Both of the men started to get up, but Lovelady quickly said, "You two boys just stay put in those chairs. Don't even think about moving. We're federal agents, and we're looking for anyone who might be dealing with illegal whiskey. Now, neither one of you boys would know anything about any of that, would you?" The two black men looked at each other and both began shaking their heads in the negative.

"Nah suh, boss. We don't know nothing bout anythang like dat. We jus bury folk here. Ain't no booze or nothing else going on here cept helpin' take care of dead folks and buryin' dead folks, dats all," the slender one answered as the one next to him shook his head in agreement.

"Who owns this place?" Lovelady asked.

The two black men looked at one another again and then the slender one answered, "I guess that bees me and my brother here. Both of us own it and run it. We got it from our pappy when he passed on."

"What's your name, boy?" Lovelady asked as his men spread out around the room looking the place over.

"Ma name's Leroy Baker. Dis here is ma brotha, Elwin," answered the more slender one.

"Now Leroy, I am going to ask you again. You boys wouldn't be hiding any booze around here anywhere, now would you?" Lovelady asked as he walked over to the two black men.

"Nah suh, boss. Like I said, we just doin' our business here, buryin' folks. Dat is plenty for us to do, just doin' dat."

"Well, suppose you get yourself up and show us around your place here. Your brother can just sit there and not move while we look around," Lovelady said as he began looking around the room.

Leroy got up and, after looking at his brother one more time, said, "Dis here is our lil gathern' room, dis bein' where all da folk first come and gets together when they have a loved one pass on. They all come here and they can cry and hug and give each other all dat kissin' and stuff so the dearly departed knows ther kinfolks done cared bout em."

"All right, I get the idea. You don't have to get into all of that. What else do you have here? How many hearses do you have in that garage of yours?"

"We gots three hearses, two of them we has we gots lots of years out of. We bought a new one just a few weeks ago cause one of the old ones be trying to stop runnin. Pretty soon now, we gonna be out tryin to go to da cemetery, and one of dem olda ones jus gonna quit. Then we be in a fix, I mean, we just can't have that hapnin. Folk be wantn to bury their loved one, and there they be, stuck on the side of the road in a hearse that quit," Leroy answered keeping his eyes mostly on the floor as he talked.

"Yea, I saw that new one you have, just saw it coming in off the street. That is a mighty fine looking hearse. Probably cost you and Elwin there a lot of money. Business must be pretty good for you boys, or else you are doing something you shouldn't be doing," Lovelady said as he looked at Leroy to see what type of reaction he was going to get. Lovelady had not dealt with many blacks in his career, but the ones he had dealt with could not fool him with any lying. No, sir. He knew that he could catch most anybody every time, if they ever tried.

"Naw suh, boss. We don't do nuthin like dat round here. We bees

151

known in the Negro community here for takin good care of Negro dead folk. Making sure they be all dressed and ready, you know, ready for da services and meetn their maker and all that needs to take place for a proper buryin. We just try to make sure we be servin the Negro folk round here and dats all we tries to do," Leroy said, finally looking up at Lovelady to see how he was reacting to all that was just said.

"What other rooms do you have here where you might could hide something if you wanted to?" Lovelady answered, making sure this black person was not going to waste the rest of his day explaining how all of the grieving went.

"Well, suh, we have the back room," Leroy said as he walked toward a door at the back of the room.

"Ah! The back room! Suppose you show us the back room," Lovelady said, looking and smiling at each one of his agents. They all began to show immediate interest in going toward that doorway. Leroy opened the door, and Lovelady and his agents all quickly moved into that dimly lit room. As their eyes adjusted to that darker room, they noticed three coffins sitting in the center. Open coffins. As Lovelady and his men slowly approached the coffins, they noticed that there was the body of a black person in each one, two black men and a black woman, of varying ages, but all nicely dressed and looking quite dignified for their burials, even if Lovelady had to admit it.

After quickly viewing the bodies, Lovelady and his agents began looking around the dark paneled walls of the room. Seeing a door at the back of that room, Lovelady asked, "Where does this door lead to?"

Leroy walked slowly over to the back door and said, "Dat leads out to the garage we talked bout, where our hearses be kept til dey be used for the transportin of the dearly departed to their final resting place."

Leroy opened the door and the bright glare of the outside sunlight made all of the men move quickly to shield their eyes as they walked through the door into an outside garage. There were the three hearses. A much younger black man was in the garage using an old cloth to wipe off the dust that had settled on the newest hearse from its last trip. The few containers sitting along the wall were quickly identified by the agents as holding those fluids necessary for a funeral home business.

Lovelady walked over to Leroy and, getting about a half a foot from his face, said to him, "One last time, how come it is you are so successful that you are able to buy a brand new, expensive hearse for your little business here?"

Leroy leaned backwards a little bit, and said, "Boss, black folk gots to die also. Dey sure do, jus like white folks. And thers lots of black folks in these here parts, boss. Lots of black folks. Somebody gots to bury'em. Somebody gots to do dat and dats what we does. We bury black folks. Our pappy did it, and now we does it. If you wants to come by for one of our services here, jus come on by. We does a fine job here, we really does. We bees really concerned bout the grieving and all."

Lovelady continued to look at Leroy, then shifted his look to his men who had checked everything around the garage walls.

"All right men. Let's go. We're through here," Lovelady said as he turned to walk back through the doorway, followed by his men. Leroy followed them, closing the door to the garage and then followed them past the three bodies and into the receiving room, closing that door behind him also. His brother was still seated in the same chair Lovelady had told him to stay seated in.

"You can tell your brother he can move now. You had better be showing me everything, Leroy, because if I find out you have been lying to me I am going to come back here and tear you apart. Do you understand me?" Lovelady demanded.

"Yes suh, boss. I understand. I really does. We jus bees burying black folks here, dat all," Leroy said as Lovelady and the agents headed to the front door. Leroy stood there as he watched the agents walk out the door and on toward their car. He slowly shut the door and walked over to the only window in the room, which was covered by a heavy black curtain. His brother, who had finally gotten out of his chair, walked over to the window with him. They both looked out the window after Leroy had pulled the curtain back just far enough so they could both see Lovelady's car doors being closed. They watched until the car had pulled out of sight.

After looking out of the window for a few more minutes, Leroy looked at Elwin as Elwin looked back at him. Just next to the window was a light switch which Leroy pushed up. They then both walked into the back room where the three bodies were laid out. Leroy stood in the doorway while Elwin walked over to one of the wood paneled walls, moved a small latch near a beam in the wall and began to slide the wall panel. The panel moved, hardly making a sound, over to the side until it covered another section of the same wall. Behind that panel was what now became a very bright room with three black men in it, who immediately began to move about once the panel had completed its short journey. The light in the room easily showed stack upon stack of barrels of whiskey.

"I thought they would never leave!" one of the men in the back room said.

"Me too," answered Leroy. "Now let's get this stuff loaded up. We be running behind schedule. They won't like it if we be running too far behind."

With that, the black men went into action like a well-drilled military team. Soon the new hearse was loaded up and its driver sent out to make another delivery.

Chapter Nineteen

Madeline went back out to the Red Maple late one night. This particular night, a local ruffian named Terry Lampton was there. Watching Madeline as she walked in and sat at the corner of the bar, Terry mumbled under his breath, "Unhhhh unhhhh uhhhhh." He decided right then that he wanted her to be with him, and he wasn't going to take "no" for an answer. Walking over to where Madeline was now sitting, Terry leaned over her shoulder and said, with a leering grin on his face, "Tonight is yor lucky night, honey. My name's Terry and I'm gonna take care of all your needs, and maybe a few you didn't even know you have."

Glancing over her shoulder, Madeline immediately thought this one might be a problem. She knew, from past experiences, that she had better quickly make it clear that she didn't think as much of him as he thought of himself. Maybe with his male ego crushed, he would go away and leave her alone. They usually did once she left no doubt that they were not what she was looking for. Before she had made her choice the last time she had been out there, she had broken a few hearts and several egos.

"I don't know who you think I am, but I am definitely not your 'honey.'
With your attitude, you certainly are not my type. You're too crude."

"Baby doll! Now watch yor mouth! This is Terry here and, regardless
of what you say, I'm gonna get every inch of you I can tonight," he said
while trying to nibble on her right ear. Madeline turned and pushed
Terry away with her right arm.

"Honey! What are you doing? You're gonna make Terry mad, Miss
High and Mighty! You're a good lookin' woman, but that don't give you
no right to just push me away. Now you just get your fine self off of that
stool and come on with me before I have to drag you out of here." The
last part of the sentence was said with a sneer.

Looking back at him, she said, "Maybe you didn't hear me. I said, you
are not my type. Now leave me alone."

The bar got quiet. Everybody in there, all of the men and the few
women, were watching to see what was going to happen next.

Terry quickly looked around the room and then reached with his
right hand, grabbing Madeline by the upper portion of her right arm.

"Nobody talks to me like that, honey! Nobody!" he all but yelled into
her face.

Madeline twisted her arm out of his grip and slid off of the barstool.
As she started walking toward the door she had just come in, Terry
walked right next to her, saying, "Where are you goin', sugar? You're
not leaving Terry yet. You think you're just gonna get up and leave?
You had better think about that again, honey. You ain't going nowhere
tonight without Terry being with you."

Madeline walked through the door and down the steps with Terry
moving along with her. She reached the bottom of the few stairs and
began walking toward her car. Then Terry pushed her, almost making
her fall.

"Where you goin', sugar? You think you gonna just leave Terry?
Leave him here all by himself?" he said as he walked a step behind her.
"Nawwww, honey. You're not leaving here without Terry getting that
fine ass of yours in the back seat of that car."

As they reached her car, he grabbed her and turned her around to
face him.

"Now, honey, either you are gonna get in that back seat there for me,
or I am just gonna have to make you do it. What's it gonna be?"

After looking down at his hands holding each of her arms, she said,

"Alright. You might just be the excitement I've been looking for. So big and so strong. Let me loose and I'll open the door and get in the back seat. Then we can have some fun."

"Yea, baby. Now you're talking," Terry said as he smiled and dropped his hands, letting her go. He looked around to see if anybody could hear what had been said or who might be watching. Madeline held her purse close to her as she turned and opened the car door, then bent over to get into the back seat. The ruffian stood behind her, taking another quick look around before turning his attention back to his prize.

A couple of guys had seen what had happened in the bar and followed the two outside at a distance to see what was going to take place next. What they saw was an immediate change in circumstances. Madeline pulled a gun out of her purse, turned around, and pressed the cold barrel of the pistol up under Terry's chin as he turned around and bent down to follow Madeline into the back seat. His smile immediately left his face. She pressed the gun under his chin and slowly began backing him up and then away from the car. As she moved him back, she said in a cold, calm voice, "You bastard. Now just what did you say you were going to do to me?"

His eyes were now almost as wide as silver dollars. Terry stuttered, hardly moving his jaw, saying, "Nuth... Nuth... Nuthin'. Nuthin' at all. Don't do nuthin' hasty now, okay?" Terry began trying to figure some way out of the jam he definitely was now in.

"Put your hands behind your back," she said coolly with the gun still firmly under his chin. Terry put his hands where the lady said put them.

"Now start stepping back real slowly, one step at a time," she said in an even voice. Terry stepped back one step and then another, with her stepping with him.

Then she quickly pulled the gun from under his chin and stepped back more than an arm's length away from him, now pointing her gun at his chest.

"Get on your knees," she said.

"Look lady, who do you think ... ." He never finished. Madeline lowered the pistol and pointed it between his legs.

BAM!

A cloud of dust swirled up from where the bullet had hit the ground between his legs. He quickly looked down to make sure the bullet had not struck any important body parts and just as quickly jerked his head up, his eyes now wide open, to see that the gun was again pointed at his chest.

"Now!" she said in a louder voice.

To Terry, her gun looked like a cannon pointing at him. He knew she was mad, and he could also see that, even though she was mad, her hand was not shaking at all. That was not a good sign for him, he thought. That meant she was not scared of him one little bit and she had just shown that she knew exactly how to use that gun she was holding. Being the smart man he believed he was, he knew he had better do exactly what the lady with the cannon pointed at him wanted him to do. He slowly went down on first one knee and then the other knee, a hard thing to do with his hands behind his back, but he did it.

"Please, just don't shoot me. I was just . . ."

"Shut up, asshole! And don't even think about moving," she said, still pointing the cannon at his chest. Terry shut up.

The loud sound of the gun being fired resulted in patrons of the bar now coming out of the front door of the establishment to see what had happened.

While still looking at him with her right hand steadily holding the gun pointed at him, she backed away from him and moved slowly toward her car. When she could feel the already opened car door next to her, she moved around it and got in, her gun still pointing at him. She started her car and then drove away.

The crowd that had gathered howled as Terry got up off of his knees. The ruffian yelled, "Bitch! I'll get you!" He shook his fists at her car as it sped away down the dirt road and into the darkness of the night. He would have to make sure he got even with her.

Madeline told Nick about her run-in at the Red Maple, which disturbed him when he heard what had happened. It didn't surprise him that Madeline had attracted attention. What did surprise him was the way in which it all had happened. He was not pleased with what had taken place between the ruffian and his sister.

A few nights later, Nick had other things on his mind. Not too many weeks before, on a night in late June, Nick noticed a muffled, thumping noise coming from out in the swamp. The next time he saw his attorney friend, Dudley Marquette, Nick asked him what the noise might have been. Marquette told Nick that he had probably heard the sounds on

June 24th, which is known as St. John's Eve. Marquette emphasized that St. John's Eve was a special night for those involved with voodoo. He said that Nick should be especially careful if he ever heard those sounds again. After all, Marquette said, there were a lot of voodoo symbols and things all over the swamp around Nick's compound.

Around eleven o'clock this night, Nick found himself standing next to the pool on the bluff overlooking the swamp. It was a clear night and the moon was out, which enabled Nick to see a far distance out into the swamp. He had thought he had heard a distant noise. Being unable to sleep, he had gotten dressed to go see if indeed there was a noise and, if so, was it like the noise that he had heard before. As he stood there overlooking the bayou, he heard what was definitely a muffled, consistent thumping noise that sounded somewhat like drums, just like he had heard before. The noise seemed to be coming from an area of the swamp where there appeared to be some sort of faint glow. Listening for a few minutes, Nick decided he might as well go see what was causing the noise. If it was connected in some way to voodoo activity, he thought that this may as well be the time to see what all of the discussion on that subject was about since the noise may be a recurring event.

Not necessarily wanting to make this trip into the swamp by himself, Nick walked back to the bunkhouse where his workers were staying and quietly eased in, making his way over to Tiny's bunk. He gently tugged on the big man's arm, waking him up. When Tiny looked like he might be fully awake and able to understand what Nick was going to say to him, Nick whispered, "Get your work clothes on and meet me outside. We're going out into the swamp." With that, Nick turned and eased his way out of the bunkhouse.

Several minutes later, Tiny emerged from the bunkhouse, dressed as Nick had instructed. He saw Nick standing there in his work clothes, holding a pistol. He also noticed that Nick was wearing a holster with a pistol in it, something very unusual for Nick. Tiny knew Nick generally liked to keep his weaponry out of sight. To Tiny, this was not a good sign.

"Put this under your belt," Nick said, giving him the pistol he was holding. "I don't think you are going to need it but just in case you do, you'll have it," Nick said, watching Tiny as he put it snug under his belt. Then Nick said, "Let's go" and began walking toward the pool.

Tiny followed, wondering what this was all about. Nick went down the steps leading to the cement docks below the pool with Tiny close behind him. At the bottom, Nick climbed into a small pirogue that was used sometimes by the men to go fishing. Nick had learned, after seeing Claude in his pirogue, that using pirogues for fishing was good since many of the best fishing areas in the bayous were usually narrow and shallow. Nick got in the front and then Tiny maneuvered his massive frame into the confines of the back portion of the little boat. Tiny had only been in a pirogue a few times, and Nick was concerned that Tiny may be too big for this one, but Tiny settled into his position in the boat without too much trouble.

Turning over his shoulder to talk to Tiny, Nick whispered, "We're going over to where those drum sounds are coming from to find out what's going on. Let's do it very quietly."

"Okay, boss. Sure hope you know whatcha doin'."

Both men grabbed an oar, which were always left in the various vessels at the docks so that people would have them when they wanted to use the boats. They both began paddling in the general direction of the swamp where the noise was coming from and where Nick had seen the faint glow. Nick soon learned one of the unique characteristics of the swamp. On windless nights, like this one, sound traveled over the miles of rather flat marshland much farther than normal. Nick expected to soon be near where the sound was coming from, but was he ever surprised. The more they paddled, the more it seemed that the sound stayed the same distance away.

Another thing that interfered with getting closer to the noise was the fact that had made the Bluffs attractive to Nick in the first place. It was difficult to get to. There were so many junctions of bayous and so many tributaries, in addition to the fact that it was night. They had both gotten tired of the constant paddling and had to take momentary breaks from time to time in that exercise. Granted, they were grateful the moon was full, but it was a long time, close to an hour, before Nick felt that the bayou tributary they were on was actually leading to the noise. In fact, Nick had almost been ready to give up and try to find his way back when he saw a bayou he felt might lead closer to the sound.

After they had gotten onto that bayou, the twists and turns gradually began to change into a narrower passageway. Some of the twists and turns had small sandbars, but most did not. Then, almost immediately, they entered a portion of the bayou that was so covered with vegetation that it became like a tunnel. Poles in the water with voodoo symbols attached began appearing on both sides of the narrow waterway. Nick looked over his shoulder when the first of those poles had appeared and noticed that Tiny's eyes seemed to be getting a bit wider. The foliage soon became so thick that the bright moon and star-filled sky were unable to be easily seen, if at all. The sounds were now becoming louder so Nick felt that they were on the right pathway. Paddling what Nick thought was probably another twenty minutes after the last turn had been made, the sounds gradually became louder. It was now clear to Nick that most of the sound was being made by drums, mixed in with other noises, the source of which Nick was unable to guess thus far.

Finally, a brighter light appeared in the distance, and the two men slowed their already slower pace of paddling. They eased around a bend, and Nick could see in the distance that there was a gathering of people on a small clearing. He motioned for Tiny to stop the boat, and then motioned for him to guide the boat over toward some bushes along the side of the narrow channel. Finally, positioning their little vessel where Nick wanted it, they were able to see some of what was causing all the noise as disclosed by several bonfires and torches, which were located around the clearing still some sixty yards or so down the bayou from them.

A group of about ten people, both black and white men and women, and all of them with very few clothes on, were frantically dancing to the constant and persistent beating of what appeared to be tom-toms. They were being watched by a larger group of, Nick guessed, about thirty people. The other noises, the ones that Nick had not been able to figure out the cause of, were coming from what seemed to be numerous small bells located on bindings attached around each dancers' ankles, above their knees, on their wrists, and above their elbows. The constant, quick movements of the dancers were causing the bells to ring in a hypnotic rhythm. All of the dancers and the observers were chanting things that Nick could not understand. He noticed piles of things on the ground. After studying them for a moment, he determined what they were. They were the bodies of dead chickens. Each one, as far as Nick could tell, was without a head attached to it!

Then, out of the darkness behind the dancers, appeared an extremely tall and thin, nude black man with two, almost nude, creole women dancing around and with him. Nick guessed the man was over seven feet tall, but probably weighed only about one hundred and sixty pounds or so. Nick felt the boat shift. Quickly glancing over his shoulder, he could see Tiny was leaning over to his right to look past Nick and see what was going on. When the tall black man had appeared, Tiny had apparently been surprised to the extent that he had shifted over in the boat, which quickly registered the big man's move. Nick grabbed the sides of the boat where he was sitting in an effort to stabilize their transportation. Again looking back, he could see Tiny's eyes fixated on the spectacle taking place in front of them.

As Nick also turned back to look at the show, the beat of the drums grew louder, and the movement of the dancers somehow, impossible though it seemed, got faster. Then, out of the darkness behind the dancers stepped a totally nude woman. That sight quickly got Nick's attention, but his senses were just as quickly overloaded as Nick's eyes told his brain who the woman was. It was Carlotta! Then just as quickly, with all of the sounds now at a fever pitch, his eyes focused on what was around her neck as she constantly turned around and around while surrounded by all of the dancers. It was a long, gigantic, white python! A snake that looked to be almost as big as she was!

Nick felt the boat move. He jerked his head around to see Tiny's whole body tilting over to Nick's right as Tiny stared, eyes as wide open as they could be, at the nude Carlotta with that huge snake. At that point, the laws of gravity took over as Tiny's weight, leaning so far over to watch what was happening and being shocked so much as to not be able to react fast enough, overturned the boat! The splash of them hitting the water sounded to Nick as loud as if a fireworks display had gone off. They both were now in the water, grabbing to hold on to their upside down pirogue.

Nick quickly checked on Tiny and saw in the reflections of light caused by the fires that, at least for now, Tiny had some of his wits about him as he struggled to get a good grip on the side of the overturned vessel. Nick had already accomplished that effort, "thank goodness," he thought. Then he turned his head to look back at the spectacle.

Carlotta had stopped turning, and her head was quickly moving from right to left, left to right, her eyes continually moving from side to side as quickly as was her head. Nick noticed that her eye and head movement was not now in rhythm with the continuing drum beat. She seemed to sense there had been a noise that was not part of the ceremony, and she was searching it out. Nick turned back around and waved to get Tiny's attention. Tiny finally noticed that Nick was motioning for him to move the overturned boat back towards where they had come from. Also motioning Tiny to be quiet, Nick began to slowly kick the water with his legs to move the overturned boat back out of the bayou. After a few moments, Tiny began to do the same thing. Nick turned again to see Carlotta, with the huge snake still around her neck, staring in a manner that seemed to indicate that she was now looking directly at Nick! He quickly turned his face back towards his companion, thinking that maybe, if she could indeed see him, she might not recognize him since his head would be turned.

It was only then that another thought crossed his mind: alligators! He also then had another bad thought: snakes! He quickly checked his holster and his gun was still there, useless though it now probably was. He could only guess whether Tiny still had his gun, and Nick's guess was that he didn't. There was nothing Nick could do about being in the water, at least not for the moment. The more he thought about it, he hoped that all of the snakes and alligators had moved away from the area when the noise started. That was the best he could hope for at this point.

Gradually, the two swimmers were able to move their boat back up the bayou to the nearest sand bar. There, they were able to stand up, turn the boat over and get back in it. Nick still had his paddle, but Tiny's paddle had long since disappeared. However, Nick noticed that Tiny still had his gun under his belt.

It took them over three hours to find their way home. They made numerous wrong turns. In some areas, the mosquitoes ate them alive. Swarms of mosquitoes would come over them and cover them from head to toe. A few times the two men got into the water near a sand bar just to get away from the swarms, at least for a few moments. He hadn't noticed the mosquitoes as much while they were on their way out into the swamp. It was either due to his excitement over what they might find or maybe the noise affected them. They may have been there, but not this bad. All Nick knew now was that they were about to carry Tiny and him away if they didn't find their way back soon.

Nick began to worry that they might have to wait until sunlight to find their way back, if they could do so even then. While paddling, thoughts came back to Nick about Carlotta, about that enormous snake, about the ritual dancing, chanting and drums, and about that seven foot tall, skinny black man. From time to time, he looked around to see if Tiny was alright. The first few times he checked, he thought Tiny was in some sort of shock. He was staring straight ahead, as if Nick wasn't even there. Nick thought Tiny was probably thinking, like Nick had been, about what all he had just seen. At least Nick hoped so. He didn't need Tiny so totally helpless that he might have to go into the water to get him out if Tiny somehow fell overboard or tilted the boat over again.

When they finally pulled up to the docks at the Bluffs, Nick was barely able to get himself out of the boat. Tiny could hardly move. With Nick's help, Tiny was finally able to get out of the boat. Nick helped him up the stairs and then to his bunkhouse. As Nick made his way over to the mansion, he had only one thought. He surely was glad they had made it out of there!

Chapter Twenty

Carlotta had been setting up voodoo symbols all around the Bluffs. She usually was seen with Claude or sometimes with a few of the swamp people. When Carlotta and Claude came to the Bluffs area two days after Nick had seen her with the python, Nick was worried. What if Carlotta had seen them? What if Claude or someone had found the paddle Tiny had lost out there in that bayou that night? However, neither Claude nor Carlotta showed any indication that they knew Nick and Tiny had been out there that night.

Nick was relieved. He wanted them to keep putting up more voodoo symbols in the swamp. Nick had to bite his tongue several times to keep from asking about that big snake. Every time he looked at Carlotta, he could not get the image out of his mind of her standing there nude surrounded by all of those seemingly hypnotized dancers and observers, with that monstrous snake around her neck. He also thought about that seven foot tall, skinny black man. It made him wonder what else was going on out there in the swamp he didn't know about. He had talked with Tiny the day after their trip to find out how he was handling what had happened and what he had seen, and Tiny was still shaken up. He seemed to be in some sort of shock and could not easily talk to Nick about what they had witnessed. A few days later though, Tiny finally appeared to be returning to some sense of normalcy. Nick did wonder if some effect from the events of that evening might manifest itself in Tiny at a later time.

Four days after Nick and Tiny's experience in the bayou, Helen was an early afternoon visitor to Nick's office bedroom in Bay St. Louis. She immediately noticed the mosquito bites all over Nick's body.

"Honey! What happened to you?" she asked as she examined the bites.

"I went out in the swamp to check something out the other night, and the mosquitoes were not too friendly," Nick answered with the hint of a smile.

"Aw, did some of my little southern mosquitoes get after my Yankee sweetheart?" she asked with her wonderful smile in full display as she teased him.

He had to chuckle to himself. He remembered seeing a sign in the window of a small shop downtown just a few days earlier that showed a caricature of a southern soldier holding a sword, and under the picture was the statement, "Forget hell!" He laughed and then said, "Didn't my side win that war? Your mosquitoes should be more respectful of the winners."

With a wide grin, she answered in an exaggerated southern accent, "Why sugar, you know I heard just the other day that the Yankees had won! Maybe my little mosquitoes still haven't gotten the message yet about General Lee's surrender."

Nick had to laugh again. "Forget about General Lee's surrender. Let's talk about yours," he said as he grabbed her and pushed her back onto his bed.

After being laid back on his bed, Helen said in her mocking southern accent, "Why, I do believe, sir, I am being taken advantage of by a Yankee!" That continued to be the situation for a little over the next hour in spite of the many mosquito bites.

* * *

Madeline sometimes rode her horses in some of the areas where the voodoo symbols had been placed, but she was not comfortable with her brother's dealings with Claude and Carlotta, especially after Nick had told her about what he and Tiny had seen out in the bayou that night. She did not have good feelings about the voodoo markings and hated snakes, but had been assured by Nick that, in spite of what they had seen that night, the markings would be helpful in keeping people away who might be fishing on the bayou or might have wandered into the area.

Madeline also began to see Nick talking with Carlotta alone several times and spoke with him about his being seen with her. Nick assured Madeline that everything was alright and to not worry. He had to talk with Carlotta in order to make sure the symbols were put in what he thought were the right places. Madeline still wondered if Carlotta was beginning to gain some sort of influence over her brother as a result of that trip into the bayou that night. She would have to keep an eye on that.

One day when she went down for her ride, she saw the very handsome young man who now always seemed to be waiting for her. When she walked into the barn dressed in her normal riding clothes, there stood Joey by himself. For the first time no one else was with him. Joey had managed to convince the other three men to stay away that day even though Tiny had told him, "You had better stay away from that woman, white boy. You gonna get yourself in trouble."

Joey had assured Tiny that he could take care of himself and that all he wanted was to spend a few minutes alone with that beautiful woman. Tiny was hesitant, but finally agreed. "This one time," he had said.

"Good morning," Joey said.

"Good morning," she replied, not remembering the man's name although she had noticed his good looks.

"Where is everybody?" she asked. Joey handed her the reins.

"I convinced them to go do something else this morning," Joey said.

"Oh, really? Why did you do that?" she asked looking at the young man.

"Because I wanted some time alone with you," Joey said.

Madeline stopped and looked at him. She studied him intently for a few seconds, looking at his face, his hair, those blue eyes, his build, those muscles, and his smile.

"What's your name again? I know you've probably told me, but what is it?"

"Joey Demarco," he said.

"Joey? Okay. Well, Joey," Madeline said as she turned toward the house.

"See that lattice work on the side of the main house there?" she asked as she looked at it.

"Yes," Joey said.

Madeline turned to face Joey and said, "I bet a man as strong as you are could climb up that lattice work and onto the balcony without any trouble, couldn't he."

"Yes. I think I could make that climb without any trouble," Joey said.

"If you were to make that climb to the balcony just after midnight tonight, Joey, you will find the door right there on that side of the balcony unlocked," Madeline said still looking at Joey.

"And, Joey, do you know what is on the other side of that door?" Her voice was low and sultry.

Joey could barely think.

"My bedroom," she whispered.

Joey did not immediately comprehend the meaning of what she had just said.

Madeline stepped away from him and mounted her horse. She looked down at him, smiled and rode off.

Joey was surprised. With all of his experiences with women, he now realized those experiences had been mostly with girls. This Madeline was a woman.

For the next hour Joey continually thought and thought about what had happened. Had he not heard what he had heard? What did it mean? Was there another possible meaning to what she had told him? The more he thought about it, the more he realized the woman had made him an offer. This was one offer that Joey Demarco would definitely take up. It really was an offer, wasn't it? Sure it was. Oh yes. Joey had been around enough to know that it was an offer. He could not believe his good fortune. Unbelievable! His smile grew bigger and bigger the more he thought about it all. He knew where he was going that night. Most definitely! Even if he was wrong, he would not in any way pass up the chance to find out if he was right.

About an hour later Madeline came riding in. The other men, Tiny included, had returned.

"How was your ride today, Miss Madeline?" Tiny asked as he grabbed the reins of the horse.

"Just fine, Tiny," she answered as she dismounted. Then glancing toward Joey, she said, "I enjoy my rides." With that she walked toward the mansion. The men watched her body in motion for most of the way. But then she knew that. She could sense it. Men always watched her that way. These were no different.

"She enjoys her rides!" Joey laughed to himself. Oh, this woman was something! For her to say that, in front of all of those guys! There was going to be one Joey Demarco climbing up the lattice work that night!

About fifteen minutes before midnight, Joey began to get dressed. He and the other guys living in the bunk house had played poker, as they almost always did, until about ten-thirty, and then all had gone to bed. As Joey stood up to leave, a whisper came out of the dark.

"Where do you think you're goin', white boy?" It was the unmistakable voice of Tiny.

"I've got something I have got to take care of up at the big house," Joey whispered back, smiling.

"Don't you go messin' with dat woman, white boy. You gonna get yourself in trouble. She ain't gonna be nuthin but trouble for you," Tiny whispered back.

"I'll be back in a little while. Don't wait up for me," Joey said as he slipped out of the bunk house.

Joey eased outside and used the cover of the trees to get closer to the main house. There he edged around the side of the house. He looked around to make sure there was no one watching. It was a dark night with only a small amount of light coming from the guest house across the way.

After looking around one more time to make sure no one was watching, Joey checked the lattice work to see how steady it was. Pulling on it did not move it at all so he began to climb the lattice work as if it were a ladder. He was surprised at how sturdy it was. He wondered if Madeline had told other men to do the same thing. This was almost too easy. But he was committed now. There was no turning back.

When he got to the top, he quickly swung over onto the balcony. He eased toward the door. Putting his hand ever so quietly on the door knob, he eased the door open and entered the room. He was tingling all over. Every sensor in his body was alive. Across the room was a vision he would never, ever forget. Madeline was lying on the bed in the sexiest white, sheer nightgown he had seen. By the candlelight she was more beautiful than ever.

Joey walked over to her bed. She pulled him down and, for the next hour and a half, she devoured him. It was the first time Joey was with a woman who kept control of the sex act. After Joey left, Madeline lay there and thought about how much she missed her husband, Carlo. And she cried.

The next three days Madeline did not ride, which was unusual. Joey confidently felt that it was because he had had so much stamina. On the fourth day after their rendezvous, Madeline sent word to get one of the horses ready for her to ride at ten that morning. A few minutes before that time, she came walking down in her riding outfit. Joey had made the same arrangement with the other guys that they would be busy when she came down. When she walked in and saw that only Joey was there, she walked immediately over to the horse. Joey walked over and put his hand on her arm. Madeline looked down at his hand and then up at him and said, "Don't touch me."

"That's not what you were saying the other night," Joey answered, a little surprised.

"The other night happened because I wanted it to. I made a mistake. It won't happen again," Madeline said as she pulled her arm away.

"A mistake? You seemed to like it. You seemed to like it a lot, Madeline!"

"Leave me alone, Joey!" she said, moving away from him as she tried to hold on to the reins of the skittish horse.

"How can I do that? I want you! I want to see you again! What happened between us the other night was the most wonderful thing that has ever happened to me!" Joey could not believe this was the same woman that he had spent time with three nights earlier.

"It was a mistake. Forget it ever happened," Madeline said as she stood there trying to steady her horse.

"Forget it ever happened?" Joey all but yelled out. "What do you mean, forget it ever happened?

"That is exactly what I said. Forget it ever happened, Joey. Just forget it," Madeline said in a cold, aloof voice.

"Forget it? How can I forget it?"

"You will have to, Joey! Now go away! I have to go," she said as she tried to get more reins in her hands.

Joey grabbed her around her neck with both hands and pushed her up against a stack of hay. Holding her against the hay, he said, "Go away? You don't just tell Joey Demarco to 'go away,' Madeline. Who do you think you are? Some queen or something?" Joey's infamous temper had now taken control of him.

Madeline looked back at him with a look that Joey had never seen before. It wasn't fear. He didn't know what it was.

"I am coming to see you tonight, you hear me? Tonight! You are not just going to throw me away like some old shoe. Joey Demarco does not get thrown away like that."

"Take your hands off of me, Joey," Madeline said firmly.

"Shut up! Just shut up until I am through!" he yelled.

"You are going to be there tonight! For me! Waiting for me and, if you aren't, I am going to tell everybody around here about us. I will tell your brother about you, and what we did. I will tell everybody out here about you, and what we did. Do you hear me?"

Feeling his hands tighten around her throat, Madeline said, "Okay, Joey, okay." Looking at him, she said in a low, even voice, "I see I underestimated you."

"You bet you have, Madeline," Joey said.

Joey gradually pulled his hands away, and Madeline gently rubbed her throat. She then mounted her horse as Joey said, "Midnight tonight. Be there waiting!" Madeline turned her horse until she was able to look at Joey.

"I'll be there," Madeline said in a firm voice, and then she prompted her steed to gallop off.

Watching her disappear into the woods on her horse, Joey realized he felt good. Who did she think she was? She wasn't different from any of the many women he had been with, except she was a much better sexual partner. Much better.

That night, Joey slipped out of the bunk house a little after eleven forty-five and made his way over to the main house. Again, no lights were on, just candlelight coming from Madeline's room. He climbed the lattice work as before and eased himself onto the balcony. He was cautious and took time to peer into the bedroom through the glass door. By the candlelight from the room, he could vaguely see Madeline lying on her bed waiting for him in her nightgown, just as she had before. He smiled to himself. Ol' Joey knew how to handle his women. He surely did. He opened the door and stepped into Madeline's bedroom, shutting the door behind him.

Suddenly, he felt something pulled around his throat and tightened. He had enough fighting experience to know what it was. It was a garrote. Joey reached for the thin rope choking him, but different men grabbed each one of his arms. Out of the shadows of the corner of the room walked Nick!

"I am glad you told me about Joey bothering you, Madeline. He won't be doing that any more. Get him out of here, boys," Nick said as he walked over to Madeline. Joey barely managed to catch a glimpse of Madeline's face as he was being pulled out of her bedroom. She looked at him with the hint of a smile on her face. Her look said it all without her saying a word. Her look said, "Gotcha."

Once out of the house, as he was being taken down to the barn, Tiny said, "I told you to stay away from her! I told you!"

After a few more feet, Tiny said, "I told you not to mess with dat woman. I told you, but nah, you don't listen. You be one dumb, white boy."

When they got to the barn, Joey kept waiting for them to turn him loose, but instead, one of the other men slugged him, right in the face. Joey fell to the floor of the barn with the garrote still around his neck and Tiny still holding its wooden handles.

"Mr. Nick told us to try to break as many bones in your body as we could. He didn't like what Miss Madeline told him about you," Tiny said.

For nearly all of the next hour, the three men took turns hitting Joey Demarco with an axe handle everywhere possible. After they finished with him, Joey was still alive, but no other women would ever want to look at him again. Most of the bones in his face had been broken, as were most of the other bones in his body.

At about two-thirty that morning, Joey was taken down to the cement docks and put into a boat. He was still alive, but unable to move much. He was conscious just enough to notice that Tiny and the other two men in the boat had each brought a machete with them. The three men took Joey out into the Gulf of Mexico where he was cut up and fed to the sharks, piece by piece.

Chapter Twenty-one

After what had happened with the ruffian at the Red Maple and then with Joey, Nick decided that it was time to get Madeline involved with people in New Orleans. Nick thought that one way she could meet people was for him to join the New Orleans Country Club, which he did.

A few weeks after joining, Nick took Madeline to a big "End of Summer" ball held at the club. All of New Orleans society was returning to the area after spending the summer away from the hot and humid climate of the city. Madeline was excited about going to the event. She was so happy that Nick finally understood how she felt living out in the middle of a swamp with no real friends. Before the party, she had gone shopping at all of the major stores on Canal Street in New Orleans. She wanted to make sure everyone noticed her. She wanted to show these southerners what a real woman looked like.

She found the dress she wanted at Keenan's. It was still available because of its high price, ten thousand dollars; and, both because it looked so good on her and because it was so expensive, she asked Nick if he would buy it for her and he did. The white evening gown was extremely low-cut, floor length and perfectly fit her figure. Real pearls were strategically placed all over the gown from the top to the bottom. A pearl necklace and pearl drop earrings added the finishing touches to her beautiful presentation. Her matching high heels gave her a height that bespoke of elegance. Her hair had been done by one of the finest hair stylists in New Orleans. It was up in a French twist with pearls scattered throughout it. Her posture and the air about her gave her an appearance of total confidence. She wanted to make sure that when she walked into a room, everyone knew she was there.

After they arrived at the party, it wasn't too long before there was a line of people, mostly men, waiting to make her acquaintance. Some of the men had a difficult time keeping their eyes on her face. Many of the women had thinly veiled sneers on their faces.

Not too long after arriving, Nick and Madeline ran into the two couples that she had traveled with to Italy and who had come over for their party at the Bluffs, Judge Marvin Tullos and his wife, Delores, and Judge Jonathan Parker and his wife, Betsy.

"Nick, Madeline, what a nice surprise! It is so good to see you here," Judge Tullos said as he shook Nick's hand and his wife gave Madeline a hug.

"Hello, hello. It's good to see you two here," Judge Parker said as he took his turn shaking Nick's hand while Betsy followed Delores giving Madeline a hug.

Nick said, "It was such a pleasure having all of you out at the Bluffs for our party. Thanks so much for coming out."

"Thanks for the invitation. We enjoyed seeing that magnificent house of yours. The ladies certainly enjoyed that, and Judge Parker and I enjoyed that and also the races," Judge Tullos said as the other three joined in with their agreements.

At that moment a tall, distinguished gentleman and his lovely wife joined the group. The man obviously knew both men well as he greeted them by calling them by their first names.

"Hello, Marvin, Jonathan, ladies," the nice-looking man said as he shook hands with the men and then slightly bowed respectively to their wives.

"Mayor Victorio Romano. Please allow me the honor of introducing you and Sally to our friends from Mississippi," Judge Tullos said. "This is Nick Gable and his sister, Madeline Benedetti, who live in that fabulous mansion over near Bay St. Louis that I'm sure you have heard of. It's known as the Bluffs." Nick made a point of shaking the Mayor's hand as his name was called.

Judge Tullos continued, "Vic is in his second term as mayor of the 'crescent city,' as New Orleans is sometimes called." Turning so that the mayor and Sally were now standing with the group, Judge Tullos continued, saying, "We were fortunate in meeting Madeline during our trip to Italy. We have since stayed in touch and were recently invited to their place for a little social function." Turning to Nick, Judge Tullos said, "Nick, you need to have a party at your place so you can invite the mayor and Sally over for a visit. Mayor, they have a marvelous house, one I am sure you and Sally both would enjoy seeing."

"Yes, yes," the Mayor responded. "I have heard about your place. We would love to see it some day."

Sally immediately joined in saying, "Yes. Please do let us know if you have something there that we might attend. We have heard such wonderful things about your home."

At that moment another couple walked up to the group. Judge Tullos again led the greetings.

"Ah, please allow me to introduce City Council President Theodore Young and his wife, Gail."

Handshakes and greetings were exchanged all around. Judge Tullos continued by saying to the newly arrived couple, "This is Nick Gable and his sister, Madeline Benedetti. I was just telling Mayor Romano and Sally about their fabulous house over at the Bluffs in Mississippi."

Councilman Young remembered Nick's name. He had heard that many of the office holders who were attending this party had already received "contributions" to their political campaigns from Nick. Councilman Young wanted to make sure he met Nick so that he might also possibly get a contribution. Mayor Romano felt the same way, which was why he had walked up to the group in the first place.

As the group began conversations among themselves, Councilman Young was bold enough to immediately let Madeline know he thought she was absolutely gorgeous which his wife, apparently not offended that her husband would make such a statement in her presence, pretended to ignore. When Young asked Madeline about what activities she enjoyed, she mentioned her almost daily horseback riding out at the Bluffs. After a few moments of conversation about the riding, Gail asked Madeline to come volunteer with her at one of the local hospitals if she had time.

She told Madeline how good she felt helping give comfort to those who were sick. She also mentioned how nice it was to get to know most of the leading doctors in the area since one never knew when a close acquaintance with a doctor might be helpful. Finding out Madeline was single, Gail made the point that several of the doctors in the area were also single and would surely enjoy being in the company of Madeline. Madeline recognized this was a very shrewd suggestion so as to guide her away from Gail's husband.

Madeline then began a conversation with the amiable Judge Tullos and his wife, Delores. Once again, both the judge and his wife discussed their love of golf stating they had found the sport an ideal way to meet people. They both asked Madeline to join them sometime for a golf outing to which she readily agreed. However, she said that she would first have to take some lessons to become better at the sport.

As Nick chatted with the others, Madeline discussed with Judge Parker his and Betsy's visit out to the Bluffs for the party. She also discussed with Betsy more about her work as an employee of the federal government in New Orleans and her continued involvement in several worthwhile charitable organizations.

While dancing with Mayor Romano, she learned that the mayor and his wife had met when he was in school at Tulane, which at that time was an all male university. Sally was at Sophie Newcomb, an all-girl's school located nearby. She now usually stayed at home with their two young children but sometimes made political appearances with her husband. Madeline learned from her new friends that Mayor Romano was a very popular mayor, something she could easily understand due to the mayor's smooth personality.

During the evening Madeline danced with several men. She had a great time making new friends and teasing some of the guys she met. Nick and Madeline both invited many of their new acquaintances to come out to the Bluffs for their next party, which they hoped to have in the late fall.

A few days after the party, Madeline followed up with some of the wives and planned shopping trips with them in the city. She eventually began making regular trips to New Orleans to spend time with her new friends. She enjoyed her new contacts and the fact that her trips let her escape from the boredom of Devil's Swamp and the close scrutiny of the people of Hancock County. Nick continually made it clear to her that he did not want any attention brought to any part of his operation. It had taken a lot of money and effort to set it all up and Madeline needed to continue to try and not attract too much attention, at least not at this time.

Nick ran into Dudley Marquette on the street in Bay St. Louis one day. He decided that, since he had often thought about his experience with Tiny in the swamp, he would mention parts of it to Marquette, if for no other reason than to get Marquette's reaction to what had happened. Nick also wanted to find out what else Marquette might have to say about any voodoo rituals out there. After all, Marquette had been the first one to talk with him about things happening out in the swamp.

"Dudley, have you got a minute for me to tell you about something?" Nick asked.

"Sure, Nick. Anytime one of my best clients wants to tell me about something, ol' Dudley is willing to listen. What's on your mind?"

Nick began, realizing he had to be careful how he presented it all to Marquette.

"I went out into the swamp with one of my workers one night a few weeks ago when we heard noises. I had heard the noises a few times before. Turns out it was drums coming from a place out in the swamp. We saw a group of people dancing, chanting and making strange noises with bells and things."

"Oh, my goodness, Nick. Sounds to me like you saw the real thing."

"What do you mean?" Nick asked, wondering where Marquette was going with his comment.

"Well, sounds like you witnessed one of them voodoo sessions."

"May be, Dudley. Like I said, one of my employees was with me. We were real quiet and stopped away from it all so we could watch what was going on. The dancers got more and more excited by the drums and the singing and all. But then, Dudley, you are not going to believe what happened next, and you have to keep this to yourself. Okay?"

"Sure, whatever you say."

"Not long after we got into position where we could watch everything, out came this really tall, I'd say about seven foot tall, black man. Probably the tallest black man I've ever seen."

Marquette immediately seemed taken aback.

"Are you saying this black man that you actually saw was really that tall?"

"Yes, at least seven feet tall and black as the ace of spades," Nick answered, now seeing a quizzical look on Marquette's face. "And after he came out, this totally nude woman came out, Dudley, totally nude! She was dancing around with a whole bunch of dead chickens on the ground. Those chickens, Dudley, looked like they didn't have any heads attached to their bodies."

Nick could see that, now, he had Marquette's complete attention. Lowering his voice, Nick said, "And Dudley, you will never guess what she had with her." Taking just a moment, Nick then said, "She had this really huge, white python around her neck! A big, white snake!"

Marquette stared at Nick, taking in what he had just been told as Nick watched for his reaction.

"Damnation, Nick! I hope you got the hell out of there! Oh, I hope you did right then! You were watching the real thing! You saw a voodoo ceremony! How many people were there? Where did you say this happened?"

"It happened in the swamp a few miles from the Bluffs. There were about forty people or so there."

"Oh, Nick! I hope you didn't stay too long, really."

"As a matter of fact, we didn't. We left right after that woman with that huge snake came out," Nick answered. Marquette kept looking at Nick without moving his eyes away from him. Nick could tell Marquette was trying to picture the scene.

Nick asked, "Dudley, do you know who that tall guy is, the skinny, seven foot tall, black fellow that was out there? All of those people were almost bowing down to him. Anybody would remember him if they ever saw him because he was so tall. It would be hard for anybody to forget somebody like him."

Marquette stared at Nick with a hard look. After thinking about how he was going to answer that question, he finally said, "Sounds to me like Doctor John."

"Doctor John?" Nick asked.

Taking a moment before he answered, Marquette said, "Yes. Doctor John. Doctor Jean Montenet."

"So you know him?" Nick asked.

"I know who a seven foot tall, black man is that is closely associated with voodoo," Marquette said in a determined voice. After a short pause, Marquette continued, saying slowly, "But Nick, I don't know how to tell you this."

Now Marquette really had Nick's attention. "Well, go ahead, Dudley. Just say it."

Marquette took a deep breath, looked to his left and to his right and then back at Nick, now with a really strange expression on his face.

"Nick, Jean Montenet? Known as Doctor John in these parts? Seven foot tall Doctor John? He's the only person around here I have ever even heard of that would come close to being that tall. But Nick, there's just one problem." Marquette paused and then, looking straight at Nick, said, "He's been dead for over fifty years."

Marquette, clearly not wanting to talk about it anymore, turned and walked away.

Chapter Twenty-two

Samuel Fuller, the district attorney for the New Orleans area, heard about the shipments of large quantities of liquor coming out of somewhere in Mississippi. He tried to get the United States Attorney and various Mississippi officials to do something about it, but nothing ever happened. After discussion with several of his friends in federal agencies, all who tried to discourage him, Fuller decided to send someone as an unofficial, undercover informant over to Mississippi anyway. The person was never heard from again. Fuller then decided to send a second person over to Mississippi, hoping the second informant would find out about the booze shipments and also about what may have happened to the first person. So far, he had heard nothing from the second one either, and it had been weeks since he had sent him.

Meanwhile, Lovelady and three of his fellow revenue agents finally found Simon Montgomery, who was feeding his horses in a stable on his farm in the middle of nowhere in northern Hancock County. It was near sunset when Lovelady and three of his agents confronted him. Frustrated by his lack of success in finding the source of all of the shipments that were apparently being made right under his nose,

Lovelady decided it was time to be more forceful. He was going to make this Simon Montgomery talk regardless of how he had to do it. Montgomery was going to tell the names of others working with him in shipping the booze just like the two men who had hit Lovelady on the road that night.

Lovelady and the three agents positioned themselves so that they surrounded Montgomery, thereby cutting off any avenue of escape.

"Are you Simon Montgomery?" Lovelady asked.

"Who wants to know?" Montgomery asked, looking at each of the men.

"Don't get cute with me! We are federal agents checking into the illegal trafficking of liquor and who knows what else in this area," Lovelady said with the air of a person with all the right cards in his hands, in this instance three agents with guns obviously showing from their belts.

"Yeah, I'm Simon Montgomery. Now just who in the hell are you, being out here, come barging up on my property, showing your guns and all?"

"We know all about you, Simon. We know about all of that liquor you have been shipping out of here. We got a couple of your drivers and, after a little persuasion, they talked with us, Simon. They told us all about your operation here. Now, if you want to make it easy on yourself, you'll tell us about who you work for, and who you get your shipments from. Do that and we might go easy on you," Lovelady said, enjoying having what he considered a lower than life scum surrounded by his good men.

"I don't know what you are talking about. Now get off of my property!" Montgomery knew that sometimes when he was in tough situations, if he just bowed up, people had on many occasions just left him alone. He had been in so many fights, one more would not bother him and right then, he began trying to determine if he could beat the group standing around him by himself.

"Now Simon, we are not going to waste any time with you on this. We know about you. We know what you have been doing out here. We just want to know who your boss is and any other names you might want to tell us." Lovelady was beginning to feel more and more comfortable, knowing that he had his three agents with him. He could tell that Montgomery was sizing up the situation, wondering if he could in fact whip all four of them by himself.

"Well, government man, I want you to git off of my property, right now! I ain't answering any of yor questions, so git." Simon rolled his fingers into fists on each hand, as he had done so many times before, and brought his hands up to just below his waist.

"Simon, don't think you can scare us. You had better answer my questions. Who are you working for? Who are you working with? I want some answers and I want them right now, Simon!"

Unknown to Lovelady and his agents, a black man named Ned, who worked for Montgomery, had been in an outhouse taking care of personal business when the federal agents had arrived. Ned listened to the questions Lovelady had been asking Montgomery and knew that these men were not part of Montgomery's operation. He had been helping Montgomery for months and had never seen any of them. When he heard what Lovelady was saying, he definitely knew they were not part of their business. He also noticed that Lovelady spoke with a strange accent. He most certainly was not from Hancock County.

As the agents focused their attention on Montgomery, Ned had eased himself out of the outhouse and quietly moved over to hide behind the trunk of a large oak tree. With it now being almost totally dark and with the four men concentrating on their prey, they had not noticed Ned.

"Like I said, government man, who do you think you are, coming up here on my property, wearing guns and all?" Simon said, still looking for a way out of this corner he was in.

"Listen, you hick! Answer my questions! Who are you getting your shipments from? I want an answer, now!"

Nobody called Simon names, least of all some stranger. Simon had fought in bars over much less than what had already been said. It was time to get it started. He lunged at Lovelady, with both hands going for Lovelady's throat. One of the men behind Montgomery had slipped his gun out of its holster and, using the butt of the gun handle, struck Montgomery on the back of his head right after his hands had grabbed Lovelady's throat. The blow stunned Montgomery and he crumpled to his knees, loosening his grip. The three agents quickly grabbed Montgomery's arms and pulled them behind him. Lovelady looked around the barn and saw a long length of chain over on the ground next to shovels and axes. He walked over, grabbed the chain and said to his men while pointing, "Take him over to that tree."

Lovelady walked over to a nice-sized oak tree just outside of the entrance to the barn. The three men dragged the stunned Montgomery over to the tree and forced his back against it. Lovelady began wrapping the long length of chain around Montgomery and the tree. Lovelady made sure that Montgomery's arms were wrapped and pulled tightly next to the tree so he couldn't move them.

Lovelady, now pacing back and forth in front of Montgomery, said, "You just showed me how dumb you are, hick! You are so stupid. Now, do something smart for a change and tell me who is making shipments to you. Tell me, now!" Lovelady then took his belt off and showed it to his captured target.

Montgomery was still dazed a little bit, but not so much that he couldn't launch a sizable amount of spit at Lovelady. Lovelady felt the spit hit his face and drip from his cheeks. Wiping Montgomery's spit from his face, Lovelady stood there looking at him.

"I know how to make you talk, hick. See this belt? See this big belt buckle? You are going to feel this belt and this belt buckle until you start talking!" Then he swung his belt, striking Montgomery with the belt buckle. Lovelady swung the belt over and over, striking Montgomery all over his body and his head.

When the black man saw this, he started easing slowly away from behind the tree. He soon reached a path he had taken many times before. It led to the dirt road that went to Simon's brother's place, the nearby farm of Silas Montgomery. As he left he could hear Lovelady screaming, "I want names! Give me names, hick!" Over his shoulder, he could see Lovelady swinging that belt, hitting Montgomery with each swing.

The black man ran through the woods to Montgomery's brother's house which was about a mile farther down the same road. Out of breath when he got there, he knocked loudly on the front door. Finally, Silas opened the door.

"Ned, what's wrong?"

Completely out of breath from running the whole way, he said as best he could, "White men beatn' yor brotha. Bad, Mista Silas! Bad! They gots guns. Said they was federal agents."

"Where?" Silas quickly asked.

"Yard. Behind house."

Bent over now, Ned kept trying to catch his breath. Silas asked, "How many men, Ned?"

"Four. I think four."

Silas turned and went into the house while Ned leaned against the wall next to the door. Silas soon came back to the door holding a rifle in one hand and a pistol in the other. Opening the door, he handed the pistol to Ned and motioned for him to follow. They got two horses from Silas' barn and rode bareback to the only road that Lovelady and his agents could take to get back onto the main roadway from Simon's house.

Riding down the winding road, Silas picked a spot that was a sharp curve. He knew that any car would have to slow down to make it around that curve. The two men then waited and waited.

"What are they doing to him that would take this long?" Silas kept saying over and over under his breath.

After about an hour, Lovelady's car came down the dirt road toward the two waiting horsemen. Silas waited for just the right moment and then fired the first shot, which hit the driver. The car veered off the road and came to an abrupt halt after running into a ditch. The ambushers fired more shots until a second of the agents and Lovelady were also wounded. As Silas aimed his rifle at the last unwounded agent, the rifle jammed. Seeing that agent trying to bring a shotgun around in the tight quarters of the car so he could use it, Ned yelled, "He's got a shotgun. Let's git!"

The agent finally was able to point his shotgun out of the back window and fire off a blast, but it was too late. Silas and Ned had ridden their horses off into the night.

The remaining unwounded agent checked on Lovelady and saw that he was alive but in bad shape. A portion of Lovelady's lower jaw had been shot off. The other two agents had both been hit and needed to be taken to a doctor immediately. Simon Montgomery lay unconscious on the floor next to the back seat, having been beaten all over his body during the past hour. Not once had he revealed any names.

In the days following the attack on Lovelady and the agents, the revenuers decided that if the local populace was going to be so difficult, there was only one way to deal with them and that was to be even rougher on those they found with shipments. They also decided that they needed more agents and that they should use boats even more. The previous interrogation of the two men had indicated that most of the liquor was being shipped from somewhere in the Caribbean. The beating of Montgomery had not revealed anything, but time would tell.

Montgomery was being kept in custody in the basement of Lovelady's house. He would be kept there until he talked. They were not yet finished with Simon Montgomery.

Since Lovelady was now in a hospital in New Orleans with his jaw shot off, his assistant, Andy Peterman, took over. He directed his men to buy two larger and faster boats and get them out into the Gulf of Mexico and the Mississippi Sound to find the sea lanes being used for the shipments. Peterman's men went to Biloxi where they were able to locate two boats that they deemed appropriate for performing the task of catching any shipments of booze. At least one of the two boats was sent out to sea every night carrying three men with guns at the ready.

As time passed, the men working on the new boats constituting the revenuer's fleet began to get discouraged. Not only had they not had sightings of any boats that remotely looked suspicious, they had spent hour after hour at sea getting sunburned and seasick and weathering storms with nothing to show for it. Members of their group, through beatings of the few car and truck drivers that they had been able to catch, received more and more information that the booze was being brought in by ship. However, because of the system that had been set up, none of the drivers knew anything other than who their immediate contact was.

As for the men in the boats, all they ended up doing while patrolling the Mississippi Sound was sitting around trying to fight boredom. They eventually came to believe that the information was not reliable and that all of the stories they had been told about the "ghost" ships, the fast ships bringing in the liquor, were just that, stories. The only ships they ever saw with any regularity were the huge, slow lumber ships taking timber cut from the massive pine forests in south Mississippi down to Cuba where most of it was shipped to other countries. The few times those ships had been seen on their return trips, they had been easy to spot. It was not worth the revenuers' time to concern themselves with lumber boats.

Late one night, three revenue agents were on patrol in one of their new boats bouncing on the waves of the Gulf of Mexico just off of Horn Island. They had been cruising around the Mississippi Sound and also south of the barrier islands of Petit Bois Island, Horn Island, Ship Island and Cat Island, all which constituted the southern border of the Sound.

"This is such a waste of time," one of the agents said. "You would think that our supervisors would have figured that out by now. I mean, they are supervisors. They are supposed to be smart. They know, just from what we tell them, that nothing is happening out here."

The other two voiced their agreement. One of the other agents said, "With all this thick fog, we couldn't see anything even if it was out here. We can't see the moon. We can barely see the water that is right around us. How are we supposed to see anything in this kind of weather? I don't know why they even send us out on a night like this." It was dark around Horn Island and the visibility was almost nonexistent.

"I heard that, before too long, efforts with boats like ours will probably be terminated and the manpower shifted to other functions on land," said the third one, adding his little bit of information to the discussion.

"Let's just sit here for a while and see if we can at least hear anything," the senior agent said.

After a few minutes of silence, the men laid back in their boat and began to talk again about their lack of success. Then they heard a faint sound. Each man stopped moving and turned his head to try to determine where the sound was coming from and what the sound was. It sounded like a boat cutting through the water. They all began to scan the fog around them. Suddenly, out of the darkness and the fog came a very large ship traveling so fast that it appeared only as it got almost on top of them. It was headed straight for their much smaller boat.

"It's gonna ram us!" the leader yelled. All three men immediately dove overboard. At the last second, just as the fast moving ship was about to hit their boat, it turned and brushed up against it, barely missing the revenuers' boat and disappearing into the fog as quickly as it has appeared.

The three men swam back to their boat and climbed on board. Each of the men was glad to be alive. After being assured by each other that none of them had been hurt by what had happened, the men began wondering about what it was that they had just seen. They were thankful that their own boat had not been sunk, but each of them also felt they had just seen their first boat involved in the illegal shipment of alcohol into the area. Nobody else would be out that late in those conditions unless they were up to no good.

Chapter Twenty-three

Sheriff Patterson did not like having all of these federal people in his county. They sometimes just went off on their on and did whatever they wanted to, never telling the local police anything. They were always putting themselves first and trying to make a name for themselves. The agencies checking into all of the illegal activities that had resulted from the passage of prohibition were mostly new agencies trying to justify themselves. Older agencies were also trying to set themselves up to get more money and hire more employees to deal with the problem of a lot more people getting into the liquor business.

Patterson had been in office for a long time now and knew pretty well who was doing what and where. He also knew, a lot of the time, when. He did not like things getting so out of hand in his county.

There were people in the county that the sheriff thought of as "do-gooders." They actually, if the truth be known, wanted to be the sheriff, but were not the politicians that could get elected and certainly did not have the courage to stand up and confront those who actually may be involved in such activities. They could whisper and start rumors and always wanted to tell on those that they thought were into various illegal activities. For them to actually do something rather than talk, though, was way beyond their courage level. The sheriff knew that all he had to do, when that sort of talk started, was to offer for the person talking to give him a name and then go with him to meet with that person in order that they both might find out if what the "do-gooder" was telling him was indeed true. That usually ended the conversation.

The sheriff had a good group of deputies, seven in all, and there was not much that went on, even though the county was rather large, that either he or the deputies did not know about. The deputies tended to be very loyal because the sheriff could get rid of a deputy at any time. Even though things economically were generally going well in Hancock County, the deputies seemed to appreciate not only that they had a job, but also that they were highly respected in the county. That went a long way in a county that was mostly rural.

Patterson had been sheriff for three full terms and in another year he would complete his fourth term and have to run again. He was aware that there were things going on he didn't quite know everything about because he kept hearing reports of cars riding low as they cruised the back roads of the county late at night. Some of his deputies had even stopped the cars, but could find nothing wrong with them or the drivers. In every instance, the cars or trucks were casually searched and found to be carrying nothing. If something was going on, he needed to find out more about it. After all, there was still the case of the unsolved death of Bubba Earl and elections were getting closer.

One night Patterson decided to ride with one of his most trusted deputies, David Thornton, out into the area that made up the most northern part of the county. He and David had been riding for a little over an hour when he rounded a curve on Highway 73 about ten miles from the county line. He saw headlights approaching and could tell by the way they were shining on the highway that something heavy was in that car or truck. As it passed, the sheriff could see that it was a car and that, being down so close to the shell road, the car was not sitting like it should have been. He turned his car around and turned on his police light. The low-riding car slowed down and pulled over after the sheriff had driven up behind it.

Both law enforcement officers got out of their car. The sheriff, not feeling comfortable about what he was looking at even with his deputy there, drew his gun and ordered the driver out of the car. Thornton also pulled his gun out and had it pointed at the car. The driver opened his door and as he started to get out of the car, the sheriff yelled, "Get your hands up high."

As the driver got out, he followed the sheriff's order and put his hands up in the air. Recognizing the driver as Stevie Morgan, the nineteen-year-old son of Neil Morgan who was the owner of a small farm in the area, the sheriff put his gun back in his holster. Sheriff Patterson remembered the senior Morgan as a person who had had some trouble with the law from time to time in the past, but none of it had been of a violent nature.

"Stand over there and keep an eye on this boy while I check out his car," the sheriff said to Thornton.

With the deputy now holding his gun on Morgan, the sheriff started examining the car. There was definitely something different about it. He opened the driver's side door and looked around. It was hard to see on such a dark night but, with the help of his car lights, he continued to look around for something to explain why it was sitting so low.

Tiring of his unsuccessful search, he looked back at the boy driver and said, "You want to make it easy on yourself, tell me why your car is riding so low. What are you hauling?"

"I ain't haulin' nothin', sheriff. I was just goin' home, and if you would have left me alone I would have already been there by now. Can I put my arms down? They are gettin tired."

"Listen, you little pissant! You keep your hands up until I say you can drop them. Now, be a real smart boy and tell me what you are doing with your car riding like that and I may not take you to jail."

"Aw sheriff, you gonna get me in trouble. Just let me go, okay? Just pretend you never saw me."

The sheriff had already had enough of this boy. He wasn't going to waste any more time with him. He pulled his gun back out of his holster and walked over to the boy, who was standing there with his hands still in the air, and got right in his face.

"Open your smart mouth, boy," the sheriff ordered. "Open it!"

The boy immediately did just that and the sheriff then slowly put the barrel of his .45 pistol in the boy's mouth. The boy's eyes opened wide as he next heard the clicking sound of the gun as the sheriff pulled the hammer back.

"Now boy, if you are going to tell me why your car is riding so low, nod your head up and down. But do it real slowly because this here gun has a hair trigger. If you are not going to tell me, well, in about five seconds you are going to have a hell of a bad accident here because this gun's gonna go off and a nice, big bullet is going to blow your damn head off. Now, one last time, are you going to tell me?"

The boy remembered the stories that he had heard about the sheriff. After all, the sheriff's nickname was Wild Bill. Now the man with that nickname was holding a gun in his mouth with the hammer pulled back! The boy quickly, and carefully, nodded his head up and down, his eyes still wide open and his hands high in the air. The sheriff slowly took the pistol barrel out of the boy's mouth and, with the barrel still pointing at the boy's head, he said, "I'm listening."

"The car's got a hidden tank loaded with whiskey," the kid blurted out, his eyes still wide, and with the sheriff still pointing a cocked .45 caliber pistol at him.

"Now that was real good, boy. You just might save yourself yet. Show me where this here hidden tank is."

The kid moved slowly at first and then, seeing the sheriff was not going to shoot him for moving, almost ran over to the car and opened the trunk. After pulling over the spare tire, the kid pointed to the place behind the rear seats where the hidden tank was.

"How much whiskey is in there, boy?" The sheriff still had his gun out, but he eased the hammer down and lowered the weapon just a little. The kid's hands were back up in the air as high as he could get them.

"About twenty gallons," he answered in a voice still shaking with fear. This was not a cocky kid anymore. So far he felt he had just barely managed to stay alive. He wanted to leave that way too.

"Okay," the sheriff said as he put his gun back in its holster. Pointing to Thornton, he said, "Drive this car back to the car barn. I'll follow you."

Turning to the boy, he said, "Go tell whoever you are working for that I want to see the person in charge of running this operation at this same spot next Thursday night at ten o'clock. If he doesn't want to come, I am going to come looking for you, and your daddy, so convince him. You got that?"

"Yes, sir, sheriff," the boy said as he stood there with his hands still high in the air. The sheriff turned back to Thornton as he started walking towards his car and said, "Let's go."

The boy continued to stand there looking at them with his hands still up as the two men got into the two cars. Then it dawned on him.

"Uh, sheriff. How am I supposed to get home?"

The sheriff looked at him and said, "That's your problem, boy."

The sheriff and his deputy then both drove away, leaving the boy standing there by himself in the dark.

When they got a few miles away from where they had left the boy, the sheriff flashed his headlights at his deputy in the boy's car and Thornton pulled over. The sheriff pulled up next to him and said through the open window, "Take that car to Hal Jackson's place. You know where Hal lives, don't you? Take it over there and get Hal to bring you back to the jail to pick up your car. Tell Hal I'll be in touch with him tomorrow."

"Okay, sheriff. Whatever you say," the deputy answered. He wasn't sure what was going on, but he did know that he had just seen the sheriff stick the barrel of his pistol in that boy's mouth and cock the hammer. The sheriff was his boss and so he would do whatever the sheriff wanted.

"You tell Hal that he is going to buy that car and what's in it, and to pay what it is worth or we will be back to see him," the sheriff said. The sheriff knew that he could count on Thornton. They had done a few things with Hal Jackson like this before with seized equipment to supplement their income. He knew Thornton would know how to handle it. A few days later, Hal had one of his workers go see the sheriff and drop off the cash for the sale of the car and the whiskey.

Before the Thursday night meeting though, the sheriff went back out to the same spot, this time with three of his deputies, and stopped another suspicious car in the middle of the night. The sheriff was once again able to convince the driver, more easily this time probably because the driver had heard what had happened on that road a few nights before, to show him where the hidden compartment was located in that car and how to unload it. The sheriff seized that car also and sent it to Hal, who a few days later sent the sheriff another nice amount for that car and its illegal content. This was getting to be a really nice business, the sheriff thought. He enjoyed the extra money that had begun to come his way, but he had to be careful who he let know about it or he might not be sheriff much longer.

On Thursday night a little before 10:00 p.m., the sheriff drove up to the spot where he and the deputy had seized the first car. As he was driving up there, he wondered just exactly who would be meeting him. He was more than a little worried because of all of the events that had been taking place in his county. Bubba Earl had literally been blown away, cars and trucks were traveling at all hours of the night on back roads loaded with illegal whiskey, and lots of money seemed to be flowing into the town of Bay St. Louis. He would have to be careful with whomever it was that he might be meeting.

As he pulled up in his car, he could see in the darkness the outline of a man getting out of a car parked on the side of the road. The sheriff got out of his car and approached the man. As the man lit a cigar, the sheriff recognized the features of the face of Nick Gable.

"Oh, so it's you," the sheriff said as he got closer. "Why am I not surprised. Now it all makes sense."

"Hello, sheriff. I hope you are not too disappointed," Nick said as he leaned back against his car, taking a drag on his cigar.

"No, no. I kind of figured it might be you. Spending as much money as you have leaves an impression in this little county," the sheriff said as he put his hands on his hips.

"Sheriff, I might as well get to the point. I am prepared to offer you a nice regular monthly stipend of four thousand dollars if you will leave my shipments alone." Nick leaned back against his car, taking another puff from his cigar while the sheriff looked at Nick and appeared to ponder his offer.

Nick continued, "I will need your help from time to time, but I will never put you or any of your men at any risk. All I want to do is ship my product, with the least amount of problems."

At exactly that moment, a car appeared down the road. It was riding low just like the one the sheriff had seized a few days earlier. For Nick, this was the test. Would the sheriff seize the car and try to make a little more money like he already had, or would he agree to work with Nick and let the car pass? Nick watched, leaning back against his car, but with his arms folded in front of him and his cigar firmly in his mouth. Nick did not want the sheriff to think that he was going to do anything such as pull a gun out or try somehow to keep the sheriff from stopping the car, if the sheriff attempted to do that.

The car pulled up next to the two men and, without stopping, moved on into the night with the sheriff still standing there with his hands on his hips.

The sheriff then said, "I will need another two thousand dollars each month to take care of my boys. Is that a problem?"

"No, not at all. It will be taken care of. Just make sure your boys take care of me," Nick said smiling at the sheriff.

"I guess you can say I will take care of my end of things. Just you don't go being real obvious about what all you are doing," the sheriff said looking at Nick for agreement.

Nick nodded his head in agreement and said, "Sheriff, I would not want to do anything that would hurt your chances of keeping your office or your standing in the community. Any way I can help you, I will. That is why we usually run only late at night."

Sheriff Patterson looked at Nick, stuck his hand out and said, "Very well then, we have a deal." Nick shook hands with the sheriff and the sheriff continued in a low voice, "Send the money the first Thursday of each month at around five o'clock in the afternoon to my garage. I will be there starting next month."

"Thanks, Bill, it will be there. If there are ever any questions, just contact me. Thanks for doing business with me," Nick said with a smile.

Then the sheriff yelled out, "It's okay, boys. You can come out now."

Soon three of his deputies, holding their guns up in the air so they didn't get caught on the bushes, came out of hidden positions on the side of the road opposite of where the sheriff had parked his car.

"I didn't know how this might turn out so I brought a little insurance," the sheriff said with a wide grin on his face.

"These and my other deputies will take care of you, won't you boys?" To which the three men all offered their assurances. The sheriff felt good, thinking that by having his deputies there he had outsmarted this man with so much money.

"Thanks, guys. You heard what I told the sheriff. We will take care of you, too," Nick said as each one walked by to shake hands with Nick.

After shaking their hands, Nick then turned and yelled out, "Alright, boys. You can come on out, too."

Soon five men in suits began working their way out of the bushes on the side of the road opposite where the sheriff's men had been.

"I brought a little insurance also, sheriff," Nick said as he now smiled at the sheriff. As Nick's men worked their way out of the bushes, the sheriff's chief deputy noticed that three of Nick's five men had submachine guns hanging from shoulder straps around their shoulders.

The deputy, seeing the firepower that Nick's men had, looked at the little six shot pistol still in his hand, and quickly made a move to discreetly put his small gun back in his holster. Fast! He didn't want to give any of Nick's men a reason to be concerned and raise their submachine guns.

"Shake hands with our new partners, boys," Nick said as his men approached. Soon both groups had extended greetings and shaken hands all around. As most of Nick's men began to slap around their necks and faces with their hands, one of Nick's men said to one of the deputies, "How do you guys put up with these mosquitoes? They about ate us alive! Some of them are almost as big as the birds where I come from and there are thousands of them."

The sheriff's deputies laughed and one of them said, "Aw, you'll get used to them. Right after they've bitten off about half of your hand."

Laughter again came from the sheriff's men. While Nick's men laughed also, their laughs were guarded as they wondered in the back of their minds whether the mosquitoes really would bite that much.

Nick then said to his men, "You'll get used to them. Pretty soon, you won't even think about them." He turned to the sheriff and said, "Sheriff, it is probably good that we had this meeting since now your boys will have some idea of who some of my men are and my men will know yours."

The sheriff was amazed by all of the firepower Nick's men had with them, knowing that if there had been a shootout he and his men would have been in a lot of trouble. Nodding his head, the sheriff said, "Yes, I guess that is a good thing. Well, time to go, boys."

"Thanks again," Nick said.

Sheriff Patterson got into his car as his men walked to their hidden cars. They all drove away as Nick and his men stood there on the road watching them pass by. As the cars disappeared into the night, Nick thought about how, when he had asked about Helen's husband, people had told him that the sheriff was a good man and the county had been lucky to have had him as their sheriff for over the past fourteen years. Nick remembered Capone's comment at the Pine Hills Hotel about how Capone had been told that the sheriff was known to keep his word. Nick felt that Capone would be very happy with what had just taken place. Hopefully, Nick had just taken care of something that had obviously been of great concern to Capone.

One of Nick's men standing near him, in between swats at his airborne attackers, asked after the last car had disappeared into the night, "How did you know he would bring some help, boss?"

Nick continued to lean against his car and then flicked ashes from his cigar on the ground. Looking back down the road where the sheriff and his deputy's car had gone, Nick said, "I just know these things."

Then looking back at his men, Nick said, "Thanks, guys. I know it was hard for you to stay in those bushes and be quiet with all of those mosquitoes working on you, but thanks. I didn't know how that was going to turn out, but it went well. Let's get back to the Bluffs."

The men got into Nick's car and they all rode back to the Cypress Landing dock to catch a boat back to their compound at the Bluffs. Nick wondered along the way what Helen would think if she were to ever find out about what had just taken place. He hoped that she never would. He also hoped that Sheriff Patterson would never find out about their relationship. He was more worried about that now that he and the sheriff had agreed to work together. He realized for the first time that, for his and Helen's safety, he may have to stop seeing her.

Chapter Twenty-four

Helen had fallen in love with Nick and started talking about getting divorced during one of their meetings in Nick's apartment. Nick didn't want her hurting his operation by alienating the sheriff. He thought a lot of Helen, but he also valued his own life. He knew Capone would be very upset if Nick's personal involvement with the sheriff's wife ended up causing serious problems for Capone's operations that had taken so much time and money to set up.

While he was thinking about how to deal with the situation after the meeting with the sheriff and his men, during Helen's next visit with Nick she gave him a big hug, and then backed away a step while still holding his hands.

"Nick, I have something important to tell you. I'm pregnant."

Nick looked at her as his mind quickly took that monumental piece of information and evaluated it. His first conclusion was that the news complicated an already difficult situation.

"Are you sure?" he asked, still trying to go over in his mind the ramifications of her announcement.

"Yes, I'm sure. You don't seem happy," she said with a tinge of sadness in her voice.

"Does your husband know about this?" Nick asked, still trying to think of all the problems that the news could eventually cause.

"Yes, I told him. He was startled to say the least and, I guess you could say, didn't believe it. When he saw that I was so happy about the news, he seemed to feel better about it. But Nick, what he thinks doesn't matter. I love you and I am going to get a divorce so we can get married."

Nick was shocked again! Helen had not taken the time to think about the obvious.

"Helen, how can you divorce Bill being pregnant? You think he's just going to let you walk away? Especially with what he will think is his child?"

Helen looked at Nick with a new expression of concern. After a moment, she said, "Nick, we can just go away. We can go to another state, even another country, to Europe maybe. I don't have much, but I do have a little money saved up that we could use. We don't have to stay here."

She then hugged him again and pulled Nick over to his bed. Nick almost felt the sex that day was an effort by Helen to convince him, in bed, that she was right. She was happy and they were going to do whatever it took for them to be happy together. She just knew that Nick would want to be with her and that they would get married after her divorce. Nick knew it wasn't that simple.

As Helen was leaving that day, she mentioned to Nick that she would see him again the following Tuesday morning at around ten o'clock. She could tell by the look on his face that the news she had given him earlier had not set well with him.

Nick thought about the pregnancy almost every moment until the ten o'clock hour the next Tuesday. What he had always anxiously waited for before, a visit from this beautiful, sweet woman, he almost wished would not happen this time. After thinking about it all, he knew what he had to do.

When Helen arrived that day, she could sense by Nick's cold reception that things were different. She was completely surprised and devastated by what happened next.

"Helen, we have got to stop seeing each other," Nick said after she walked in. "There are a lot of things that you don't know about me, and it will be better for you, the baby and for me, for us to stop meeting."

She answered, "Don't say that, Nick. I love you. I don't care if when you were a little boy you didn't put the nickel your parents gave you in the church collection plate. Whatever it is, it doesn't matter to me."

"Oh, if it were only that simple," Nick answered. "You have no idea how complicated it is and also how dangerous this situation now is."

"It's not like I've got yellow fever or something, Nick. Whatever it is you are talking about can't be that bad. I am pregnant, and when I get divorced we can go away and live the rest of our lives together. We will be so happy, Nick. I just know it, and with a child to raise, I can't wait to see you playing with our child, Nick."

"Stop it! Just stop it!" he all but yelled. Helen drew back in shock. He had never raised his voice with her until now.

In a slow, but stern voice, looking directly into her eyes, he said, "I am not going to marry you, even if you were to get divorced, Helen, because I can't."

Helen had never seen Nick like this, nor had she heard the low, even tone of voice he was now using.

"I will say it again. Now listen to me. There are things that you do not know and cannot know. If you were to know them at all, your life would be in danger, the baby's life would be in danger, and my life would be in danger. I love you, and that is exactly the reason I am telling you this. I had no idea I was going to fall in love with you, and I certainly didn't know you were going to get pregnant. But your getting pregnant has nothing, nothing at all, to do with why I am now doing this. Other things have happened that would have made me tell you this anyway."

"Yeah, Nick, sure. Now that I'm pregnant, you just decided you don't want to deal with this situation so now you'll very conveniently let me deal with it by myself! Thanks, you bastard! You know, you are right. I don't know you. I love you, and I thought you loved me too. Outside of my love for you, the only thing I have to keep me going is my love for playing the organ and piano at church, and now I will have this baby. I want you to be there with me, with us. Now, I find out that because I am pregnant, you are not going to have anything to do with me!" As she finished her last sentence, she began to cry.

Nick put his arms around her and tried to comfort her as she sobbed deeply.

"I can't blame you for feeling like you do, but please believe me. This is not happening because you are pregnant. It has to happen because of things that you do not know about that affect how I have to deal with my relationship with you. If I could tell you I would, but I simply can't. One day maybe you will understand, but please know that I am doing this because I do love you. I know that sounds strange, but please believe me. It is best this way for you, the baby and me."

After he finished that sentence, only then did Helen, being an intelligent woman, begin to figure out that maybe he was telling the truth.

There was one thing, though, that Nick felt he had to know and the only way to find out was to ask.

"Helen, I have to know. Is the baby mine?"

"Nick! Oh! How could you ask me that? Yes, it's yours!" She pushed him away and began crying again.

Nick felt badly. He felt she was telling him the truth and that made it even worse.

"Helen, I want you to know that, somehow, I will try to help in some way with the baby. Maybe it could be with the baby's education. I don't know how yet, but I will do something."

Nick looked at the crying woman after he had said that. Yes, he had gotten valuable information from her at important times while setting up the operation, but he now realized, after having said it to her twice now, that he had grown to love her. His past experience with what he thought was love had not ended well, and he made sure that he guarded himself. If he was capable of loving a woman after those experiences, he loved Helen. He wanted to tell her the truth about himself, but the more he thought about it, he knew that, if he did, all of them would be in danger. By bringing their relationship to an end right now, maybe she and the baby would be alright.

Having thought about it as much as he had, he had decided one thing for sure. He could not tell her about Capone. If Capone found out that Nick had told her, he would probably have them both killed. Capone was known to solve sticky problems himself, and he had no tolerance for loose ends. The rumor had been around before Nick had left up north that Capone had already killed several people, some said at least seventeen, himself. Nick knew that number was not right. It was way too low.

Nick and Helen stopped seeing each other that day.

Chapter Twenty-five

After seeing how well things had gone for Madeline at the New Orleans Country Club party, Nick knew it would be better for her to widen her social circle in that city rather than run the risk of having another run-in with the ruffian or some other person similar to him at places like the Red Maple. He told her to go into New Orleans more often to see some of her new friends, and also try to meet people who may provide information that might be helpful to him and his operations.

Madeline agreed and began making trips more often to New Orleans. She regularly went by boat to the Cypress Landing dock and was met there by a limousine usually driven by Tiny, who would take her to New Orleans. She went to receptions and parties held at the elegant New Orleans Country Club and began to meet new people and make new friends. She danced and flirted with many men, married and unmarried, and talked with their wives and with their girlfriends.

Madeline soon became the talk of the party circuit in New Orleans, just as Nick had felt she would. All of the men wanted to be seen with her because she was so beautiful and interesting. She was not like the more conservative southern ladies at the parties. Madeline always wore the tightest dresses that were very low cut and, because of her figure, she was quickly resented, not only by some of the more prim and proper women of the New Orleans social set, but also by those who considered her as competition for attention. A few of the more confident women did not feel threatened by her. They were even glad she was present at the parties so that their own flirtations and romantic adventures would be less obvious. They hoped she got all of the attention she could handle, which helped them avoid intense scrutiny of their own activities.

As she attended more parties and social events, Madeline began to see people that she had met before and became comfortable being with them. She continued to enjoy her conversations with Judge Tullos and his wife, Delores, and never tired of hearing about their golfing adventures. Judge Tullos was delightful to be around with his easy smile and background knowledge of everybody and everything. She also noted that he was always discreet in checking out her cleavage. His wife, Delores, was interesting to listen to as she discussed how she enjoyed taking golf lessons from her cute golfing instructors. Madeline noticed that Delores mentioned her golfing lessons only when her husband was not around. She also noticed that the golfing instructors Delores specifically mentioned were usually college graduate students using their golfing instructors' positions to help them pay their way through graduate school.

City Councilman Young could always be expected to give them both a big welcome to what he called "my city," and immediately asked how things were in the lovely little town of Bay St. Louis. Though he was a city councilman for New Orleans, Madeline was amazed at how much he knew about things that were happening on the Mississippi Gulf Coast. His wife, Gail, was always among the first to greet Nick and Madeline. She never failed to tell Madeline that she needed to do volunteer work with her at the hospitals where there were a few doctors that she knew were eligible bachelors. She continuously offered to arrange dates for Madeline with some of her doctor friends. She just knew that they would find Madeline to be someone they would like to get to know better.

Judge Parker was always interesting with his tales of past political campaigns that had resulted in contacts that had helped him get his appointment as a federal judge. Madeline could easily understand why the Judge with his reserved demeanor had been successful in his judicial life. Judge Parker's wife, Betsy, was completely overshadowed by her husband. Many times Madeline would catch herself wondering how

Betsy had ever ended up with Judge Parker. She was always surprised by Betsy's intelligence and insight into or observation of some event or person. Madeline began to notice that Betsy's intellect only made its appearance occasionally, and that was usually when her husband was not around. Betsy talked a little about her job with the Treasury Department, but had to be encouraged to talk about herself. The more time Madeline spent around Judge Parker and Betsy, the more she realized that Betsy was a much smarter person than anyone first meeting her would ever imagine.

Mayor Romano always made sure that, if it were at all possible, he danced at least two dances with Madeline. With her beauty and his general good looks, they appeared as if they were meant for each other, especially when their dance steps were perfectly in unison. He was suave and charming, but because he was the Mayor, his attention was constantly being directed toward people who almost always demanded his immediate presence, usually in an attempt to make that particular person appear important. His wife, Sally, did not attend many of the social events because of their kids. When Madeline asked him about her absence from one of the parties, the Mayor answered that Sally did not enjoy the constant social demands of being the mayor's wife. She often told people that, before they had gotten married, she had never expected her husband to be involved in something, such as politics, that would require her to deal with the public so much.

Other notable citizens became people Nick and Madeline considered as friends. However, Nick constantly reminded Madeline that she had to be careful about what she said around them. Many of the men at the various parties had heard about Madeline's brother's extreme amount of wealth and how everything he touched seemed to involve a large amount of money. Nick had certainly gotten the attention of the local power brokers and soon many of the women were attempting to be as attentive to his every need as were the men for Madeline. Whenever they made an appearance together, there was usually a pause in whatever activities were taking place because so much attention was focused on them. Except for the fact that they were brother and sister, they appeared to be a wonderful couple.

Madeline continued to ride horses at the Bluffs, though for a while she felt less comfortable going to the stables after what had happened with Joey. She knew that she had manipulated Joey, but he had gone too far.

He had been so handsome and she had been lonely. It was a spur of the moment thing that she had done before. However, once he grabbed her by her throat, the situation had gotten out of control and there was only one solution. She had done what was necessary to remove him from being the problem he had become. Besides, who did that barnyard worker think he was? She had done what she had to do. In a way, the more she thought about it the better she felt about it.

She remembered when Johnny Scabelli, the son of a wealthy family in her home town in Sicily, had always been after her when no one was around. When other people were around though, he acted like he didn't know her and that she wasn't good enough for him to be seen talking with her. She had always hated that. Now, she made sure men paid attention to her and she could care less what the women thought. They weren't ever going to do anything except be jealous of her looks and upset with the people trying to please her.

Madeline soon put what had happened to Joey behind her. There was simply too much going on now to dwell on that. She tried to think about things and to observe things while riding. She continued to see Nick talking with Carlotta near the bayou from time to time. When she had asked Nick about seeing him with Carlotta, Nick just said he was trying to find out more about the voodoo markings, especially the meaning behind certain ones that had been put in what seemed to be key places in the bayou. Madeline decided to not say anything at this time since she felt that soon there may be someone coming to see her at the Bluffs. She did not want anything to interfere with those visits, if and when they began to take place.

The jealousy and envy of Madeline among the socialites who had positions in New Orleans society grew with each party or social gathering that took place. Not many of them had the personality that Madeline possessed and none of them had her looks. Women, whose husbands or dates were lucky enough to get some of Madeline's attention or were the recipients of some of Madeline's most obvious flirtations, regularly got together and talked about the new beauty. Every little bit of gossip became more and more animated with every tease by Madeline. Some of the men knew that talking with her would immediately lead to their wives' or girlfriends' disapproval. Now, everything about Madeline was discussed, especially her living in Mississippi at what was reported to be a fabulous mansion on the water. All aspects of her private life were the subject of detailed discussions with alleged instances of various sorts reported as fact, though the alleged instances never came close to Madeline's actual activities.

At one party held by the Krewe of Nobles at the New Orleans Country Club, all of local society was present which of course included most of the members of the other krewes in the New Orleans area. Madeline and Nick made another grand entrance with the immediate result that Madeline was surrounded by admirers who were constantly giving her compliments, bringing her drinks, and asking her to dance.

Nick made his rounds separately, expressing his greetings and exchanging pleasantries with powerful men and the women accompanying them. He always made sure to never appear to be flirting with any of the women at these parties. He needed to have the appearance of a close friendship with many of the people there and did not ever want to give any of them a reason to think badly of him. Madeline, on the other hand, was very capable of stirring up adverse sentiment even though Nick had warned her time and time again to not be so flirtatious.

As the evening wore on, Madeline slipped into the powder room. It was a refuge where she could take a few moments to relax before returning to the activities of the party. As Madeline took one last look at herself to critique her face, the restroom door flew open and in walked Gertrude Hensley, known as "Gertie" to her friends. With her was Amanda Whiteside, another socialite who had been a friend of Gertie's since elementary school days at a local Catholic all-girl school.

Gertie was a slight woman whose five foot three inch frame had never had over one hundred and four pounds on it. Everyone had always commented, very discreetly of course, on how Gertie had no figure to speak of and had never done anything of consequence, except that she was probably the most widely-known gossip in New Orleans. Some of her closest friends, who from time to time were the targets of some of her harshest criticisms, were the first to comment on how her jaw muscles were probably the strongest muscles in her body because she always exercised them and hardly ever any other.

Her friend, Amanda, a much better looking woman who was a bit taller, was a lot less talkative than Gertie mainly because no one ever had any time to say anything around Gertie. Gertie always monopolized any conversation and was constantly interrupting anyone who ever had something to say so she could have her say on the subject. On this occasion, having had several drinks while watching her husband be a member of one of the groups of men attempting to take care of Madeline's every need, Gertie had become a little tipsy. She had also become furious because of the attention her husband showed toward Madeline. Her speech had become slurred, but that did not stop her from having already presided over a long, critical discussion of the object of her husband's interest.

Walking through the door to the restroom, Gertie saw Madeline at the long mirror. Immediately upon seeing her, Gertie slurred, "Well, look what da cat drug in!"

Madeline saw that Gertie was looking in her direction but, since the comment completely caught her by surprise, she paused and looked around to see who else in the powder room could possibly be the object of such a statement. There was no one else.

Madeline looked back at Gertie, knowing now that her statement was referring to her. Gertie staggered over toward the sink next to where Madeline was standing.

Amanda realized that she might not want to hear what her longtime friend, Gertie, might say next. She had seen and heard Gertie's mouth in action many times before, so Amanda said, "I think I'll wait outside," and made a hasty retreat out of the room.

"You have every man in this place, including my sorry husband, thinking you are just the greatest thing even though you slithered out of some swamp in Mississippi," Gertie slurred.

"You think just because your brother has all that money that you have class and that you can get whoever you want and do whatever you want," Gertie continued, leaning on the sink for support.

"You wouldn't be jealous, would you?" Madeline said with a tilt of her head.

"Not at all, honey. Everybody can see that you are nothing but a tramp!"

At first, Madeline was stunned, then she got mad. Quickly livid with anger, she reached over and grabbed Gertie's hair on the back of her head. Using both hands, she pulled her head back and then slammed her face down on the vanity shelf that ran under the mirror. When Gertie's face hit the vanity, the cracking of her front teeth could clearly be heard.

Blood splattered all over the front of Gertie's dress, but Gertie didn't notice that since all one hundred and four pounds of her body was now being pulled around by her hair and next flung face first into a wall. Again, there was a cracking sound. Madeline let go of Gertie's hair when she hit the wall. Gertie slid down the wall like a clump of wet mud. A messy trail of blood ran from the vanity over to the wall and onto the floor.

Madeline stepped back, breathing heavily from both anger and her exertion, but mostly from anger. Gertie had blood all over herself, but Madeline was not satisfied. At all! How dare this ugly bag of bones say something like that to her! Madeline didn't even know her. She reached into Gertie's evening bag and pulled out her lipstick. Madeline bent down and, using the bright red lipstick, wrote her initials "MB" on Gertie's forehead. She stood up, threw the lipstick on the floor and, after taking one last look at Gertie, walked out the door.

Entering the corridor outside the powder room, Madeline noticed Amanda near the entrance talking with another woman. Walking over to Amanda, Madeline said, "Your friend needs help. She really can't hold her liquor very well."

Amanda and the other woman rushed to the powder room and looked inside. They saw Gertie on the floor leaning up against the wall.

"Gertie! What happened?" Amanda exclaimed as Madeline walked back into the ballroom.

Chapter Twenty-six

In Chicago, Bugsy Moran called in members of his gang to talk about what he had heard concerning Capone's whiskey smuggling in the South. They had heard about all of the money Capone's operations were making down there off of the shipment of booze. Moran knew that, sooner or later, his gang and Capone's were going to have a turf war in Chicago. They were both competing for total control of illegal liquor shipments in the greater Chicago area. Occasionally, something would happen to one side with the result being something happening to the opposite side. So far, outright gang warfare had not broken out, at least not yet in Chicago. Moran decided he wanted to weaken Capone's position by hurting his operations on the Gulf Coast because Capone was now, literally, taking in suitcases of money almost every day.

Calling in three of the members of his Northside Gang, Moran said, "We need to do something about Capone's operations down south. He's getting too strong from the money he's making down there. All of that money has allowed him to be a real problem for us here in Chicago. He keeps horning in on our territory. So let's give him something to worry about somewhere else. You boys catch a train to New Orleans and find out from our friends down there where his whiskey is being shipped out of and put it out of business. Harry, you will be the head of this little operation. Take care of it. I am sick of the bastard! You hear me? Sick!"

"I'll take care of it, Mr. Moran. I'll let you know when it's over," Harry said. "Do you care about how we do it?"

"Yes, I care! I want him to know his operation there was taken out by us. Leave this calling card."

With that, he reached into his coat and pulled out one of his business cards from his wallet. After writing something on the card, he gave it to Harry.

"Leave that somewhere where it can be found after it's over. I want him to know who did it. Call and let me know when you have shut it down so we can be ready in case he tries to do something up here." Harry took the card and put it in his wallet.

"We'll make sure he knows. When it's too late," said Harry with a sly smile on his face.

"Okay. Good luck, boys. Happy hunting." With that, the three men left the presence of Bugsy Moran.

Two days later, the men boarded a train to New Orleans. Along with their suitcases, they carried other cases, musical instrument cases, which, in fact, held something much more dangerous.

When the men arrived in New Orleans, they found out from friends that Capone's whiskey operations were coming out of Mississippi, in particular from the Bay St. Louis area known as the Bluffs. The three men borrowed a car to drive to Bay St. Louis. They checked into the Bayside Hotel and spent a couple of days asking around town about how they could get out to the Bluffs. The next afternoon Harry asked one of the boatmen down at the city docks if he would like to make some extra money, say a hundred dollars, by taking Harry and his two friends up the bayou to a place called the Bluffs at sunset.

With the mention of the hundred dollars, the boatman said it would take more than that for him to make that trip, with all of those voodoo symbols all over the bayou around the Bluffs.

"Voodoo symbols? All around the place?" Harry asked with a quizzical look on his face.

"Lots of 'um. Everywhar up thar. Won't do it for less than two hundred dollars and I wants ma money in cash fore we leave. It's real spooky up thar," the boatman said. He figured if he was going to go into that area of that swamp at sunset, he was going to get paid and paid well for it, before they left the docks.

"Alright. Alright. Two hundred it is. I'll pay you when we leave the dock. How long will it take us to get up there?" Harry asked.

"It'll take every bit of an hour, ifn thar ain't no problems or nuthin," the boatman answered. "Be here bout five o'clock. Dat way we can git thar a little fore sunset.

At five o'clock the three men were back at the dock. Each carried an instrument case. The boatman felt better about taking them up the bayou once he saw them dressed in suits with their instrument cases. As he guided the boat away from the dock, he couldn't help but ask the obvious question.

"Are y'all goin' out thar to the Bluffs to play fer sum kind of party?" The boatman got a few stares. Trying one more time he said, "Thars been some great ones out thar, I'm told."

Harry finally answered. "Yeah, I guess you could say that. We are gonna make a lot of noise up in this old swamp."

The boatman thought about that answer for a few moments. It really didn't make any sense to him so he decided he wouldn't ask anything else.

As they were being taken up the bayou on its many turns and twists, it got darker and darker. The farther they rode into the swamp, they began to see things hanging from posts sticking out of the water.

"Are the things on these posts what you were talking about being voodoo symbols?" Harry asked the boatman.

The boatman answered, "Yep. Those be the voodoo signs and they are all over the place. I don't like'um at all."

"What is all of that stuff hanging from those posts?" Harry asked as they went by one.

"I thank its parts of pigs and goats and all. Some of dat over thar be chicken guts. Dat over there be markins with blood from chickens," the boatman said as they passed another post with things hanging from it.

"I don't like this, Harry," one of the men said with a little shake in his voice. "This is all really weird."

Harry agreed, but he didn't say so. They had a job to do and they were going to do it. As they got closer to the Bluffs, a fog began to roll in. When Harry finally saw through the now dense fog two large cement docks, he asked, "Is this the place?"

The boatman said, "Yep. Sure is."

Harry then said, "Take us to that pier on the left there."

As the boat approached the dock to their left, two of the men opened their cases and each one took out a machine gun. The boatman was so shocked that he almost rammed the little boat into the dock.

Up above the docks, peacocks screamed out their alarm as the boat neared the cement fixture. The boat then struck the dock and the men jumped onto the landing, each one nearly falling on the dock because of the darkness now completely covering the swamp. One of Nick's men heard the boat hit the dock and called out, "Who's there?" The three men answered by opening fire toward where the voice had come from. As soon as the shooting started, the boatman made the smart decision that he wanted no part of this fight and pushed his little boat back away from the dock and disappeared into the night, leaving the gunfire behind him.

The two submachine guns fired almost continuously as the men worked their way up the stairs next to the dock to the top of the bluff. They began to spread out with one man advancing off to the left of their leader and the other man advancing off to the right. A few of the kerosene lamps had already been lit and provided a background of partial light and shadows for the shooters.

Nick's men were caught completely off guard. Their automatic weapons were locked in a gun closet in one of the barns where they were usually kept because there was no need to always have them available out in the swamp. Nick did not want those types of weapons ever seen around the Bluffs. Now, his men could not get to them because they would have been illuminated by the kerosene lamps and become perfect targets for the overwhelming fire power from the two submachine guns.

Nick had been at one of the barns checking on his barrels of inventory when the firing started. When he ran outside to see what was going on, he was quickly pinned down behind a water trough. Tiny was hiding behind a small haystack while Rocko, who had been carrying his pistol, fired two shots back from behind the corner of the barn. Those shots only led to more bullets being aimed in his direction. Rocko quickly figured out it was better to save his few remaining bullets and not just shoot to be shooting.

Madeline was downstairs overseeing the preparation of dinner when the shooting began. She made her way to the front window of the dining room and peered out from behind its curtain. From time to time, even though fog had settled in, she could make out where the shooting was coming from. After seeing that gunfire from submachine guns was being directed at where she thought Nick and his men were, Madeline told Nehemiah, the black butler, to get her the sawed off double-barreled shotgun that was kept in the pantry in the kitchen. Nehemiah got the gun, loaded it and brought it back to her. She then assumed a position behind the front door with the loaded shotgun in her hands. If the shooters were going to come through the front door, some of them were going to be in for a big surprise.

The firing by Moran's men was sporadic, but deadly, for what had now been almost fifteen minutes as they gradually began to work their way in the thick fog toward the stables and the mansion. Moran's men had already reloaded several times. Nick saw one of his men get hit by the submachine gun fire early in the shooting and knew that he had probably been killed. He had also seen two of his men get wounded. Only the two shots by Rocko and occasional shots from another of Nick's men had been fired in return. Things were beginning to look bleak for everyone at the compound. It was just a matter of time until they all would be killed if something wasn't done, but there was really nothing they could do.

As the man on Harry's left was firing his submachine gun at two of Nick's men trying to hide near the front of the stables, out of the fog behind the gunner a voice yelled out, *"Monsieur!"* Hearing that word and the man's accent, the gunner turned around and was surprised to be looking at a man wearing a long red coat, a white shirt and white trousers and holding a musket. The man in the long coat fired his weapon, knocking the gunner to the ground with a big hole in his chest.

Upon hearing the loud shot, the second gunner called out to his friend. Not too long after the loud shot, behind the second gunner a man appeared out of the fog dressed in a pirate's outfit and also carrying a musket. The figure yelled out, *"Monsieur, je suis ici!"* As the second gunner turned to see where the voice was coming from, the figure fired his weapon. The second gunner was blown completely over by the close blast of the powerful musket.

There was silence. Harry called out, "Ben! Sam!" but there was no response. As he continued calling out for his two associates, another man slipped up out of the fog behind Harry with a long dagger raised high above his head and quickly brought the dagger down using both hands, stabbing Harry in the back between his shoulder blades. Harry yelled out a blood-curdling scream and fell dead to the ground. The area was now completely quiet.

After a few moments Nick and his men, cautiously, began to come out from where they had been hiding. They walked over toward where they had heard the scream. They saw Claude standing there with the blood-stained dagger in his hands. They also saw the two strangely dressed men slowly appear from the fog, each holding his musket at the ready. Nick had never seen either one of the men before.

Claude turned and said to the two men, *"C'est fini."*

After looking from one to the other of the two men and then at Claude, Nick said gratefully, "Thank you. Thank you so much. You saved our lives."

Claude said, "I saw them coming through the fog in the swamp. They deet not look like people you would be expecting, especially so early in the week and on a night like thees. When I heard the shooting, I got my two friends here and we came to see if we could help out."

Nick's men were speechless. Nick finally broke the silence by telling his men, "Check the pockets of these guys. See if you can find out who they are."

Nick's men, after once again looking at the strangely dressed men who had just saved their lives, bent over and began going through the pockets of the dead men.

Soon one of Nick's men stood up, walked over to him, and said, "Boss, look at this!" He showed Nick a business card that had writing on the back of it. The writing said, "To Al from Bugsy."

As Nick and his men looked at the card, the man in the pirate outfit began speaking rapidly in French to Claude. The other man also said something to Claude in French. Claude turned to Nick and said in his heavy French accent, "They want to know if they can take the bodies of the men they killed with them because, in the swamp, they usually get to keep what they kill."

Nick looked at Claude in disbelief and, although stunned by what he had just heard, after a moment said, "Claude, these were bad men. If their friends know where they were, other bad men will come looking for them. I think it would be better if you just let us take care of getting rid of the bodies. That way, nobody will ever find them."

Claude looked at Nick and said, "*Monsieur,* I can assure you, if my men take them, nobody will ever find them either."

Nick did not say anything. He began to have some idea what the implications were from what Claude had said. He looked away in deep thought. Claude saw Nick's reaction and finally said, "But since they are on your land here, you take care of them."

Claude turned and said a few words in French. The two men with the muskets looked at Nick and his men and then gradually began stepping backward into the fog, still holding their muskets at the ready, until both had completely disappeared.

Nick turned to Claude and said, "Claude, where did they get those muskets?"

Claude looked at the ground for a moment and then, lifting his eyes to Nick, answered, "The same place that long red coat came from, off of dead British soldiers at the battle of New Orleans." Pausing for a brief moment to look at a nearby body, Claude then looked at Nick and said, "*Au revoir, mon ami.*" He turned and also disappeared into the fog.

Nick's men looked at each other and one of them said, under his breath, "Did you see those guys?! They disappeared like they were ghosts!"

As Nick and his men slowly began moving the bodies, Claude's voice called out of the fog saying, "*Monsieur* Neek, now we are even."

Chapter Twenty-seven

One night in late August, Tiny drove a Rolls-Royce Phantom limousine in at Cypress Landing. He loved driving the Phantom. The luxury car, built at the Rolls-Royce plant in Springfield, Massachusetts, was one of the ultimate limousines of the day. The car had an open cab for the chauffeur and a cabin for its travelers that had upholstery in embroidered tapestry with silver plating finishing off the fittings. The extravagant and expensive car had an automatic engine control that could be set to keep the car going at a speed determined by its driver.

Nick loved automobiles, especially those that were top of the line cars built with special care such as the Phantom. Anytime he and Madeline now took part in the New Orleans social scene, Nick saw to it that the car was brought out and made available for their use. He made arrangements for the Phantom to be kept and cared for at the Lambert Garage, a very exclusive garage in New Orleans where it was maintained and stored when it was not in service. Madeline, with Nick's permission, saw to it that the car was available for use this particular night.

Out of the limousine stepped a mysterious figure who wore black riding boots, a black cape, and a black hat. The figure boarded a waiting boat and was taken in a thick fog to the Bluffs. At the boat dock at the Bluffs the figure was met by Madeline and escorted to the guest house, where the two stayed together for two days. Madeline instructed the cook to deliver meals on a tray and leave them on the porch at specified times. After the two days, in the late evening, the figure, again dressed in black, left the Bluffs' dock by boat and was taken to meet Tiny, who was waiting with the limousine at Cypress Landing.

Nick now spent most of his time out at the Bluffs. The operation was going very well and, with most of the shipping activities taking place from there, it was not as necessary for him to be in town as much. He spent a lot of time checking shipments that were brought in to make sure he was getting what had been ordered. He had to hand it to Fernando. Each shipment was almost exactly what Nick had been notified would be on a particular ship. There had been only slight discrepancies so far which made Nick's job much easier. His only worry was getting and keeping their products stored in the barns at the Bluffs until there were transport vehicles, whether cars or trucks, either at or on their way to Cypress Landing.

It wasn't too long before there was a need to have a dock on the opposite, or eastern, side of the Bay of St. Louis. Nick positioned this dock about three quarters of a mile up a body of water called Rotten Bayou. Through negotiations conducted by Marquette, Nick purchased a four hundred and eighty acre tract of land bordering the bayou which was only about three miles from a county road. This location provided a better departure point than Cypress Landing for the delivery of booze to the honky-tonks, speakeasies and other locations in southern, central and eastern Mississippi, as well as coastal Alabama and, eventually, even portions of the panhandle of Florida. Shipments to southern Louisiana, southwest Mississippi and a portion of Texas continued to be made from the existing facilities at Cypress Landing.

At first, the demand for the liquor was much more than could be supplied so Nick had the task of making sure his shipping efforts became large enough to meet demand, were timely, efficient, and, of course, as discreet as possible. Madeline assisted with some of the scheduling for the shipments and, occasionally, checked the cargo as it arrived at the Bluffs. She also spent time at Cypress Landing watching the transfers of the booze from the boats to the waiting cars and trucks. She was amazed at how resourceful Nick had been by equipping cars, a few at first and then many more, with hidden tanks so that their products could be put directly into the tanks and then carried to their destination. She watched her brother deal with the problem of cars riding low to the ground when their hidden tanks were fully loaded. Many of the cars were refitted with stronger suspension springs so the cars would have less of a look of being loaded down.

Madeline spent more of her time overseeing the functions of the staff of the Bluffs. She made sure that enough food was purchased to feed all of their employees, not only at the mansion, but also those involved in the shipping portion of their activities, which was a major undertaking. There were four employees who took care of work requirements at the Bluffs and any other matters that Nick or Madeline needed taken care of. Those employees consisted of two black females who cooked and cleaned, a black man who was assigned to the cooks to assist them, and a creole man who served as butler and general problem-solver.

There were two workers, both black men, at the barns and docks as well as the now five "visitors" from up north. The two dock workers unloaded boats and took care of the barns. They reported to Tiny, who reported to Nick. The five "visitors," which included Tiny, reported directly to Nick. All of them, as well as the mansion workers, stayed in one of the two bunk houses on the backside of the property. Nick eventually had a smaller building constructed not too far from the rear of the mansion, which he set aside for the black female workers.

Nick and Madeline usually shared meals together, using those times to catch up on how things were running. Nick spent more and more time with the business at the Bluffs location, especially once it had become so successful, while Madeline circulated more and more in New Orleans. Very seldom did she go into the little town of Bay St. Louis, mainly because she had no interest in going there when she could go to the big city of New Orleans. Having lived in Chicago and Detroit, she was used to being in a big city and having access to all of the shopping and things to do that go along with a large city. She would occasionally go to some of the bigger parties held in the Bay St. Louis area, but she always attended with Nick and they never stayed too long at any of them.

As the business became more and more successful, demand increased for their products with the result that even more time was spent unloading and loading shipments. Barrel upon barrel was unloaded from the ships from Cuba and kept in the barns at the Bluffs until vehicles were available at Cypress Landing, and eventually at Rotten Bayou, to take the cargo to its final destinations. The ships left, usually after spending a day or so at the Bluffs, and went to the various loading docks for the timber companies. From there they made their trips to Cuba packed with pine lumber.

Nick occasionally sent someone, in the early days usually one of the muscle men Capone had sent from up north, on trips throughout their service area to find new markets for their products. After developing local contacts Nick felt they could trust, those local contacts were sent out looking for businesses that might have an interest in what Nick's operation could supply them.

Nick was not seeing Helen any more, but he missed her. He had always been concerned about the sheriff finding out about them, and with the sheriff and his men now being such a good addition to his operation, the more he thought about it the more Nick knew he had made the right decision about ending their relationship. He did realize with every passing day, though, how much he had loved her and what a void not seeing her had left in his life.

When Nick spent time at his Bay St. Louis office, he dealt mostly with the legitimate aspects of his lumber business. He hired an older woman, Bessie Howell, to keep his books and occasionally work in the downtown office. Nick had looked long and hard to find just the right person for that part-time job and finally was told about Bessie by one of the men that Nick sent out to find new locations for his products. Bessie, in her late fifties, Nick guessed, was the man's sister, She was hired by Nick once he became convinced from talking with her that she could keep quiet about what all was going on and would know how to look out after things when Nick was not around.

One day when he was working out of his office downtown, Nick left to go get lunch at the Bay Café. While he was walking over to the restaurant from his office, he saw Helen, who now had the appearance of a pregnant woman, as she walked down the street near the courthouse. Nick crossed the street to talk with her, although she almost made an effort to avoid him, but at the last minute changed her mind.

"Hi, Helen. It's great to see you."

"Hello, Mr. Gable. It is nice to see you too."

There was formality in her voice, but a warm smile was on her face.

"How is the new prospect for the family doing?"

"It would be doing better if its mother could see its father," she replied looking straight at Nick.

"I am sure its father is thinking about it every day, and its mother," Nick said after briefly looking around him and her to make sure no one was overhearing their conversation.

"I really miss its father, Nick. I really do. It's breaking my heart. I am so lonely. Don't get me wrong. My husband has been very understanding with my condition. He just doesn't understand why I am so sad most of the time and, of course, I can't tell him. Playing the organ and the piano at church services has been a blessing because it takes my mind off of everything."

Nick nodded his head and said, "I have heard that the music you play for the church services is really something special." Then, leaning closer to Helen, he softly said, "I just want you to know that I am going to set up the education fund that I mentioned, Helen. The money will be provided indirectly somehow for the baby. I just wanted you to know that."

She answered, "Now how are you going to do that, Nick, when you can't even talk to me, much less leave a trail leading back to you? How are you going to take care of that, Nick?"

"I don't know yet, Helen. I really don't. All I know is I am going to do it. I will find a way somehow. I am looking into it. If I knew it wouldn't possibly cost the lives of you and your baby, as well as mine, I would do a lot of things so differently, Helen. Please believe me when I say that. I really mean it."

"I have no idea what you are talking about, Nick. I really don't. All I know is I fell in love with you and wanted to be with you for the rest of my life and, when I got pregnant, you deserted me. You just left me."

As she said that, Helen's eyes filled with tears. Nick didn't want this to take place on the main street of Bay St. Louis. He would much rather have her in his arms in the upstairs bedroom of his office, but he knew that was impossible and would probably never happen again. There was simply too much danger, for all of them, for that to happen now, if ever again.

At the same time, he truly missed her. Did he ever, ever miss her. It had been over nine weeks now since he had last seen her. He missed just being with her. He missed her wonderful personality and laughing with her, not to mention the fabulous sex. He also missed the information he could occasionally coax from her. But most of all, he just missed her.

Now that Sheriff Patterson was part of his business in Hancock County, there was no need to get any further information from Helen. Instead, Sheriff Patterson passed the information needed to protect Nick's activities directly to him. The sheriff's information was much more detailed and accurate. Seeing the tears well up in her eyes, he knew he would have to leave. Just walk away, as he had before, and it was a heart breaking thought. But he had no option and the worst thing about it was, he would have to seem callous about it. She would never, and should never, have any idea why he did not have an option.

"Helen, I have to go. Please take care of yourself. And I promise things will be taken care of." With that he turned and walked away, but he missed her the moment he took the first step.

* * *

A few days later, Claude was out in a particularly swampy area near the Bluffs checking on voodoo symbols. Nick saw this as an opportunity to talk with Carlotta alone as she stood at the edge of the main bluff watching Claude. Once again he noticed that she was, in her own way, a striking woman, a pure natural beauty. Her olive skin was enhanced by her dark brown eyes and black hair. Nick had thought, the few times Carlotta had pulled her hair back, her classic features were such that he would have been more than happy to be seen with her at any social function. However, when he thought about her, the first thing that always popped up in his mind was her dancing nude out in the swamp that night with that huge snake. He could never seem to get that thought out of his mind.

"Hi, Carlotta. How are things?" Nick asked as he walked onto the last piece of dry land near the Bluffs where Claude had left Carlotta while he took the boat farther into the swamp.

"Hello, Mr. Nick," she answered. "Good. Claude is putting up a few more symbols," she said, pointing over in the general direction of their boat.

"Okay. Again, thank you for your help with all of this. You know you are the first voodoo priestess I have ever been around," he said.

"I do what I have to do," she responded.

"What do you mean by that?" Nick asked.

"I was born in this swamp, Mr. Nick. I was raised in this swamp," she said looking back out over the vast swamp.

"Please call me Nick, okay?" Nick said.

"Okay, Nick," she said, smiling her beautiful smile at the same time. Nick had to remind himself to not forget that Carlotta was Claude's woman. He remembered how forcibly Claude had made that point to him when he had first introduced Carlotta to him.

"There are lots of things that happen out here that you and your people will never know about. I do what I have been raised to do. It is important to my people. I am not going to disappoint them, but some of what I get called on to do is, how do you say it, a pretend," she said.

"Oh, you mean like a fantasy," Nick said.

She slowly nodded her head "yes," being careful to not look at Nick as she did.

Nick began to feel better about what he had seen that night in the bayou. He was beginning to understand what she was trying to tell him. She may be a voodoo priestess but a lot of it, at least her involvement, may be something that she did because of how she was raised in the swamp. It could mean, he thought, that she didn't necessarily believe all she was called upon to do. Yet she could not say anything because it might cause her problems with those she called "my people."

Nick noticed Claude was headed back in. He had to be quick about what he was going to say next, and at the same time be very careful in his choice of words. He did not want to presume anything and did not want to say something that could upset his relationship with Claude.

"Carlotta, I appreciate both your and Claude's friendship. If there is anyway I can ever help either of you, all you have to do is let me know."

Nick wanted her to know that if she, specifically, ever needed help, he would do whatever he could. From the look on her face, he could tell she understood. Her wonderful smile brightened up her beautiful face, but she said nothing since Claude was now within hearing distance.

"Hello, Claude," Nick offered as Claude made his way up the bluff.

"*Bonjour, Monsieur* Neek," Claude responded with a broad smile.

"How is your work coming along?" Nick asked as Claude reached the top of the bluff.

"*Je suis finis.*" Claude said in French, almost as if to see if Nick really did understand much French.

"*Tres bien,*" Nick answered with a big smile. "Is the place pretty well surrounded with symbols now?"

"*Oui, Monsieur,*" Claude responded. "The symbols are now everywhere."

"Claude, you know that area around Bayou Michele, where the channel splits into five different streams and bayous?"

"*Oui, Monsieur. Tout le monde* gets lost there. Everybody. A person must really know the bayou to get to here from there," Claude said, clearly knowing exactly where Nick was talking about.

"If you would, just make sure there are symbols on each one of those open water areas as they come out of Bayou Michele. Leave unmarked only the main channel going away from the Bluffs."

"*Oui, Monsieur.* I will have to go back and pick a few up," he answered laughing. "I marked them all, *Monsieur!*"

Nick joined in the laughter as Carlotta smiled.

"If you will take care of that, then we should be set. Anyone who gets lost up in here would probably follow the unmarked way out and that will help them go the right way."

Claude nodded his head in agreement.

"I will take care of eet," he said.

"Well, I must be going. Good to see you both," Nick said, nodding first to Carlotta and then to Claude. "Thanks again, Claude."

"*Il n'y a pas de quoi,*" Claude answered.

As he left, Nick's mind went back to his conversation with Carlotta. That conversation was something he would spend a lot of time thinking about for the next several days, trying to interpret just exactly what she might have meant by what she had said.

Madeline had been out riding the Bluffs area and had seen Nick talking with Carlotta. She had not seen Claude in the boat several yards away and only noticed him when he had waved. Madeline felt that it was time to do something about Nick and Carlotta. He was having too much to do with her. Madeline did not want to let her big brother get too close with some voodoo priestess of dubious heritage, for several reasons. The primary reason was that if word ever got back to Sicily that her brother was seeing a voodoo queen, the entire family would probably be ostracized by the members of their church. There were other reasons as well. At the right time, she would be more forceful about making sure the relationship went no further.

Chapter Twenty-eight

New Orleans District Attorney Fuller did not know what had happened to his informants. The first one he sent over to the Mississippi Coast had disappeared and the second one had been missing now for several weeks. He had no idea where either one of them were or what had happened to them. The only thing he did know was that illegal booze was all over south Louisiana and New Orleans. He knew that because some of his close friends and supporters had told him they had seen it and wanted to know what he was going to do about it. It seemed to be everywhere.

Even though the revenuers had made some progress with their arrests of the two men who had almost broken Lovelady's leg when they hit him with their car, Lovelady's men had beaten Simon Montgomery so badly that he eventually had died. Lovelady was still recovering from having had his jaw shot off in the shootout. No other information had been uncovered since Lovelady had been put in the hospital. Nothing had happened except for the supposed sighting by the three agents in the boat of what may have been one of the "ghost" ships. The people in Hancock County were not willing to cooperate with the revenuers because word had spread around like wildfire about the violent tactics they had been using.

Fuller was not getting any cooperation out of anybody in Louisiana. No one was saying anything. The people of both states were enjoying their easy access to alcohol and did not seem to want that pleasure interrupted, even though it was illegal. He was beginning to wonder if he would ever find out what had happened to his undercover informants.

* * *

After a lot of thought, Nick decided that he had to have something fun to do for those who worked for him. He began wondering about what he could do to provide some type of entertainment for them in the mostly rural Hancock County. It would be to his benefit if he could keep them in the area and not have to continuously take them over to New Orleans every weekend. He decided that the entertainment he needed was a boat that had gambling on it. Boats that cruised the Mississippi River generally had gambling on board, as well as prostitution along with bars that served food and illegal liquor. Nick also realized that such a boat might give its owner, in this case that meant him, the opportunity to relieve the workers of some of the money they had been paid by him due to their work in his growing business. With a boat, he would be accomplishing two things at the same time. He would get back some of that money, and he would be providing them with a diversion from the mosquitoes and hot working conditions that they faced daily. He began putting his plan into action.

While in New Orleans he inquired about any river boats that might be for sale and was told about the *Excalibur*. The *Excalibur* was a river boat that, Nick thought, was the perfect size for what he had in mind. It was a version of the famous *Robert E. Lee* paddle wheel river boat, being just over two hundred sixty feet long and about thirty-five feet wide. It had twin smoke stacks and an upper deck with the bottom being an open area for any livestock that could be transported to various locations along the river. The upper deck had a walkway with a railing that went all the way around the boat, giving it a nice appearance. At the rear of the boat, the walkway provided an area that overlooked the paddlewheel. The boat, which had been only one of many just like it on the river at one time, was coming to the end of its usefulness as a transport since the paddlewheel era had long since passed.

Before purchasing the *Excalibur* for a price he just could not pass up, Nick quietly, through Marquette, bought five hundred sixty acres of land mixed in with swamp land along the north shore of Bayou Caddy. Bayou Caddy was a rather large bayou located about ten miles south of the town of Bay St. Louis. On the south side of the bayou, opposite the land Nick bought, was a long, slender island known as Point Clear Island. Point Clear Island ran, generally, east and west for about twelve miles parallel to the bayou. Nick's property had a little under a mile of water frontage along the north shore of the bayou. At one of the small inlets along the undulating north shoreline of Bayou Caddy, Nick had constructed a rather large and sturdy wooden dock.

With the cooperation of a riverboat pilot from New Orleans that Nick hired to bring the boat around from that city to Bayou Caddy, the *Excalibur* arrived just before dusk on a Monday evening in late September. It was taken up the bayou to the dock and positioned there through the expert seamanship of the pilot. Traveling up any bayou was dangerous for a boat the size of the *Excalibur* and especially on a bayou as shallow and narrow as Bayou Caddy. However, the boat was a flat-bottomed vessel and, under the guidance of the experienced pilot, the *Excalibur* made the trip without any problems.

Soon Nick had his builders spending time at the site cleaning off the bottom floor of the vessel and putting a wooden layer on top of the floor that was made from some of the pine timber from the area near the boat and its pier. This also had the effect of opening up the land next to the pier so that wagons and cars could be parked nearby, depending on the mode of transportation used to get there. About three-quarters of a mile from the landing was a local dirt and shell road that eventually ran to the east to a county road. That county road then went north along the edge of the Mississippi Sound to the town of Bay St. Louis. There was no question that, in order to get to Nick's boat, a person had to know where it was and which turns to make and roads to take to get there. There was simply no way to just stumble upon the *Excalibur*, and that was exactly what Nick wanted, just like at the Bluffs.

Nick had to find someone who could run the gambling operation he was going to put on the first floor and the bordello he planned for the second floor. He spent time in New Orleans talking with people and going into the French Quarter, which had numerous places that housed both operations. During one of his trips, in an out of the way nightclub he watched a short, almost round woman named Lillie, who wore garish makeup and had on more jewelry than he had ever seen on one woman before, stop a fight by clubbing a drunk patron on his head with a bottle holding the remnants of a fifth of scotch as she sat in a tall chair near the piano. With one motion of her left hand, two men showed up immediately and carried the offender out the front door and, literally, threw him out on the street. A man showed up to clean up the remains of the bottle and its contents and the party got back underway. Nick's conversations with two of the bar girls revealed an almost love for the short, portly woman by everyone who had ever worked for her. He concluded that he needed to see if he could hire this woman to come work for him on the *Excalibur*.

On his third trip back to the establishment, he noticed that she recognized he had been there before. As he walked through the door past her post on the tall chair next to the end of the bar, she said with a big smile, "Welcome back, honey." He laughed to himself as he walked over to a table and chair near the far corner of the room, almost exactly where he sat before. He knew she called everybody "honey." After watching her direct traffic for about an hour, Nick decided the next time she walked around the room, which she did with some regularity, he would try to talk with her. It wasn't too much later, he had his chance.

When she walked by his table, he stood up and said, "Could I buy the lady a drink?"

She looked at him with a look that told Nick that this short, extremely wide woman was quickly evaluating him.

"Why, honey, when a man as good looking as you are, stands up, and calls me a lady, he can buy me just about whatever he wants."

Nick had to laugh. She knew what she was doing, and doing it well. This woman had a sharp wit and probably had good judgment. Both would come in handy out on the bayou.

"My name is Lillie," she said as Nick pulled a chair out for her at his table. She maneuvered her large frame into the chair, adjusting the top of her dress in an attempt to cover her rather large endowments. She had her garish makeup on again, he noticed, along with so much jewelry she could hardly walk under all of its weight. Then, before the next word was mentioned, he noticed her perfume. Oh, did he ever notice that perfume. It almost took his breath away.

"I'm Nick Gable. What would you like to drink?" he asked as she settled in.

"Nice to meet you, honey. They know what I drink." With that, she raised her hand and one of the bartenders sprung into action.

"What are you drinking?" she asked as if to hurry up and get past that point.

"I will take whatever you are having," Nick said, with the passing thought that his decision might not have been a wise one. She raised her hand this time holding up two fingers, obviously having given that signal before.

"What's on your mind, honey?" she said getting right down to business. He had to laugh again to himself. This woman did not waste time. The more he smelled her perfume, the more he decided he did not have any time to waste. If he had to smell her perfume for very long, it was going to give him a headache, at the very least.

"I know you have been in here at least three times, including tonight. Are you a cop?" she asked, looking at him intently. Nick chuckled out loud this time.

"No, no! I am not a cop."

"Well, they come in here all the time wanting money. I just figured you were the next one." If she was going to be so direct, then he was going to be direct also.

"I want you to come to work for me," Nick said, watching her for a reaction.

"Now, honey!" She stopped and started laughing. Then she continued, "Just what is it you want me to do for you?"

"I want you to run a place just like this, except over in Mississippi." The drinks came and were placed on the table by a bartender who quickly disappeared.

"Honey, the last time I checked, and it hasn't been recently, they don't even have any places over in Mississippi like this one, at least not any that I would want to work at."

With that, she took a long swig from her drink. Nick looked at her as he picked up his drink, and said, "Well, they do now." He took one sip of the drink and knew that was the last time he would ever order what she ordered. After putting the drink down on the table, he said, "Tomorrow morning at ten o'clock, I will pick you up out front and take you for a visit. It will take us most of the day to make the round-trip."

"You are serious, aren't you?" she said, taking another sip from her terrible drink.

He leaned forward and said, "I will pay you twice whatever you are making here." He definitely got her attention with that statement.

"Honey, are you alright? Don't joke with me about something like that."

"I am not joking. Just come take a look at the set-up. Tomorrow at ten o'clock. Okay?"

Looking at him with an expression on her face that indicated she was willing to, at least, hear more, she said, "Okay, then. Ten o'clock sharp tomorrow it is."

Nick then got up, left a large bill on the table, and walked out. He hoped she took the job. She would be good to have around but he would have to get her to do something about that perfume.

Lillie was standing there waiting for him at ten o'clock the next morning. Nick quickly noticed that she was not wearing as much perfume, which really made him happy, nor was she wearing a garish outfit. No, instead, she wore a long, loose skirt, blouse and boots.

Nick drove her to Bay St. Louis in his car and, using the cutoff, took her directly to the *Excalibur*. She was impressed by what she saw. She had seen the boat before and saw how it had been fixed up so that it was now a rather nice boat, especially for one that was out in the middle of a bayou just south of nowhere. Nick told her she could run it and only had him to report to. When he again mentioned that he would double her pay, she agreed to Nick's proposition. Nick also told her that she would be responsible for recruiting the prostitutes and that no local girls were ever to be hired. Her girls should only come from New Orleans and even then, preferably, they should be girls new to the area from other parts of the country.

Soon the *Excalibur* was open for business. All of Nick's employees, their business associates and their guests and friends were told about the boat and encouraged to visit. Select visitors enjoyed themselves with all of the gambling and prostitution. Nick made sure that, at least for the first few months, there was a lot of winning by those visiting the *Excalibur*. Lillie made sure her girls were somewhat attractive, but most of all, they were friendly and available. It wasn't too long before there were good crowds every night, especially Friday and Saturday nights.

Nick had decided Sundays would be closed days for the *Excalibur*. He didn't want to do anything that might cause an uproar with the churches in the area. He felt, and it turned out that he was right, that most of the people would not be concerned with his operation on the bayou. To begin with, it was away from Bay St. Louis and Waveland, and everything else for that matter. For those who were interested in what the *Excalibur* had to offer, the place was in good shape and did provide something for people to do, which was definitely something new to Hancock County.

Nick was amazed at how much additional money he began making from this endeavor. Capone was also surprised by its success, but was pleased that Nick had consulted with him for his approval before he had put this plan into action. Nick provided Capone with most of its profits, roughly seventy-five percent after expenses, but Capone allowed Nick to keep the rest for himself as a reward for doing so well in providing this additional source of income.

As for Madeline, Nick told her about the *Excalibur* and why he had brought the boat over from New Orleans. Although the boat was exactly what was needed to provide the area with at least some entertainment, Nick told Madeline that it was not a place where a lady of Madeline's newly found social standing should be seen. Since her social life in the New Orleans area had become so active and was also becoming important to the entire operation, Madeline easily agreed that she should not be seen at the *Excalibur*.

Not too long after the boat had opened, Nick was contacted by Sheriff Patterson and told to meet him at the boat on the next Tuesday night at around eight-thirty. Nick did not like to spend a lot of time out at the boat, which was just about as far south in the county as a person could go and was not in any way close to the Bluffs. However, he did go out there from time to time to see how the operation was doing. He wanted to keep an eye on things, especially at the beginning, and make sure that Lillie was running the activities at the boat the way they should be.

While out at the boat, Nick always tried to stay mostly on the second floor of the boat in the stern area. That way he could discreetly observe who was coming to the boat without being easily seen. He noticed that Lillie was an excellent manager, especially with the help of the two men from the Bluffs, and on the weekends sometimes three, that he had assigned to be at the boat. They were there to help her, if she should need it, with drunks, bar fights, and anything else that might come up.

At eight-thirty this particular Tuesday night as Nick slowly walked the back portion of the upper deck, he periodically looked down toward that part of the landing near the entrance to the gambling area. Eventually, he saw Sheriff Patterson appear out of the darkness, all complete wearing his western hat and with a big gun in its holster on his right hip. As far as Nick knew, this was the sheriff's first visit to the boat. Nick had instructed his men up the road at the gate to the property to let Sheriff Patterson through when he appeared. He had told them that the sheriff could probably be identified by the western hat that he usually wore. Nick went downstairs to meet his visitor. By the time he got down the stairs and into the gambling room, the sheriff was already inside. Lillie was sitting on her stool at the end of the bar and stayed there, having been told by Nick to let him handle this situation.

"Hello, sheriff," Nick said, wondering again to himself why the sheriff had wanted this meeting to take place out here. Nick had noticed that the sheriff seemed to be by himself.

"Hello, Nick. Just wanted to come take a look at what you got going on out here," he said as he constantly moved his eyes around the room.

"Well, as you can see, it's just people enjoying some time off from their worries," Nick replied, trying to put a good face on what the sheriff was looking at.

After a quick look, the sheriff walked through the room toward the side of the boat opposite from where he had entered. Nick followed him and soon they were on the lower walkway outside of the gambling room. After using a set of stairs to go up to the second floor walkway of the boat, they walked over to the railing where the sheriff raised his big, cowboy-booted foot and put it on the middle rail. That caused Nick to remember what he had previously been told, which was that the sheriff always wore cowboy boots. Nick wondered what Helen's comment would have been about that.

"Nick, you've got some operation here. Cost you a lot of money to put this all together."

The sheriff was now lighting up a cigarette as he looked southward out over the bayou toward Point Clear Island in the distance. Turning to look at Nick after lighting his cigarette, Wild Bill said, "I am going to assume you have four thousand dollars a month set aside for me and the boys for this little operation."

Nick, nodding his head in agreement, said, "Always had that in my plans, sheriff. It will be delivered the same time as the other, if that's alright with you. Just didn't know exactly how much it should be."

Wild Bill took his boot off of the railing, turned to face Nick, and said, "Now you know. I am glad we have that little piece of business out of the way."

Looking down the stairway they had just come up, the sheriff continued. "Nick, I don't want any problems out here. This is different from your other operations. You keep a tight rein on this one, okay? I don't want something cropping up in the community because of all of this. Are we in agreement on that?"

Nick nodded his head in the affirmative. He had no choice. Besides, that was not too much to ask, Patterson being the sheriff and all.

"Don't worry, sheriff. If at all possible, any problems from out here will be dealt with here. I will let you know if something comes up that we can't handle for whatever the reason. And if you would, sheriff, let me know if something is brought to your attention that I need to be aware of or take care of out here."

"You can count on that, Nick. I don't want any of my citizens being taken advantage of by any of your games on this boat. Is that clear?"

"That's clear, sheriff. We'll keep all the games fair."

"Good," the sheriff said as he shifted his eyes back to Nick.

"One more thing, Nick. I understand you've got some girls on this second floor here. Get them checked out by a doctor in New Orleans every now and then, okay? There are plenty of them over there that will do that."

"You got it, sheriff."

As the sheriff began to move to go downstairs, Nick said, "Sheriff, could I ask you about something else before we go back downstairs?"

"Sure, Nick. What's on your mind?"

"One night not too long ago, I heard a sound coming from out in the swamp and noticed a faint light a good distance away from my house. I got one of my men and we went to check it out. When we got there, we stopped along the edge of this small bayou close to where the noise was coming from. We saw a group of people dancing to the beat of drums with what looked like dead chickens on the ground all around them. I think it was some sort of voodoo ceremony. It wasn't too long and out came this woman with a huge, white python around her neck."

The sheriff looked at Nick, but did not offer any comment on what had been said so Nick continued.

"I had met her before and had actually gotten her and her boyfriend to put up more voodoo symbols around my place out there to keep people away. She is not the one I want to ask you about though."

Now making sure he was watching the sheriff's face to see what kind of expression was going to take place, Nick said, "I also saw a really tall black man dancing around out there. He was at least seven feet tall and was very thin. I asked Dudley Marquette about who the guy might be and he said that it could have been a man known as Dr. John Montenet."

Nick could see that the sheriff was now paying closer attention to what he was saying so he continued.

"Then, Dudley told me that Dr. John has been dead for over fifty years or so."

Hearing that, the sheriff did something that Nick was not expecting. He laughed. Not just a little chuckle, but a complete belly laugh.

"Dudley told you that, did he?" the sheriff said with a big smile on his face.

"Yes, he did, as a matter of fact," Nick answered, now completely puzzled by the sheriff's response.

"And you have been wondering ever since then about how that seven foot tall Negro, that you know you saw, could be out there if ol' Dudley told you he had died so long ago."

The sheriff made his statement with the smile still on his face. Nick was now even more interested in how this conversation was going to come out.

"As a matter of fact, sheriff, I have been wondering about all of it because I know I saw a seven foot tall black man out there dancing that night."

The sheriff chuckled and said, "I have no doubt you did see a seven foot tall Negro out there, and I don't doubt that Dudley got you thinking that it was ol' Dr. John himself." He chuckled again.

Taking a moment, the sheriff then said, "Nick, when a body was found in the swamp a few months ago, I looked into things out there and even had some interesting conversations with a few friends of mine in New Orleans who know a little something about voodoo. During those conversations we talked about Dr. John. He's a legend in these parts as far as voodoo is concerned."

The sheriff then looked at Nick with the hint of a smile on his face and said, "What I found out was that it's true that Dr. John is supposed to have passed away some time ago. But Nick, he had fifteen children. What you saw out there was probably one of his sons, who is also into voodoo."

Nick immediately felt embarrassed, but he had to admit to himself that he also felt relieved. At least he had an explanation that he could understand of a situation that he had thought about several times since he had talked with Marquette.

The sheriff added, now with a wide grin on his face, "That ought to help you sleep a little bit better at night out there, Nick."

Smiling, the sheriff turned, went down the stairs to the first floor and walked into the gambling room with Nick following close behind him. Just as he walked inside, one of the players at a nearby roulette wheel, being more than a little drunk and slurring his words, said, "Sheriff, looks like a whole lot of illegal stuff goin' on in here. Dis gamblin here and all dis illegal whiskey." He then held up his shot glass which was half full and said, "Whacha gonna do bout it, sheriff?"

Nick could have shot the guy for putting the sheriff, and Nick, on the spot like that. The room got almost quiet as everyone waited for the sheriff's answer. The sheriff looked at the fool that had asked the question, and then moved his eyes around the room.

Looking back at the fool, the sheriff said, "The only thing I see here is a bunch of my voters having a good time. But if you ask any more stupid questions, I just might have to take you in for being drunk."

The room broke out with howls of laughter. Hoots and even a few cheers followed as the sheriff continued his walk toward the doorway leading out to the dock. Nick had to smile as he watched Wild Bill leave the boat. Patterson had been elected sheriff for exactly the reason he had just shown. He had incredible common sense and knew how to handle people and situations just like that one. The county was lucky to have him. Patterson was lucky to have Helen.

* * *

Bobby Thornton owned and operated a large seafood processing plant, named Thornton Seafood of course, near downtown Bay St.

237

Louis. He was one of the few people in that town who had a little money in the local bank. Of course, a bad year in the seafood industry always affected how much the Thornton family had in that bank. Some years they were closer to being bankrupt than anyone ever knew, but they always kept a good face on for the benefit of the community. Pledges to the church were always made and kept, even when it was really not very comfortable for them to do so.

Benny Thornton, Bobby and Hilda Thornton's first of four children, seemed to always know that his dad was thought of as an important man in the community. He had been told that on several occasions while growing up by various grown-ups, usually men who wanted his dad to do something for them. His dad was always one of the first people to be approached by someone asking for a contribution for their favorite charity or maybe even a short term loan to carry them over to pay day. His dad was regularly seen having a cup of coffee with Mayor Foucher, Sheriff Patterson and other community leaders at Josie's Diner on Main Street not too far from the courthouse.

As Benny grew up he saw how the local leaders paid attention to what his dad had to say and would often consult him before taking any action affecting the little town. Seeing this, Benny just naturally began to assume he was important also and in fifth grade began to let everybody know that.

The teachers noticed it at school, but were worried about saying something to the oldest son of one of Bay St. Louis's leading citizens. The only teacher who did, Benny's sixth grade teacher Miss Harriett Chandler, soon found herself confronted by the boy's father. Benny heard all about how his dad had talked in such a loud voice in the teacher's room the day after she had corrected the boy's behavior in front of the class. He noticed how she walked around after that like she was scared of seeing his dad again in such a foul mood.

For Benny, that was all he needed to encourage him to try to get away with things that other kids his age would not even think about, much less dare to do. Benny would do things like call out in the dark to someone, usually of a very senior age, who might be in their house enjoying a nice peaceful evening. When they came to the door, Benny and one or two of his friends would enjoy throwing rocks at their door or on their house just to watch them react in surprise, anger, or sometimes even fear. The boys would immediately run down the road yelling and laughing at the commotion they had just caused.

As he grew older, Benny's pranks became more serious. Benny graduated from throwing rocks at the houses of elderly people to throwing eggs at people on the front porches of those houses while they were relaxing during the evening. Eventually, he began to do things such as trying to scare a horse drawn wagon or cutting the tires of the few automobiles in town. Benny enjoyed watching as the car's owner would come up to his car and find out, either as he first walked up or shortly after he tried to go down the street, that he was in for a lot of work fixing what had happened to his tires.

When at the age of seventeen and in his senior year of high school Benny was allowed to use his dad's car, he was the envy of every boy his age in town. All the girls wanted to ride in Benny's car, even though some of them knew that Benny had been rumored to do things that they should be worried about. Benny had used his car to get dates with different girls in his senior class and, along with his good friend Pete Dyson, or "Peety" as he was called by his classmates, they began to go through the female population of Bay St. Louis high school. Soon, Bessie Mae Walters became a regular for Benny's weekend dating and Peety would bring along Alice Biggers. They were both cute girls who were allowed the freedom to go out with a boy driving a car and his best friend. After all, everyone knew Bobby and Hilda Thornton and how important they were in the community so their oldest son had to be a good boy, despite what was said from time to time about his exploits.

Word about the *Excalibur* had begun to spread all over the county. Most people did not know exactly where it was located, but many did and others tried hard to find it. Nick had gone to great lengths to see that it was difficult to get to the boat, unless you knew where it was docked. That didn't keep people from trying, including Benny Thornton.

Chapter Twenty-nine

Because of the information sources he had established and the contacts that Madeline had developed in New Orleans, Nick knew the same time as the revenuers what information had been revealed to the investigators and usually who had revealed it. He had also found out that the revenuers had not been happy with no seizures by their boat crews and were planning to reassign those agents to land duty.

Nick decided it was time for his little fleet to make an appearance and arranged for a boat carrying a shipment to make a run by one of the revenuer's boats. If they actually thought they saw a boat, maybe the revenuers would not shift those men back to duty on shore. He was not worried about the revenuers out-sailing his local crews. He had seen how good his crews were and how they could sail those boats in almost any weather. He was also impressed with how fast those big boats could travel, even when loaded with barrels of rum and whiskey. Because of the increase in demand for his products, Nick began to also use small boats to bring in booze to the Bluffs that had been unloaded from newer, much larger mother ships. Those ships made the trips from Cuba also, but they were much too large to navigate on the shallow, narrow bayous. Instead, they anchored more than twelve miles south of the barrier islands, which put them outside of State of Mississippi waters. Nick felt, though, that it was about time for one of his boats to be sighted again. Eventually, one of them would probably get caught. He would have to make plans to deal with that the best way he could.

Capone let Nick know that he was very satisfied with the way operations were being run and the amount of money the operations were producing. He also let Nick know that he would do a few things to keep Bugsy Moran occupied in Chicago. Capone had not liked it that Bugsy had tried to sabotage his operations in Mississippi. Bugsy would have to be repaid in some way, somehow, and it would have to be in such a way as to make a point.

Madeline's mysterious guest was now a consistent visitor to the Bluffs, generally arriving with the passage of every two or three weeks at the most. Her guest always wore a black cape, black boots and a black hat. Tiny was always the driver of the Rolls-Royce Phantom limousine that brought Madeline's guest, and the stay was usually of two days' duration. After each stay, the guest was always taken back to Cypress Landing where Tiny was waiting with the limousine.

In the Mississippi Sound, not too far from the old Civil War era Fort Massachusetts on Ship Island, sat a boat on this night carrying the same three revenue agents who had been out there when their boat was almost rammed by the "ghost" ship. Tonight, they all had their guns easily accessible. They had been out there for several nights in a row now, waiting for the ships smuggling illegal liquor to the Mississippi Gulf Coast from somewhere south of state waters. After jumping into the water that night several weeks ago when they had almost been rammed, they had been kidded by all of the other agents about how they had literally bailed out of their boat so as to not get hit.

They promised each other that they would be tougher next time, if there ever was a next time. They still believed that their patrol boat duty was a waste of time, but they could not convince their superiors of that. So there they sat, in a rocking boat night after night, with just the one sighting to their credit, and they were not sure about it. At least that boat had not waited around to help them, which could indicate that it might have had something to hide. If there was another time, they would, at least, shoot at the ship if it tried to ram them. With the small motor on their boat, they felt they could catch any rumrunner who might venture into the waters they guarded.

They had seen nothing for so long though and were again lying around onboard, talking about how they were never going to see the boats, if indeed that was the way illegal shipments were coming into the coast. The fog was thick, as it sometimes was, and they could not see much. They hoped it would clear up later in the evening.

Suddenly, out of the fog came a huge boat and it was flying. It was so close to their own boat when they first saw it, and it was headed straight for them again! Then through the air came a dark round object that was making a hissing sound. It was the noise of a fuse burning.

"It's a grenade!" one of the men yelled while looking at the object that had landed at his feet. He dove overboard, quickly followed by the other two men. As they swam away from their boat, they heard the laughter of those on the passing ship as it continued flying on into the fog of the night. The bomb fizzed until the fuse burned up and then the noise stopped. As the men worked to keep themselves afloat in the water, a voice came from out of the fog where the passing ship had disappeared, "Y'all enjoy yur swim!" followed by howls of laughter.

* * *

As fall arrived, Carmine made one of his visits to the area to check on things for Mr. Capone. He and Madeline had known each other in Detroit, and he had known her late husband very well. He invited her to meet him at Genico's, a restaurant in the French Quarter in New Orleans, where Carmine knew a few people and they could have a few drinks after their meal. Madeline agreed and met him at the restaurant, which was just off of Canal Street not too far from the famed Pirate's Alley, where General Andrew Jackson met with the pirate Jean Lafitte to plan the defense of New Orleans at the end of the War of 1812. She was looking forward to seeing this important man in Capone's operations, who had been one of her husband's good friends from Detroit before he had been killed.

They gave each other a big hug when she arrived at the restaurant. Once seated at their table in the back where they could have some privacy, they ordered drinks and began to reminisce about their times in Detroit. With more drinks, Carmine guided the conversation away from Detroit and began to try to impress this beautiful widow of his friend by telling her the story of how he had become one of Capone's right hand men and how important he now was.

After dinner, as they waited for more drinks to be delivered, Carmine said, "I heard you had a little problem at a party at the New Orleans Country Club with one of this city's fine, upstanding southern belles." He let forth with a solid laugh after completing his sentence.

"What, these southern girls don't like a little competition from a Detroit girl?"

"She couldn't handle her liquor," Madeline answered.

Carmine chuckled and said, "Yeah! Sure, Madeline. Go tell that to somebody else."

The bar maid appeared and placed their next round of drinks on their table as they both sat there not saying anything while she was there. When she had left, Carmine said, "I bet, Madeline, that she had more of a problem dealing with your probably being by far the best looking woman there than she did handling her liquor." Madeline took a sip from her drink and said nothing, continuing to sit there looking at the crowd in the restaurant.

"For what it's worth, Madeline, my sources down here tell me that a lot of people were happy about what you did to that woman," Carmine continued. He took a swig from his glass and, putting it back on the table, said, "It seems that her mouth has offended a lot of people down here at one time or another. You actually did what a lot of those so-called 'southern ladies' would have loved to have done, but didn't have the guts to do."

Laughing, Carmine continued, "Hell, Madeline. You could probably be elected President of one of the women's clubs down here right now if you wanted to." With that, he let out another boisterous laugh.

Madeline looked at Carmine while he was laughing. She had to admit it made her feel good to know that some of the women in this town liked what she had done. The one thing about it all though was, she didn't care whether people, men or women, liked what she had done or not. Nobody, especially some ugly, thin woman with a tongue too big for her mouth, was going to talk to her like that woman had.

Carmine and Madeline ended up dancing in one of the bars close to Genico's and getting totally drunk. At least Carmine did. As they danced, Carmine enjoyed looking at Madeline's cleavage and rubbing up against her from time to time, especially as they slow danced. Madeline was getting ready to politely stop some of that rubbing up against her when Carmine slurred, "I know about what happened to those two men sent undercover over to Mississippi by the district attorney."

Madeline quickly recognized this as another attempt by Carmine to demonstrate to her how important he had become. Looking intently at her to watch her reaction to what he was going to say next, Carmine mumbled softly so only she could hear him, "Both found out way too much and had to be taken care of. Each one was taken out into the Gulf of Mexico where they were cut up and fed to the sharks."

Looking at Madeline and seeing her attention was momentarily kept by this news, Carmine continued.

"I have heard that the same thing happened to one of the stable boys Nick hired out at the Bluffs."

Seeing that passing on this last tidbit of information clearly captivated Madeline's attention, Carmine now felt much more important.

Madeline was tipsy, but her head was clear enough to hear everything Carmine had said. As they danced one of the few slow dances, they were leaning heavily on each other, Carmine because he could hardly stand up and Madeline holding him up because she did not want Carmine to stop talking.

Trying to impress the woman with the cleavage even more, Carmine said, "I know how Carlo was killed, Madeline. It was not how everybody was told."

Even though Carmine was slurring his words badly, Madeline had heard enough to understand what he had said. She had always been told her husband had died in a shootout with members of the Purple Gang in Detroit in the closing days of Capone's war with them, but she had never been told any details. Now Carmine was saying that was not true?

"What happened, Carmine? I need to know. You know how much I loved Carlo. I have to know, Carmine. Tell me, please tell me." She said all of it in a pleading voice.

Here Carmine was, standing on a dance floor in a bar in New Orleans with one of the most beautiful women he had ever seen and that woman was pleading with him to tell her about how her husband had really been killed in Detroit.

After thinking in his dazed state about it for a moment, Carmine said, "Okay, I'll tell you, Madeline. Mr. Capone ordered it."

With that, Madeline could not keep her mouth from falling open. After a few seconds to let the shock wear off, he continued, "It's true, Madeline, he ordered it, but he had no choice, at all. Now I can't say any more than that."

"Carmine, you can't do this to me. You tell me this and then you say you can't say any more. You were one of Carlo's best friends. I was his wife, Carmine. I have to know what happened. You can't just say that and not tell me anything else. Please tell me. I loved him so much. You know how much I loved him."

Carmine broke away from her and staggered over to their table. He sat down in the booth on one side of their table and Madeline slid over next to him. She continued to look at him as he took several swallows from his drink. Carmine turned to look at Madeline, his gaze not missing the now obviously loose top Madeline was wearing that was showing a great deal more than it had just a few moments earlier. Wanting to continue to impress this beautiful woman with such wonderful cleavage, and at the same time knowing the effect of what he was getting ready to say, Carmine took his time, but finally said, "Carlo was a government informant, Madeline."

Madeline was stunned! For a moment, the fact that her top was almost completely open wasn't anywhere in her mind.

"Mr. Capone ordered Carlo killed, Madeline, because he was telling the government everything about what we were doing. Everything, Madeline. We lost several good men because of what he did." Carmine paused to take another sip of his drink and then continued.

"The Purple Gang knew he was an informant and told us about it when we agreed to a truce with them and started to work together. They told us we had to take care of our problem, so Mr. Capone did."

Madeline still could not move. She could only stare at Carmine as he talked.

"When Mr. Capone found out, he said that whoever had sponsored Carlo had to take care of him. And you know who sponsored Carlo, Madeline." Madeline's mind quickly thought about what was being said. Her mind gave her the answer at the same moment Carmine said, "It was your brother, Madeline. It was Nick."

Madeline slumped back on the bench, how much of her cleavage was showing being all but forgotten for the moment.

Thinking for a moment, realizing she would probably only have this one opportunity to find out as much as she could, she asked, "Who did it,

Carmine?"

Carmine looked away, clearly not wanting to answer that question.

"Carmine, who shot him? Please, Carmine, who actually did it?"

"Madeline, I can't tell you. You know that."

Leaning forward, her cleavage now obviously back in play, Madeline said, "Carmine, I would do anything to know that. Anything." The implication was perfectly clear.

"Anything, Madeline?"

Pausing a moment and then looking Carmine directly in the eye, Madeline said, "Anything."

After looking around the room one more time and taking a full swallow from his drink, Carmine looked at Madeline and said, "It was Nick."

Madeline almost fainted. Her husband had been killed by her brother? Madeline gasped for air, trying to hide it from this drunk next to her as much as possible.

Breaking the silence after a few moments, Carmine said, "He had no choice, Madeline. None." She shifted her attention back to Carmine, now with a little more air in her lungs.

"When Mr. Capone found out, he told Nick, who had sponsored Carlo for membership, remember Madeline? Nick had done that because of you, Madeline. Because you are his sister. Well, Mr. Capone told Nick that either Nick had to cure the problem, take care of it himself or Mr. Capone would take care of both of them himself, Madeline. Both of them."

Taking another big swallow from his drink, Carmine said, "You know about Mr. Capone, Madeline. I mean, he has already killed nineteen people and those are just the ones I know about. He would have killed both of them, Madeline. In a heartbeat. Both of them. And thought nothing about it."

Madeline was numb from what she had been told. Somehow, she continued to show Carmine a good time after hearing this devastating information from her husband's old friend. When thinking about what Carmine had said about Joey, she felt that he did not seem to know the real reason why Joey had been taken out into the gulf. At least he wasn't bringing up the reason if he did know.

Within thirty minutes, Carmine took Madeline to his hotel room to collect on her agreement with him. After Madeline spent only a short amount of time with him in his bed, Carmine passed out. After making sure he was soundly asleep, Madeline got out of bed and sat at a table in a corner of the room, deep in thought as she went over and over everything that she had just been told.

* * *

Benny Thornton now felt like he could do almost anything he wanted. His dad was a person everyone wanted to remain friends with because he ran that business down on the waterfront that employed all of those workers. Since Benny was the son of such an important man in the community, Benny just knew that he was special. If the truth were to be known, Benny actually looked down on the workers that made money for his father and their family. The few times his dad had taken him down to the plant, Benny felt contempt for the employees and their families and did not think any of them deserved so much as a nod of his head in recognition. He did try to say and do a few things to please his dad though. After all, his dad let him use a car to run around town with his friend Peety.

This particular Saturday night, Benny and Peety had dates with Bessie Mae and Alice. Benny had the evening all planned for the group. The first thing they were going to do was go to the beach and later they would get some liquor. That's what the grown-ups were doing on the weekends, at least the ones who were so much smarter than everyone else and knew how to easily get what they wanted to drink. Benny had asked Kirk, the foreman at his father's plant, where someone might go to get some of the booze that seemed to be so off-limits to younger people like him and his friends. He told Kirk that he and his best friend wanted to impress their dates for the coming Saturday night by showing them that they could get something to drink during the evening. Kirk had told him he knew where they could go. Benny would have to be quiet about it and not mention it to anyone else, but since he was the boss's son, he would tell him. Benny was all ears.

"Since yor dad lets you drive that car when you go out on yor dates and all, after about nine at night go to the black funeral home there on Sixth Avenue," Kirk said under his breath.

"The black funeral home? Are you sure?" Billy asked almost in disbelief.

"Yeah, I'm sure. I bought some there last week," Kirk answered.

"Where do I go there, the front door?" Benny asked, still not sure about this information.

"No! Not the front door! Drive around back where they have bodies displayed in that big window there," Kirk said with a serious tone in his voice.

"You mean I have to drive up under that shed behind the funeral home where they all go to look at dead people to get a bottle of something?" Benny asked, still somewhat in doubt.

"Yeah. Just pull up back there like you are going to sign the visitor's book in that drawer they have right next to that big picture window there. Write your order on a piece of paper that will be in the drawer there and put your money in the drawer and you can get what you want. If the curtains are pulled so that you can't see the body, that means they are not open."

Benny knew he had to try doing this. It was exciting, getting a bottle of something illegal. He had never been drunk before but the few people he had seen who had been drinking seemed to be having a good time. Besides, both of the girls would be impressed, he was sure.

The following Saturday night, the two couples got together and went to a beach on the edge of town as they usually did. They put blankets out on the sand and started a small fire. As it got closer to nine o'clock, Benny said, "Peety, you and Allison stay here and keep the fire going. Bessie Mae and I are going to go pick up something."

"Where are you going," Peety asked.

"I am going to pick up a little something for our party here," he answered. With a confident look on his face, he said, "When we get back, we'll really have a party. Come on, Bessie Mae." Looking at the other two, he said, "We'll be back in a little bit."

"Don't be gone too long," Peety said.

"Don't forget us," Allison said.

Benny walked across the beach to the car. Bessie Mae followed a step behind. She liked doing things that other kids her age had not yet experienced. That was why she had started dating Benny. His reputation for doing things that caused trouble meant there was a good possibility that there was usually going to be some excitement, and Bessie Mae loved excitement. Her family was relatively poor, but her parents were happy she was now going out with the son of one of the leading families of the community. Yes, there were rumors that floated around about Benny from time to time, but he was the oldest son of a very respected couple. After all, his family did own that factory and had a lot of money. As Bessie Mae's mother told her when she first started dating Benny, if they ended up getting married, she would be fixed for the rest of her life.

When she got in the car with Benny, she said, "Where are we going?"

With a sly smile, Benny answered, "You are not going to believe it. Just wait and see."

Benny drove the car back toward town, eventually pulling up to the rear of the local black funeral home.

"What on earth are you doing, Benny Thornton?" Bessie Mae asked, not knowing what to expect for an answer. She had some idea of where they were, which was somewhere on the colored side of town, the side where no whites were supposed to be after dark, especially white kids like them.

Benny pulled up under the overhang. After he stopped, they both looked to their left through a big picture window and saw the body of a black man dressed in a suit laid out in a casket! Both of their mouths dropped opened. Bright lights inside the room focused on the body. Dark blue curtains hung on three sides of the casket.

Eventually, after recovering from seeing a body laid out in a casket, Benny reached down and pulled the handle of what seemed to be a drawer that was located just below and to the left of the picture window. He looked in the drawer and saw a leather bound book with several pages in it. He pulled the book out and opened it. On the first page were what appeared to be signatures in various types of handwriting. Looking back in the drawer he saw a small stack of paper and a pencil.

After quickly looking around, Benny took the pencil and one of the small sheets of paper and wrote the word "fifth of whiskey" on it. He pulled his wallet out of his pants pocket and took out a twenty dollar bill. He put the book back into the drawer. On top of the book he put the note and the money. He then slid the drawer back in.

They both waited. The seconds seemed like minutes to Benny. Bessie Mae was nervous.

"Benny, what are you doing? Tell me!"

"Be quiet, Bessie Mae! Shhhhhhhh!"

"Why did you put that money in there?" she whispered.

No answer was given by Benny.

They both began to look around them and then back at the body behind the window. Benny also moved his eyes to the drawer, but the drawer was still closed. Again, they looked around. Nothing was happening, around them or in the building. It was beginning to get spooky for both of them.

Thirty seconds went by. It seemed like a half hour. Then a minute had gone by. Now, it seemed like an hour. Nothing.

"Let's go, Benny Thornton," Bessie Mae pleaded, in almost a whisper.

Benny began to think about what he was going to do to Kirk when he saw him. For sure, he would come up with some reason to try and get his dad to fire him for telling him about this.

Then the drawer slid back open. Benny looked in. On top of the leather bound book was a paper sack with something in it. Benny grabbed the sack and pulled it and its contents inside his car. Opening it up, he took out a strangely shaped bottle with an official looking label on it. He also saw dollar bills in the sack and heard change making its special clinking noise. Benny quickly put the car in gear and drove off.

Behind the curtain in the funeral home, Leroy watched the car pull away. These kids had not been there before, but he thought he knew who they were, the boy for sure. He did not like new buyers, especially if they were kids, and these two were definitely kids. He didn't want any trouble, but he had finally made the decision to go ahead and fill their order. After all, he was in business to make money.

He had looked at them from behind the blue curtain. With the lights in the ceiling angled toward the window, it was almost impossible for the buyers to tell that someone, in this case Leroy, was checking them out. Because this was their first visit and because they were kids, he added a little premium to the price. After all, he was taking a chance selling to them. So he made what he called to himself a "business" decision and charged them almost twice as much as a regular customer. He felt they would never know the difference. The speed with which they had pulled away from the window convinced him that he had made the right decision.

There was that one thing though. It always seemed to happen with new customers, especially the younger ones. They usually pulled away so quickly that they left the drawer open, just like these had done. That convinced him that these two were new customers. It left him with the same problem, though, that he had dealt with many times. The drawer was still open. The next customer might hit the drawer with their car and break it. That had happened quite a few times. Before, that is, Leroy had Elwin tie a rope to a nail on the back of the drawer so it could be pulled and closed without the need to get up out of the chair and go do it. Leroy pulled on the rope and the drawer smoothly closed. Now he was ready for the next customer.

* * *

The ruffian went out drinking at the Red Maple again, hoping he was going to see the woman who had put that gun under his chin. He was going to take care of her, do things to her she would never forget if he could just find her. Sitting at the bar, he began talking about her with a man who had come in and sat next to him. The ruffian went into great detail about how beautiful the woman had been and what all she had done with him in the back seat of her car. The more he drank, the more he talked about what all he was going to do to her when he saw her again. He was going to fix her so no man would ever look at her again. He would make sure of that.

The man he was talking to bought him several drinks while the ruffian raged on more and more about the woman. As the hours went by, the ruffian began to realize the woman was not going to be there that night so he finally decided to leave. He got off of his barstool, struggling to stand up, and started shuffling toward the front door of the building. The man he had been talking to also got up and moved to help him as he walked, but the ruffian told the man that he didn't need any help and was all right.

As the ruffian opened the door to the bar and started to step down the three stairs at the front of the building, he felt a sharp pain as he was hit on his left leg by a fence post. He tumbled down the stairs and onto the ground. As he tried to get himself up to fight with whoever had hit him, he was hit on his right leg, this time by another man with fence post.

Now, he was mad and although both of his legs were really hurting, he made another effort to get up, only to get a kick in the rear that sent him back face down in the dirt. Then he heard the voice of the man who had been sitting next to him all that time, he thought he had said his name was Rocko, as the voice said, "You never should have been so ugly to the woman you have been talking about. You need to learn how to act around a lady."

Then the ruffian felt another blow as he tried to turn around to get up, this one on his right ribs, with a fence post from the man who had been sitting with him. After numerous other blows were delivered all over the ruffian's body from the three men with fence posts, he was left lying in the dirt conscious, but barely able to move. The man who had been sitting next to him in the bar bent down to the ruffian and, pulling his head back by his long hair said in a firm, threatening voice only inches away from the ruffian's face, "Didn't yor mamma ever teach you any manners? Never act like you did around a lady. If that particular lady ever lays her eyes on you again, you are a dead man."

The man then turned loose of the ruffian's hair, brushed his hands off as if to rid himself of dirt, and stood up. The three men then beat the ruffian unconscious with the fence posts. After they were finished they walked, each one still carrying his fence post, over to their car at the edge of the parking lot. After putting the fence posts in the trunk, the three got into the car and drove down the dirt road into the night.

* * *

The men of the IRS navy hoped that the time was coming when they would capture their first boat. They had what they believed were two sightings and, but for their responses to those sightings, they might have already had their first capture. They sincerely felt that, so far, they had mostly themselves to blame.

One night, a night during which the fog was not so thick and the moon was out, the revenuers were bouncing around in their boat offshore from Biloxi when one of them saw with his eyeglasses what he thought was a boat that they should more closely examine. It was riding low in the water and seemed to be trying to stay away from the government boat.

"Let's go check her out," said their leader for the evening. They turned their vessel toward the ship and gave chase. After trying to turn away, those on the thirty-five foot boat, which on its stern had the name *Green Lizard*, seemed to realize they could not get away and, eventually, the revenuer's boat pulled alongside. All three agents held their pistols up ready for action. The two men aboard the *Green Lizard* offered no resistance and were soon standing there with their hands up in the air. Two of the agents jumped on board the vessel and tied the two boats together. After directing the two men with their hands in the air toward the bow of the vessel, the agents began to conduct a search while the agent remaining on their own boat held a gun on the two men. They soon found what they were looking for, barrel upon barrel of booze. They had finally captured a rum-runner.

The agents quickly put the two men in handcuffs and put the now seized boat under tow. They took the boat to Biloxi which was the nearest port from the site of the seizure. After docking both vessels and making sure the two criminals were in the custody of the U. S. Marshal for that area, the three revenuers notified their superiors, who were ecstatic.

A ceremony was held the next week celebrating the seizure. All of the agents were honored and articles were printed in the local newspapers about their successful effort. The articles also announced that the seized vessel would be offered at auction to the highest bidder the very next week. The amount received for the seized ship would go toward offsetting the operational costs of the efforts by the IRS. In addition, pictures were taken of the barrels of booze being smashed with sledge hammers and the illegal booze running into the drains of the city of Biloxi. The IRS announced that severe prison sentences would be sought for the two men arrested during the seizure of the *Green Lizard*.

When the day arrived for the auction of the *Green Lizard*, there was a crowd at the Biloxi small craft harbor to witness the event. The auctioneer began by singing the praises of those who had been involved in the success of assisting in stopping the flow of, as he called it, the "demon brew." He then presided over a lively bidding contest in which three determined buyers challenged each other with consistently higher prices for the boat. Finally, two of the potential buyers fell by the way-side and the winner, George Whitaker, was announced. He was immediately told by the governmental agents to pay in cash, which the advertisement for sale had mentioned, if he wanted final title to the vessel.

Whitaker had come prepared and paid the bid amount on the spot and was told he could take possession of his newly acquired vessel as soon as that very day. With the sale concluded, all observers gradually dispersed and the IRS agents speedily traveled to a local bank to deposit the money just received from their efforts. Success was in the air for the IRS and they made sure everyone knew about it. Before too long the agents were back out in their boat looking for their next big seizure.

Chapter Thirty

Madeline was out riding her horse as usual around the Bluffs when she came upon Claude and Carlotta as they were repairing some voodoo markers and putting up more. She was still not comfortable with either of the two, and, after she had asked them what they were doing, told them that if it were up to her they wouldn't be allowed on the property. Then she rode off as the two continued their work.

Madeline continued meeting her mysterious guest now at least once every other week at the Bluffs' boat dock. As before, the guest was always brought there by Tiny from Cypress Landing. Nick and the other people at the Bluffs knew, when the shadowy figure arrived at the Bluffs, to stay away from the guest house as Madeline had made it clear that no one was allowed near there during those visits. Madeline always seemed to have at least some information of benefit to them after each visit.

The Mardi Gras krewe that Nick had decided to join, the Krewe of Nobles, was one of the oldest and largest in the New Orleans' area. It was a krewe made up mostly of what was known as old-line families, which were families that for many years had exercised significant influence in

New Orleans. After Nick had made the appropriate contributions to the right political campaigns in New Orleans, the powers in control of the krewe decided that a person of Nick's obvious good judgment should be considered for membership in their krewe and not in one of the others.

Of course, the fact that the men who made those decisions had either directly or indirectly benefited from his substantial contributions was not something that worked against Nick. The amount of money he had been spending in the New Orleans area quickly made Nick a person office holders wanted to know much better. Old money could conveniently forget about certain rules that kept out those who had worked their way up the financial ladder. Maybe a person was from the wrong side of town or had a family association that might not be that attractive because of past transgressions, either public or private. New money, the more of it the better, seemed to overcome most of that. Good common sense prevailing, Nick was personally notified by City Councilman Young that he had been voted into the Krewe of Nobles.

As for Madeline, what she had done to Gertie Hensley, while certainly shocking to New Orleans society, was generally acclaimed as something that Gertie had coming to her. In fact, several of those who had been the target of Gertie's previous verbal assaults quietly cheered what Madeline had done and a few even made sure that their husbands, some of whom had also been the target of Gertie's sharp tongue, were aware of what the woman from the Mississippi Gulf Coast had done. Meanwhile, Gertie had to visit a surgeon to have her nose repaired and a dentist to have her two front teeth replaced. After the word had raced around New Orleans about what had been written on her forehead, Gertie's reputation needed to be repaired as well.

Gertie finally began to realize that the depth of the dislike for her was more than she had ever imagined. Although at first she wanted her husband to sue Madeline, she was finally convinced by her few close friends that maybe the best thing for her to do at the moment was to quietly take on a lower profile and possibly even disappear from the New Orleans social scene for a while, at least until her face had healed completely. After several discussions about it all and feeling horrible about her appearance, she decided that her friends' advice was something she needed to follow. She dropped completely out of the social scene in New Orleans.

Her absence was acclaimed by some people. Madeline was actually seen as almost a heroine who should be admired for what she had done. More than one socialite wished that she had been the one that had slammed Gertie's face onto the wooden shelf and then into the wall. The bit about Madeline putting her initials on Gertie's forehead had topped it all off.

Having cultivated several good sources of information both in the Bay St. Louis area and in New Orleans, Nick was notified by some of those sources that the revenuers were beginning to find out more and more about his operation. He had no idea how the information was getting to them. The two men arrested on the *Green Lizard* had provided some bits and pieces before their sentencing and the judge in their case had given them both just three months in recognition of their cooperation with the authorities. However, they had not known that much. Nick felt that something else was going on. Somehow, information about the operation was beginning to get out.

While the leadership of the IRS was upset with the judge's lenient sentences, the judge noted that the efforts by the IRS had resulted in the seizure of the *Green Lizard* itself which was a financial loss to the bootleggers. The two men, when questioned, had talked and what little they had known they had shared with investigators. Therefore, the judge saw no need to crowd the jails with people who had cooperated with the authorities. For that decision the judge was lauded and commended since, hopefully, the success of the whole operation might lead to further cooperation from those arrested in the future and to additional information being provided by members of the public in general.

Just over two weeks after the auction of the *Green Lizard*, at close to nine o'clock at night, the successful bidder, George Whitaker, docked the boat at a small wharf on the Wolfe River near Pass Christian, not too far from the Bay of St. Louis. Out of the darkness walked the huge black man that Whitaker worked for. Recognizing the man, Whitaker greeted his associate.

"Hello, Tiny," Whitaker said, glad to be seeing his contact.

"Hi, George," Tiny said as he ambled toward George, holding a wooden name plate in his left hand with the word *Electra* on it. Looking over the boat, Tiny said, "Is she in good shape?"

"Good as ever," George said smiling. "But next time, we need to set it up so the three bidders don't drive the price up so high. They almost drove the price out of sight! I thought they were gonna stop sooner than they did."

"I know, I know. But Mr. Nick wanted the revenuers to really think that was an auction with real people bidding up the price. The next time the price won't get so high," Tiny said looking at first the boat and then back at George.

"Okay, let's put her name plate back on her. They will never know what happened."

With that, the two men took the *Green Lizard* name plate off of the boat and put the *Electra* name plate that Tiny had brought with him firmly on the stern in its place. The vessel was now again named the *Electra*. Within three days the boat was back in the business of carrying lumber down to Cuba. Once the ship left Havana's harbor on its next trip carrying booze back to the Bluffs, the ship's name plate for the trip north was changed to *Blue Moon*.

Four months from the date of their sentencing, the two men who had been arrested on the ship were back on their jobs, working on boats that were carrying whiskey. They had been welcomed back very quietly with generous bonuses that were discreetly provided to each man.

Word was starting to make the rounds of those responsible for the investigation of the illegal booze shipping activity that Nick might somehow be involved. The problem was that none of those receiving that information wanted to do anything at all about what they were being told. On the contrary, most wanted to make sure that, as far as they were concerned, Nick didn't have anything to worry about.

District Attorney Fuller had still not heard back from either of the undercover informants he had sent over to Mississippi. He knew he had no jurisdiction over there, but what little information he had consistently indicated that the source of most, if not all, of the shipments coming into New Orleans and the rest of Louisiana was from over in that area. Also, he was not getting much information because the federal agents responsible for investigating the manufacture and shipping of illegal liquor would not share any of the information they might have with him. When Fuller finally did hear that Nick Gable might be involved in the shipping operations, he had been strongly encouraged to not go after Nick by such people as federal and state judges in Louisiana and the U. S. Attorney in New Orleans, who had told him on several different occasions, "Let us handle those investigations. You stay out of it. That is beyond your responsibilities and you know that. We will take care of it."

* * *

Down near Bayou Caddy, on this particular Friday night when the car pulled up to the gate on the road leading to the *Excalibur*, Elrod just knew it was going to be trouble. In the car were four kids, all about age seventeen or eighteen, two boys and two girls, none probably out of high school yet, he guessed. Out of the driver's side stumbled the driver. Elrod had seen his kind before, not recently, but before, and more than once.

He knew that Mr. Nick wanted him to do his job, which was keeping people away from the *Excalibur* unless he had been specifically told to let them into the area and onto the boat. He also knew by now that doing his job meant no exceptions. Being a poor black man, this job was important to him. He had been a little worried when he first took the job, but it had not been hard to do, and working for Mr. Nick had been alright so far, as long as he did exactly what Mr. Nick wanted. What Mr. Nick had told him, more than once, was to make sure no one, no one at all, came in unless Elrod already knew who they were or had something from Mr. Nick saying they could come. From the looks of things, he knew quickly that he did not know these four kids and they were not going to have anything that would admit them to the boat. He hoped this would go easily.

He stepped out from under the big oak tree a few feet down the fence line from the gate, walked over to the young boy and said, "Wat's yor bizness?"

The white boy stumbled over to him and said, in an obnoxious tone of voice, "I wanna get to tha gamblin' boat."

Elrod looked at the boy and slowly said, "You needs to git beck in yo car and go beck up dat dare road."

The boy answered, his words very slurred, "Look, I know they's a boat down this road, a gamblin' boat, and me and my friends want to go to it."

The girls in the car both giggled and the boy with them yelled out, "Yeah! We want to go to the gambling boat!"

Elrod looked around the boy standing in front of him at the car with the boy's three friends in it. The motor was still running. Elrod could tell by the smell on the boy's breath and the way he was speaking that

261

the boy had had too many drinks already. By the way the boy's friends sounded, they had not missed too many drinks either.

"Thar's nuthin har for ya, so go on, turn dat thang round and git."

The boy answered, "Now don't be talking to me like dat! Do you know who my daddy is? Do ya? My daddy's Bobby Thornton, the Bobby Thornton! Now er ya gonna let me in?"

The black man had seen white boys like this before. He had seen them do stupid things when they had a few too many drinks in them. It gave them courage, made them feel like they could conquer the world, and gave them mouths their mothers would never believe. It looked like this one was not going to give up easily because he thought he was so special. Most of the ones who drove up finally just gave up and left. This one was probably going to be different.

"Nah, there's nuthin here fer yus to see. Now go on home."

"I don't think you heard me! I said, do you know who my daddy is?"

About that time, from behind the same big oak tree Elrod had appeared from walked a huge, fat white man. Charlie was almost six feet tall and he weighed about three hundred forty pounds, give or take fifteen pounds depending on what he had to eat for his last meal. Charlie was also carrying a long barreled shotgun draped over his right forearm.

"Didn't you hear what he told you, son?" Charlie said as he walked the few steps over to where Elrod and Benny were standing.

"Who are you, Mista?" Benny asked.

"Don't matter, son," said Charlie as he got closer.

"You know my daddy, don't you? You know who my daddy is. Tell him to let me in or I surely am gonna let him know about all of this."

Charlie looked at the boy and said, "Go away, boy."

The boy kept standing there, swaying from side to side, and answered back saying, "Don't be telling me …."

At that point Charlie pulled the shotgun up, pulled the hammer back and pointed it at the boy. In that split second, the boy realized, even as drunk as he was, that the long barrel of that shotgun was pointed right at him and the hammer on it had just been cocked. Benny closed his eyes and moved to turn his left side toward the man with the shotgun when he heard it.

WHAM!

The girls screamed and the boy in the car yelled, "No!"

Benny cringed. After a long moment, he began to realize that he was not feeling any pain. He slowly opened his eyes and looked up. The big white man was still standing there, only now smoke was coming out of his shotgun. Benny knew that he was drunk, but he thought that if he had been shot, he would have been hurting a lot more. Then he saw Charlie looking past him and Benny slowly turned to look over his left shoulder to see what Charlie was looking at. Everybody was quiet. It was then that Benny realized what had happened.

"You shot my car," Benny slowly said as he continued to look over his left shoulder.

Smoke was now coming up from the hood at the front of the car where the radiator had been, except now it was partially blown away.

Looking back at Charlie, Benny said again, slowly, incredulously, "You shot my car."

Charlie already had the barrel of the shotgun open and was pulling out the spent casing. Looking at the car as he reached into his pants pocket, Charlie said, "Yep. Sure did." He put a new shell into the barrel of the shotgun and closed it up with a click.

"Had a choice, son," Charlie said as he took a step closer to Benny. "Shoot you or the car."

Laying the shotgun again over his forearm, he said, "Picked the car."

Both of the girl's mouths were open. Peety's mouth was open. All four of the kids kept looking at the motor of the car and back at Charlie.

Charlie looked at the car motor, looked at the two girls and the boy in the car, then at Benny who was still just standing there. He turned to Elrod and said, "I guess you may as well go get Adam and Eve."

Elrod nodded his head ever so slightly and walked back into the darkness past the oak tree.

"Adam and Eve?" Benny asked out loud. Looking at Peety, he said, "Aren't they dead?"

Peety's eyes got as big as Benny's. Benny began to think that maybe he had been shot after all and that Peety was dead too. Then he saw the girls and they looked alright. Seeing that they were alright made him feel better, but he still could not believe what he was seeing.

Benny looked back at Charlie and said again, "Mista, I can't believe you shot my car." He then added, in a more sober voice, "And I am not your son."

Charlie looked back at him, and for a few moments at Peety. The girls began to wonder if Benny was actually going to be the next target.

"Well, for that you sure are lucky, because if you were my son, I would jerk a knot in your head, right now, for being out here and bringing those girls."

Out of the darkness came Elrod, carrying harnesses and rope and holding the reins of what appeared out of the darkness next, which were two mules. Elrod began the task of putting the harnesses on each one.

"That's Adam and Eve, dummy!" Charlie said, pointing to the two mules.

Benny finally turned and stumbled, quietly, back to the car, still looking at the shot engine. Then he shifted his eyes back to Charlie. Finally, he asked, "What are you doing with the mules?"

"Well, Mr. Smart Mouth, do you want to push your car all the way to the coast road or would you rather have Adam and Eve here pull it for you?"

Benny still could not believe it. Something else began to dawn on him. How in the world was he going to explain this to his daddy?

As the car was being pulled back toward the coast road by the two mules, Benny asked Elrod, who was walking next to the mules, "Why do you use two of them? You only need one."

Elrod didn't even turn around to face Benny as he answered. "They work as a team. He won't work on pullin' heavy thangs without her thar with him."

That was the last thing said until they got to the coast road. The whole trip was made in silence as each of the four thought about what had happened and what was ahead of them the next few days.

Finally, after Elrod had left and the four of them were walking back to Bay St. Louis, Benny said, "Look, y'all have got to keep quiet about this." They each assured him that they would.

"You can never say anything about this to anyone, okay? Just tell your parents we had a flat tire. Don't tell anybody about this." They all nodded their heads in agreement.

At about nine o'clock the next morning, one of the workers from the boat appeared at Nick's office building in Bay St. Louis. He had been sent by Lillie to see Nick. When he opened the door and walked into Nick's office, Nick was surprised to see him. After taking him to the back of his office, Nick asked, "Is something wrong down at the boat?"

"No, not really," the man answered. "Ms. Lillie just wanted you to know that Charlie shot a car last night."

Nick was at a loss for words.

By noon the next day, word had made it all over Bay St. Louis that Benny Thornton had gotten his daddy's car shot out near the gambling boat.

Chapter Thirty-one

Shipments of illegal whiskey in Hancock County were now being made even in police cars. Sheriff Patterson decided that since his deputies were all in on the scheme anyway, there was no sense in wasting the gas used by their police cars while they were on patrol. Nick had agreed with the sheriff's suggestion about the police cars since they were on the roads anyway. Soon changes and alterations were made to the police cars so that they could be loaded up with booze like any other car that might be carrying the cargo. The cars were driven by deputies who greatly appreciated the substantial extra income they received for making each shipment. Some deputies went so far as to modify their police cars with extra heavy suspension systems so that they could carry more liquor on each trip and not appear to be loaded down, which usually raised the attention of the ever vigilant federal agents.

Nick went by the church office of Father Ryan to see if the money he had made available to the church for scholarships for kids had worked out alright. He hoped it had because he wanted to plan ahead for the next year and do the same thing again, if possible. Upon being let in by the Father's door guardian and secretary, Mrs. Mueller, again on a

Tuesday, the Father greeted Nick as an old friend.

"Welcome, Nick," the Father said with his comfortable smile. "It's good to see you and thanks so much for what you did for the kids here. So many of them would not have been able to attend school here if it had not been for you and your contribution. On behalf of all of them, thank you," the Father said with genuine sincerity.

"You're welcome, Father. I am just glad it all worked out. I am glad I was able to do it and I am glad you helped make it all happen."

Now seated in front of the Father, Nick continued, "Let's try to do some more good again next year. By discussing it with you now, maybe we can get this taken care of sooner. Do you have any idea at all about how much you might need for the school year beginning in the fall next year?"

"Not yet, but we would greatly appreciate it if you could do the same thing, or something similar, for next year as you did for this year," the Father said with a hopeful tone to his voice.

"Father, this is something that is close to my heart. Just let me know when you have some idea and I will try to go ahead and do the same type of thing that we did this year."

"Oh, Nick! That would be wonderful if you could! So wonderful. In a few weeks we should have some idea about what that amount might be. I will let you know when we do. Thanks again so much for offering to help," the Father said with an obvious appreciation in his voice.

"How are things going for you otherwise?" Nick asked, wondering if there was anything else the Father might have on his mind. The answer he got surprised him.

"Nick, I am really worried about our community here. I am so glad that you want to work through the church to do something worthwhile to help it. It needs it. I don't know how much you keep up with local happenings and all, but there is so much illegal whiskey being made available here that it is having a really bad effect on families and jobs and the very kids you are interested in helping."

Nick was not expecting this response and listened closely to see how Father Ryan was going to deal with the subject that he had just brought up. He was further surprised.

"I have never seen anything like it in all my life. The consumption of all of the illegal liquor that is available around here is something that is working against the members of our church and the community.

But what has really gotten me greatly concerned is all of the just plain evil that seems to have come into our community and involved itself in almost everybody's lives. We have kids not knowing where their parents are at all hours of the night. We have men deserting their wives and families. We have so many couples wanting to get divorced and you know how frowned upon that is by the Church. We have men and women losing their jobs because of their drinking. We have illegal gambling and prostitution going on in our county. It all does nothing but hurt our community and the families living here. These are horrible problems. There is just a pervasive evil here now. It's everywhere, and it seems to all be tied to the rampant availability of alcohol." The Father's mood had changed completely.

Then Father Ryan said something that would stay in Nick's mind for a long time. Leaning forward in his chair, he said in a quiet, but firm voice, while looking straight at Nick, "I know one thing though. In the Bible in Genesis it says the Lord saw how great man's wickedness had become and how the thoughts in the heart of man were only evil all the time and the Lord was grieved. Genesis then says the Lord's heart was filled with pain and that He would destroy and wipe mankind from the face of the earth. His only exception was Noah who was warned by the Lord to build the ark for himself and his family and the animals. Then, as you might remember, there was a great flood."

Nick looked at Father Ryan and could tell how serious he was now as he spoke in a tone of voice that was not harsh, but very clear.

"Nick, the Lord is not going to let those who are pushing this liquor on our families and our children go on about their lives without something devastating happening. When it does happen, when He decides it is time to deal with it, it will be something that we all will know about. The Lord will not allow this to go on endlessly. They will all eventually pay a heavy price for what they are doing. A very heavy price."

Nick did not think Father Ryan had any idea that he was at the center of what was going on. Then again, maybe he was sending Nick a message. And sending it right now.

Nick decided it was time for him to leave and said, "Father, I am sorry to hear all of that. I hope things get better." Beginning to stand up, Nick said, "I know you are really busy and have so many things you need to be tending to. Let me get out of your way so you can deal with them."

Sticking out his hand, Nick said, "Thanks for taking the time to see me. We will try to see to it that you get enough to help the kids next year that really can't afford to be here. At the least, enough to get them started in school for their first year. This next time, I will try to get the money to you a lot earlier. That is one reason I wanted to mention it to you now, so we could begin making plans and I would know sooner how much you might need. So when you can, just have Mrs. Mueller let me know what the approximate amount might be to get as many kids in as possible. I'll try to take care of it, at least, by spring time. And please, keep all of this to yourself."

The priest stood up and walked around his small desk to shake Nick's hand and to see Nick to the door.

"I will, Nick. Thanks for coming by. You have no idea how great it is to have you wanting to help our kids like that. And thanks for your past generosity. We really appreciate your getting involved," the priest said as Nick began leaving the small room.

"You are most welcome. Thanks for your time. We have done something good here. Let's do more if we can," Nick said as he walked over by Mrs. Mueller. "Nice to have seen you, Mrs. Mueller," he said as he now passed her on his way to the door.

"Thanks for coming by, Mr. Gable," she answered.

"Good day to you both," Nick said.

On his way back to his office, Nick focused on what Father Ryan had told him. He had started thinking in just the past few weeks about whether there was more to life than running an illegal operation for a murderer. He liked to think of himself as having the ability to be a success at whatever he might do, but he had been drawn into the life he now led because of the limited opportunities that had been available to him as he grew up. He had done things he was not proud of and, in some instances, witnessed extreme brutality and, yes, also the evil that Father Ryan had talked about. It had not been pretty, but it had been something that he had just had to deal with.

His way of life had given him a good existence, if having lots of money and all of the women that a man could ever need was the test for that. The bad side of it was not good at all though. If he had ever wanted to settle down, as he had thought about doing with Helen, and do something else with his life, what else could he do? He had no education and no one would hire him once they found out about what he had been doing for a living. Despite the fact that he had done what he did well, he was limited in what he could do legitimately.

Yet, he was tired of it all. He was tired of constantly having to watch his back. He was tired of not being able to talk about the successes of what he really did. Mostly, he was tired of making so much money for a man who would probably have him killed if he knew that Nick was even thinking these things. The worst thing of all was that, knowing Capone, and Nick definitely knew how he thought, Capone would probably make sure that he killed Nick himself. Capone would not run the risk, if Nick just announced one day that he was quitting, of having Nick perhaps show up in a courtroom one day and tell everything he knew. That was exactly what he had not been able to tell Helen. There was so much pressure being put on Capone now by the various federal agencies that Capone would do whatever it took to protect himself. He would have no patience with a guy who just wanted to stop working for him, especially one who knew everything Nick knew.

As Nick got into his Lincoln, he took a moment to look around. Bay St. Louis would be a wonderful place to be married and raise a family. Helen would have been the perfect wife. Those types of thoughts were thoughts that Nick seldom had. Father Ryan had gotten him to start thinking again about all of that. He wondered if that was what the priest had really been trying to get him to think about when the priest had said all that he had. Nick now realized that there was no way he would ever be able to enjoy what so many thought of as a normal life. For the first time in his life, as he pulled away from Father Ryan's church, Nick thought about all of that and was sad.

Chapter Thrity-two

Madeline was riding at the Bluffs after spending time with her visitor. She felt alive and refreshed. She had started seeing her visitor, with Nick's encouragement, initially in order to get information. She had seen men, especially mafia men, use sexual relationships to gather information. If the men she was most familiar with did that, she could do it also. She had not counted on the way things in her life had twisted and turned, and she definitely had not counted on falling in love. Now for the first time since her husband had been killed, she was enjoying some real happiness in her life. Time spent with her frequent visitor was something she looked forward to every trip. She marveled at how blue the sky was and how beautiful the marsh grass looked today. She knew she must be experiencing something special if she was thinking that marsh grass looked good.

Her day quickly took a turn for the worse. She spotted Carlotta by herself on the edge of the farthest bluff. Now was the opportunity for her to go deal with Carlotta. She did not like the voodoo priestess being around. It was time that she did what was necessary to isolate Nick from her, if she could. She did not want this woman to be a friend to her brother.

She was just too dangerous and might get in Madeline's way. Madeline spurred her horse into a gallop toward Carlotta's location.

Riding up to where Carlotta stood, Madeline reined in her horse and said, "Carlotta, I know my brother is working with you and Claude about all of those things you are putting around the property, but don't go thinking you are going to get closer and closer to him. He doesn't need a woman like you around, so I want you to stop meeting with him. Besides, you've got Claude."

Madeline's horse seemed to sense the hostility between the two women. It kept moving around and when Madeline would try to rein him in, he would suddenly twist another direction causing Madeline's back to then be toward Carlotta. Madeline did not want her back to Carlotta during this conversation or at any other time for that matter. She could also see Claude in the distance on the bayou and it looked like he might be coming back to Carlotta's location there on the bluff.

"I have no intention of being with your brother. Claude is my man. You know that," Carlotta said facing Madeline as Madeline tried to control her constantly turning horse.

"Honey, I know people. I've seen the way you flirt with my brother. Claude may not see it and my brother, bless his little heart, may not even know it, but I do. Stay away from him!" Madeline said in a loud voice causing her horse to become even more agitated.

"Who do you think you are, miss high and mighty on a horse? Who are you to talk to me like that?" Carlotta yelled back at the twisting horse's rider.

It was then that it happened with the blink of an eye.

ZZZZZZWWWWWWWHHHPPP!!!!!

Madeline had swung her riding crop across Carlotta's face and caught her full on the left cheek of her face. Madeline's horse reared up, its hooves flying and kicking. Carlotta ducked away grabbing her face, feeling the blood now flowing from her cheek. Madeline then struck her horse twice with the same riding crop and the horse stopped rearing itself on its hind legs.

Carlotta looked down at her bloody hands and then up at Madeline with a look of complete disbelief. Madeline yelled at her, "I said stay away!" Then she galloped off into the woods as Claude pulled up in his boat.

When Claude got out of his boat, he saw Carlotta crying with blood all over her face and her blouse. He then saw the four inch long deep gash left on Carlotta's face by Madeline's riding crop. Pure hatred filled his heart as he looked off toward where Madeline had ridden.

Nick was very upset with Madeline when he found out at the stables from one of his workers what Claude had told them that Madeline had done to Carlotta. He immediately went to the big house and caught Madeline as she was leaving to go to New Orleans.

"What did you do?" he yelled at Madeline. "Why did you do that? Are you crazy? How could you have done that?"

"I was trying to protect you, big brother. That is all I was trying to do," she said trying to be at least a little conciliatory.

"You didn't have to hit her face, Madeline! Why would you do that?" he exclaimed in total disbelief.

"You don't know what she has been trying to do to you. She wants you to be with her," Madeline said, knowing her brother was upset, but she had known before that he would probably get upset once she had confronted Carlotta.

"So what, Madeline? That is not your business!" he exclaimed, yelling right in her face. "How could you do that to her?"

"Wake up, big brother. I was just trying to protect you. She knew what she was doing."

"Madeline, she is Claude's woman! You know that!"

"Big brother, you are so stupid sometimes. She doesn't want Claude, she wants you! The bad thing about all of this is you can't even see it!"

"Madeline, so what? That is not something for you to deal with! That is my business, not yours."

"Listen, big brother. Whoever you want to be with is fine with me. It's just not going to be some voodoo queen from the middle of a Mississippi swamp. If I didn't love you, I would just let her go on and ruin your life. That is exactly what she was going to do. Ruin your life! You can go be with any woman you want to be with. Just not her! All she wants is to get control, through you, of the Bluffs and all of the area around here for herself and her swamp people."

"Madeline, they already have control of this area! They don't need me!"

Nick stood there shaking. He could not believe what his sister had done. All of the ramifications of her action were going through his mind. None of them were good. Not one! He continued shaking his head, looking down at the ground. He could not believe it.

"You will thank me one day, big brother," Madeline said as she turned and started walking toward the dock to be taken to Cypress Landing.

"Madeline, stay away from her! Let me deal with Carlotta!" Nick yelled as Madeline continued to walk toward the dock. With a wave of her left hand, she continued walking away, not even bothering to look back.

Nick had absolutely no idea what he was going to do about this situation. He also had no idea how this incident was going to affect his operation. Time would tell but Nick was not hopeful at all. Nothing good was going to come from this. Nothing.

In addition to the situation with Carlotta, the next day an envelope was delivered to Nick at his office by a deputy. After the deputy left, Nick opened the envelope and unfolded the piece of paper inside. The note read, "Meeting tomorrow at boat two p.m..." Nick knew that the sheriff would be there and he knew that the sheriff expected him to be there also.

At the appointed time the next day, Nick was waiting on the stern of the second deck of the *Excalibur*. He could see the sheriff walk up to the boat and knew the sheriff would walk through the gaming area which, due to the time of day, was mostly deserted and then climb the stairs to where he was.

"Good afternoon, sheriff," Nick said as the sheriff walked onto the second deck from the downstairs gaming area.

"Hello, Nick," the sheriff said as he assumed his familiar position of his right boot being on the middle railing of the boat, wearing his gun in his holster and western hat on his head. Lighting up the cigarette now in his mouth, the sheriff took a puff and looked at Nick.

"Your boys have got to stop beating up my citizens."

"What are you talking about?" Nick asked.

"You know damn good and well what I'm talking about, Nick," the sheriff said, obviously irritated.

"A guy comes out of a bar and gets beat up by three guys carrying fence posts. Are you going to tell me that's not some of your people doing that?"

"Sheriff, the guy almost raped my sister. Yes, those were my guys, but he deserved it."

"Well, I don't care how much he deserved it. Save that kind of thing for your own people. I'll take care of everything else."

"Okay, Sheriff. The next time someone tries to rape my sister, I will come to see you," Nick said in a sarcastic tone.

The sheriff jerked his head around and looked right at Nick and said, "Nick, you leave that kind of stuff to me for everybody except your people. Understood?"

"Okay, okay. Understood," Nick said, with a different tone in his voice. "So tell me, sheriff, what caused all of this concern?"

"You boys have managed to upset a lot of people, most of them I don't care about, but some I do. That beating, along with everything else that the revenuers have been doing to try to intimidate everybody, was just not a good thing. We are getting more and more federal agents all over this county. You keep beating up on the locals, for whatever the reason, and you are going to have people start turning you in. Hell, I might even do it if you don't stop. So take care of that!"

With that, the sheriff flicked what remained of his cigarette into the waters of the bayou and turned to leave.

"I'll take care of it, sheriff," Nick said.

"Yes. You make sure you do that, Nick," the sheriff said over his shoulder as he walked back down the stairs.

Nick thought about that short meeting for quite a while. He finally reached the conclusion that the sheriff may know of a few dangers that Nick might not be aware of. He and his men would have to be more on guard. Everything had been going so well. Now things were beginning to get out of control.

* * *

One of the old line New Orleans families, the Walker family, had been very successful in the hotel business in the New Orleans area. The patriarch of that family, Basil Walker, had been after District Attorney Fuller to find out where all of the illegal booze was coming from. Abigail Walker, one of two Walker children, had just graduated four months earlier from a local, exclusive, all-girl's school where she had been a part of all of the social activities.

Abigail had been bored since her graduation though. She had not been dating anyone and her family would not let her work at most places she could have because they felt that those particular places and positions were beneath her status in life. At one of the recent receptions she had attended, Abigail heard her father and District Attorney Fuller talking about all of the things they thought might be going on out at the Bluffs in

Mississippi and with Nick Gable.

Abigail listened to their conversation and decided that she was the one person who could go to one of the parties occasionally held at the Bluffs and find out things that someone else might not be able to discover. After all, Abigail had made the highest grades in college and had been awarded several of her school's top scholastic awards at graduation. Abigail was sure she could deal with anything that might come up from a bunch of uneducated people living in a swamp who just happened somehow to have a lot of money. That was almost not even a worthwhile challenge for such a smart, well-educated, upper class graduate of one of the finest schools in the country.

Abigail mentioned all of her reasons for being sent over to the Bluffs soon after she had heard the two men talking at the reception. Basil Walker was not in favor of Abigail doing such a thing and told District Attorney Fuller exactly that. For his part, Fuller was not in favor of it either, although he would like to find out what had happened to the two undercover people he had sent over to the Mississippi Gulf Coast. Abigail, having nothing of interest to occupy her time, constantly brought up the matter to her father after the reception. Almost daily, she pleaded with him to let her get involved and altered between begging, whining and nagging about being allowed to do something to help get information. It all seemed like a big game to her with no thought that there could be any serious consequences.

Abigail continued to focus on getting the two men's approval of what she considered to be an opportunity for her to do something exciting. Not only would she get to attend another party, which she, of course, had plenty of experience with, it was also an opportunity for her to do something that nobody else apparently had been able to do and that was maybe find out about what happened to the two men who had been sent over there.

The situation was all brought to a head at a wedding reception after the marriage of one of Abigail's college friends. She attended the wedding and reception with her father and mother where they ran into District Attorney Fuller. After more prodding from her, the two men finally agreed that Abigail, being such a smart girl, could surely handle any situation she might find herself in. Having originally objected vigorously to such an idea, Fuller agreed, once Walker had finally said it was all right with him, to let Abigail try to get an invitation to an "End of Fall" party that Nick Gable was throwing soon at the Bluffs. Surely there was not much that could happen to her at a party of that size anyway. With an invitation, Abigail could make the trip out to the Bluffs and have a look around while she was there. Her next opportunity to approach Nick would be at the upcoming New Orleans Country Club's "Halloween" party that Fuller found out Nick would be attending.

* * *

Madeline continued to meet her mysterious friend at the Bluffs' dock. The visits were discreet with the visitor usually arriving early in the evening, always wearing black boots, black pants, a black cloak and a black hat. The guest house continued to be off limits to everyone when the visits took place. The visits usually lasted for a couple of days with the visitor returning at night to Cypress Landing where Tiny would be waiting with the limousine.

Finally, Madeline was able to talk to Nick without him getting upset by the situation her actions with Carlotta had put him in. She didn't want to think about what had taken place any more. It had happened, she had planned for it to happen, and she was glad it had happened the way it did. She didn't really care how Nick handled it, as long as he didn't end up seeing Carlotta any more. She wanted Nick isolated from that swamp woman and her friends.

For his part, Nick didn't want to talk to Madeline about it any more either. It only created problems with her screaming and yelling that her brother was not going to end up with someone who was a voodoo queen. Madeline did have time to tell him, really just to change the subject, that she felt that she was in love for the first time since the death of her husband. She told him that being in love made her feel wonderful and alive again. While Nick was happy for his sister, he still pondered how he was going to deal with the potential major problem his sister had created by her actions. Meanwhile, more vital information was passed on to Nick by Madeline after each trip to the Bluffs by Madeline's guest.

* * *

Somewhere deep in the swamp, a face looked into a faded mirror to once again examine the scar. The scar was deep and it ran for most of the length of her left cheek. The scar had ruined Carlotta's once beautiful face. She put her hand up to it, tenderly, gingerly feeling the edges of the deep cut in her face. Then she cried. Every time she looked at herself now, she cried. The scar would be with her for the rest of her life. She cried more. And then she cried out.

* * *

The members of the revenue service's little navy had been so excited about their success capturing the *Green Lizard* that they were ready for another one. However, that had not immediately happened. The vessels carrying the booze were once again more than able to not even let the agents see them. Mostly, it was due to the expertise of the sailors on the ships carrying the booze. Those seafarers had years of experience under their belts and were using that experience to perfection.

That was what worried Nick to some extent. The IRS agents needed to be allowed limited success from time to time so that they did not place their manpower where it could really do some damage, which was on shore at the shipment points. So Nick decided it was time to let the government's little navy have some success once again.

Soon, on another fairly clear night, the revenuers were once again just off of Biloxi, which is where they figured they would have more success since that was where they had seized their first boat. They determined that with the first seizure being near Biloxi, that must mean that the shipments' destination was somewhere in that area. In reality, Biloxi was nowhere near the Bluffs, but Nick did not want them to think otherwise. Besides, as long as his big sixty-five foot boats were not getting caught if he didn't want them caught, he could afford to let a boat get seized every now and then, for the good of the operation. So now it was time for another seizure in the Biloxi area.

On a night like this one, even the revenuers could not miss the ship and miss it they did not. Spotting a vessel as it loomed in the distance on a moonlit night, the revenuers pointed their boat in its direction, eventually reaching what had been seen. Following the same procedures as before, the two crewmen were handcuffed once the booze had been found. The boat was once again taken into Biloxi harbor and a few days later auctioned off. The IRS was glad its navy was so efficient now and again sent press releases out to all of the local papers.

On the day of the auction, a lot of people once again attended, but not as many as the first time. The word had gotten out that there had been no bargains at the first auction. The bidding there had been so fierce that no person in their right mind would consider taking part in the second auction. Only two bidders actually bid on the boat and then it was only a matter of minutes before one of them dropped out. The new owner, Pops Blanchard, dutifully paid his money, picked up his newly purchased boat and soon disappeared with it.

The comment was overheard from one of the IRS supervisors, who had been at the first auction and attended the second auction also, that the ship being auctioned looked a lot like the one that had been auctioned before. He was quickly assured by one of his agents that, yes it did, but it was the agent's understanding that the booze runners used what amounted to a small fleet of boats that were all alike since they had been so successful with their shipping. Having that assurance, the supervisor felt much better.

When Pops took the boat he had bought at the auction, which was named the *Blue Moon*, to the boat dock on the Wolfe River, he was met there by none other than Tiny, who had another new wooden name plate with him in his hand. The same boat, again with the name plate *Electra* on it, was back in business making a trip down to Havana in two days. On its way back north this time, its new name plate said *Cajun Lady*. The two man crew arrested when the boat had the name *Blue Moon* on it received the same treatment by the same judge that the prior crew had received. Within a week of their release after serving their three month sentence, they were back working in the shipping business. Each man enjoyed spending the bonus money provided upon their release from prison.

One night as one of the county patrol cars was carrying its load of booze to a distribution point on the other side of the county, the car was stopped by the revenuers who forced the deputy out of the car at gun point and began to take the car apart on the spot. They found the hidden booze and immediately began to push the deputy around, trying to make him talk. The revenuers were ordered by Lovelady, who could not talk because of his jaw having been partially shot off but who could write messages, to take the deputy back to Lovelady's place and make him talk.

Nick was immediately told about the seizure of the patrol car and the deputy and was concerned. It seemed that somehow information about his operation was getting into the hands of the revenuers. How had the agents found out about the patrol cars being used for shipments? They had to have had that information provided to them. It had been too specific and too accurate. More and more things were beginning to go wrong. They would have to be really careful now when they made their shipments, at least for a while. In addition, he had not seen Claude so that he could talk with him about Carlotta. Nick wanted to somehow make amends to Carlotta, but he didn't know what to do until he saw Claude. It was unusual for him not to see Claude for such a long period of time. That was not a good sign.

Chapter Thirty-three

Nick and Madeline attended the "Halloween" party at the New Orleans Country Club. Over a thousand people were there. Everyone was in a costume and having a great time. All of the power brokers came by Nick's table to greet him and his sister. Those who wanted to befriend Nick knew they had to pay homage to him. They had been told that, if he liked them, he would do things to support their causes. Others knew that he might do things to support their private needs.

During the party he was introduced to Abigail, who just insisted that she be invited to the next party that Nick threw at the Bluffs. Since the "Fall Fest" party Nick was throwing was going to be given in less than three weeks, Abigail was invited once she identified her ties to her well-known family. Madeline had several men seeking her attention, and she danced with and was entertained by each of them at some point during the evening.

The next week one of the large trucks carrying a shipment of booze was stopped by the revenuers. The contents were taken off and smashed and the driver and his rider were both taken to Lovelady's place for intense questioning. The information obtained from that questioning caused

Lovelady to call his supervisor in New Orleans and ask for permission from his supervisor in that office to go after the sheriff. After three days and two follow-up phone calls, he was finally given permission to go see the sheriff. Lovelady had one of his agents call Patterson and find out when the sheriff was going to be at his office because Lovelady wanted to come by and see him. When told by a deputy that the sheriff was out, but would be in his office at ten o'clock the next morning, which was a Saturday, the agent said to tell the sheriff that Lovelady would be there to see him then.

Lovelady still had his face taped from losing part of his jaw during the shootout. He looked like something out of those new comic books, except he was for real. He had difficulty eating, but was still trying to be active so as to show that neither he nor his men could be intimidated into not doing their job. He had to get someone to speak for him or he used a notepad to write notes on so that whoever he was dealing with would know what he was saying or at least wanted to say.

The next morning at ten o'clock, Lovelady arrived at the Hancock County Sheriff's Office just across the street from the courthouse. With him were three of his revenue officers and Peterman, all armed. As they parked in front of the jail, they noticed that not many people were on the street that was usually very busy during the week. Looking over their shoulders as they went into the sheriff's office, they realized that the street was, in fact, almost completely deserted, which was good for them and what they had to do.

Lovelady opened the door and he and Peterman were the first two inside, followed by the three other agents. The sheriff was sitting alone behind his desk with a pencil in his hand doing some paper work.

"Hello, boys, what can I do for you?" asked the sheriff as he put his pencil down on the desk and leaned back in his chair.

Lovelady wrote out something on one of his pads and handed it to Peterman who read it to the sheriff.

"Sheriff, we are here to talk to you about your deputies using patrol cars to carry illegal liquor all over this county," Peterman said reading from the piece of paper given to him by Lovelady. Then Peterman said, "You probably know that we caught one of them the other day red-handed." Lovelady then wrote again on another sheet of paper.

"We want to know how you could let such a thing happen," Peterman said, again reading Lovelady's note.

"Well, I knew that you had grabbed one of my men, but I hope you aren't holding me responsible for all of the actions of my deputies. That would mean that you should be held responsible for all of the actions of your agents, now wouldn't it?" said the sheriff, looking at the man with part of his lower jaw missing.

Peterman was handed another note by Lovelady and, after reading the note, said, "Agent Lovelady wants to know how much money you have made covering for your deputies delivering bootleg whiskey around this county."

The other revenue agents had now spread themselves in the room in front of the sheriff sitting at his desk. They all faced the sheriff and stood in such a way that if the sheriff were going to try to fight his way out of his office, he might get one or maybe even two, but with all of them facing him, he did not have a chance of making any kind of escape.

"You come into my office and ask me about cover-ups? I thought we were going to have a friendly meeting, maybe talk about how we might work together. I didn't expect you to come see me and start right off with all of this," the sheriff said now folding his arms.

With all of the agents now standing almost in a row facing the sheriff, Peterman said, "Let's just get to the bottom of all of this. Sheriff, get out of your chair and come along with us."

"Where are we going?" the sheriff asked as he looked across his desk at the five men.

"Well, we are going to take you back to Mr. Lovelady's house for a talk. We think you need to have a serious talk with us, one that won't be interrupted for a while," Peterman said as he leaned forward with both of his hands now on the sheriff's desk.

"And what are you going to do if I don't want to go with you?" the sheriff asked, now also leaning forward and looking Peterman right in his eyes. Peterman glanced at Lovelady, who was slightly nodding his head up and down, then turned to face the sheriff and said, "We are going to put you in handcuffs and take you out of here, in front of everybody."

The sheriff looked at Peterman and then at Lovelady and said, "Do you boys have anything like a warrant for my arrest, because that is really what you are talking about, isn't it? An arrest? Am I being arrested?"

Peterman looked at Lovelady again and then back at the sheriff.

"Sheriff, you are being taken into custody for questioning. Now get up and come along with us or we will drag your sorry ass out of here and everybody will see you being hauled off in handcuffs. What is it going to be?"

One of the agents standing to the sheriff's left moved his hand so that it was now on his gun in its holster. The other agents stood in front of him almost sneering at him. Peterman clearly was trying to show his boss, Lovelady, that he could handle this situation. The sheriff thought for a moment that this was probably something Peterman was counting on to get a big pay raise and promotion. The sheriff had both of his elbows now on his thighs as he leaned forward, which let him push with his left forefinger the small button under his desk that turned on a light in the back of the holding area of the jail.

"Mr. Lovelady, is this man doing something you are in agreement with?" the sheriff asked as he looked at Lovelady with what Lovelady thought was a plea for mercy.

Lovelady vigorously nodded his head up and down and motioned for Peterman to grab the sheriff. Then Peterman and the agent closest to the sheriff moved forward to grab their prey.

"Don't do that! Boys!" the sheriff yelled out.

When he did, two doors behind the agents opened and out came six deputies carrying pistols and shotguns. The noise of the doors opening caused all of the agents to turn around to see what was happening. As the agent with his hand on his gun started to pull that gun out of his holster, the sheriff grabbed his hand and shouted, "Don't even think about it, hotshot! Get your hands up! All of ya!" The sheriff's deputies clearly had the drop on the revenue agents.

"Get their guns, boys!" the sheriff said. The deputies searched the agents and made sure that they took all of the guns from the agents that they had, including two small derringers that two of the agents had up their sleeves and one gun that was found in an ankle holster.

"Back up against the wall! And keep your hands up!" shouted the sheriff. The agents all backed against the wall with the deputies holding guns and shotguns on them.

"Ronnie, put all of those guns of theirs in one of our canvas bags," the sheriff said to one of his deputies. The deputy did so and put the bag on the sheriff's desk. The sheriff then faced the lineup of agents as they continued to hold their hands up.

"You scumbags! I know what you boys have been doing to the citizens of my county here. I know you've been beating people up and keeping people for days without food and water and not letting them talk to anybody. I ought to put all of you thugs in jail for violating the United States constitution which, I think, you were sworn to uphold. If I hear one more thing about any of our citizens getting beat up in your house up there where you have been takin'em, I am going to come arrest all of ya. If I have to call the governor and get the state national guard down here to stop you, I'll do that too!"

Walking over to Peterman, the sheriff got right in his face and said, "You had better find another line of work, boy." Pointing at Lovelady, he continued, "Hanging around this guy is going to get you in trouble. It got him part of his jaw shot off."

Walking over to Lovelady, the sheriff got in his face and said, "You gutless piece of shit. Who in the hell do you think you are? Coming into my county and treating the people of my county like you do."

Then getting his face not inches from where Lovelady's jaw used to be, the sheriff said in a low monotone voice, "If I hear about you beating up one more person in my county, I am coming after you, boy. You hear me? I will arrest you just like anybody else and throw your sorry ass in jail and we will have a trial, convict you and send you to prison, unless you get killed in some sort of accident first."

Backing a step away from Lovelady, but still looking at him, the sheriff continued, "And if you mess with me anymore, you are gonna find yourself with a lot more serious problems than just part of your jaw missing."

Stepping back further, the sheriff said, "Your guns will be delivered to you in a few hours at that hellhole your boss here calls home."

Motioning to his deputies, he then said, "Get these assholes out of here."

One of his deputies opened the front door and the agents were let out of the sheriff's office one by one. They were thankful there weren't many people on the street to see them coming out of the sheriff's office with their hands up.

The sheriff's deputies, carrying their shotguns and pistols at the ready, walked the agents out to their car. They stood there watching as the agents got into the car, started the engine, and pulled off.

Walking back into the jail, one of the deputies asked the sheriff, "How did you know they were going to do that, sheriff?"

The sheriff sat down in his chair, much more comfortable now, leaned back in it and said, "Let's just say our friends were looking out for us."

Chapter Thirty-four

Nick was told by the sheriff about what had happened, but decided to go ahead with his Friday night "Fall Fest" party as if everything was normal. After all, the IRS had talked to the sheriff, not Nick. The party would go on. There was no reason to cancel it. That would just raise questions.

The party at the Bluffs was well underway by seven p.m. The barges carrying the visitors were greeted at the dock by a Dixieland jazz band playing loudly and continuously. Attendees included people from New Orleans, as well as those from the local area. The band eventually paraded up to the mansion where the big dining room had been cleared of furniture for dancing. The fall weather not being too chilly yet, the French doors of the living room were opened onto the veranda and traffic flowed freely.

Abigail arrived on one of the regular barges from Cypress Landing at about eight-thirty and was amazed by what all she saw. She had been worried that she might be overdressed by wearing one of her very expensive dance dresses. However, once she looked around and saw that most of the other women there were equally well-dressed, if not even more so, she felt better. She had seen a lot of elegance during her young years, but to see all of the attendees in what was surely some of their finest attire impressed her. Something else that impressed her was finding this mansion and extensive set of other buildings out in the middle of a swamp.

Knowing some of the people at the party, she tried to move from small group to small group and yet not allow herself to constantly have someone from New Orleans standing by her side. She recognized several people who knew her family rather well and spent time talking with various ones, mostly in an attempt to hide her efforts to observe attendees and at the same time to look at the layout of the place.

After about two hours of going from group to group and exchanging the small talk so common at parties like this one, Abigail felt that it was getting late and now was as good of an opportunity as she was probably going to get to look for Nick's office. If she was lucky, she might find something that showed what types of businesses Nick was involved in. She was actually excited that she also might find that part of those businesses involved something illegal.

She had noticed down an adjacent hallway what she thought might be the door to a room she wanted to examine more closely. When the opportunity presented itself, she excused herself from those with whom she was conversing to retire to a nearby restroom. After checking to make sure no one was in the hallway, she left the restroom and walked over to the door. Quietly turning the knob, she was able to determine that the door was not locked. She eased the door open and entered the room, quickly closing it behind her.

It was totally dark inside the room except for the reflections of light from the kerosene lamps and lighted torches around the grounds outside the house, which served the dual purpose of keeping the flies and mosquitoes away and also providing light for the guests. The lighting cast an eerie glow. It reminded her of the stories of voodoo in the swamp that she had heard about when she was a child. Seeing the flickering shadows from the fiery sticks caused a chill to run through her body.

Abigail groped her way around the room until she reached a desk sitting near the center of the room. The big window behind the desk provided some light. She sensed that she might have the right room for her purposes.

She managed to work her way around the desk to get behind it, but stayed at the left corner of the desk so that her back would not be to the window behind the desk. She did not want anyone who might be outside to notice that there was someone in that office going through what she now assumed was Nick's desk. She pulled open the top drawer and was able to see that there was nothing but blank sheets of paper, envelopes and pens in that drawer. Quietly shutting that drawer, she opened the drawer below it.

The second drawer contained several documents that looked to be legal papers, all stacked very neatly. She took the top document and moved closer to the window to read it. After quickly scanning the document, she noticed the Chicago address at the top of the first page.

A moment after she saw the address, she heard the click of a door latch. She looked up from the document and got the shock of her young life. Madeline was standing at the door, looking straight at Abigail.

"What do you think you are doing?" Madeline demanded.

"Oh, I was just looking around. This room is so interesting," Abigail said as she slowly lowered the document to the top of the desk.

"No, you weren't. You were going through papers in that desk," Madeline said as she began slowly walking toward Abigail.

"Why, I don't know what you are talking about! How dare you accuse me of that," Abigail said. She moved from behind the desk to make a quick dash for the doorway.

Madeline moved, blocking Abigail's escape route, and said, "Not so fast, dear. Where do you think you're going? Do you think you can just come in here and go through somebody's papers and then pretend nothing happened?"

As Madeline took another step toward her, Abigail saw a reflection off of a silver letter opener lying on the desk. She grabbed it, and then raised it like a knife, saying, "Stay away from me!"

Backing away a step, Madeline said, "My, my, my, little girl."

Madeline had seen knife fights before and knew about how far a person could reach holding a weapon the size of the letter opener. She made sure she was standing at least far enough away so that if Abigail were to lunge at her with the letter opener, Madeline would have time to react.

Looking at her, Madeline said, "What do you think you're going to do now? Just walk out of here?"

Abigail hoped so. This had not turned out right. Here she was in the middle of a swamp in the middle of nowhere, holding a letter opener like a knife on the sister of the man who had invited her. She had to find some way to get away from this woman and back to the party and get on a boat back to Cypress Landing.

She backed away from Madeline very slowly and moved toward the door, poised to strike.

"I saw you when you first got here," Madeline taunted. "You didn't fit the type of girl my brother usually asks out here, so it made me wonder just exactly what a little girl like you was doing here."

Abigail continued to gradually edge herself toward the door while still facing Madeline. Madeline folded her arms and took a couple of small steps to the side, which made Abigail turn so that she still was facing her.

"I saw you constantly looking around, but not always at people. Then I saw you leave the room, but didn't see you come back. When I came to see where the little girl had gone, I saw the door to this room being closed. I wondered if the little girl had gone into this room and, if she had, what the little girl was up to."

"Shut up, you piece of white trash! And stay away from me!"

"My, my! Such language! Do your parents know you use such rude language, little girl?"

"If you know who my parents are, then you know what they would do to you, and your brother, if anything happens to me out here. And I am not a little girl. So leave me alone!" Abigail said. Mentioning her parents was reassuring to her and she now felt that talking about them may be her way out of her situation.

"I know who your parents ---."

Abigail did not hear the rest-she suddenly felt her head explode. She fell unconscious on the floor. Tiny had come in behind her as Madeline distracted her. He had slugged her with the wooden handle of one of the umbrellas from Nick's umbrella holder next to the door.

"Pick her up. Take her down to the stables, to the tack room in the back," Madeline said as she put the letter opener back on the desk and the umbrella back in its holder.

"Keep her quiet down there, Tiny. We don't need her to wake up and start screaming."

"Yessum," Tiny said as he picked up the woman and put her over his shoulder.

Madeline stepped outside and looked both ways down the hall. No one was coming. She motioned for Tiny to come through the door and then go out the back door.

"And, Tiny, start the fire," she said as he walked past her.

Madeline went back into the office and looked at the stack of documents. Now the question was what all had Abigail read in those documents. Looking over the papers Abigail had left on Nick's desk, she could not tell. Hopefully not much, but they would have to find out later, after the guests left.

When Madeline returned to the party, the guests had begun to leave. Madeline knew she would have to tell Nick about what had happened in his office. She was finally able to mention it to him in a lull between seeing guests off while standing on the veranda at the front of the house.

"Remember the girl named Abigail that I asked you about earlier?" Madeline asked.

"Yes. I haven't seen her lately. She must have left. Did you see her leave?"

"She's not leaving just yet," Madeline said softly.

"What do you mean," Nick said, now looking at Madeline.

"I caught her going through some papers in your desk. She grabbed your letter opener and was going to stab me with it."

"What? She did what?" Nick wanted to know more, now.

"She grabbed your letter opener when I found her going through your papers in your desk. I had seen her go into your office. Before I went in to see what she was up to, I told Tiny to follow me. While I kept her attention, Tiny slipped in behind her. She was holding your letter opener on me like a knife. He hit her with the handle of one of your umbrellas. Knocked her out. He took her down to the tack room and is keeping her there until we decide what we are going to do."

"Madeline! Abigail is the daughter of one of the most well-known families in New Orleans! How are we going to explain this? What is he doing with her down at the tack room?" So many questions were going through Nick's mind.

"Tiny is not doing anything but holding her down there so far. I had been keeping an eye on her because I thought she was acting strange. Looking and walking around, not really with anyone in particular but taking everything in. Not enjoying the party at all. It was like she was looking for something. I thought maybe she was looking for somebody, but she never connected with anyone. It really got to be obvious. She wanted to snoop around this house."

Their conversation stopped as another group of people said their goodbyes. When those guests headed for the dock, Madeline said, "Meet me right here after everyone has left. Don't go down to the stables. Don't let Abigail see you until you and I talk." She then returned to what was left of the party.

It was a little after midnight when the last barge left carrying the remaining, mostly drunken, guests. Nick was anxious for everyone to leave so he could find out more about the office incident and what needed to be done. His sister had again caused him a severe problem. He had no idea how he was going to solve this one. Nick knew who Abigail was and now Madeline had her, the daughter of one of New Orleans' most well-known families, being held in the stables at his place. How in the world was he going to explain this one?

He was standing on the veranda when Madeline came downstairs dressed in riding clothes. The jodhpurs and white blouse she had on were what she wore to enjoy the outdoors while riding horses around the Bluffs. This time, the outfit was not being worn for a happy occasion. It was being worn because Madeline did not have any idea what was going to happen. She did know one thing though. The girl at the stables had no idea who or what she was dealing with.

When he saw Madeline, Nick knew that she was expecting the worst. She never liked being seen by someone from the so-called upper class, such as this girl now in the tack room, unless she was dressed like she was part of that class. The way Madeline was dressed now meant that things were probably not going to go well. Madeline was not trying at all to impress the girl in the stables with what she was wearing.

As they walked from the house down toward the stables, Madeline said, "Nick, you asked for trouble by inviting her. She had no business being here. You created this problem. Why don't you go back to the house and let me handle this."

"You have got to be kidding me! You put the kid of one of the most important families in New Orleans in one of our stables and you want me to let you handle it? Madeline, this is your brother talking to you. What happens to that girl may determine what happens to me! And to you! "

"Listen to me! Listen to me!" Madeline said as she grabbed Nick's arm and stopped walking.

"She has not seen you. She doesn't know if you even know about what has happened. Don't let her see you. Let her think it's only me involved with all of this, if she even thinks that."

Nick gave it some thought.

"Let me take care of it, Nick. I have always tried to help you, haven't I? Let me take care of this. Go back to the house. I'll let you know what I find out."

Nick thought about what his sister had just said. It was true that Abigail did not know if he was involved with her being in the situation she found herself. Maybe Madeline was right.

"Okay. Okay. I'll go back to the house, but be gentle, okay?"

Madeline smiled at him and nodded her head. Nick turned and left. It was up to Madeline now.

Madeline walked into the tack area of the back stable and saw Tiny and two of the stable men sitting on bales of hay. Abigail, lying on the dirt floor in front of them, was still unconscious. One of her high heeled shoes was missing, causing Madeline to wonder where it was. But there were more important things on her mind at the moment.

"Get a bucket of water and throw it on her. Let's see if we can wake her up," Madeline said. Tiny got up and walked over to one of the wooden buckets on the ground, picked it up and filled it from a nearby trough. After carrying the filled bucket back over to where Abigail was, he splashed her with the water. She moved slightly and began to moan. She lay there trying to get her well-educated brain to work again.

"Get her up and lean her back against that post," Madeline ordered. As Tiny pulled her up and leaned her against the post, Madeline sat on one of the bales of hay facing the now wet and soiled young woman.

Abigail leaned her head back against the post and moaned.

"Can you hear me?" Madeline said looking at her. Tiny must have really hit her hard, she thought. It was good that the girl was moaning. At least he hadn't killed her.

"Can you hear me?" Madeline asked again.

Finally blinking her eyes ever so slowly, Abigail tried to say something.

"Wha hapnd?" she tried to mumble.

"Why were you prying into Nick's desk?" Madeline asked. There was no response. Madeline repeated the question again. And again.

Abigail finally slowly spoke, "You'd better let me go. My parents are going to be so angry with you. You had better let me go right now." She then tried to get up, but Tiny pushed her back down next to the post.

"Look. Don't make this hard on yourself. Just tell me why you were looking in Nick's desk and you can leave." Madeline hoped this would make sense to a girl in Abigail's precarious situation.

Abigail looked at Madeline through glazed eyes. She had a pounding headache, but she was alert enough to know she did not want to answer that question.

"If you let me go right now, you might not spend too much time in jail after my family gets through with you. Let me go," Abigail said.

Madeline had had enough. She was not going to waste any more time with this insolent little girl. If this girl had any sense, any common sense at all, she would have shown it by now. Madeline decided she needed to try another tact with this one. She stood up and walked over to the fire that had been started in the pit nearby. She pulled gloves on that were near the pit and grabbed one of the branding irons, putting it in the fire. Then she turned around to face Abigail and said, "Tiny, hold her arms."

Tiny grabbed her arms from behind her, just above her elbows, and held them tightly in his big hands so Abigail's back was firmly against the post.

"I have asked you very nicely-and repeatedly- what you were looking for in Nick's desk. You have one more chance to answer me," Madeline said in a voice that was calm but firm.

"Let go of me! Tell him to get his hands off of me! You think you're scaring me?" Abigail bluffed. "If you don't let me go right now, you could spend the rest of your life in jail for kidnapping at least, and your sorry brother too. Let me go!" She tried to get up, but Tiny held her in place against the post.

Madeline walked over, now holding the steaming hot iron in her gloved right hand. She bent over about three feet in front of Abigail and, holding the iron in front of Abigail's face, said, "You have one last chance, dearie."

Abigail looked at Madeline and needed no more than a fraction of a second to know that her options were nonexistent. She knew this Madeline person meant business.

"Okay. Okay. Enough of this. Okay!"

Taking a brief moment to again assess her situation, she decided she had better start talking or things were quickly going to get really bad for her. She took a big breath, resigned that she was going to have to say something because she did not want that hot piece of iron to touch her. She just knew that if she gave Madeline a reason, that was exactly what was going to happen. Abigail's game was over. Maybe she would just be let go if she would tell everything.

"I am working for the district attorney of New Orleans. I offered to get invited to this party over here because they could not get anybody that they trusted out to this place. They think that Nick is running illegal liquor through here somehow. I was to try to find something that would show that. The only document that I had time to read was the one showing the money that has been sent to Chicago because of the rum shipments that have been made from here. Then you came in. Now, let me go!"

"Not so fast, dearie. Exactly who are the 'they' you are talking about?" Madeline asked, still holding the smoldering hot iron.

"District Attorney Fuller and other law enforcement people over there in New Orleans. District Attorney Fuller knows a lot about Nick. Now, let me go, please?"

Madeline was having a hard time understanding if this society girl really understood the ramifications of what she had just said.

"So you came over here for the District Attorney of New Orleans to find out more about Nick running liquor from here?"

"Yes! Now, let me go!" Abigail tried to move again, but Tiny held her in place against the post.

"I ought to use this branding iron on you just for your being so obvious and stupid!"

Madeline thought for a moment and then stood up. She walked over and put the branding iron back in the pit. Walking back by Tiny and the girl, she said to Tiny, "I don't care what you do to her. You boys have some fun. Just don't kill her yet." With a glance back at Abigail, Madeline began walking out of the barn.

"Wait! You said I could leave! You told me that!" Abigail shouted.

Madeline glanced back over her shoulder and said, "I lied," and kept walking.

"You lied? Don't leave me here with them!"

Madeline heard Abigail screaming all the way back to the mansion.

Chapter Thirty-five

Basil Walker appeared at the District Attorney's office at seven o'clock Saturday morning. Fuller got there about twenty minutes later. When Walker had called Fuller earlier that morning to tell him that Abigail had not returned from Mississippi during the night, Fuller did not know what to do and had suggested that they get together at his office.

"Go find her, Sam! You have got to go find her!" Walker all but yelled.

"I just can't go over there and do that. I really can't. My jurisdiction is here in New Orleans. I just can't go flying off over there." Fuller did not like having these types of conversations, especially with one of his chief political and financial backers.

"Yes, you can, Sam. She went over there to help you! Now, go find her! I don't care how you do it, but do it!"

"I told you to not let her go do that, Basil. I didn't want to send her over there in the first place. I told you that!" Fuller answered.

He could see it now. He had finally agreed to let her go after her father, of all people, pressured him into doing it. Now he was catching it for letting her go. He was going to get all of the blame.

"That doesn't matter! Not now!" Basil said, almost yelling. "Go find her!"

"How do you expect me to do that, Basil? I told you. I have no jurisdiction over there. How do you propose I handle it?"

"Sam, she is my daughter. If you don't do something, every newspaper around here for miles is going to know that Abigail went over there for you and you did nothing to find her! Nothing!"

"All right. All right. I will call a few judges I know and see if I can get some sort of order authorizing me to go over there."

Fuller began using the phone in his office while Walker went over to a secretary's desk outside of Fuller's office. Using a phone there, he began making a few calls himself. Fuller called two state judges and even a federal district judge who owed him a few favors, but each one told him they could not do anything. One of the judges did tell him that a place called Cypress Landing, at the end of the third dirt road off of U. S. Highway 90 after entering Mississippi, was the closest place to get a boat out to the Bluffs.

Walker called the U. S. Attorney, Jack Montgomery, another good friend, but upon finding Montgomery, he was told the same thing Fuller had said, that he could not do anything over in Mississippi. Being a big political supporter of Sheriff Tom Miller, Walker also called him and, after telling him the situation, got Miller to agree to come over to Fuller's office as soon as he could get there.

When Walker and Fuller got back together again about thirty minutes after their first meeting, Sheriff Tom Miller walked into Fuller's office. Fuller knew Miller well. Miller was a long-time friend and was well-respected by not only Fuller but almost everybody.

After hand shakes all around, Walker said, "Sam, Sheriff Miller here has agreed to get a few of his deputies and go over there with you. He told me he would go but you have to ask him and you have to go too. You have to tell him it's alright. You have got to do that, Sam. You have got to do something! You've just got to!"

"Basil, let Tom and me discuss this, okay? Just stay here while we talk." Fuller then took Sheriff Miller into an adjacent office and shut the door.

"Tom, you know we don't have any jurisdiction over there. How can we do that? I don't want to lead you into something you and I both know is not right." Fuller said, shaking his head and looking at the floor.

"I have had two undercover people disappear over there. There is no telling what happened to Basil's daughter. I feel so bad about it. I watched Abigail grow up. But I know what you and I can and cannot legally do."

After a moment of thought, Tom said, "Yeah, Sam, you're right. You and I both know what we can and cannot do legally. But what about being human beings, Sam? What about being friends? We know where she went. We know when she went. I made a few calls to some people I know who went over there to that party and they are all back. We know she didn't come back. Now, she may have just met some ol' boy over there and is with him now, although you and I both know that is probably not the situation, knowing her. So then maybe it's some type of an emergency. Maybe it even involves a kidnapping. If that's the case, then she may be in a lot of trouble already and not live very long if we don't do something about it right now. Let's just go check into it and see if we can find her. Not officially, but as friends. But, let's assume the worst. Let's take a few of my men just in case. I think they would agree to come along."

Fuller looked at his old friend. Tom Miller was one of the most decent people he had ever known. Leave it to Tom to put it all in perspective. It was simply about going to find a friend's daughter. If it were Fuller's daughter who was missing, Fuller knew Tom and probably Basil also would both do whatever it took to find her.

"How soon can you get your men together?" Fuller asked.

"Some of them are already at my office for the morning roll call. Let me talk with them and maybe a few more and I'll meet you at the Pearl River ferry on Highway 90 at the state line in about two hours," Miller said.

"Okay. Get going. I'll see you there. And Tom, tell your men to bring a lot of firepower. If this involves who I think it might, this may be much bigger than we can imagine."

"I was thinking the same thing. I've heard a few things about that situation over there also. I'll make sure they are ready," Miller said as he turned to leave. Opening the door, Miller said smiling, "Sam, we are going to find out just how good a lawyer you are with this one."

"Come see me in jail, okay?" Fuller said with a chuckle.

"Come see you? Hell, I'm gonna be right in there with you," Miller said laughing.

Going back into the room where Walker was waiting, Fuller said, "Okay, Basil. We are going over there. But only if you stay here."

"Not on your life! That's my daughter we're talking about. I'm going, too!"

Fuller looked at Miller and then back at Walker. "I would have been disappointed in you if you hadn't said that. Okay, see you in two hours, Tom. Let's go Basil. It's not everyday I get the chance to throw my political career away."

Chapter Thirty-six

The meeting just after ten-thirty a.m. at the Highway 90 Pearl River ferry at the Mississippi-Louisiana border looked like what preparations for a small invasion might have looked like. There were five cars in all. Three of them were Orleans Parish police cars each carrying four of Tom Miller's deputies, those who had been at the morning roll call and a few others who had been summoned by Miller to come help out. One of the cars was Miller's personal car with three more of his men in it. Fuller and Walker came in Fuller's car along with one of Fuller's assistant district attorneys, whom Fuller made sure knew that he was coming strictly as a volunteer.

The men gathered around as Fuller told them where the cutoff road was to Cypress Landing. Once there, they might have to force themselves onto the boats that were normally kept there to shuttle people back and forth to the Bluffs. Several of the deputies had brought shotguns, and two even had submachine guns that no one could ever remember having been taken out of their locked case in the sheriff's office. A few of the men had brought along their favorite hunting rifles and all had handguns in their holsters.

Fuller briefly told them about Walker's daughter being missing and what she had been trying to find out for his office. He also told them about the other two people he had sent over to the Mississippi coast undercover who were also missing and had never returned. Fuller made it clear to them that if they went with him and Miller, they would probably not be legally protected as law enforcement officers. In fact, they could get into a lot of trouble for crossing the border and using force. However, if there had been a kidnapping, he would try to put together a legal argument to protect whoever went with them, if they could somehow get the kidnappers back to Louisiana. He then asked for a show of hands of all those who would still go with him and their sheriff over into Mississippi to see if they could find Walker's daughter. The vote was unanimous.

Smiling, Fuller said, "Well, Tom, it looks like we might have some company in that jail cell we talked about."

The men all chuckled and then Miller said, "You all know why we are doing this. Thank you all for volunteering. Now, let's go find that girl."

The group dispersed to their various cars. With Fuller leading and Walker's car bringing up the rear, the caravan began its invasion of the Mississippi Gulf Coast. The cars were loaded onto the ferry and transported over to the Mississippi side of the Pearl River, the dividing line between the two states at that location. Once all of the cars were unloaded on the Mississippi side, Fuller drove as fast as possible. After about forty minutes, the line of cars turned off of the main highway and onto a dirt road, becoming covered in a cloud of dust that almost immediately shrouded the group. They went as quickly as they could, taking the many turns in the road that was covered by the canopy of numerous trees.

The cars quickly pulled up at Cypress Landing. The group caught the two men lounging next to the dock totally by surprise. One of the men was quickly handcuffed around one of the smaller live oak trees near the dock. The other one was convinced that it was in his best interest to take them by the most direct route to the Bluffs. His cooperation had been quickly obtained once he had watched a shotgun being placed about six inches from his face. Two deputies were left to stand guard at Cypress Landing as the group moved quickly to get into the two boats. Fuller prevailed on Walker to also stay at Cypress Landing because of the possibility of gunfire at the Bluffs. If they were successful in finding

Abigail, he did not want an emotional father jeopardizing the rescue and maybe being shot in the process.

"Y'all hurry back, you hear?" Walker said as they loaded into the boats. "Watch out for my girl!" Walker yelled as the group floated away from the dock.

The group took the boats down the bayou as quickly as they could. As the boats landed at the cement docks at the Bluffs, the men jumped out with weapons in hand and rushed up the Bluffs and onto the flat, open ground. The attack was so quick that even the peacocks did not have much time to sound a warning. Only six gunshots were fired by Nick's men, and most of those were in the first few moments of the takeover. Hearing the first shots, Nick came out of the mansion with a gun in his hand. He immediately saw the two men with submachine guns and realized it was useless to resist. He dropped his gun and put up his hands. He was handcuffed along with the two men who had fired the shots. Three of the deputies stood guard over them, two of them holding shotguns, while the others began searching the grounds.

Nick's unarmed men were not handcuffed. They were checked for weapons, separated from the others, and then told to sit on the ground next to a big oak under the watchful guard of four deputies with guns drawn. Rocko was included in this group because at the beginning of the attack, like Nick, he had quickly evaluated the weapons carried by the deputies and knew that shooting his handgun would have been futile. When he had walked out of one of the barns, he made sure he did not have any guns on him and that his hands were high up in the air.

Madeline had run out of the house to see if the sound she had heard was gunfire and quickly had a gun pointed at her by one of the deputies. Looking at the particularly handsome young deputy holding the gun, Madeline said, as only Madeline would say in such a situation, "You don't have to point that thing at me, honey. If you want to, you can search me just to make sure I'm not carrying any guns."

Her smile made the deputy feel more comfortable with her but, after visibly checking her out, he answered, "No, ma'am. I don't think that will be necessary but still, if you would, just stand over there with the others for the time being."

Madeline walked over to the tree and stood there with the others who had not resisted and were now sitting on the ground.

The search of the premises quickly revealed barrel upon barrel of bootleg whiskey stored in the two barns and in a small, new warehouse behind the stables. In the rear of the warehouse near the back stable, the deputies stopped Tiny and two other men as they attempted to run into the woods. Inside the last stable, a partially nude Abigail was found on the floor. She was breathing, but that was about it. Tiny and the two men were handcuffed and a deputy took them to join Nick's group.

The men covered Abigail with a blanket from the stables and hurriedly carried her to one of the boats. She had to be carried because she couldn't walk. Although barely conscious, she couldn't talk either. The vacant stare in her eyes indicated that she was, at the very least, in a total state of shock.

Fuller instructed a few of the deputies to load some of the barrels of booze onto the boats so they could take them back to Louisiana as evidence. With some difficulty, the men loaded several of the barrels on the barge that was carrying Nick and his handcuffed associates. Madeline and the men who had not resisted were left where they were and not taken to the boats. The men conducting this possibly illegal raid felt they had enough to take back as it was. The two vessels were soon on their way back up the bayou to Cypress Landing.

As the group docked back at Cypress Landing, Walker broke down when he saw his daughter. He took her from the two deputies carrying her and held her close. He constantly talked to her, trying to comfort her and telling her over and over that he would get her the best medical help possible when they got back to New Orleans.

Miller assigned a deputy to drive Walker and his daughter in Walker's car back to Louisiana. The other men all quickly piled into their cars after assigning Nick and the other prisoners one by one to separate cars. The two men at the landing were left there, not sure they had actually seen everything that they had.

When they arrived back in New Orleans, Miller put Nick and the prisoners in his jail. Fuller immediately began making calls and visiting with judges to determine what to do with those he had picked up and brought back. Finally, the U.S. Attorney for New Orleans agreed to take the cases since there had been a kidnapping and also since so much illegal liquor had been found at the Bluffs. Some of the markings on the barrels brought over from Mississippi were found to match up with markings on barrels that had been confiscated in Louisiana. When two of the men who had been arrested in New Orleans with the marked barrels were interviewed, once they were assured of shorter sentences if they helped the investigation, both men identified Nick as the head of the operation shipping the booze they had brought into New Orleans. The U.S. Attorney in New Orleans then filed charges against Nick and each of the men that had been brought back into Louisiana.

Chapter Thirty-seven

Abigail was not going to be of any help to the U. S. Attorney. Her mental condition was such that, once in New Orleans, she had been taken directly to the Community Hospital. Her hours of abuse in the barn at the hands of Tiny and the other two men after Madeline had left had taken a severe toll on Abigail. She was now in a state of total shock, unconscious and unable to speak. Her family, her doctors and the U. S. Attorney felt that if she were able to have peace and quiet that maybe she could recover enough to, hopefully, tell them who was responsible for what had happened to her and also tell them what she had found out at the Bluffs.

At the hospital, she was put in a room on the second floor and U. S. Marshals were assigned to protect her. Since her father did not want her location known to the public, it was decided to try to keep as low a profile as possible and, therefore, only two marshals were actually on duty at any one time. That way, she might not become exposed to the intense scrutiny of the local press, who were trying to get the details of exactly what had happened and had begun to search for her.

Madeline was worried about Abigail; specifically, what Abigail might say about Madeline's role in what all had happened. Yes, Nick was in jail, but Madeline was not and she wanted to stay that way. After the raiders had left the Bluffs area, Madeline conferred with Rocko about what to do.

"She read some of the papers in Nick's desk," Madeline said while standing with Rocko in front of the main house at the Bluffs. Knowing that Rocko was usually the one man Nick had counted on to do the extremely dirty work that had occasionally been performed, and also having observed that Rocko had always been a loyal soldier, so to speak, for Nick, Madeline pressed that point.

"You have to go do something, Rocko. You have to go find out where that girl is being kept. It would have to be at some hospital, I would guess. It would have to be. Go over there, Rocko, and ask some of our friends and find out where she is," Madeline said earnestly. "We have to protect Nick, Rocko. He would do the same for us, you know he would." She noticed Rocko shaking his head slowly in agreement.

"You have got to go over there now. Find out where she is. Take one of the men with you, but go. Don't let time go by or that little girl can fix it so Nick cannot get out of this," Madeline said watching for more reaction. She kept to herself the fact that Abigail could do as much harm, if not more, to her than to Nick if she were ever able to begin relating her recent experiences.

"Okay," Rocko said. "If that's what you think I should do, I'll get one of the boys and we'll go over there. We'll see if we can find out anything."

"Good, Rocko. Good. That is exactly what Nick would want you to do. He would want you to go help him by finding out where she is." Then, in a firm voice, Madeline said, "And Rocko, once you find out where she is, take care of the problem." Rocko's head quickly turned toward Madeline and she slowly said it again, "Take care of the problem."

The next night, a light drizzle settled in over New Orleans. This often happened during this time of year, the late fall, when cooler weather moved in to mix with the balmy warm weather left over from the hot summer. The newly paved road and parking lot in front of the Community Hospital, with the coating of rain, reflected the occasional street lights in the area. The area had a peaceful appearance since what few automobiles that had been present had departed once visiting hours were over at eight p.m. The quietness was only broken by the light, steady downpour and the wind that blew in with the change in temperature.

At about three-thirty a.m., an automobile moved slowly along the street on the east side of the hospital and came to a stop next to a big live oak tree, one of several in the area that were as old as the city itself. Out of the car stepped an individual who quickly eased into the shadow of the huge tree as the car began to move again down the side street. The person waited until the car made its turn onto the street running in front of the hospital and drove down that street until it arrived in the half moon drive-way in front of the hospital. The figure then walked across the side street in the drizzle of the rain and stood next to the door leading to the fire escape that ran the height of the five-story building. After checking in all directions, the person opened the door to the fire escape and entered the stairway area, quickly closing the door behind them.

At the front of the hospital, a man got out of the automobile and went to the door, opened it and walked into the lobby area.

"Who's in charge here?" he demanded as he walked up to the desk located not too far from the front door.

The nurse sitting at that desk replied, "It's after visiting hours, sir," she said very politely.

"I am Beasley with the Times Picayune. We just heard y'all have that Abigail Walker girl here. Is that true?"

"Mr. Beasley, we are not permitted to give out information about our patients. So I can't answer your question about any of that," the nurse said now standing up.

"We heard y'all have her here on the second floor, is that true? You know the girl, the one that was brought back over from Mississippi?"

A large man with "Deputy-Marshal" on a badge on the left front pocket of his shirt stood up from his slumber in the seating area to the left of the man and began walking over. As he did, Beasley moved quickly toward the stairway behind the desk.

"I am going to go up to the second floor and see if she's here," he said as he moved up the stairs, now followed by the deputy-marshal.

"Sir, you can't go up there!" the nurse yelled out to the man as he bounded up the stairs and disappeared past the landing in the flight of stairs with the deputy in pursuit.

While the commotion at the flight of stairs was taking place, Rocko made it up the fire escape stairs, stopping at the doorway to the second floor. It was unlocked, as he had been told it would be because the doors were never locked. They had to always be open so they could be used in case of a fire. No one in a position of responsibility wanted to get everyone trapped inside if there was indeed a fire of any significance.

Easing the fire escape door slightly open, Rocko peered down the hallway and saw a man in a uniform sitting in a straight-back chair which had been placed in the hallway next to the door to room 205. The officer had his attention directed toward the center stairway since a lot of noise was being made by a man coming up that stairway. The officer got up from his chair and went down the hallway to stop the man who had just come up to the second floor. Soon they were joined by the deputy-marshal from the first floor and by the second floor nurse. All were trying to calm the intruder down and fend off his flood of questions. The center stairway was situated so that the privacy of the rooms along the hallways was protected. A person standing at the desk on each floor could not see down the hallways of that floor.

As the three people continued to be asked about Abigail Walker's presence, Rocko eased down the hallway to the room with the chair in front of its doorway. As he slowly pushed against the door to room 205, he looked in and saw a woman who appeared to be sleeping and was undisturbed by the voices at the end of the hallway. Walking silently over to the chart hanging from a hook on the metal frame at the foot of the bed, Rocko took it and held it up to available light. He saw at the top of the chart the name, "Abigail Walker."

Easing the chart back onto its hook, Rocko walked over to the side of the bed and picked up a pillow from the bed that was not being used by its sleeping occupant. He looked at the woman for a moment and then slowly pressed the pillow over the woman's head. There was almost no reaction at all from her. Only after he had held the pillow in place for a few seconds was there any stirring, and then it was just for a moment. Soon her covers were no longer moving up and down with her breathing. Everything was still. After keeping the pillow in place for a few extra seconds just to make sure, Rocko then pulled the pillow up and put it back in its place at the head of the bed next to the one being used by the bed's occupant. He then eased back to the door.

Peering through the crack in the doorway, Rocko heard the continuing discussion down the hallway in the desk area. He slipped out of the room, making sure the door was in the same position as before he had entered. He hastily made his way to the fire escape door at the end of the hallway, opened it quietly, and after getting into that stairway, closed the door without making a sound. He had left his raincoat on the railing of the stairway so there would be no water from the rain left on the hallway floor. He slipped the coat back on while silently descending the stairway. Soon he was back outside standing next to the familiar large oak tree.

The discussion at the desk on the second floor continued for a few minutes more. Then Beasley announced, "Look, I understand you guys have a job to do. So do I. But, you guys being here tells me what I need to know. I won't bother you any more. She's here and that's what I needed to know right now for my story. You are all just doing your jobs."

The two marshals looked at each other. They didn't like this guard duty, but the U. S. Attorney had gotten them into it. They were more than willing to just let this newspaper guy go away, as long as he did it right now, which he did. Going down the stairs, apologizing all the way, Beasley left the building and got into his automobile. Driving away in the now misting rain, he pulled around to go down the side street he had come in on, stopping to pick up his passenger. Once Rocko was in the car, they disappeared into the night.

When the ruckus was over at the desk on the second floor, the officer who had been on duty sitting in the chair in front of room 205 returned to his post. Taking a moment, he eased the door open and saw the girl inside sleeping very peacefully, he thought, just as before the disturbance. He returned to his chair and took a big breath, relaxing once again. This really was not that bad a duty to pull if that was all that happened, he thought.

The next morning, the morning of the second day after the raid, when the floor nurse came down the hallway at six-thirty a.m. to make her rounds, she noticed the officer sleeping in the chair in the hallway next to the door to room 205. She opened the room's door and walked in. The occupant seemed peaceful enough, although upon further thought maybe too peaceful. As she moved closer to examine the female figure, she noticed something that immediately shocked her. The woman wasn't breathing. She was dead.

Chapter Thirty-eight

The Wednesday after the raid, and three days after Abigail Walker was found dead in her hospital bed, Madeline was taken in the Rolls-Royce Phantom limousine driven by Rocko to Judge Parker's house on St. Charles Street in New Orleans. The judge answered the knock on the door to his house and recognized Madeline, who was carrying a large black bag.

"Hello, Judge Parker." Madeline said as the judge peered through his partially opened door.

"Hello, Madeline. Good to see you. Come on in," the judge said pulling the door open wider to accommodate Madeline and her case. The opening of the door also let him check and see if anyone happened to be watching from the street. He only saw Madeline's driver who was now leaning back against the limousine with his arms folded. Closing the door, Judge Parker motioned her into his reading room, a comfortable room with many books in shelves along the walls and a fireplace. He turned a chair in her direction and she sat down while he moved over to occupy his favorite reading chair.

"Our maid is in the kitchen, just so you know," the judge said in a soft tone. Continuing after he glanced toward the kitchen he said, "I suppose you want Nick to be able to get out on bail. I could probably make arrangements for him to be out until his trial. I would imagine that during that time he could find some place to go where he might not be found."

"Thanks, Judge. I appreciate your saying that, but that's not why I called to meet with you." Pausing a moment, Madeline then said in a low, firm voice, while looking the judge straight in his eyes, "I want you to make sure Nick stays where he is for a very long time."

She watched the judge absorb this shocking piece of news. She then reached by the side of her chair and pushed forward the large black briefcase she had placed on the floor there. She bent over, opened the case and pulled out an envelope and gave it to the judge.

"That should give you some encouragement to do that," she said. Then she got up from her chair and said, "Let me know if there are any problems doing what I asked. I don't expect that there will be."

With that she turned and walked toward the front door. The judge followed her to the door and opened it for her.

Madeline said, "Goodbye, Judge."

She walked down the front stairs of the house and got into the limousine after the back door was opened for her by her driver. Then the car drove off down St. Charles Avenue.

The judge had watched Madeline as she walked to her car and then departed. Shutting his front door, he walked back into his study and opened the envelope to look at its contents. He pulled out pictures which he studied for a few moments and then put them back inside the envelope. He looked inside the brief case and saw stack upon stack of money which almost completely filled the case. The judge took the brief case and the envelope and walked over to a picture on the wall. There he gently pulled on the lower right edge of the frame, causing the entire frame and the picture to swing out away from the wall. Behind the picture was the door of a safe, which the judge opened with a few twists of the safe's dial. He put the stacks of money into the safe along with the envelope and then shut its door. He put the empty briefcase next to his desk and, after settling back in his chair, returned to his reading.

Madeline spent the next few weeks watching the legal system deal with Nick's case. There was a tremendous amount of sympathy for Abigail and the more information about what had happened to her over at the Bluffs got around, the more public sentiment there was that there should be quick retribution. Nick's case seemed to get on a fast track and go even faster. In no time at all Nick pled guilty and was sentenced to twenty-five years in jail for trafficking in illegal liquor and a host of minor offenses that the U. S. Attorney had decided should also be added to Nick's charges. Tiny and the others also pled guilty and received sentences of twenty years for trafficking in illegal booze, and other violations of various laws. Since Abigail was dead, nothing ever came up about Madeline.

Nick was able to get his lawyer to meet with Tiny and the two men seized behind the stables and convince them that it was in their best interest to not say anything about Madeline's involvement with Abigail. Besides, Madeline had continued to live in Mississippi and had not made any trips to Louisiana, except for that one quick trip to see Judge Parker. She was not going to make any more trips until everything with Nick, Tiny and the others had settled down. She didn't need to take the chance of some over-zealous law enforcement agency trying to tie her in with all that was going on concerning Nick and his associates.

Nick continually asked his lawyer to tell Madeline to come see him, but she never did. He thought she was too scared to come see him because of everything that had happened. Each time a message came from Nick, Madeline thought again about what Carmine had told her about Nick killing her husband, so she did nothing. She felt that was basically what Nick had done for her after he had killed the man that she had enjoyed such a fun life with and who had always spent so much money on her.

When the New Year arrived, Madeline decided to contact Carmine and ask him if Capone would let her run the operation in Nick's absence. Capone was worried because of all the publicity the Bluffs had received due to Nick's arrest. After thinking about it for a few weeks and seeing how things had quieted down, Capone decided he had too large of an investment at the Bluffs and on the coast to let it go to waste and that it might be worth at least exploring if it were possible to put the operation back together. It had, after all, made so much money. He told Carmine to tell Madeline that if she could re-establish all of the connections that had been part of Nick's operation, she should let Carmine know and then Capone would take starting the operation back up under consideration.

Madeline went to see each of the two cooperative timber company owners and got them to continue the agreement they had previously had with her brother. They were very happy that their supplemental income was possibly going to begin again. She made sure that the ships that were part of the lumbering operation remained available for the shipment of booze on their return trips from Cuba.

She re-established the agreement with the sheriff, although she did have to increase the amount that the sheriff and his deputies were receiving and the frequency. It seemed the sheriff did not have the confidence that a woman could run the operation like Nick had. She also saw the sheriff's wife, Helen, on the streets of Bay St. Louis with her new baby, a boy named Bart.

Continuing her effort to keep the whole operation functioning that Nick had been running, Madeline contacted the black funeral home operator and his brother. They were more than happy to continue their part of the operation. They had never even been stopped and enjoyed having the extra money. The ambulance drivers also agreed to keep doing their part in the shipping operations.

Notifying Carmine of her success in re-establishing the operation, she asked Carmine to set up a meeting for her with Capone. She wanted to talk to him herself about what all she had been able to accomplish in re-establishing the operation and try to convince him to let her, a woman, run it. Carmine reluctantly agreed, but told Madeline that she would have to convince Capone that she should run it because Capone had never before let any woman run a part of his operation. He generally did not trust women and thought they should limit their activities to the bedroom, the kitchen and raising children.

Carmine was able to get Capone to agree to, at least, meet with Madeline on his next trip to the area. Capone was going to be in New Orleans in the next three weeks on his way back to Chicago from Florida and told Carmine to tell Madeline that he would meet with her sometime during that trip. He would be staying at the Monteleon Hotel in the French Quarter and she was to meet with him there.

Madeline realized that this was her chance. She knew that she could do everything her brother had put together, supervised, and had done. She had always been smarter than Nick anyway. She hoped Capone would take her seriously. She had gotten to know him a little bit while she had been in Detroit. She knew about his opinion concerning women and what they should be limited to doing with their lives. She would just have to convince him she was different.

On March 15th, Carmine notified Madeline that Capone would be in New Orleans the following Thursday for a two day visit. He would be registered at the Hotel Monteleon under the name of Eddie Harris. She was to go to the front desk and ask for his room number and then go to that room at eight o'clock sharp that night.

On Wednesday, Madeline had the chauffeur pick her up and drive her to New Orleans in the Rolls-Royce Phantom for shopping and a hair appointment. She enjoyed the Phantom and was using it more and more in Nick's absence. Its extremely quiet engine allowed for easy conversation while traveling around New Orleans with her friends. She enjoyed the very elegant and cozy coach portion of the limousine. She found that, while riding in the coach, she could monitor a gauge located on the back of the front seat that showed her how fast her driver was going. If the speed needed any correction, all she had to do was knock on the small glass window on top of the front seat and the driver could slide the glass aside enough to hear directions from the rider. With the inside drapes that could be pulled over the windows, there was ultimate privacy for the passengers as they were being driven to their destinations, which on special occasions she especially loved.

Arrival at any location caused quite a stir because there were so few of the cars in that area of the country, especially in Louisiana and Mississippi. Its fine lines had rarely been seen. Any time Madeline arrived at a restaurant for dinner, her transportation was greatly admired and when the chauffeur opened the door to the coach area, Madeline made sure that her exit from the car was something that one of the new so-called movie stars in California would have been proud of.

On Thursday evening she arrived promptly at eight o'clock at the Monteleon Hotel. Several people stopped to watch this beautiful woman get out of the very elaborate Rolls-Royce Phantom limousine dressed in a gray business suit of tasteful design. Her dark hair was up and the heels she wore were business like. What only a few people would know, the people who knew those sorts of things, was that the rings on her fingers together cost more than most people's houses.

Her chauffeur held the car door open for her and then walked her up the set of stairs to the glass doors to the hotel. There he left her as she entered the hotel and made her way to the front desk. Arriving at the front desk, she asked for Mr. Harris's room and was quickly directed to proceed to Suite 301. Apparently, Mr. Harris had told the front desk to be looking for this visitor.

Arriving at Capone's room, she knocked on the door. Soon it was opened by Capone himself, dressed, Madeline noticed, in an expensive business suit. She quickly made her entrance into his suite. Closing the door behind her, Capone said, "Hello, Madeline. You look wonderful, as always."

"Why thank you," she said as she reached the center of the room. Motioning toward one of the two chairs next to a small round table, Capone said, "Sit down, Madeline, and I'll get us a drink. What would you like?"

"Anything with bourbon would be fine." She moved to sit in one of the chairs next to a writing table and Capone walked over to pull the chair out for her. After seating her, Capone went over to a cabinet, opened the doors and started mixing their drinks.

"Carmine tells me you have made a lot of progress in setting things back up. He says you have done more than he would have ever expected." Capone related as he continued mixing their drinks.

"Everything is back in place, just like before. It did take a lot of effort, but everybody came around and things finally fell into place," Madeline said in her smooth, but now business-like voice. She had to be careful how she approached this, knowing Capone's predisposition for not wanting a woman running any part of his operation. She felt she had to appear to know what to do and how to get it done, but not appear to be too smart or else she might cause Capone to feel uneasy. She really had to watch what she said and how she said it.

"How should I feel about what all you have done, Madeline?" he turned and asked with two drinks in his hands.

"I would hope that you would be pleased. It really just needed the right person to do it and I was able to get it done. Now the whole operation can start back up at any time you say. Since I put it back together for you, I hope you will consider letting me run it for you."

Capone walked over to her with their drinks in his hands and handed Madeline her drink. She eased her drink to her lips, watching one of the most powerful men she had ever known study her and think about what she had just said. After setting his drink on the small table next to their chairs, Capone pulled his chair over closer to where Madeline was sitting and sat down, immediately taking a sip from his drink. He sat there looking at Madeline for a few moments and then said, "I don't like how everything happened down here, Madeline. I don't like how things were getting out about our operation. Somebody had to have been talking, Madeline, and I don't like that. I don't like that at all."

Madeline looked at Capone and could tell he was very serious. He was being quite up front.

"I have been around long enough to see things, Madeline, to recognize when things are not right. Something went wrong down here. We suffered a big loss and it didn't have to be that way."

Capone took another sip from his drink and Madeline did likewise, not wanting to not respond until she knew where Capone was going with the conversation. After pausing a moment, he continued.

"There was a problem down here, Madeline. There had to have been a leak. Maybe there is someone we can't trust anymore. Something, something, somehow went wrong. What do you think that something was, Madeline?" Now Capone was watching for her reaction to what he had been saying.

The room was quiet for a moment as Madeline shifted herself in her chair and crossed her legs. Then she said, "There may be something to what you say but, especially after all you have put together with the whole business, sometimes people are just going to talk. Regardless of what you or someone else, like Carmine or whoever, might do to try to not let it happen. Eventually, somebody is always going to say something that can cause a problem. I am sure you have probably had that happen in Chicago or other places."

Capone let out a chuckle, then another one after taking a sip from his drink.

"Yes, that is very true. In Detroit, you remember how the revenuers knew a lot about what we were going to do before we had even made final decisions to do it."

Madeline nodded her head. She remembered. She remembered well. That was why her husband was dead. Capone didn't know she knew why, but she did. Capone definitely knew though that it had been Madeline's husband that had provided information to the revenuers in Detroit. Now, it seemed like there had been a leak down here. Seated next to him was the wife, of all people, of the man who had betrayed him in Detroit. Capone had never thought, though, that Madeline was part of her husband's betrayal of him in Detroit. In fact, he was almost positive Madeline had known nothing about her husband's betrayal activities.

Down here Capone was worried enough about what had happened that he was at the point of leaving it all closed down. He might start it back up, but only when he had some answers. He had made so much money from Nick's activities that he really did not want to keep it shut down. He wanted very much to get it all back in operation, if it could be done without too much unnecessary risk.

For Madeline's part, she knew that if she was going to be successful in getting Capone's backing to take over what Nick had been doing, she had to get Capone to start thinking at this point in their meeting about positive things. The negative things could be dealt with later.

Madeline said, "Yes, it did seem like the revenuers were getting more and more information. But after all, they did work some of our people over, you know." Madeline realized she was now at a critical point in their meeting. She needed to give Capone some reason he could believe in and agree with so he might re-establish the operation.

Capone seized on her suggestion and said, "Yeah! That's right! The feds were beating up our guys at that house they had there in Bay St. Louis. Of all things, they were the ones beating people up."

Madeline sensed that Capone had provided her with a chance for her to further encourage that the operations be continued. Feeling that she had to keep pushing, she said, "All I know is that the complete operation is still in place. It can begin again any time you want. I have talked with everybody. They are all ready to go. All we need is for you to say it is okay."

At that point, she put her drink down and stood up in front of Capone. Turning to face him, she took the jacket of her suit off. Capone sat watching her as she then slowly unbuttoned her blouse and took it off while she watched his reaction. Then she reached behind her to the zipper on her skirt and started pulling it down ever so slowly.

"And I want you to know that I come with the deal. All of me." As

Madeline said that, her skirt slipped off and fell to the floor.

Capone admired the view for a moment and then said, "You know how to convince me. Alright, Madeline. If I give the 'okay' for you to run the coast operation, I want you to be available for me every time I come down here. Whenever I want you. Do you understand?"

Madeline smiled at Capone, and began walking toward the bedroom in the back of the suite, letting her hair down as she walked. She stayed in Capone's hotel bedroom until late afternoon of the next day.

Before he left for Chicago, Capone authorized the resumption of shipments and for Madeline to run the operation. He realized, when he thought about it, that his operation had received no interference from any of the authorities in Mississippi. With that in mind, he was willing to let activities get started again. Madeline assured him that she would make every effort to see that there were no problems, and that there would be only total satisfaction with how things were run. And yes, she knew that she was to be available for Capone whenever he was in the area and wanted her. For his part, Capone was willing to let her try to run things, at least for a while. He had made so much money from their operations in Mississippi and had so much invested in the Bluffs, it was at least worth the try.

* * *

The next day at the Patterson house in Bay St. Louis, the sheriff walked into the baby's room and saw Helen holding the baby. Looking at both of them, Patterson said, "Helen, put the baby in its crib and come into the den for a minute."

Helen saw the look on her husband's face and knew there was something serious he wanted to talk about with her. She put the baby in his crib and walked into the den. Patterson shut the door behind her and turned to face her.

"Helen, this is going to be the only time we are ever going to talk about this. I want you to know that outside of this room, I will always be known as the father of that child you were just holding. But I also want you to know that since I was a senior in high school, when I had surgery for an injury I got playing football, I have always known that I would be unable to father a child. So I know, without a doubt, that child is not mine."

With an astonished look on her face, Helen stared back at her husband, speechless. With that, Patterson turned, opened the door and walked out of the room and left the house.

Helen was devastated. She had no idea what he might do next. Later that evening when Patterson came home, he conducted himself as if nothing had happened.

* * *

The following Sunday afternoon, when visitors were allowed at the facility, Madeline finally went by the jail in New Orleans to see Nick. She had been told that Nick would be sent in the next few days to a prison in rural southern Louisiana where he would serve his sentence. She dressed in a demure, dark blue business suit with a matching wide-brimmed hat. She looked as if she had just been to church.

She was guided into a large room with a row of desks in the middle. She went over and sat at one of the desks, as directed by one of the prison guards. She had not been sitting there long when Nick was led in dressed in a grey prison uniform with hand cuffs and leg cuffs on. He was very happy to see Madeline and began smiling at her the minute he saw her.

"Hi, Madeline. Thanks so much for coming."

"Hi, big brother." Her tone of voice was one of indifference.

"I had hoped you would have come by to see me before now. I never even saw you when I pled guilty," Nick said, wondering as he had so many times how she was going to answer that statement.

"Mr. Capone has agreed to let me take over and run things in your absence," Madeline said, changing the subject from under her wide-brimmed hat.

Nick was shocked. Capone never let women run things. And he was going to let Madeline run the operation on the Gulf Coast? Which he, Nick, had turned into one of Capone's largest operations in the country?

"How did that happen?" Nick asked, surprised at hearing that news.

"I asked him," Madeline answered. "You obviously can't do it. You're in jail or haven't you noticed?"

Nick looked at his sister. Why was he getting such an arrogant attitude from her? There were a lot of things here all of a sudden that he just was not understanding.

"But why you? Why not Carmine or Rocko or one of the other boys? Why you, Madeline?" he asked.

"You are not happy to hear that, big brother? I thought you would be happy for me, proud for me. But you don't seem to be. Why is that?" she asked with a sarcastic tone.

"Madeline, I am proud for you, but you have never run anything like that in your life. Besides, you need to be trying to get me out of here. What have you done to get me out of here? You haven't been to see me. You didn't try to help me before I pled guilty. You left me out there, Madeline, dangling in the wind. I didn't tell them anything about your knowing about it all. Why didn't you help me, Madeline? You've got to start putting things together to help get me out of here. Maybe you can start trying to get a pardon for me or some kind of early release. The president could do that."

Madeline looked at her brother. He was waiting for her to say something. She waited for a moment. She knew that what she said next would change things between them forever. But then, that was why she was there.

"Nick, I know about Carlo." She watched his face, looking for the moment when he realized what she was saying.

"What about Carlo, Madeline?"

"I know what you did to Carlo, Nick."

She was now leaning forward so she wouldn't have to speak so loudly, but she also wanted him to remember this moment.

"I know you killed my husband, Nick, and I hope you rot in hell!" She then stood up and yelled, "Guard!"

The guard came and she turned and started walking out. Nick was in total shock. He had not known she knew. He had been told that she would never find out. How had that happened? How long had she known? When did she find out? Who told her? All of those questions popped into his mind. Yet, she was walking out. Now! He yelled out to her.

"Madeline, you don't understand!"

She kept walking.

"We both would have been killed if I hadn't done it!"

Madeline kept walking. Why didn't she stop and listen to him? She could hear him. Why didn't she stop walking?

"I had to, Madeline!" he yelled.

She continued to walk.

"He betrayed us both, Madeline!"

There was now a guard by Nick's side, grabbing his arm and pulling on him.

"Madeline!"

She disappeared through a doorway, gone.

"Madeline!"

Nick was now restrained by two guards and pulled through a back door.

As Madeline passed through the doorway, she smirked. It had gone just as she had planned months earlier. The taste of revenge was so sweet.

Chapter Thirty-nine

Madeline returned to the Bluffs and operations resumed. Soon the amount being shipped was up to the same level it had been before the raid. Suitcases full of cash were once again being delivered to Chicago twice a week. It was almost as if there had been no interruption

On Friday night the second weekend in July, four months after her visit with Capone, Madeline's mysterious, cloaked guest again arrived at the guest house, just as high winds began announcing the arrival of a coastal storm that was the first hurricane of the year. No one ever knew exactly when a hurricane would arrive or how bad it might be, but this one seemed to have all of the capabilities of being something special. Having been told that her friend had arrived, Madeline left the main house and worked her way in the strong winds over to the guest house to see her now regular visitor.

In an area not too far from the guest house, the shadow of a figure moved across the grounds in the darkness, having difficulty moving in the high winds of the approaching hurricane. The figure saw Madeline as she went into the guest house. The figure then worked its way toward the guest house and, after finally making its way onto the porch of that house, gradually began to open the front door. This was made more difficult because of the long dagger that was being held in one hand. Everything was dark and the howling winds muffled almost every other sound.

As the figure opened the front door, the sound of the wind coming through the opened door caused the person standing just inside the door to turn around toward where the sound was coming from. It was at that precise moment that the figure holding the dagger plunged the sharp knife through the dark air and into the chest of the person standing at the door. At that same moment, a flash of lightening showed Carlotta that who she had just stabbed was NOT Madeline! Carlotta looked up and, by the light provided by the same flash of lightening, saw Madeline coming out of a back room. Carlotta turned and ran out through the doorway, disappearing into the darkness of the storm.

Madeline saw Carlotta run from the room and quickly rushed over to the person now lying on the floor. She went to the floor on her knees, trying to cradle her lover's head in her lap. She could do nothing but look at the dagger lodged deep in Betsy Parker's chest. She cried watching as Betsy died in her arms. Finally realizing Betsy's life was over, Madeline screamed,

"NOOOOOOOOOOOOOOO," as the winds howled louder and louder.

* * *

Several days later a man in a three piece suit knocked on the door to Judge Parker's house on St. Charles Avenue in New Orleans. The judge opened the door and the man identified himself as Mike Harrington, a federal investigator. The judge let the agent in, shutting the door behind him. Harrington followed the judge into his study and, after the judge had seated himself, he sat down. Feeling awkward, the agent felt he had to begin the conversation.

"Judge, I am sure you know that anytime someone in the position of Assistant to the Director of the Investigative Branch of the Internal Revenue Service, like your wife Betsy Parker was, is killed, especially with all that has been going on in New Orleans and along the coast, a special investigation has to be done. We have been conducting that investigation and are about to bring it to a close, but we felt we needed to talk to you before doing that. This won't take but a few minutes and

I do appreciate your taking the time to meet with me."

"I understand. Thank you for meeting me here at my house instead of at my office. My wife's death has been very hard for me," the judge said.

"I am so sorry about her passing, judge. She was such a fine person and so well-liked by all of those who knew her and worked with her. Everyone we talked to has had nothing but good things to say about her."

Harrington paused for just a moment to allow the judge to compose himself and then continued.

"Judge, in order for us to bring this investigation to a close, we really need to know one thing. Why was your wife out at the Bluffs that night?"

The judge had known that at some point he was going to be asked that question and was almost relieved that he was now going to have the opportunity to answer it.

"My wife and I became acquainted with Madeline Benedetti last year. We first met her during a trip we took to Italy along with Judge Tullos and his wife, Delores. At one of the parties put on by the Krewe of Nobles last year, we met Madeline's brother, Nick Gable, who later became a member of that krewe. We used to see Madeline with Nick at the functions of the krewe," the judge said leaning back in his chair.

Harrington knew about the Krewe of Nobles all right. He knew that everybody who was anybody was a member of that krewe. He also knew that the political powers in that krewe were most anxious for his investigation to quietly be brought to a conclusion and for him to move on to other things.

The judge continued, "At one of those functions Madeline, who enjoyed riding horses like Betsy did, invited her to go out to the Bluffs to ride. There was a nice area for them to ride out there and Betsy enjoyed Madeline and Nick's hospitality. So she was out at the Bluffs from time to time riding horses, which she loved doing. She never had any idea, and she certainly would have mentioned it to me and to her supervisor if she had, about those things that were recently revealed as having gone on out there in those areas away from where she always stayed. As you probably know, Madeline was never indicted or even charged with anything. Apparently, it was all her brother's operation. True friends don't cut off friends because a relative messes up. Betsy liked being outdoors in the fresh air and riding horses, as did Madeline.

They both just enjoyed each other's friendship."

Agent Harrington felt a relief after the judge had given his answer. Interviewing a federal judge was something he had never had to do, especially one who was the chief district judge for the New Orleans area. Interviewing any federal judge whose wife had just been killed was something he hoped he never had to do again. The answer he had just been given would allow the investigators to bring this matter to a close.

The judge then asked, "How is Madeline doing?"

"She is heartbroken, Judge. She is absolutely sick about what happened to your wife. Just like you said, as we found it out during our investigation, they were good friends. She has not gotten over your wife's death at all. She is very quiet, eats very little, and when we went to talk with her, judge, she could hardly function. Riding out a hurricane sometimes does that to people. It changes them. Some people are mentally never the same again after suffering through a hurricane. I guess with everything that happened to her brother and then with your wife's murder and going through that hurricane and all, she pretty much doesn't even know where she is. We have decided, like you just said, that your wife really didn't know about what all Madeline's brother and his friends were doing. If Madeline had been involved, we are sure your wife would have reported it."

"I know she would have," the judge said slowly, while staring at the floor in front of him.

Seeing how the judge was now tearfully reacting to his last statement and wanting to get away from that subject, Harrington said, "There has never been a hurricane like this one, Judge. I can't get over the devastation out there. This hurricane was like a broom. You know how they usually blow on through and go on. Well, this one stayed there for a while. I mean, it just went back and forth through that area three times over a twenty-four hour period. Nobody has ever seen anything like it. With all of that voodoo going on out there in the swamp and with all of the strange things that have happened out there, it was as if the Lord just decided to sweep the place clean."

Thinking for a moment, the agent said, "It was really interesting, Judge. That church school in Bay St. Louis, you know the one."

The judge nodded his head affirmatively.

"That school was hardly damaged. Now it does sit up on a little ridge there, but it almost didn't have any damage at all, even from the wind."

Continuing, Harrington said, "Those swamp people that lived out there in that Devil's Swamp, a lot of them were killed. Bodies have been washing up all over the place out there. There are bodies of people that nobody has ever even seen before or can identify. They just seem to have come from out of nowhere."

Pausing to take a breath, the agent continued. "We found out about this gambling boat that was down there on Bayou Caddy. Well, Judge, when I saw that boat, it was like it had been picked up, turned upside down and slammed down into the ground. Nothing was showing but the bottom of the hull. The smoke-stacks of that boat were stuck down in the mud."

Shaking his head in disbelief, he added, "All of those buildings out at the Bluffs, all of them, were almost completely destroyed. A small portion of what they call the guest house was about the only thing left standing. Madeline lives in that part and just sits for most of the day on what is left of the front porch, rocking back and forth in a rocking chair. Staring out into the swamp. That's all she does every day. It's really sad."

The judge nodded his head slightly. He knew about part of the guest house being left because that was where they had found Madeline and his wife after the hurricane had finally gone away.

Harrington then said, "Judge, based on what you have said and our own investigation, we think your wife's death was a case of mistaken identity. The murder weapon had several voodoo markings on it. We believe that a voodoo priestess named Carlotta probably did it intending to kill Madeline. Apparently, it was no secret that there had been a serious confrontation at the Bluffs between them. We have tried to find this Carlotta woman, but have been told that she did not survive the hurricane."

Harrington then stood up and stuck out his hand. The judge slowly stood up also and Harrington, while shaking the judge's hand, said, "That's all I needed, Judge. Thanks for your time. Sorry to have bothered you with this."

As they moved toward the front door, Harrington continued, "I think we can bring this investigation to a close now. Again, please accept my condolences."

After the judge walked Harrington out onto the front porch of his house, he watched as the agent got into his car and drove away. The judge went back inside, closed the front door and locked it. He slowly made his way back into his study and went over to the framed picture and pulled it away from the wall. Opening the safe behind the picture, he took out the envelope that had been given to him by Madeline. He took out the pictures of his wife and looked at them. She looked so unlike herself posed in the various stages of undress.

He started a little fire in the fireplace and put the pictures on the fire, watching them burn into nothing. He checked on the stacks of money still in the safe and then closed it, locking it and pushing the picture back against the wall. He took a metal poker from its stand near the fireplace and stirred the ashes of the small fire. Satisfied everything was burned, he went over to his favorite chair and sat down, picking up the book he had been reading when the agent had arrived.

* * *

At the Bluffs, Madeline sat in a rocking chair on the dilapidated front porch of what remained of the guest cottage. She looked off in the distance with a vacant gaze, slowly rocking, rocking, rocking.

Epilogue

Carlotta, the voodoo priestess, and Claude were never seen again.

The southeastern cove of Cat Island is identified on United States Geological Survey maps to this day as "Smuggler's Cove."

In Chicago in 1929, seven members of Bugsy Moran's northside gang were lined up against a wall and machine gunned to death in what became known as the St. Valentine's Day massacre. It has always been thought that members of Al Capone's gang were responsible.

Nick was serving his twenty-five year sentence when, in 1943, he was allowed to leave prison and eventually sent to Sicily to serve in a special unit of the United States Army dealing with members of the mafia during the allied invasions in that area. Four days before the end of the war in Europe, Nick Gable was reportedly killed in a car accident in southern Italy. His body was never found.

Sheriff Wild Bill Patterson served as sheriff of Hancock County for thirty-seven years, dying of natural causes while still in office. His funeral was attended by his widow, Helen Patterson; his son, Bart Patterson; and over six hundred people.

Helen Patterson played the organ and piano at St. Richard's Catholic Church for over forty-five years. People would come from miles around on Sundays just to hear her play the church's music so beautifully.

Bart Patterson graduated from St. Richard's high school in Bay St. Louis. After driving a tank in General George Patton's U. S. army during World War II, he attended Louisiana State University on a full scholarship, which was funded by an anonymous donor. Upon graduation, he returned to Hancock County to serve as Deputy Sheriff, following in his father's footsteps.

Over the years, numerous hurricanes have gone through the Bay St. Louis area. The St. Richard's church school has sometimes been slightly damaged but, through God's favor, it has never been destroyed.

In 1974, one of the largest oil and gas fields ever discovered in the state of Mississippi was found in Devil's Swamp under the land bought by Nick.

Madeline lived by herself at the Bluffs in the guest cottage until she died in 1976. At her death, her estate was valued at over one hundred ninety million dollars.

Thirty-three people attended the reading of Madeline's will at the Bluffs. They came from New York, Cleveland, Detroit, Chicago, Miami, Kansas City, Dallas, Phoenix, Las Vegas, ... and Sicily.

Author's Notes

This book is fiction. Though rumors have persisted over the years of Al Capone's ownership of various properties on the Mississippi Gulf Coast and of his regular visitations to the area during the roaring twenties, no effort was made by this author to verify or substantiate those rumors.

Some geographical locations as described in this book were different in the real world. For example, the best information available seems to indicate that in the 1920s, while there was a road going from New Orleans to the Mississippi Gulf Coast, an individual driving a car would have been required to deal with several ferry crossings over the following: the Chef Menteur; the Rigolets; the West Pearl River; the West Middle Pearl River; the Middle Middle Pearl River (that's correct, Middle Middle); the East Middle Pearl River; and the East Pearl River. The East Pearl River is generally recognized as the location of the state boundary. For the sake of this story, only the crossing of the Pearl River at the state boundary location was utilized.

Devil's Swamp is the name that has been assigned by map makers to an area of Hancock County, Mississippi that consists of thousands of acres of swamp land with only occasional high ground. Those high grounds, or bluff areas, were created by the deposition of soil during the numerous years that ice or water covered the area. Many of them appear as islands today and are readily apparent when a person is traveling in certain parts of Hancock County.

As with any time consuming endeavor, the support of one's family and friends are absolutely necessary. For their patience, encouragement and support, I sincerely thank them.

There was a great deal of enjoyment in writing this book. The author hopes that you enjoy reading the story.

About the Author

Mack Cameron was born and raised in Laurel, Mississippi. He was on crutches as a child from the first grade to the middle of the fourth grade. Through the grace of God, he got off crutches and took up tennis. He went to the state high school singles finals four consecutive years, winning the championship two times.

He attended Mississippi State University (MSU), receiving a Bachelor's Degree and a Master's Degree in Political Science. At Mississippi State, he won four Southeastern Conference (SEC) individual tennis championships while a member of MSU teams that won two SEC team championships and finished as high as number three in the nation.

Upon graduation, he worked in Washington, D.C. as Staff Assistant to U.S. Senator John C. Stennis. He then served as an officer in U.S. Army Military Intelligence. After completion of his active duty military service, he attended law school at the University of Mississippi (Ole Miss) where he won the American Jurisprudence Award in International Law, served on the Law School Honor Council, and coached the tennis team.

After graduation from Ole Miss, Mr. Cameron served as Assistant Legal Counsel for the United States Secret Service under Presidents Nixon, Ford and Carter. He returned to Mississippi and worked as a Special Assistant Attorney General in the Mississippi Attorney General's Office under three Attorneys General.

Mr. Cameron has served on the Mississippi State Bar Ethics Committee and is in the State of Mississippi Sports Hall of Fame and the Mississippi State University Sports Hall of Fame. He and his father, C. B. "Buck" Cameron, are the only father-son duo in the State of Mississippi Sports Hall of Fame. He is a member of the Mississippi State Bar Association and is a real estate broker.

Made in the USA
San Bernardino, CA
22 July 2016